STOLLING

CW01507690

IN

WINTER

STORKS
IN
WINTER

MIKE KRAWIEC

atmosphere press

To my wife Agnieszka
who made me see that I could be more
than I thought I could.

CHAPTER 1
ARRIVAL

As the squeaking rattling army lorry lurched to a halt Jan awoke. 'We're here mate' shouted the driver from the cab. Emerging from the dark shroud of the tarpaulin covered rear Jan was blinded by the sunshine of a spring morning. Dropping his kit bag onto the ground he vaulted down into this new bright day.

"We're going for a cup of tea mate" said one of the two drivers gesturing to a low building with the welcoming sign 'Canteen' over its entrance. "You need to go there" said one of the drivers pointing to a small cottage adjacent to the gates of the camp "he'll sort you out in there".

Jan picked up his kit bag and threw it onto his shoulder. He walked up the gravel path to the door and rapped on the knocker and waited. After a moment a short dumpy man came to the door. He was balding, and his wire rimmed spectacles were perched on the end of his nose.

"Can I help you?" he enquired as he scanned Jan over the top of his spectacles.

"I'm Jan Kot, and I'm here to take up my job as a shepherd for farmer Dyke in this area".

"One moment," said the man, and pushing the door he disappeared back into the cottage. After what seemed like an eternity the man reappeared dressed in a pinstriped business suit sporting a gold watch and chain in his waistcoat pocket. He held a clip board which he perused with a stern eye. "You are not supposed to be here until Monday," he said.

"I had the chance of a free ride on a military transport that had come up at short notice," said Jan, "and so I took up the offer to save the train fare."

"Well, I am Mr Monk the manager of this hostel, and I represent the Ministry of Labour and National Service, if you have any requests regarding your employment you must direct them to me for approval hence forth. I will need to formally confirm who you are; we cannot have just anybody coming in here. Papers!"

"Here are my documents from the co-ordinators office in Havant, I think you'll find them in order-"

"Aha as I thought," declared monk, stabbing the paper-work with his pen triumphantly as he scanned the documents, "you should not be here till Monday 29th March 1948 at 4 pm"

"But as I explained-"

"I will have to telephone farmer Dyke to see if it is con-venient for you to go over there today. Go to the canteen and find a cup of tea and I will send for you when I have word"

As Jan walked towards the canteen Monk summoned him back to the cottage.

"You have no family, no children I presume?"

"No," replied Jan, "I'm not sure where my wife is, or even if she is alive, The Red Cross is helping me look. We had no children before the war, so I'm alone."

"Quite," said Monk and once again disappeared into the cottage.

Once more Jan threw his kitbag onto his shoulder and walked over to the canteen.

As he pushed his way through the double doors, he was welcomed by the sight of rows of white enamelled metal tables with wooden benches running up both sides of them. In the far distance his travelling companions were sat on the table nearest the tea urn. They both looked around and beckoned him over.

"Tea?" asked one of the drivers.

"Yes please, black no sugar,"

"Sorry mate, it only comes white from the urn." Jan dismissively gestured that that was OK, and he sat down and waited. The driver took a mug from the pile and filled it with an evil brew that you could stand a spoon in, if the spoon, as in this case, hadn't been chained to the table. Handing Jan his tea the driver asked, "So, what you up to here then?" "I'm sorry I don't know what you mean, my English is not that good yet" replied Jan.

"In my opinion," said the second soldier, "I was thinking how good it was, where did you learn to speak so well?"

" Well, I've spent the last three years working for the American army in southern Germany as a liaison officer with Polish refugees. Recently, we'd been given the chance to return to America with the battalion as the need for our work had ceased. But, after the previous three years I'd had enough of them and instead, I decided to come to England as a European Voluntary Worker to help rebuild the country after the war. My contract is for two years, after that, if I haven't found out what has happened to my wife, I'll decide what to do."

"Yeah, bloody Yanks, overpaid, oversexed, and over here." The first soldier quipped unkindly. He grinned and carried on. "Can't you go back to Poland then?"

"No, the part of Poland I lived in is now part of the Ukraine under Soviet rule."

The three men continued to exchange stories about where they'd got 'their lot' during the war until the drivers decided

3

that they had better continue on their way north. "We need to reach the airfield by lunch time as it's Saturday and Saturday is toad in the hole day." It appeared that the two had a culinary knowledge of which were the best camps to dine at and on which days to attend.

"Well, good luck mate," said the first soldier. Jan shook his new-found friends hands and they promised to meet again at some point on their travels as new-found friends do.

Jan followed the men outside and watched as their lorry made its' noisy progress north down the country lanes. At this point, Mr Monk emerged from his office beckoning to Jan with his clipboard to come over to him.

"Mr Kot! I have arranged for farmer Dyke to call in on his way to the village just before noon today."

"Can I leave my kit bag in your office till then?"

"I am afraid that is out of the question, it would not be appropriate, my office is a place of work not a storeroom. You can leave your belongings at the post office." Monk pointed to a bungalow type building across the entrance road of the camp to the right of the gate. "Rosemary the post-mistress will be here at nine o'clock so you can leave your bag with her till noon when she closes."

Jan once more hoisted his kit bag onto his shoulder and wandered over to the post-office. There he waited in the warm spring sunshine, the sounds and smells of the English countryside reminding him of his home on the farm in Poland. His mind wandered back to that summers' day when he had sent his wife to friends in Lublin for her own safety while he had rushed to the nearby town to sign up to fight.

After that, he had returned to the farm to say farewell to his parents before leaving for the front. His father had spent a lifetime on the farm and was a resourceful man who Jan knew would do his best to protect the family and farm. That was the last time Jan had seen any of his family and, despite lodging paperwork with the Red Cross in Germany, he had still heard nothing of their fate. Jan knew he was one of millions searching for loved ones but while the search continued he at least had hope. He knew his father would do all in his power to keep the family together and safe if it was humanly possible.

"Good morning," a shrill voice declared, jolting him from his past into the present with a start. "I don't open till nine o'clock, so you'll have to wait. I have to set up my till you know."

Jan gazed at the elderly lady astride her bike, its wicker basket stuffed full of large ledgers. "No, it's OK, I don't want anything. Mr Monk said I could leave my kit bag here until you close at noon" Jan informed the lady.

"Are you sure he didn't say you could ask me if it was all right to leave your kit bag in my office?"

"No" replied Jan, "he definitely said I would be able to."

The post-mistress looked at Jan disapprovingly, "I can't have you coming into my office it is a secure area! Whatever next."

"I can leave it in the canteen, it isn't a problem for me." Jan replied hastily, aware that he had elicited some kind of diplomatic incident.

"Sir, your bag won't be safe in there, not with all these types about." She snatched the bag from him. "However, as a matter of kindness, I'll keep it behind my counter."

Jan scratched his head. "Why-, thank you very much I appreciate it." Jan introduced himself to the lady. "My name's Jan Kot, and I'm new here, I have come to work for farmer Dyke."

In turn the old lady introduced herself. "I'm Rosemary." She gave him a wisp of a smile that suggested that their altercation was behind them now.

Jan decided that with this positive sign it might be time to embark on an attempt at conversation, so at a loss to think of any stunning conversation openers he glibly asked her "So, how long have you worked for the Post Office." Feigning interest.

"I've worked for the post office since I left school," Rosemary declared as she pulled a large bunch of keys out of her basket that looked like they belonged to a castle rather than a small wooden bungalow. "I've worked my way up to post mistress," she announced in a moment of solemn pride.

"Oh! That's quite an achievement." Jan acknowledged with a sideways nod of his head. He decided that he had done enough to save their relationship and so, having now successfully stored his bag behind the counter he exchanged a polite farewell, once again expressed his gratitude, and walked away waving as he retreated.

Jan decided that as he had some time to spare, he would explore the camp and the rows of Nissen huts that spread out before him in militarily precise ranks. He could see that the perimeter fence had been removed and that all that remained of its existence were periodic tufts of grass.

As he slowly walked down the central main road the curved huts gave up their steaming condensation to the heat of a new spring day. Each hut was tethered to its neighbour by a number of clothes lines. On each side of the huts, running their full length, were neatly tended gardens fenced in against careless passers-by with sticks and any other material that could be scavenged. Old, glazed windowpanes substituted for cloches, and despite the early season, prized vegetables pressed up against the glass eager for freedom and the breeze.

Each hut had a broad wooden porch astride its entrance. Bright yellow tobacco leaves hung in profusion, drying on the creaking eves that bore them. At the rear end of some huts chicken runs had been constructed from the redundant fence wire rolls left to rust in the long grass. Their occupants clucked their displeasure at their confinement, necks

stretched through the wire trying to peck the elusive greenery beyond their reach. The camp had an air of order about it,
yet Jan noticed that it seemed those responsible for that order
were nowhere to be seen. As he pondered the reason for this
he heard a high-pitched squeak of a rusty hinge behind him
and, as he turned to investigate an old man emerged through
the entrance from the hut and made his way towards Jan.

The man looked distinguished, but his jacket appeared
threadbare and overused. Clearly the man had seen success at
some point in his life, but now it had faded and left him in a
less affluent situation.

"Can I help you?" the old man asked in broken English.

Jan, recognised his mother tongue in the old man's falter-
ing English. "My name is Jan Kot, and I'll be working in the
area. I'm waiting to be picked up by the farmer now. Where is
everybody? "The camp seems deserted?"

The old man began to speak, punctuating his answer by
pointing at specific huts. "The unmarried men will be working
or sleeping, the families will be at church, the children will be
at Saturday school or with the nuns for religious education,
and the single women will be working or also at church."

"There are children?" queried Jan, "I thought that no children were allowed here." " Most of these huts hold ex-servicemen from the Polish Second Corps who're being joined
by their families. They're classed as displaced persons under
the Geneva Convention, some are voluntary workers and are
contracted, and, as such, are viewed as financial migrants or
adventurers by us in the camp."

Jan decided that he had better introduce himself before
making further enquiries. "My name's Jan Kot" he informed
the old man in a manner calculated to elicit a response as to
who he was. None was forthcoming. "I'm one of the adventurers," said Jan smiling, however, there was no sign of an
impending smile from his companion just a long awkward

silence that was broken by the man when the tension became unbearable.

"I'm Professor Kaminski."

"Professor," exclaimed Jan with palpable surprise.

"Yes" continued the old man. "I'm the scientific advisor to the camp committee. I keep them informed on scientific developments, which may affect our return to Poland in the future".

"Why on earth would this be required in rural England in 1948?"

The professor snapped back at Jan in disbelief, "We all know that there will be a third world-war, and we must have the most up-to-date information to hand if we are to prevail and drive the Soviets from Poland and back over the old borders."

Jan was at a loss to understand the professor's reasoning given the political situation in Europe as Jan understood it.

"What rank are you?"

"I've no rank as I'm a civilian, but when I was captured by the Germans in France in 1940, I was a captain in the infantry."

"French infantry or Polish?" quizzed Kaminski.

"Polish."

"Excellent, we'll soon need good men like you."

Jan decided that these were the musings of an old man and that he should pay them little heed. "Well, it was nice to meet you professor, however, I think that I'll continue to look around the area now. Which way's the village?" The professor indicated to the camp gate and signalled right. Jan bade the professor farewell and resumed his tour of the local area.

As Jan sauntered down the lane in the shade of the elm trees, the cold of the March morning sought him out. He pulled his jacket closed and waited for the sun's rays to return in the next clearing. The aroma of the emerald banks of lush spring shoots signalled that Mother Nature had a tenuous hold on her new season, but the cool shade was a constant reminder that all could be lost in a frozen moment. Jan had been walking for some time and still could not see any sign of the village, so he retraced his steps back to the camp.

On arriving back at the camp gates, he was shocked to suddenly hear an alarm bell ringing, however, the bell did not ring in frantic confusion but at a lethargic rhythmic pace. He peered over the hedge and there, in splendid isolation, was a single Nissen hut. On its roof, a wooden bell tower perched, constructed from pallet wood some of which still bore the name of its supplier, USA. It was this tower that was home to the alarm bell. As the sun streamed into this rudimentary belfry, Jan could clearly see the red painted bell with the word fire emblazoned on it.

As Jan watched, the doors were flung open by two boys in red cassocks with white linen copes, and the hut disgorged its excited crowd, chatting animatedly into the morning air. Jan stood and stared at the throng as they crossed the road back into the camp hoping to catch the eye of someone with a fixed grin on his face as a sign that he was open to association with any who cared to look his way. Yet not one of this eager congregation paid him the slightest attention.

It was as if he was invisible. Perhaps, thought Jan, the vision of a man dressed in an assortment of ex-military garb and wearing worn out work boots was such a common sight around here that nobody gave it a second thought. However, Jan soon settled on the opinion that there was apparently no gain to be had from befriending a traveller who was bereft of material goods and influence, and based on this supposition, Jan decided to remain aloof and keep his own counsel.

As the last of the throng processed through the camp gate, Mr Monk emerged from the gate office and beckoned Jan over to him.

"Farmer Dyke will be here shortly so can I ask you to wait here until he arrives?"

Jan made a move to walk into the office, at which point Monk held up his hand in the style of a traffic policeman on point duty.

"No, if you could wait please."

So, Jan acquiesced to this last command. He waited in expectation of a new chapter starting in his life, and yet as the familiar smells of Polish dishes cooking in the kitchen wafted about the place he was immediately taken back to home, hearth, and family. As Jan mused over his family's fate, from across the road, his eye was caught by Rosemary the post mistress who signalled that he should pick up his kit bag by deftly tapping on an imaginary wristwatch. Jan walked over to collect his chattel and returned to his spot by the gate office to wait for his new employer.

After a time, a small Morris car pulled up at the gate entrance. A short elderly man got out dressed in a grey checked suit with highly polished, brown brogue shoes. This, thought Jan, must be the farmer as he watched the man walk to the gate office and, as if on cue, Monk appeared from the office clutching his clip board laden with sheets of official paperwork.

"Good morning, farmer Dyke."

Dyke replied "Ow bist?"

Jan had heard what he thought was Dyke speaking German and, in an instant, eager to make a good impression, in a genial tone he asked Dyke, "*Sprechen sie Deutsche?*" "*Sprechen sie* bloody *Deutsche?* I don't speak that Gerry lingo," protested Dyke. He looked at Monk as if to admonish him. "I thought you said this bugger could speak English"

"He does, but you will have to be patient with him" counselled Monk.

Dyke paused for a moment, as if to gain some inner

equilibrium and tried again. "So, you are my new *Tegman* are you?"

Jan looked at Monk for guidance and Monk looked at Dyke for the same. "Farmer Dyke, I have been speaking the King's English all my life but have no idea what you are talking about."

"Well, down in these'ere parts it's a bloody shepherd. I don't know what you posh buggers in London call it, but down ere that's what it is."

At this point Monk decided to return to a world that he fully understood, government administration formalities. He handed Dyke the clipboard full of paperwork and asked him to sign for his new charge. Dyke fumbled in his jacket pocket. "Where's my bloody fountain pen, ah *yer-tiz*," Pen in hand he gave the paperwork a cursory glance. "So, his name's Jan," Dyke said, using a hard J.

"No" replied Monk, "you pronounce his name Jan as in yacht, not as in jam."

"So, his name means yacht in Polish does it?"

"No, it is Polish for John" explained Monk.

Jan interrupted this lexical conundrum and said, "it doesn't matter how you say it, I get this all the time it is not a problem."

Dyke shrugged his shoulders, "I dunno what the world is coming to when we have to get foreigners to do the work of honest British men-"

"Farmer Dyke," Monk interjected quickly, "the problem is that the honest British men don not want to do the dirty work. The world's changing, and these people are coming here to help us rebuild after our war losses."

"I s'pose so," replied Dyke in a tone of resignation, "but it seems a bloody, pity don't it."

Jan had become aware that his welcome to the area might not be quite as rapturous as he had expected. He had made his way here to work for money, he thought, but it was work that no one else had signed up to do. He had not taken someone else's job, he was only allowed to work in mining, steel works, chemical plants, or agriculture, and as that was all he knew about that is what he was contracted to do.

Dyke, now silenced, pulled a small aluminium box from his waistcoat pocket lifted the lid and offered its contents to the assembly. "Hedges?" he enquired of his cohorts.

"No thank you farmer Dyke, I never take snuff."

"I'm sorry but I've no idea how to take snuff," said Jan.

"It's easy, young-un," said Dyke and then gave a demonstration that only a connoisseur of snuff-taking could. After the brown dust had been laid out in the joint of his finger and thumb on the back of his hand, he brought the dust up to his nose and sniffed, first the left nostril and then the right. He then prepared to deal with the aftermath of his inhalation. He began to gasp in large quantities of air while at the same time fumbling for his handkerchief. He held on as long as possible until he was able to produce a brown kerchief of enormous volume. He then attempted to facilitate control of the sheet in order to control the ensuing issue. After what seemed like an eternity, Dyke finally produced an enormous nasal retrogression that could be heard all over the camp. As Dyke removed his hanky from his sniffling face, the visage that welcomed both Monk and Jan reminded Monk why he never took snuff and left Jan wondering why anybody would ever take snuff.

Dykes face was contorted and streaming with tears that welled up from his eyes which were caked with his wet eyelashes. His eyes looked like some kind of yellow molluscs filtering the salty brine that had opportunely presented itself. The moist hairs in his nose were now coated in the excess snuff powder hanging there like miniature brown stalactites glistening in the noon day sun. Dyke wiped and wiped again sniffing and snorting until some kind of symmetry had returned to his face.

"You buggers don't know what you're missing" wheezed Dyke as he screwed up his hanky and forced its soggy volume back into his pocket.

With order restored, Monk returned to the business at hand, the housing of Jan. "Will you be taking Jan back with you now?" enquired Monk.

"No, I bloody won't," replied Dyke. "I'm off to the village pub now, and anyway I don't want this randy bugger living at the farm in case he tries tupping our Chastity like that last article did".

Monk looked dismayed. "If you are not prepared to provide the worker with lodgings, you'll have to pay him his full remuneration and he'll have to pay for his own keep here."

"That's all right, I'll tell the missus to change the paperwork."

"So, how'll I get to work each day?" asked Jan.

"That last un left a bike, so you can have the use of that," suggested Dyke.

"So, when can Mr Kot come over to the farm to look around and be informed of his duties?" Monk asked.

"Who is this bloke Kot?"

"This is Mr Kot". Monk gestured to Jan in frustration.

Jan smiled at Dyke as if they had just met for the first time. "It's nice to meet you."

"He can come over to the farm with that other shifty sod from the hospital. He's bringing me some soot tomorrow morning" Dyke suggested.

"Fine," retorted Monk, "I now have the odious job of changing a plethora of forms, files, ration cards, and a phone call to inform the police where you will now be staying. First however, I will have to inform the kitchens and housekeeping staff of your change of circumstances at the camp."

Having wreaked administrative havoc, Dyke returned to

his car and sped off to the pub.

"Wait here," instructed Monk, and he disappeared into the office, re-emerging with a plan of the camp folded in such a way as to expose the area of the camp Monk was making for. Jan could see that each hut had a grid on it with names pencilled in with an accompanying date.

Monk led Jan across the road from the gate office to a hut directly alongside the post office by the entrance gate. They entered the hut and Monk consulted his map. He then led Jan to the back end of the hut to the last bed on the right.

"This will be yours; you can use this wardrobe but give me anything of high value to keep in my security cage in my office."

"I'm pretty sure that after four years as a prisoner of war and three more as a refugee I will have little of value." laughed Jan. "Very convenient just inside the gate though."

"That is not why you are here. We have had problems with drunken single men coming home late at night and waking the other residents and their children, this then caused fights to break out. So, we keep all the single men here. It is for a similar reason that all the single women are kept at the other end of the camp next to the priest. I think you will settle in here as you are older, but some of these boys have seen terrible things, in Siberia, in combat, and in the Soviet army and they need a good deal of discipline to keep them out of trouble."

Monk took Jan back outside to continue his induction. "Next to the kitchen block you will see the men's shower block and lavaboes."

"Lavaboes?" asked Jan.

"The facilities for ablutions," replied Monk. "On my way back to the office I will inform the kitchen committee that, from today, they must cater for you, and I'll pass them your food ration book."

Jan thanked Monk and started to sort his meagre belongings. He hung his three shirts on hangers which were emblazoned with the motif of the White Star Line. Sadly, he thought the hangers had fallen on hard times. With trousers hung and the rest of his belongings put away Jan looked around the room. Each bed had a curtain that could be pulled around it for a modicum of privacy in the same manner as a hospital. The wooden floor was swept and polished to a high shine and in the middle of the room there lived a pot-bellied stove, against which was stacked a pile of kindling and some dry logs atop which was a box of Swan-Vesta matches. The hut appeared to be run with military precision despite what Monk had alluded to.

It had been a long day, and Jan thought that prior to having lunch, he would take a nap. Lying on his bed he took stock of his situation. Thinking through the events of the day he closed his eyes. After a while he was aware that someone was standing by his bed. He opened his eyes to see who or what was intruding on his rest. To his surprise, a Boy Scout was standing there bedecked in a crisp uniform with highly polished shoes.

He saluted Jan with martial precision and said in Polish "Excuse me captain, I have a message from the security committee. Major Bialy wants to see you please."

"But I was going to have my lunch, can't he wait?"

"Lunch is served late on a Saturday to allow everybody to get back from work, if we all eat at the same time it is more efficient. please follow me. By the way captain, you're not allowed to wear your boots on your bed."

Jan was about to apologise, but he decided that would be taking the countenance of the polite newcomer just one step too far.

Jan followed the boy to the community centre hut, where he had earlier met Professor Kaminski. The boy opened the door, ushered him in, and then waited outside in case he was needed. At the far end of the hall, in front of the stage, was a row of trestle tables covered in green baize. Sat behind these tables were several men, all of whom were trying to make an instant assessment of him. As Jan got within six feet of the assembly, the central figure spoke.

"That will do, captain, stand there please."

"I'm not a captain," protested Jan. "I've held no military rank for eight years"

"Captain!" Major Bialy interrupted, "it is clear to those who are interested in such matters that a third world war is imminent therefore we must all be ready to do our part when the time comes. Our journey isn't over. We represent the official Polish nation, uninfected by Soviet lies and treachery, abandoned by the allies that we fought and died for,. We've to make the last part of the journey on our own to a free Poland. Do you still have your uniform and insignia?"

"No. When the French surrendered, my unit was in the field, we were ordered to remove our uniform jackets and hand them and all our weapons to the Germans."

"Did you try to escape?"

"Yes, we'd been told that the British were sending ships to pick up as many Poles as possible, so we tried to get to the coast. However, when we arrived at the port many of the places had been taken by staff officers who had no active role in the French forces, and the ships had left.

"I and some of my comrades started moving south, ahead of the advance trying to get to Portugal or Spain. We saw a French military unit on the road south and asked for help. They arrested us and handed us over to the Germans."

"Did you make contact with the French resistance?"

"No"

"What about communist partisans?"

"No" Jan exclaimed most emphatically, finding it hard to understand why he was being subjected to this line of questioning three years after the war.

Bialy continued his line of questioning. "Captain, we've been in touch with London since your arrival. You were highly regarded by your superiors. We'll need reliable men like you soon so you must be ready to act at a moment's notice."

Jan once more tried to explain that those opinions counted for very little now, three years after the war. He turned and proceeded to walk out of the hall. Undeterred, the major turned to a functionary at the end of the table and barked,

"Corporal, find the captain a uniform and some insignia." The functionary hastily jotted down assumed measurements on a piece of thin yellowing paper with the stub of a pencil as Jan receded from view.

"Captain, be careful who you speak to and what you say, our enemy is amongst us sending reports back to Moscow of our preparations, plans, and intentions. Many of our countrymen are confused and have disorganised minds, some, who are not patriots are returning home giving support to Moscow's lie that all is normal in the Motherland."

"I'll keep my eye out," confirmed Jan sarcastically and he left the hall.

As Jan walked the short distance back to his hut, the camp buzzed with activity. Mothers steered young children towards the canteen, followed by old men who spoke on the weighty topics of that day's political developments. Jan took this as a sign that lunch was ready, and he followed the throng of people into the canteen where all still seemed impervious to his presence as before.

On entering the canteen, it became apparent that there

existed a system of social boundaries that divided the diners into selected classes and perceived statuses. Families with children were seated near to the serving hatch, to the right of them at what looked like the top table sat many of the committee men that Jan had met earlier plus Professor Kaminski and a priest. Next came the single men and women, kept from association by two tables that divided them for the old and infirm, one allotted to men and one to women. All took to their assigned tables and waited patiently.

Jan sat at the single men's table, looked across at his dining companion nodded, and introduced himself, "Jan."

"Marek," came the reply, and this was followed by a broad grin.

At last, a friendly face he thought. He felt that based on the grin alone, this reaction warranted further investigation, but before he could utter his first enquiry, his new companion started his own interrogation.

"You are new here, yes?" asked the inquisitor.

"Yes."

"I will be taking you to farmer Dyke in the morning after breakfast, as I have some merchandise for him."

"Soot?"

"Yes, but it's not just soot, everything has a value. Everything is merchandise; there's money to be made everywhere if you know what is wanted and where it can be found. If a man can find what people want and sell it to them, he can become very rich."

Jan nodded in such a way as to show an understanding of his new friend's creed. At this point, the food hatch was slammed open by a member of the kitchen staff sending a cloud of steam-laden aromas into the seating area.

This action was the trigger for the whole of the single women's table to rise as one and file up to the hatch. Jan made a move to stand up as he wanted to be sure not to miss his first chance of food that day. Marek signalled with the flat of his hand that he should remain seated. The young women then took the first bowls of soup to the elderly on the table next to them.

This service was then extended to the 'top table' which included many of the security committee, Professor Kaminski, and the priest. Eventually, after the family tables had been served, the single men finally got their soup. Jan made a move to pick up his spoon to begin, and again Marek signalled that he was to wait.

Finally, as the single women sat down with their soup the priest stood up and chanted grace in Polish and gestured over the whole canteen with an expansive sign of the cross to which many replied, "Amen." Conversations halted all over the hall as the hurried clinking of spoons on dishes signalled a satisfactory soup had been provided. A wicker basket with just enough rye bread in it for one piece for each diner was positioned centrally on the table, Jan could see that eager eyes policed this rationing, to ensure equitable and fair apportioning of this meagre feast.

As the soup was consumed, the level of chatter in the canteen began to rise. This was the sign for a member of the kitchen staff to come out with a trolley to collect up the empty vessels and spoons. Those who had not finished clung to their bowls protecting them from her eager grasp.

She disappeared into the kitchen with her laden trolley only to reappear moments after with an empty one for those slow consumers to place their bowls on when finished. All at once the kitchen shutter slammed open again and the single women sprang to their feet to perform their catering duties once more as before.

After lunch Marek followed Jan back to his hut and sat on the bed next to him, to talk.

"Are you sure you can sit on that bed?" Jan asked sarcastically.

"Of course, it's mine,"

Around them, an assortment of young men slept, read Polish language newspapers, or changed into their tidy clothes in preparation for some outing or romantic assignation. "Would you like me to show you around the area this afternoon? We can travel in style as I have my own transport."

"That'll be great, but first could I steal an hour or two's sleep as I have been up since 4 a.m."

"Of course, I have some business to attend to anyway, so I'll pick you up at 4 p.m." said Marek. With that sorted, Jan slipped into the arms of Morpheus.

In what seemed like an instant, Jan was wakened by a polite cough. He opened his eyes to see Marek standing over him.

"Ready to go?" he asked cheerfully.

"What's the weather like?"

"You'll need a coat" Marek informed him, and with that the intrepid travellers stepped outside into an indifferent afternoon. There, parked outside the hut, was an American army motorbike and sidecar still in its olive-green colour, it did however, have its white star painted out in a green that was about ten shades deeper. Jan looked at the hastily painted star with such a glare of disbelief that Marek was able to pre-empt his question.

"British Army gloss green, it was all I could get, and the police told me that if I didn't paint out the star they would confiscate my bike." Marek gestured to Jan to climb in, and two things struck Jan immediately. Firstly, how much room there was in the sidecar and secondly, the strong smell of mashed potatoes that pervaded the inner sidecar seating area.

"Where did you buy this?" asked Jan, expecting some long, drawn-out epistle on Marek's miraculous discovery of it in an empty barn.

"Army and navy surplus" was the matter-of-fact reply. "When I came to Britain, earlier this year, I had a large number of dollars in cash. When I tried to deposit them in a post office account at the camp, she asked too many questions about how I had come by that much cash. I then tried a bank in the town, but they too were interested in how I had accumulated such a large amount of dollars, so I decided to invest the money in a motorbike as a way of 'kick starting' my business endeavours."

Jan decided to press no harder on this line of questioning, and they set off.

"First," announced Marek, as if he were delivering a tour itinerary, "we must check the traps." They turned left out of the gate of the camp and started to climb the gentle slope that would eventually take them to the chalk downland. Marek drove his charge with great care and propriety. Suddenly his arm shot out to the left, and they turned down a narrow lane, then right, and then left again. Marek navigated the maze of country lanes like a local who'd grown up in the village. After a while, Jan could see a column of white steamy smoke moving swiftly through the folds of the landscape, betraying the presence of a railway line and its burden forging southwest on its permanent way. After a short while the boys arrived at a crossing point over the track. It was constructed of sleepers that provided a level surface for farm wagons to cross on.

The crossing was situated on the inside curve of a long sweeping track which could only be crossed safely if there was an observer on the far side of the outside curve of the tracks which benefited from a clear view in both directions. The cant of the twin tracks, banked up on aggregate to allow the trains to take the long curve at speed, were carved into a hillside which rose seventy feet like a green amphitheatre.

"Shall I go across and see if it's clear?"

"No need" replied Marek pulling a timetable from his inside coat pocket. He studied it, interrogating its confusion of tables, folded it shut, replaced it in his inside pocket, and proceeded across with utmost caution.

They left the bike on the farm track and having both decamped their transport, started to climb the steep bank which disappeared to their left and out of view. Marek pointed to a brown warning sign.

"That sign is from the old Great Western Railway it is called British Railways now. During the war, due to pressure on the system, the banking was neglected and became infested with rabbits. The rabbits were safe from hunters as the banks had been off limits, had a breeding explosion, and had burrowed into the banks causing landslides.

Now the new owners are trying to bring the system back to some kind of order. I answered an advert, placed by British Railways, in the local press for an agent to control the vermin. I was the successful applicant and am paid ten shillings a month to control the rabbits by trapping."

Marek scaled the embankment like a mountain goat. Every now and then he would extricate a dead rabbit from a snare and, when his burden became too cumbersome, he would summon Jan over to take the quarry off him.

"Jan; hold the heads down with their back legs tied with this sisal twine. That will keep the carcasses in good condition," instructed Marek. Some of the rabbits were still pliant and, in one case, still warm. After about half an hour, they had harvested around a dozen of the unfortunates and Marek returned with his snares and they loaded their bounty into the sidecar.

"Aren't you going to re-set the snares?"

"No, I don't have time to return today, and any rabbit trapped would spoil overnight and the butcher will only pay a shilling for rabbits in good condition, so they have to be fresh."

The hunters returned to their transport. A satisfied Marek threw his leg over the saddle of his bike, adjusted his position, and with a contented smile on his face prepared to make the journey towards more profit.

CHAPTER 2
A CAUSE FOR CELEBRATION

As the motorbike was kicked into life, Jan sat with his dead travelling companions and took in the scenery. Eventually, they arrived in the local market town. As they passed through the market square, the costermongers were frantically wrapping and packing their produce for the journey home. Marek left the square and made his way up a narrow side street, eventually turning into the back yard of a butcher's shop. The butcher was waiting for him, Marek took the carcasses over. After a short while, money changed hands and Marek was on his way. Retracing their steps, back to the marketplace, they left by another road and started to leave the town. Just as the houses began to dissolve into tree-lined countryside, the bike was steered through a pair of imposing iron gates that hung on monumental stone pillars.

Jan shouted at Marek, "Where are we?" as he was sure they had arrived at a palace. Marek pointed to a large sign, in the bushes, that indicated that they had, in fact, arrived at a psychiatric hospital. As the two rode through the extensive parkland, they eventually started to encounter those unfortunate souls who were under its care, walking in silent contemplation of their lot, some staring at the ground, some staring to a distant horizon fixed in what Jan knew to be the thousand-yard stare, an indication that some past horror had been visited on that poor, hopeless case.

In the middle of the estate, there was set a large house, as big and imposing as any Jan had seen. Adjacent to the house but discreetly masked by trees was a large boiler house, its chimney belching yellow grey smoke. Marek pulled up by a side door.

"Wait here," instructed Marek, and disappeared into the hissing, steaming bowels of the building. He eventually re-emerged, carrying a sack. "Soot," Marek declared, indicating to Jan to move his body so that the sack could be stowed at the front of the sidecar.

"How are you able to just walk into a boiler house and come out with a sack of soot?" enquired Jan.

"It's easy, I work here."

As the young men sped out of the estate Marek left by a muddy farm track that carried them out into the countryside once more. Jan was convinced that they were lost, but after an uncomfortable ten minutes of bone-shaking purgatory, they emerged onto the farm track which took them back to the outside curve of the railway line they had visited earlier. With their view unimpaired, they rode over the tracks and made their way back to the camp.

However, instead of turning into the camp, Marek sped past the gates and after a while they arrived at the village. Marek pulled up on the village green opposite a pub named 'The Bell', which the sign proclaimed was a purveyor of fine beers, wines and spirits. The young men parked their transport and walked into the pubs bar.

"Good evening chaps" said the landlord politely, "what'll it be?"

"Two pints and one for yourself," declared Marek.

"That's very kind of you, but it's a bit early for me. Do you mind if I have it later?" Marek nodded his approval, and the two travellers quenched the dust of the trail with two foaming glasses of Indian pale ale.

"You bought him a drink; do you know the landlord well?"

"No, but he is a businessman, and I may need to sell him something one day," replied Marek with entrepreneurial vigour.

The pints slipped down with speed and audible approval, and Marek signalled his host that two more were required.

"It's a new barrel that I put on this morning" said the landlord, in the manner of a man who knew how to keep a good pint of beer.

"I can't have another; I have no cash on me."

"Don't worry, this is payment for your help this afternoon, and don't worry, you'll soon get a chance to buy me a beer."

As the two quaffed another pint the landlord took this opportunity to get to know his customers. "I'm James," he said, as he lovingly dried a pint glass. "I was in the RAF during the war, and I promised myself that if I survived, I would settle down in a nice quiet village and run a pub. Little did I realise, that my pub would be at the end of a runway."

This irony was not lost on his two customers who signalled this by rolling their eyes while still sipping beer. James's monologue continued, in the way of a barber or travelling companion on a train, the weather, sport, or local news, but never straying into religion or politics. As the evening light faded, James switched on some lights to illuminate the proceedings. The bulbs yellowed with smoke cast out an opaque light no brighter than the light that faded through the small windows of the pub.

This peaceful scene was, at once, interrupted by a gang of young men who had come in and walked over to the bar in excited expectation. Their voices were not those of the vowel filled locals but were clipped with a finesse which betrayed the fact that these were from an educated class that saw itself as separate and did not feel privy to the politeness of keeping quiet in a public place.

Filled with this same confidence the first young man came over and said,

"Hello," to Marek who gave a wave of salutation. The youth then turned to Jan and introduced himself.

"Hello old boy, my name's Tony Sharpe, I'm one of the lads from the university group who've come down to help out with the spring planting and who'll stay till the harvest is in." "Ah, so you and I are doing the same thing. I've come here to help out too. I've just arrived. I'm farmer Dyke's new shepherd."

"Ah Dyke, I know him, good man, good man," replied Sharpe, at which point he was called away by his cohorts, but as he returned to them, he spun around.

"Maybe we could meet again soon, you can tell me all about yourself, where you are from, your family, what your plans are. I would love to know as I am conducting a study into diaspora at Cambridge." Jan nodded and the encounter was over.

Marek signalled to Jan that it was time to go, and as they left the bar, the two bade their host goodnight and returned to the camp. The pair had missed dinner due to their excursion, however. As they dismounted from the parked motorbike, Marek, ever resourceful, pulled two pork pies from his jacket pocket.

"A gift from the butcher." He smiled as the pies were eaten on the walk back to their hut.

"How did you get your job at the hospital?"

"Before the war, back in Poland, I had been a storeman for a coal mine in the south of the country, buying pit props, electrical equipment and the like. I put this information on my application sheet for work in Britain in the hope that I would get a high paid job in mining. When my job allocation came through, I was informed that I would be a stoker at a boiler house at the hospital we visited earlier. While I was unhappy at first, it turned out that the job had many fringe benefits and so I decided to stay there.

"Could we be at the farm as early as possible tomorrow Jan? I want to get back for the mass at eleven o'clock."

Jan looked at Marek.

"You don't seem to be a particularly religious individual."

"I'm not" Marek confirmed, "but tomorrow is Easter Sunday, and I feel the need to continue a tradition that started back home in Poland. There, my whole family would attend at least one mass together a year and that was the mass."

"My goodness! I had no idea it was Easter. Life in the transit camp, the journey, the upheaval had all caused me to forget what day it was."

"Do you take an interest in religion?"

"Not really, but like you, I hope my family in Poland will be at church, and in this way I will feel closer to them. We can go to the farm straight after breakfast I'll be ready when you are."

"You really aren't religious are you? There is no breakfast, it's Easter Sunday and it'll be after church tomorrow as everyone'll be fasting for communion."

Both men felt this an imposition having to wait for breakfast due to a religious practice that neither of them particularly ascribed to. They wished each other good night and entered the darkened hut, and made their way to bed.

Bright and early, they rose, made use of the shower block which was empty due to the hour and set off for the farm armed with good intentions and soot. As they followed the lane straight towards the downs it slowly began to rise until, after a couple of miles it levelled out and it was on this plateau to the left of the lane that the farm was situated.

"Priory farm," announced Marek. It was eight o'clock and the farmyard was silent. "I don't know where everyone is," said Marek, "Sid, the cowman, should be here somewhere. I'll put the soot on a cart in the cart shed and we can have a look around."

The pair set off around the farm buildings, their red brick glowing orange in the morning sun and the pan-tiled roofs flaking with frost damage that had been etched into them over the centuries. Jan thought, however, that the farm seemed in good order. Yards were swept, muck was piled, and hay was stacked. The equipment, although old was well maintained and protected under cover. He felt that Dyke must know the value of his equipment and, hopefully, his workers, and this made him feel more at ease about the coming days and months.

As they walked deeper into the complex of low buildings they came upon the empty milking parlour. Its glistening floor and strong smell of chlorine suggested that the milking was over for now. Opposite to the milking parlour and across the stock yard were the stables. The young men walked across and as they approached the giant heads of two shire horses emerged from their respective stables.

"This is Dolly, and this is Bubbles. Bubbles is so named because her mane is tight and curly, and Dolly is named after Dyke's wife, Dorothy, although I am not sure if she knows that."

The pair laughed and moved out of the yard and over to a great tithe barn set on a slight rise. Marek opened one of the giant oak doors to reveal an assault on the senses that flooded Jan's memory of home. The sweet smell of meadow hay filled the air, and this was mixed with the pungency of linseed oil-rich sacks of cattle cake, the sacks stacked on a platform of wire milk crates to keep them out of the reach of the damp. A clamp of potatoes and another, larger one of swedes and sugar beet was stored next to a hand cranked machine to chip them for the cattle feed. Jan could appreciate that this was a farm where animal husbandry was a priority, and that he would fit in well.

As the men walked towards the pig sties a shrill voice hailed them.

"Morning boys."

"That is Chastity, Dyke's daughter," Marek informed Jan quietly from the corner of his mouth. "We're very close," Marek whispered.

"Hello Marek, are we still going today?"

Marek nodded confirmation and took this opportunity to introduce Jan.

"Chastity, this is Jan Kot, your new shepherd."

After a handshake, Jan stood back to let the young couple talk about their plans for the day and he watched her as she sidled up to Marek. Chastity was bubbly with smiling eyes, and she appeared to have no sense of propriety. She was fulsome in her bounty, and much of that bounty was on show, but Jan could see that she had a good heart.

She radiated human warmth that Jan had found in short supply since his arrival, and it made him happy that his new friend could find such a girl in the desert of despair that infused camp life.

"Chastity, I was wondering where Sid was, as I wanted Jan to meet him to find out what his duties would be."

"Oh, as it is Easter Sunday, Sid milked early and has gone home. Father will milk later and get ready for the Monday collection of churns. We hadn't expected Jan to start till Tuesday as we assumed he would travel up from Havant during Monday. Why don't you come back on Tuesday morning at eight o'clock, Jan? Sid will have finished milking by then and the two of you could spend the day together learning the ropes."

"That sounds fine. Could I ask where the bike might be so that I could ride back to the camp?"

Chasitity directed him towards the cart shed where he found his transport leaning up against a wagon. Jan dusted off the saddle, which had a small pouch full of tools suspended from it, and astride his new charge, attempted to ride out of the shed, but to his dismay, both tyres were flat.

Marek, by this time, had disappeared through a large box hedge and was sitting on a bench outside the farmhouse, which was concealed by the neatly trimmed hedge, and so, Jan decided to push the bike back to the camp and make any necessary repairs.

By ten o'clock, Jan had washed the bike, adjusted the saddle, tensioned the chain, and had removed the tyres and tubes to effect repairs. He decided that if he was going to church, he had better get cleaned up and put on his one good shirt and his best, and only, smart trousers. As Jan changed by his bed Marek came in and handed him a small sack which contained rubber patches, rubber solution glue, a chain, padlock, and key.

"Where did you get this from, and how much do I owe you?"

"I've borrowed it from the farm workshop so that you can repair your tyres. You can take it back on Tuesday. But keep the padlock and chain as I am not the only 'business-man' around here, and if you don't chain up your bike, it'll go missing."

The boys made their way outside and walked over to the church where Chastity was waiting for them by the entrance. The church was crowded, but they managed to find a space at the end of the bench in the last row at the back. The day was sunny and warm, and so, Chastity had decided to wear a summer dress in a floral print, which did not meet with the approval of many with more Catholic tastes. Chastity was attracting glances of admiration and admonishment in equal measure. It was only the beginning of the service that served to quell the muttering and murmuring.

With the sudden chimes of a set of altar bells the celebrants began to process into the small church, first, an honour guard of Boy Scouts, followed by the children's choir singing a Polish hymn. As the vanguard of the procession moved up the aisle, they were followed by six altar boys, the last two of whom held poles and silk ropes that were attached to a canopy under which the priest walked. This canopy was stabilised at the rear by two more altar boys gripping poles and silk ropes trying to keep an even tension on the canopy so that it neither sagged nor swayed as they walked.

As this caravan progressed, it was followed by a group of men in suits with red-and-white sashes across their chests, many resplendent with a row of clinking shiny medals, proof, if it was needed that these men had endured many harsh days at war. At their front was the flag bearing party, the bearer holding the Polish flag at forty-five degrees. This was followed by several other flags of differing Corps and ex-combatants' associations.

As the column dissipated to their allotted areas at the front of the church the flags were placed in holders on the wall and all and sundry took their place so that the service could begin.

As Jan watched, It became clear to him that Chastity was out of her religious depth. Chastity, he thought, associated church with a social function, a chance to be seen, a place to proclaim one's loyalty to the establishment and to preserve its Protestant values and traditions.

Jan had seen the Protestant Church at work within the

British forces. While the core message of Easter Sunday was the same, it was expressed here in a totally alien way to anything that she had witnessed at church fetes or evensong over the years. Jan realised that most confusing for her was the fact that the whole proceeding was spoken in Latin, and when, on occasion it wasn't, it was in Polish.

As the mass progressed, Jan, Marek and the congregation seemed to know instinctively when to stand, sit, and kneel. For most of them, this was the product of a lifetime's devotion that began in childhood.

Jan began to smile as he watched Chastity, as the moves were carried out with such speed and accuracy that Chastity always found herself one move behind, sitting when she should be kneeling and standing when she should be sitting. It reminded Jan of a bad chorus line dancer who had missed one too many rehearsals and this was opening night. The bells, the clouds of incense, the solemn hymns, the overt spiritual devotion were overwhelming her, and its intensity seemed to be unsettling her greatly.

After what must have seemed like an eternity to her, the mass finished. However, this was not the end of the spectacle. Instead of drifting out of the church for a chat in the porch area like Chastity was prone to do after church, the exiting was a rerun of the original entry. The Scouts first formed a guard of honour on the path outside the church, then the priest in his mobile marquee with his altar boys plus some other sides men hitherto unseen processed down the aisle.

Flags were then unfurled, and the military detachment marched away followed by the choir and then from the front pews the notables emerged followed by the rest of the congregation, row after row peeling away all joining in a solemn dirge as they walked. Jan, Marek and Chastity took their places at the rear of this column.

"Are you OK Chastity? you seemed a bit overwhelmed in there."

"It was a bit much," Chastity confided quietly, out of ear-shot of Marek. "I'm not sure that I could get used to it."

Still singing, the pageant of colour and devoted emotion made its way across the road to the canteen where an Easter breakfast had been prepared by the ladies of the camp. When Jan and Marek entered the canteen they could not believe their eyes.

The seating was still based on status, but the tables were decorated with greenery and daffodils, and baskets of deco-rated, nut-brown, hard-boiled eggs were placed on each table. There were jugs of fruit compote on all the tables and platters of poppy seed cake glazed in icing and dried fruits. Clearly, this was a departure from the austere normality that had greeted the boys so far.

There was an air of celebration that was palpable, which lifted the spirits in the room. As soon as the boys and their guest were seated, the younger women, as normal, distributed bowls of traditional hot soup, a kind of white *barszcz*, which had halves of hard-boiled eggs and Polish sausage in it. A sec-ond young woman placed large baskets of rye bread on each table, triple the normal ration.

"You won't see anything like this in an English restaurant, Chasity!" Marek said, unaware of the effect his world was hav-ing on hers.

Jan watched as she examined the bowl's contents with a degree of suspicion while her hosts alongside her seemed to revel in its appearance. Jan could see that Chastity, who had been brought up with good manners and a modicum of eti-quette, had resigned herself to eating the dish.

However, just as she had come to this conclusion a third young lady floated by at speed charging each bowl with fresh cream from a large jug. Jan felt so sorry for her, Chastity stilled herself to consume this witch's brew and picked up her spoon, an action which was greeted by a sea of waving hands from her hosts imploring her to put down the spoon. Chastity's face turned bright red, and she sat looking down at her lap.

As the chanting of grace subsided, the room was enveloped in excited chatter, clinking spoons and a sense of bonhomie which neither of the boys had witnessed since their arrival. The second course was quartered roast rabbit with potatoes sprinkled with fennel shoots and mixed vegetables with a rich gravy. Jan looked at Marek and smiled.

"Let's just call it a marketing exercise."

Chastity was on familiar culinary territory now and happily consumed the game.

As plates were cleared away and cups of tea were served to accompany the cakes, the hum of voices rose to an excited peak which only abated with the high-pitched clinking of a knife on glass and the room fell silent. Major Bialy rose to his feet and spoke in Polish.

"I would like to start by thanking those responsible for preparing and providing the meal that we have enjoyed. But my address must turn to more serious matters." His speech was impassioned and calculated to raise the emotions of his audience.

"First, I must address the betrayal of the Poles by their allies which had led to the Poles spending another Easter away from their motherland. Secondly, by the committees assessment, a third world war must soon come, and we exiled Poles must be ready to join their brothers in Poland in the final struggle.

"Finally, I can't stress enough how important it is that we preserve our culture, traditions and religion as these are the pillars of our nation. On Easter Monday evening at six o'clock there will be a public meeting in the camp dance hall followed by entertainment and dancing. As this is a public holiday most, if not all, of the camp residents should be able to attend. Mr Monk will attend to make some announcements and answer questions."

As the meal came to an end, the young women moved to clear away the empty dishes and straighten the room, whilst the throng of diners returned to their huts or gathered outside in the sunshine to chat.

"I'm taking Chastity for a ride in the countryside. Would you like to come Jan?"

Jan, sensing that this invitation was more out of politeness than desire, declined,

"No thanks, Marek, I think I'll spend my afternoon fixing my bike. You two get off."

So, as Marek and Chastity disappeared down the lane in a cloud of blue smoke, Jan returned to his hut, got changed, and continued to repair his newfound mode of transport. As he did so, he mused that it was good to be using his hands again to be building something of use as not only was the bike providing him with transport for work but also giving him some independence.

With his repairs completed and filled with a positivity he had not felt for a long time, Jan washed his hands and returned to his hut for a sleep. As he sat on his bed to remove his boots, he smiled to himself and thought, "Bloody Boy Scout."

Jan's sleep was not, on the whole, a satisfactory one as it was as though he was balanced on the cusp of consciousness. It was punctuated by the sudden screams of playing children, the murmur of conversations, and the excited chatter of women in the next hut preparing the next evening's festivities. The bright sun streaming in through the huts windows eventually persuaded him to get up and make the most of the day.

As Jan left the hut, he noticed Professor Kaminski sat on

the porch of the hall hut, writing a letter. Jan decided to try and reacquaint himself with the professor, so he wandered over to him and sat next to him.

"Good afternoon professor,"

The professor acknowledged him with the briefest of smiles and a nod.

"Are you writing a letter home?"

"No, I am writing to an old work colleague whom I corresponded with before the war at Oxford University. I have written to him on several occasions in the hope that he could help me find work at his university."

"Any luck?"

"No. The work we did together just before the war was of the utmost importance and we made a number of breakthroughs which I am unable to speak about now."

"It must have been very important work" said Jan, but not wishing to pry, he changed the subject. "Do you have work here?" Jan enquired.

"No, I don't, I exist on a small amount of money from the British government and that is supplemented with money from the Polish army who donate one day's pay to help those without work."

Before Jan could respond he heard a familiar voice call across the camp compound. "Hello, old chap, nice to see you again!" Jan recognised the voice of Tony Sharpe who walked across to him and the professor.

"Good evening, professor, are you ready for our game?" The professor nodded and Tony pulled a chess board and box of pieces out of a pouch he had slung over his shoulder.

"Do you play, Jan?"

"No, I have never learnt."

"Maybe I could teach you and we could meet up sometimes?"

"No thank you, Tony, I don't think I will have the time now."

"If you change your mind, just let the professor know. We meet each Sunday to play, and we exchange all the gossip in the camp and discuss world affairs. You will be most welcome."

Jan decided to leave the two of them on the porch in the soft evening sunshine, and, as the faithful returned to the church for the second time that day, he wandered on around the camp. After wandering aimlessly for several minutes, Jan became aware that the quiet order of the camp had perceptibly changed to a scene comparable to near unruly disorder.

Outside the last two huts at the rear of the camp, groups of men sat on wooden crates smoking and gambling. Small shot glasses littered the makeshift tables, bottles of spirits were concealed within the packing cases, a ruse that fooled nobody. Men spoke in excited tones and across the camp road some women sat peeling vegetables on the porch chatting and laughing in what Jan recognised as at least three languages.

No vegetables grew, no chickens clucked, no tobacco dried, weeds grew in between the kerbstones, and the area around the huts was unkempt and unmown.

"Hey Polish!" shouted one of the women on the porch, "why have you come here to the foreigner's huts?"

"I'm sorry to interrupt you but who are you all?"

At this, one of the gamblers put down his hand of cards and spoke.

"We are Hungarians, Czechs, Germans, Latvians, Lithuanians, Ukrainians, we are the forgotten. We have come here to work to help Britain get back on her feet while some of our countries remain under the communist boot, and how do they thank us?

"They put us in cold huts in the middle of nowhere and charge us for the privilege, and the pay we receive doesn't allow us any hope of a future, that is who we are."

Jan was by now feeling like a foreigner himself, like someone who had stumbled into a bizarre chaotic scene such was

37

the difference in conditions within just feet from each other.

He bade the throng "good evening" and returned to his ordered world.

As Jan passed the professor and Tony on the hall porch, he thought he might enquire as to why the foreigners appeared to be on the margins of camp life. The professor was quick to answer.

"They're financial adventurers; not political refugees like us. They choose not to involve themselves in camp life and always demand special treatment."

"We hardly ever see them," Tony added, "as they work most of the time leaving early and coming back late. It's only because of the Easter holidays that they are about."

"Do they all work on farms around here?"

"No" said Tony, "most of the women work at the flax factory in town and the men mostly work in food processing at the milk and bacon factories near here. So, in a sense I suppose they do work in agriculture."

Tony returned to his chess game, and Jan returned to his hut, which was now full as church was over, and most had availed themselves of a light supper and retired. Jan chatted with the other men, and after a while, Marek returned to his bed, threw off his boots and lay on his back with his head cushioned in his hands, so Jan wandered over to chat to him. "Everything OK?" asked Jan as he could see that Marek was uncharacteristically quiet and pensive.

"Well, I'm not sure if it is, I've known Chastity for three months now and we have had some fun, going to dances, the cinema, and trips out into the countryside at weekends when I am not working. Today I mentioned to her that I liked her and would like to make our friendship more formal."

"What did she say?" asked Jan fearing the answer that was to come.

"She said that I was sweet, and that she enjoyed my company

but that her parents would not agree to her becoming involved with a foreigner as we had nothing in common and that she would be expected to marry into a farming family."

"I can see why you are so upset."

"Yes," said an exasperated Marek, "I was so close to marrying into a farming family, but after months of planning and hard work, it was all for nothing-"

"Hold on a minute! Do you mean to tell me that you don't love her but were just trying to get hold of the farm?"

"Well, you can learn to love somebody over time, but you can't find a farm going for free every day," reasoned Marek.

"Are you crazy?" Jan exclaimed through gritted teeth, as quietly as he could. "We don't belong here; these people don't want us here and no matter how nice they are to us we will never be treated as equals here. Everything we get we will have to work hard for, and none of these people will make it any easier for us. We are not living in a new country, Marek, we are living in a new world!"

At once Jan realised he may have crossed a line in dishing out his sage advice so abruptly. Marek was the one person who had befriended him and offered him help and kindness since his arrival at the camp, and Jan felt that maybe he should have tempered his admonishment to reflect this.

"Look, it's great that you want to get on and make a success of your life but maybe there are easier ways of doing it than the way you have chosen"

"Like what?" demanded Marek.

"Well, there are some nice single Polish girls here on the camp and any of them would make an ideal wife. They're young, hardworking, and they've come here to start a new life. Why don't you get to know one of them and see where that takes you?"

Already half considering the suggestion, and having instantly weighed up his options, Marek said,

"That Marta is the only girl on the camp that I feel could meet my needs, however, she is seeing the son of her employers at the manor, and he's a pilot, and I don't think my ex-army motorbike can compete with his sports car and lifestyle."

"Ah, that could be a problem," said Jan, but he thought to himself that having now planted that seed, he would allow it to germinate.

**

The next morning Jan was disturbed by Marek as he dressed for the early shift at the boiler house. It was still dark, and as Jan heard Marek's motorbike splutter to life, he rolled over and went back to sleep. What seemed like a moment later, he was awakened by girls screaming and running in all directions, chased by young men spraying water on them and a busy throng in his hut chatting, dressing and getting ready for breakfast. It was wet Monday, and for many the Easter holiday still bestowed one last day of leisure, so Jan decided to spend his on his bike, riding around the country lanes and exploring. Jan now had a general understanding of the area, so he decided he would visit the one place he had seen from his very first day but was yet to explore, the down land.

After breakfast, he unchained his bike and set off up the lane. Soon he was passing the farm on his left as he slowly climbed the hill, then, on his right, a field of sheep with a donkey in attendance with a crude metal bell hanging from a collar clanking as it fed on the grass. In a short while, the hill became so steep that Jan had to dismount and push his bike until after, what seemed like an eternity Jan reached the top of the hill.

Jan stood and took in the view that greeted him. The steep green escarpment of the downs was corrugated with horizontal animal tracks and every mile or so beech woods crouched and clung in the lee of the hills for the protection it afforded them. Stretched out before him was a sea of grassland where this undulating vista stretched to the horizon which was dotted with juniper and gorse bushes. It reminded him of the Russian Steppes that he had trudged over in 1939, day after day of relentless struggle into an uncertain future. But these lands seemed benign, almost benevolent, with their mild breezes and soft sunlight and the air filled with lark song as spring took hold.

However, as Jan pushed on, he came to a barbed-wire fence that stretched out of sight to left and right. Periodically, a small triangular sign attached to an angle iron was driven into the unyielding chalk. Jan walked along to one of these signs and read it, 'Danger of Death', it proclaimed, 'Unexploded Ordinance', 'Keep Out'. Suddenly, this rural idyll had come into sharp focus with the sobering realities that persisted in post-war Britain.

Barred from proceeding further ahead, Jan mounted his bike and rode east along the chalk track that ran along the edge of the downs. After riding for a while he heard what he thought was the squealing of pigs coming from the wooded slopes below. As a farmer himself, Jan decided to investigate. Dismounting, Jan carefully guided his bike down the furrowed slope and entered the wood. In a small chalk cleft, Jan found a pig stie fashioned from rusty iron sheeting, steel angle posts and various other materials cobbled together into a shelter.

The stie contained a well-fed sow and eight healthy piglets, proof Jan thought that these were the property of some smallholder who lived locally in the village. However, Jan was puzzled that the pigs were in such an isolated area away from habitation and this he thought must make it very inconvenient to feed and care for them, but they seemed content and so Jan retraced his steps and continued on his way.

On reaching the track, Jan decided to head in the opposite direction to explore the western reaches of the down land track. He rode on, eventually passing his point of entry onto the downs, and then carried on along the track for a few miles more. Eventually, Jan decided that as beautiful as it was, the downs were not going to offer up any more surprises, and he stopped to rest, leaning his bike up against a metal post. It was then that he noticed that without the rattle of the bike, he was suddenly immersed in perfect peace, just him and the soaring larks shared this tranquil utopia. Jan found a certain solace in this landscape and instantly knew that he would enjoy his time there.

After spending a while absorbing his surroundings, Jan was aware of a rhythmic whooshing noise invading his peace. He turned and looked down into the valley below. It was a train on the mainline forging its way up to London. Jolted back to reality, Jan looked at his watch and decided it was time to return to the camp for dinner and hopefully an after-dinner snooze.

CHAPTER 3
LIKE OLD TIMES

L ater that same evening Jan and Marek made their way to the community hall for the camp meeting. All the seats were taken so they stood at the back of the hall and chatted. After a short wait a long line of officials processed onto the stage and assumed their seats in order of seniority, shuffling their papers and files into some kind of order. It appeared that the more important the position of the council member, the bigger their pile of papers appeared to be.

The expectant hum of voices in the hall slowly died away as the stage filled with the lesser officials and it became apparent that the evening's business was about to commence. The meeting was called to order and the priest stood and offered a prayer to the assembly hoping for good counsel and successful outcomes. The chairman, Major Bialy, then announced the agenda details apologising for the lack of copies for the audience, explaining that this was due to paper rationing.

"As our first order of business, I will introduce Mr Monk."

Monk, who was sat in the front row of the audience, was accompanied by an interpreter. As the whole proceeding was conducted in Polish ,it was only when he heard his name that

Monk jumped up and turned to face the gathering. He gave a nervous cough and launched into his report, waiting for a moment or so for it to be repeated in Polish.

"The major and I met earlier today, and this is a synopsis of the information I gave to the major. Firstly, with the except for a few single females, the last of the European voluntary worker's living on the camp will soon be leaving for an empty POW camp in the next village." This was met with stifled approval by his audience.

"Secondly, this is being done so that more Polish families can be settled in the vacant huts." This comment also attracted muted approval.

Monk then went on to say,

"if any camp members are trying to trace missing relatives, the Red Cross liaison officer, Mrs Jarvis, will be attending the camp the following Saturday to review their cases."

Then Monk dropped his bombshell!

"Sadly, I have had a number of complaints that a young English woman was brought onto the camp this weekend without the approval of the committee or myself."

As this announcement was made, Marek, who was leaning on the hut wall at the back of the hall with Jan, stood bolt upright looking for signs of approval from members of the audience that might betray the mischief maker. None were forthcoming, so he looked at Jan and rolled his eyes up into his eye sockets as a silent gesture of disgust.

Monk raised his finger in the air as if to quell disquiet

"May I just say that I can vouch for the propriety of the young lady concerned as she comes from a well-respected local family who are from a certain class that are beyond reproach.

"However, there are rules at issue here that must be obeyed for the security of all those on the camp, especially the reputation of the single girls and the camp within the local community. It is impossible to validate a strangers' reasons for coming onto the camp without first making enquiry and this takes time. Therefore due to the circumstances on this occasion, no further action will be taken, but future transgressions will be punished."

Monk then moved on to his next order of business.

"I have been approached by His Majesty's Customs and Excise with a complaint about the supply of rolling tobacco within the area. It has come to their attention that numerous members of the camp are growing and supplying tobacco to work colleagues and the local community without paying the excise duty required by law.

"You are reminded that you may only produce enough tobacco for your own private use, and it is illegal to sell any surplus for financial gain without paying the tax due." This comment elicited the loudest reaction of the evening so far.

Undaunted Monk continued.

"May I remind you that fines can be made by the Excise for which there is no appeal, an estimated tax burden of several hundred pounds could be levied and a criminal record would decimate an individual's chances of staying in this country. In addition," here Monk raised his finger again waving it as if it were a judge's gavel, "we must not forget that these kinds of transactions are closely related to the sordid business of the black market and could attract the wrong kind of attention from the seedier types of criminals. This would reflect on the camp as a whole and all those who are innocent and blameless alongside those who are guilty."

The hall fell silent after this message was translated.

Also, Monk complained,

"The village school mistress has complained that a number of Polish children, who are allocated time in the state school, are not taking advantage of the English classes being offered. It is crucial that your children learn English as soon as possible so that they can fit into the English education system. So, please ensure that they attend at the allotted times from here on.

"Finally, I have received an invitation from the Rural District Council who have invited your camp orchestra to play as part of the May Day celebrations in the local market town. I have placed this invitation before the camp committee who have assured me that it will be discussed at this meeting and a decision passed to me later this week.

"I would just like to take this opportunity to remind you all of the great effort made by many in this community to provide you with instruments and sheet music for your orchestra and suggest that this would be an appropriate way to repay that kindness."

Just as Monk was about to turn and leave the hall he remembered he had one last announcement.

"I have been informed by the Western National Bus Company in Cheltenham that a second bus service will start on the first of next month leaving the camp gate at 10 am. and returning at 3 pm. This is to allow camp dwellers to go into town for shopping, especially on market days. The early morning bus will remain in operation for workers as will the early evening service for those returning from work."

With that Monk spun on his heels and left the hall with no acknowledgement to the camp committee or any of the assembly.

While Monk was still making his way out of the hall, Major Bialy took to his feet and, without acknowledging Mr Monk, started to speak.

"As far as the tax payments are concerned I say, 'render unto Caesar what is Caesar's' and will make no further comment on the matter. To those of you who are not sending your children to the English lessons but are bringing up your children to be true patriots I say we the committee support you.

"The committee are convinced that a third world-war will come when the Western leaders realise that they have chosen a poor bedfellow. Until that moment approaches, we must use the time to prepare ourselves for the conflict that is surely to come, and which will see us return to the warm, sunlit fields of our homeland. Until then we must stay here, like storks in winter, unable to fly home, kept in this wet, cold country by our erstwhile allies to do their bidding.

"But we must not relax our guard, we know that we are surrounded by enemies of a free Poland and, we know that their spies are amongst us, which brings me to the next item of camp security as there can be no exceptions to our strict rules on guests. Only those authorised by the committee and Monk will be allowed in with no exceptions made."

Once again Marek moved to interrupt Bialy's monologue, but with Jan's hand on his shoulder restraining him and a silent gesture to leave made with the other hand, the two exited the hall. As they walked down the steps to return to their hut they passed Marta and her two friends entering the hall.

"Have they finished talking?" asked Marta. "We have come for the music and refreshments."

"No," Marek replied, "they are still preaching to the faithful."

"Or trying to keep the faithful, faithful," added Jan.

The girls decided that they would come back later when they could hear some music, and Jan, nudging Marek in the ribs, agreed that would be a good idea.

As Jan and Marek lay on their beds discussing the merits of a Polish wife, they were aware that the sound of music had started coming from the community hall. They rose as one from their beds and both made their way to the small mirror screwed to Jan's wardrobe door. They swept their hair into some sort of order using their fingers as combs, tucked in their shirts, and made their way to the hall.

On entering, they were met by a distinctly different atmosphere to the one they had left earlier. On the stage were at least a dozen musicians playing a variety of instruments including an accordion, four violins, drums, brass instruments and clarinet and oboe players. Their age's ranged from early teens to mid-forties, and all seemed accomplished with a good command of their instruments.

"Where have all of these come from?"

"Mostly army band musicians," said Marek, "but some of the older ones were professional players before the war and they teach the younger members for a small fee."

Marek saw Marta and her two friends sat at a table being entertained by Tony Sharpe and so he steered Jan by the arm over to their table.

Jan greeted Tony. "Hello, Mr Sharpe," he said, in a manner that invited Tony to vacate his seat at the table.

"Tony please call me Tony," the seated guest insisted. "I'm just catching up on all the camp news from the girls before the committee arrive."

"Ah" Jan retorted, again in a manner calculated to suggest that it was already time to move on.

At that moment, Major Bialy, the professor, the priest Father Graboski, and several other functionaries of the committee arrived and made their way to a large table set aside for them away from the music. This ensemble stood to attention by their chairs, and as if by magic, the dance music stopped, and the Polish national anthem rang out around the hall.

Everybody stood, whilst many of the men stood to attention and saluted the Polish and regimental flags as they sang out with gusto. Even Jan and Marek felt moved to sing along with the rest of the table with the exception of Tony who stood silent and motionless.

After the anthem, there were no speeches and no ceremony. The orchestra resumed playing old Polish tunes interlaced with some regional rural ones which nobody felt the urge to dance to. Tony had now moved to the committee table and was in deep conversation with the professor, so the boys embarked on a charm offensive in support of Marek.

"So" asked Jan, "what do you do for a living Marta?"

"I work at the manor house in the next village."

"Is it a good job?" Jan asked rather lamely.

"Oh yes, there's nothing I like more than cleaning up rich peoples mess and dirty laundry."

At this point, Kinga, one of Marta's friends, butted in.

"She doesn't have to worry as she'll soon be marrying her boss's son. He is a pilot, you know, so she'll be able to afford to pay someone else to clean up after her!"

"A pilot you say. I can see why she'd want to marry a man with prospects and a manor house, can't you Marek?"

Marek answered in a wise and profound tone,

"A good friend once told me that you should marry for love and not profit." Marek gave Marta a benevolent smile and braced himself for her riposte.

"Well, I'd rather ride around in an open-topped Riley sports car than a motorbike and sidecar."

"My sidecar is open topped too," replied Marek, but it was too late, the pilot had won the first dogfight.

As the orchestra fell silent and left the stage for a break, the accordion player and a violinist slowly made their way to the front of the stage and struck up a tango. Immediately most of the adults sprang to their feet and started to dance. Jan decided to help Marek out and thin the field of available dancers.

"Would you like a dance, Kinga?"

"That would be nice."

The two left the rest at the table in the hope that there might be a ceasefire called by their return. The tango did not lend itself to talking while dancing it, so Jan decided to wait until they were back at the table before continuing 'operation Marek'.

They found Marta sat on her own drinking homemade compote, but within seconds a breathless Marek appeared with her other friend Kasia and all the revellers sat down and the chat continued.

"Are you married?" Kinga asked.

"Yes, I am," Jan replied, "I am trying to trace where my wife is now, and I am hoping for some good news soon. I intend to meet Mrs Jarvis on Saturday to see if she can find something out. One of the problems is that I've been moving around a lot and so my case keeps being handed on to the next official and then I'm gone again, but, hopefully, that'll change now I am settled here for the next two years."

"Do you have family?" Jan asked.

Kinga shrugged dismissively and Jan knew to pursue the matter no further.

As the orchestra threaded its way back on stage, a group of colourfully clad dancers stepped onto the empty dance floor and took up their positions with a flourish of outstretched arms and swirling dresses. The costumes represented some of the traditional regional styles of Poland, and the dancers were skilled in their portrayal of several long-established polonaise and dizzying mazurkas. As feet stamped and heels clicked the dancers disappeared into a kaleidoscope of colour, spinning in ever faster circles, their yipping and screeching filling the hall.

Marek turned to speak to Marta, but before he could utter a word, she stood up.

"It's late, and I've work in the morning."

Marek assumed from her abrupt exit that the lady was not ready to be wooed, as a glance at his watch showed that it was only nine o'clock.

"Any chance of a beer?"

"Sorry, just ginger beer and cordial', Jan replied. "We could go to the pub if you don't mind using the motorbike."

"It will be closed due to the Easter holiday." Marek sighed. "Grab a couple of glasses of cordial and meet me outside." Marek gestured to the door whilst tapping the side of his nose.

Jan exited the hall and sat on the steps. After a short while, Marek arrived from behind their hut with a small bottle of clear liquid.

"Bimber?" proffered Marek.

Jan thrust the two glasses forward and the liquor disappeared into the anonymous fruit cordial. The boys spent a happy hour drinking and not caring, while camp dwellers came and went, and Polish music infused the cooling air. As the bimber worked its magic both boys' thoughts left the steps of the hut and drifted east to their homeland and, as bimber is apt to do, their hearts filled with melancholy and a sad silence engulfed them. After a time, Jan looked at Marek.

"We both have work in the morning."

In unison, they drained their glasses and made their way to the hut to ready themselves for a new day.

The day dawned fair, and Jan ate breakfast with the early workers who needed to catch the six o'clock bus into town. At seven, he unchained his bike and took a leisurely ride to the farm ready to meet Sid and learn his new duties. It soon became clear to Jan that Sid was a man of few words.

"Morning" he exclaimed in a broad Wiltshire drawl, "you the new bloke?"

"I am," Jan confirmed. He offered a hand of greeting to Sid.

"You don't want to be grabbing my and yet, my old mate, it's covered in cow shite." Sid laughed. "Dyke told me you were coming today. You bide on'ere, I will clean up, and we can get underway."

Underway, thought Jan, there must be a journey in the offing. Sid returned after a while and beckoned Jan over to the stables. As Jan drew nearer to Sid, he picked up the slight odour of chlorine and animal excrement pervading the air, an aroma he would soon come to be familiar with.

"You drive osses?" enquired Sid.

Jan nodded that he had, so Sid carefully showed him how to tack them up and get them onto the cart shaft.

"Mind out on Monday mornings," warned Sid. "Miss Chastity feeds the old girls over the weekend, and she gives'em too many oats, and when they ain't been working they can get a bit hot and skittish."

Jan nodded that he understood, and the pair loaded some tools and the soot onto the cart, and they set off.

As the cart moved slowly up the lane towards the downs accompanied by the languid rhythm of the horses' hooves, time seemed to stand still for Jan. The last few hectic days seemed a world away and Jan was transported back to a speed of life he had not experienced for nearly a decade.

As the cart was passing the sheep fold, Sid pulled the cart over into the gateway and he slid down off the cart in a way which suggested that his back, ravished by a lifetime of farming, would not allow him to dismount in any other manner without pain.

"Once we get the dew pond fixed, these daft buggers will be edding up the hill for the summer and then it'll be your job to look after'em every day,"

"Where are the dogs for controlling them?" Jan asked.

"Oh, we don't have dogs, Dyke doesn't like'em because they scare the sheep," explained Sid, and, pointing at the donkey which was grazing with the flock, he said "We have Teddy, he's as good as gold, and they follow him anywhere he goes no fuss. Miss Chastity had him as a pet when he was a foal, but as they both got bigger, she lost interest, so we stuck him in with the sheep and found out that he seemed to control them. The daft old bugger probably thinks he's a brown sheep by now, but he is calm and keeps the sheep calm."

"The sheep seem strange to me," said Jan, "they are bigger than any I have seen before, and their coats look different."

"That's because they're Wiltshire sheep," Sid informed Jan. "They're good for meat and can convert any old grass into muscle rather than fat. They are hardy, so they cope with the exposed down land, and they shed their coat in summer, so there is no buggering around shearing them. They lamb easily and are good milky mothers. They aren't that popular, but they are easy to keep and around springtime the lambs will bring in a load of cash for Dyke."

Jan feigned a face that said, 'I am impressed', and they both climbed onto the cart.

As the two set off again Jan began to understand the power of silence and how it had been in very short supply for him over the last few years. With Sid as his travelling companion few words were required, and the pair slowly made their way uphill soaking up the solemnity of the simple life. As is inevitable when silence exists, folk take to thinking and thinking leads to questions and the seeking of answers and it was at this moment that Jan broke the unyielding silence.

"Chastity is a strange name, what does it mean?"

"Well," started Sid, with the eagerness of a man with a good yarn to spin, "Dorothy, Dyke's wife, comes from a wealthy farming family down Dorset way. At a Young Farmers dance she had a little accident in a drunken moment of weakness with Dyke when he was a young man. That is how she came to marry below her station as it were, and as a reminder to her own daughter of the care to be taken in choosing a partner, she named her Chastity. It sort of means pure or chaste, but, unfortunately, the fruit doesn't fall far from the tree and the only time Chastity was chased was by American airmen during the war." Sid smirked and returned to his stoic thoughts.

Jan felt that this was an unfair assessment of Chastity and that she had been judged too harshly, but he kept his own counsel and returned to his own thoughts.

After Dolly and Bubbles had laboured away for an hour or more, they eventually delivered their load to the top of the downs and Sid halted them next to the half-empty dew pond. There was a cool breeze at the top of the hill, so Sid and Jan put the horse blankets on their charges so that their sweaty bulk would not chill.

Sid took a leather bucket from under the cart seat, filled it with pond water and let the girl's drink.

"Right," said Sid in a commanding tone, "let's get this done so we can get back for dinner. Jan, get that mattock out and crack the chalk basin in those areas over there. I'll take some dry grass from around the pond and moisten it with water.

Now, I'll sprinkle the soot on the area you have exposed and then I'll lay the wet grass down on top." Sid then spread the remainder of the soot on the grass.

"Right young-un," said Sid, "you take the chalk that you dug out and put it in one of them wheel tracks."

The wheel tracks had been hewn from the solid chalk over countless centuries as wagon after wagon had passed that way. As soon as this was done, Sid sprinkled water on the broken chalk lining and urged Dolly and Bubbles forward so that the cartwheel crushed chalk pieces into a white pasty marl.

"Right, my boy!" Sid said, "take that marl and re-plaster it into the gaps you made earlier until it is level and perfectly sealed around the edges." Jan did as instructed until Sid was happy.

"That'll do" Sid announced with a note of satisfaction. "By the time that dries out, it will be watertight again, let's hope we don't have another'ard winter to bugger it all up again."

Jan nodded in agreement.

With this the two remounted the cart and began to make their way back to the farm. Once more it was Jan who felt he had to break the silence and ask Sid just one question.

"I'm sorry but why did we put soot on the base?" he enquired of Sid, in the manner of an apprentice seeking knowledge from his master.

"Don't be sorry, if you don't ask, I'll assume you know. It's to stop the worms burrowing into the chalk and making it leak again." Jan nodded and the two returned to their tranquil journey home.

At the farm, the horses were stabled as they were not required again, and Sid continued to methodically teach Jan his duties and Jan continued to listen intently, only interrupting Sid when it seemed most pertinent. Jan was no stranger to farm work, but Sid was pedantic and organised, and Jan was sensitive to his ways.

Dinner for Jan was back at the camp, but he returned to the farm for afternoon milking and when that was done, he was free to go for the day. A visit to the farm office to sign his work chitty for the day and then a freewheel ride down the hill and back to camp.

**

As his week of tuition continued, Jan began to understand the politics of the farm. Jan reported to Sid, Sid reported to Chastity, Chastity reported to farmer Dyke, and Mrs Dyke signed the cheques. The week sped by and by the Friday afternoon, Sid deemed Jan ready to "go it alone and not bugger it up." Jan was pleased with this robust validation of his capabilities as Sid did not shower praise on anyone at any time without good reason

***

By chance, it was Jan's weekend off that week. As Marek was working, Jan planned to meet with Mrs Jarvis from the Red Cross on the Saturday morning and then explore further afield on his bike, but life was not going to be that simple for Jan. It started well enough as Jan and Marek ate together at the early breakfast sitting, and when Marek had disappeared off to work with the ubiquitous cloud of blue smoke on his motorbike, Jan returned to his hut to sort out his Red Cross paperwork.

At nine o'clock Jan went next door to the community hall to see Mrs Jarvis where to his surprise the queue was very short. Within the hour, Jan was beckoned to the table where Mrs Jarvis sat with piles of files and registers laid out before her. Jan introduced himself and handed over his bundle of documents for Mrs Jarvis's perusal. As Mrs Jarvis flipped from document to document, she made small noises to herself.

Jan listened in silence but was heartened when Mrs Jarvis uttered

"Ah,"

and less so when she uttered,

"Oh dear."

It was several minutes before Mrs Jarvis finished consulting Jan's papers and made some rudimentary notes in her notebook, at which point she stared Jan squarely in the eyes.

"Is it bad news?" enquired Jan with a perceptible tremor in his voice.

"No, not really" replied Mrs Jarvis in a practiced tone that she had become used to in delivering life changing news both good and bad.

"I have a record here from the Salvation Army that your wife has been trying to trace you since May 1942. This request was made from a transit camp in Iran, however, although her details match your paperwork the Salvation Army file shows her as married but alone with two baby children."

Jan rocked back in his chair so hard that the front legs came off the ground.

"Are you sure of this?" he asked Mrs Jarvis.

"Quite sure," she replied. "The information is taken from the records of the priest who performed the matrimony and christened the babies on the same day in Russia in April 1942. Your wife, if that is who she is, uses the name Kot-Dudek on her official paperwork after the date of her marriage and on the children's paperwork too."

Jan sat stunned, questions racing through his mind. Clearly, his wife had been taken to Russia, but what about his family, why weren't they with her? Why had his wife ,Eva, only waited such a short time after parting to start a new life? Did she think he was dead? If so, why was she trying to find him now? Unless the children were twins, how had she coped with two pregnancies in Russia? Had she settled down there, was the father a Russian, had she been raped? Jan's mind was a kaleidoscope of questions, but he was suddenly aware of a voice in his head calling him.

"Mr Kot, Mr Kot, Mr Kot, I need an answer from you on how to proceed with your enquiry, and do I have your permission to notify your wife that I have found you?"

Jan took a deep breath, and without really trying to understand the reason, he answered.

"Yes, I will sign the documents and put the procedures in motion to get my wife to England."

"Thank you, Mr Kot; this will take some time as your wife may have moved several times by now. Transport is scarce, but I will hope to have news for you in a month or two. Goodbye for now, I will be in touch."

Jan stood and, clutching his paperwork, walked trancelike

from the hall, returned to his hut and slumped on the bed trying to make sense of this new information. His mind juggled with the negatives and positives of the last hour in an attempt to control his emotional state. He felt elated that, at last he had found his wife after so long but disheartened that she had chosen another so soon after parting and now had children with this man.

He questioned his own rationale for agreeing to send for her when it might be that she would be a stranger to him who was only looking for security for another man's children. However, as the morning passed, reason returned to calm his mind and Jan took comfort from the fact that, hopefully, he would soon see his wife at last and that all the other questions would then be answered.

Jan decided to wait at the hut for Marek to come back from work and maybe they could talk things over, as; reasoned Jan, two heads are better than one and this would be a good chance for Marek to put his quick mind to some real good. Jan sat on the porch in the fresh spring air and watched the world go by. In time Jan heard the familiar sound of Marek's motorbike coming down the lane so Jan walked towards the gate to meet him to ensure that he would not get involved in some other business before he had helped Jan with his problem.

Marek removed his goggles and could see from his friends face that the morning had not gone well. In an effort not to pre-empt bad news Marek greeted Jan with a cautionary

"'Well, how did it go?"

Jan, who at last felt that he could release his emotional outpourings, replied,

"My wife has been unfaithful to me!" This single statement encapsulated his innermost feelings and was distilled from hours of wrestling with reason and the logic of the very extraordinary situation that he now found himself in. It did not help him to know that others in that very camp were facing a similar quandary or even worse.

"Calm down," said Marek, "let me have a shower and we'll go for a drink and sort this out together."

After Marek's shower, the boys had dinner at the canteen and then set off by foot into the village for an early evening drink.

"No rabbiting today?" enquired Jan in an attempt to defuse the abnormal atmosphere with banalities.

"Not on a work weekend, I can't collect them and get them to the butcher in good condition. Anyway, they aren't going anywhere, and they'll just get fatter for next time." Marek smiled and his smile released the tension and the rest of the amble to the pub was in better heart.

Jan bought the pints, and the pair sat outside to afford them some privacy whilst Marek started by trying to make some sense of the little information Jan had.

"Firstly, your wife has kept your name, her married name. Why, if she'd given up hope of finding you, did she not use her maiden name on the documents? I think it was because she knew if you were alive, it would make it easier to find her.

Secondly, she has been looking for you for six years. Why has she not given up if you meant so little to her? We've all heard the stories in the camp about conditions in Siberia.

"Yes," agreed Jan, "but what about the marriage, how can I forgive her for lying with another man, especially as she was still hoping to find me at some point in the future?"

Marek knew that, at this point, he needed more time to think and gave Jan half a crown to get two more beers.

Jan returned with the beer, and as he sat astride the bench placing the glasses on the wooden table, Marek continued with his reasoned response to Jan's earlier question.

"The problem here is, that we are dealing with paperwork that has changed hands many times, it has been copied and re-copied. First by a priest in Siberia or somewhere else in Russia, then after he made his way to North Africa with the Second Corps, he would have followed them up through Italy. At this point he is still holding the documentation, but after the end of the war, he would have allowed the Salvation Army to copy his records whilst still holding the original documents.

"The Salvation Army, at some point, would then have allowed the Red Cross to copy the documents onto their central tracing records. Then, in England, the information would have been transcribed into the local Red Cross officer's records. All of this copying from Polish to possibly French and then English means there is a good chance that the information is incorrect."

This explanation seemed plausible to Jan, and it calmed him somewhat, allowing the boys to finish their beer in a better humour and to enjoy the rest of their evening at the pub.

CHAPTER 4
STORMS ON THE HORIZON

The next day dawned bright and sunny, and Jan decided to take the planned bike ride that he had abandoned the day before. He set off into the Wiltshire lanes with no real plan and no destination in mind but found himself instinctively riding towards the downs. He arrived at the dew pond after a leisurely walk and ride and surveyed his work from earlier in the week. The chalky repair looked dry and sound, but as there had been no rain, the pond was still low.

Jan gazed out across the wide open landscape. It had a cathartic effect on him; here he could make sense of the world and his place in it. Spring had wrapped her warming cowl around the earth, and everything was filled with the zest for life and re-birth. Imbued with this spirit of optimism, Jan took some time to take stock of his situation and tried to put the last nine years into some kind of perspective.

Jan reasoned that for nearly a decade everything and everyone that he knew or loved had been torn away from him by the dislocation of a world war. It had cleaved his homeland from him, and after so much turmoil, he had at last washed up on a shore that offered the prospect of peace and safety.

Despite all of this mayhem, he had, at last, found a connection to his old life in the form of his wife. Surely, he mused, he would be crazy to just push her aside because of his silly pride. A woman, whom he loved and who knew his world before its untimely destruction, when he had the chance to rebuild his life with her and regain some resemblance of normality in their shared displacement.

Now convinced of his new path, Jan sat on the grass and soaked up the sun, and as his mind hovered between the conscious and unconscious world, he gazed with pleasure on his old life and wondered how much of that life he could retrieve in his new one. Rested and with his mind at peace at last, Jan decided to forge on with his bike ride, stopping only to take dinner at the camp before resuming his Sunday outing.

As Jan pedalled, he reflected on his first week at the camp, pleased that he had made a good friend in Marek and glad that he had settled into his work at the farm. He had a good feeling about his future here in the village and resolved to take every opportunity he could to better his chances of success. The one cloud on the horizon was the uncertainty surrounding the discovery of his wife, but Jan resolved to cross that bridge when he got to it and, in the meantime to labour as hard as he could to build a future.

Infused with optimism, Jan immersed himself in the Wiltshire countryside riding at a steady pace that seemed in tune with his surroundings. To mark this new beginning, Jan decided that, at the first opportunity, he would open a post office account with Rosemary to keep his money safe and would direct all of his energies io making his savings grow as fast as possible.

As his peaceful Sunday receded into a pleasant memory and the working week began, Jan threw himself with renewed vigour into the farm work, often arriving early and leaving late. It was not an imposition for him as it was a pleasure to follow the familiar rhythms of nature and to rekindle memories of his old life back home. He especially enjoyed working the horses, Dolly and Bubbles, who seemed to absorb whatever work he threw at them with ease. They even started to learn his commands in Polish, such was their close working relationship.

***

The spring rains came, and the dew pond filled up and, at last, it was time to set the sheep loose on the fresh green sward that had appeared. One Monday morning when Jan arrived at work, Sid called out to him across the yard.

"Oi! Young-un, hitch up the shepherd's caravan and make ready for the move to the downs. Wait for the mid-morning bus to go by and then call me,"

Jan collected the girls from their stables and hitched them to the caravan, and while he waited, he took a look inside what would be his new home from time to time.

The inside contained a small wooden bed, an enamel bowl in a built-in wooden stand with a small cupboard also in this stand. A table was situated under the only window and at the far end a small stove for heating food and boiling water for tea and to wash. Jan thought that as a starting point there was enough to work with, so he latched the door closed and climbed down the steps at the rear. At this point, Sid appeared.

"You might want to soak them wheels, that bugger has been in the cart shed for a while and they might be a bit dry."

Jan got Dolly and Bubbles to reverse the caravan nearer to the dairy and hosed down the wheels for a while, stopping now and again to allow them to soak up the water. When Jan was content that all was well, he turned off the hose and sat on the front dashboard awaiting further instructions.

In time, the bus passed the farm on its way to the village

and Jan took this as the signal to open the dairy door and call Sid. Sid duly arrived and threw some wedge-shaped blocks of wood onto the caravan seat and a bucket of cow cake.

"We will need these blocks of wood later up yonder," Sid advised Jan.

Both men took a seat on the caravan and Jan urged Dolly and Bubbles forward in Polish. "*Wio koniku wio,*" Jan commanded, and the girls burst into life straining against the weight of their burden.

"Bloody'ell!" exclaimed Sid. "You have taught them Polish, by Christ!"

"No," replied Jan, "they are clever girls who've learned quickly."

Turning to the left out of the farmyard gate, they made their way to the sheep fold up the lane, which was heavy with the scent of May flowers, the lotus blossom of Wiltshire, thought Jan. The girls soon delivered their master's to the gates of the fold. Sid purposefully descended from his lofty perch slowly and carefully to avoid the pain of his descent, while Jan adopted his usual vault to the ground.

"Right," said Sid, "you take the bucket of cattle cake and call Teddy over to you, lead him to the open gate and the rest of the flock will follow. Then lead him up the hill and keep moving at a steady pace as he is a lazy bugger. I will close the gate when the field is empty and follow behind to block any traffic."

Jan did as he was instructed, and Teddy complied. Like the pied piper, Jan set off with his new charges bleating and baa-ing excitedly, the odyssey had begun. Progress was slow but it was uneventful, and, eventually, the flock arrived at its new summer home on top of the downs.

***

As the gate closed behind them, the flock and Teddy spread out to explore and find the tastiest grasses. Sid, watched by

Jan, got the girls to reverse the caravan onto a flat piece of land next to the dew pond which was set into the dip created by the natural slope of the land. Sid then hammered the wooden wedges under the steel wheel rims to stop the caravan from moving.

"This is the best place for you here, out of the worst of the wind, close to the water and low down in case of thunderstorms. There'll be plenty of wood in the copse left by winter storms, so, if it gets chilly, you can light a fire."

"How much time do I have to spend up here?" Jan asked.

"You'll need to be up here every day to at least check the flock and fences and look for problems with the ewes. They'll be tupped by our ram Percy. You may get problems with one or two of those in lamb if the autumn is wet and cold."

"Where can they shelter from the sun and heat?" asked Jan.

"They'll wonder off into the beech copses in the midday sun, but they only have that short curly coat which will start to fall out soon, so they don't mind a bit of heat. We'll make two crops of hay in the sheep fold this summer and then they'll go back down in October ready to lamb."

Jan decided he knew all he needed to know, so the pair checked the fences, and then strolled back to the farm leading Dolly and Bubbles.

As the unhurried rhythms of rural life slowly moved on in harmony with the seasons, Jan knew that at last he had found a place where he could embrace life in peace. But for some Poles there was another rhythm that dominated their lives and very being. One day in late May, Jan came home from work to find the camp in a state of frenzied activity. Scouts ran around with armfuls of birch sapling greenery; in differing areas of the camp there was the sound of hammering and sawing and excited voices offering advice and suggestion.

As Jan stood astride his bicycle in the gateway, surveying this scene, Marek came towards him on his motorbike making his way to his nightshift at the hospital, so Jan waved him down. Marek stopped when he saw his friend and raised his goggles.

"What's going on here then?"

"Corpus Christi tomorrow!" exclaimed Marek, in a tone that suggested he may have been kept awake for much of the day.

"Ah," replied Jan as if these two words explained everything.

As Jan walked back to his hut he was reminded of his time as an altar boy when every year different church groups would decorate four altars around the village and the congregation would process to each one to hear a mass. This, it was believed, was to protect those within the village from pestilence for the year to come and to protect their crops. While the reasons might not be valid anymore, thought Jan, the symbolism was a welcome reminder of happier times and of hearth and home, and a lifestyle that was probably gone forever.

But not all the camp dwellers were lucky enough to find such solace in this place. One Saturday afternoon in early June, as Jan returned from work, he was met at the camp gate by a cacophony of screaming and crying coming from the back door of the camp office. He could see a woman gesticulating with her hands, a tear-soaked hanky gripped in one, and Mr Monk desperately trying to pacify her.

"Frau Swartz," Monk pleaded, "I have told you this matter is out of my control; you signed a two-year contract to work at the flax factory and that is that. If you do not want to work there any-more, you will have to return to Germany."

Frau Swartz screamed back in protest, "I've told you my home is now in Poland. not Germany, how can I return to a country that I don't belong in? My family are dead; I have no one except a sister in Austria who I've not heard from since the end of the war, even though I've written to her asking for help many times.

I'm the daughter of a doctor, I shouldn't be made to work in that stinking, steamy place with women who all hate me and treat me cruelly."

Jan decided that it would be rude to listen any longer and sped up his pedalling to put some distance between him and the altercation. He resolved instead to get a full account of events surrounding the story from Marek later.

Luckily for Frau Swartz, Marta, who was making her way from the bus stop, displayed a greater level of empathy than Jan, and walked over and put an arm around her shoulder.

"Come with me Frau Swartz, we'll go back to the hut, and you can have a lie down, that'll make you feel better." Marta led the still sobbing Frau to the single lady's hut and laid her on her bed and sat with her until she fell asleep.

Then Marta, Kinga, and Kasia walked to the canteen for Saturday dinner just as Jan and Marek emerged from their hut.

"How is she?" enquired Jan of Frau Swartz.

"Asleep now, we've had to keep an eye on her since Monk moved her into our hut."

"Why is she in your hut?" queried Jan.

"Some months ago, while she was in with the other women at the top of the camp, she had a nervous breakdown. They blamed Germany for all their ills and as Frau Swartz was German, she'd received the butt of their angst."

As Marta pointed out, "No Poles in the camp had any love of the Germans, but no one felt that Frau Swartz was solely responsible."

As the group separated in the canteen, Marek took his chance.

"Fancy a drink at the pub later Marta?"

"No," came the steely reply, "I'm out with my pilot tonight."

Marek's eyes rolled back into his head while Jan smirked at him, and the boys sat down.

Later that day, the boys set off for the railway embankment to check the freshly lain snares and to harvest the catch.

Marek looked with concern at Jan.

"I think I may have to cease trapping for a few weeks. The younger rabbits are too small, and I think I may've over-trapped the adults."

"Yes, but isn't that the point Marek, surely the railway company are paying you to do just that?"

Marek sucked air in through his teeth in a way that suggested that it wasn't that simple.

"You see, this is about keeping the railway happy, the butcher happy, and me happy. If I clear the rabbits, then I lose an income and so does the butcher, but if I'm able to manage the rabbit problem in a certain way to keep the railway company happy but also maintain both of our incomes, then I'm a successful businessman."

"Ah," acknowledged Jan, "so, what're you going to do?"

"I'll stop for now and give the rabbits a bit of time to recover before I start to trap them again. We'd better go into town and tell the butcher."

So, with that, the boys set off to break the bad news to the butcher before returning to the village pub to drown Marek's sorrows.

On entering the pub, the boys found Tony Sharpe propping up one end of the bar on his own, so they headed for the opposite end of the bar to place their order for beer. However, Tony beckoned them to him and reached into his pocket to pay for their beer.

"That's OK Tony, I'll get these," said Jan, at which point Tony drained his glass and placed it on the bar.

"Thank you, old chap, very decent of you."

Jan wasn't quite sure how it had happened, but he paid for the three beers and the three men sat on the bar stools and began the polite chit-chat that was typical of bars all over the world.

Tony opened, "I hear that Captain Kronski is leaving the camp and returning to Poland. Do you know much about him, Marek?

"I know nothing about Kronski or where he came from in Poland."

Tony then enquired about the boys' homes and how they had been affected by the war. Both responded by explaining that due to the turmoil of war, neither was sure if they still had family in Poland or even if their part of Poland was still Poland.

Jan then offered some news to lighten the mood by explaining that he had at least found his wife and that plans were afoot to bring her to England.

"At last!" cried Tony. "Something to celebrate. I'll get the next round, and we can drink to a happy reunion." Jan, who was not so sure of that, accepted the offer in good faith.

As the boys chatted with Tony, the saloon bar door opened and in walked Marta with her airman. The dashing young man made straight for the lounge bar door, opened it and ushered Marta into the relative luxury behind its etched glass.

Tony excused himself, jumped up from his stool and made to follow them into the lounge bar.

"It's no good," shouted Marek, "she's smitten with her pilot. She won't be interested in you." Tony smiled and disappeared through the door.

Jan and Marek slowly sipped their pints and tried to right all the wrongs life had beset them with. A group of young men from the village came in for a drink and all seemed in high spirits. At once, Jan and Marek started speaking in English to each other so as not to attract too much attention.

"Evening, lads," hailed James the landlord.

"All right?" answered the eldest young man. "Crikey, lads, something smells sweet in here!" He joshed with his mates.

"Yeah, it must be nice to have hot and cold running water, showers, indoor privies, and free food provided, mustn't it?"

Jan and Marek knew at once that these comments, however inaccurate, were aimed at them but kept quiet.

"Right, lads, keep it down; we don't want any trouble in here!"

"Or what?" asked the leader of the group.

Before James could answer, Tony appeared with Marta and the pilot through the lounge door.

"Problems, landlord?" asked the pilot.

"Nothing I can't handle, captain," replied James, and with that, the lads fell silent and Jan and Marek, along with Tony, resumed their evening and the pilot and Marta returned to the lounge to continue their courtship.

After a short while, the gang of lads got up to leave.

"Let's go to the Nags Head," announced one of the group loudly, "where we can be amongst our own!"

At this point, Tony stood up, and despite the boys' attempts to stop him, he launched a tirade of chastisement at the village lads.

"Listen you lot!" he said in his clipped tones. "While you were still in shorts, these men were fighting their way across North Africa, and then Italy and Europe. Their airmen were defending our shores when no one else came to our aid. They were our one and only ally. You should show them some respect or shut up!"

As the leader of the group left the pub he muttered, "Posh git," and amid a chorus of laughter, they were gone.

"Sorry lads," said James but you should pay them no heed.

"Please, don't worry," said Jan, "we know how they feel

about us here, but we are where we are and that is the end of it."

"I hope you don't mind my outburst," said Tony, "but when I think of what you boys have been through, it makes my blood boil. Did I reflect your experiences accurately to some degree?" asked Tony.

'Not really," the boys laughed, and they carried on uninterrupted for the rest of the evening.

**

The next day Jan and Marek ate breakfast together. Being a Sunday, there were few diners as most were fasting before Holy Communion.

As Marek went up to get a cup of tea, Frau Swartz came in accompanied by Marta and the girls.

"I see that your flyboy has some competition," laughed Marek at Marta.

"I don't know what you mean."

"I saw Tony creeping around you both last night at the pub," Marek parried in return.

"He's not interested in me, all they talked about was aeroplanes without propellers," Marta responded in a tone that reflected her boredom on the subject.

There the conversation ended, but, thought Marek, at least he knew that he would not have to tackle two suiters in his pursuit of Marta, which he felt was a positive note to end on.

The following Monday dawned fair as Jan set off for work as normal. On arrival, he made his way to the dairy to help Sid clean up before setting off to check the sheep. As he threw open the door of the churn room, he was shocked to find Chastity scrubbing away on the equipment.

"Hello Jan!" she said, sweeping the hair off of her face as

she stood up to greet him with her beaming smile.

"Oh" declared a shocked Jan, "I didn't know Sid was away."

"Yes, he has gone to spend a week with his sister in Weymouth before the haymaking and harvest begins."

"You should have told me, I could have done the milking for the whole week,"

"No, I like to keep my hand in, and anyway, Mother doesn't like paying holiday money at the best of times so by me standing in, she thinks she is saving money." Chastity laughed and the churn room lit up with her smile. Jan was bathed by a feeling of bonhomie from her friendly open spirit, and without thinking he blurted out,

"I think it's a real shame you and Marek couldn't make it work."

Chastity seemed taken aback by his candid remark, but she responded even so.

"Marek is a lovely man you know, but I had to stop things in their tracks before it became too serious to protect both of us. How is he anyway?"

"His pride is hurt, but there is no permanent damage, I think." Jan smiled.

"Good," replied Chastity, "say hello from me when you see him." Jan nodded that he would, and he closed the churn room door as the two parted company.

As Jan headed out up the lane towards the downs, he was immersed in the bird song of early summer. In the marshy, chalk spring paddock, the ghostly trill of the curlews infused the air, and the pee-wits wolf whistled as they flipped and tumbled disturbed by Jan's progress. On top of the downs the skylarks song sored and fell, whilst yellow hammers pleaded for a little bit of bread and no cheese in the juniper bushes.

The verdant chalk lands played host to a myriad of wildflowers, which were being busily visited by blue butterflies and industrious bees, their lot in stark contrast to Jan's lethargic pace of life. As he sat on the steps of his shepherd's caravan surveying his flock, it seemed to Jan that at that moment everything in the world was in its place. The warm sunshine made it increasingly hard to stay awake, so he climbed down from his vantage point and lay on the grass up against a fence post and allowed himself some slumber.

As he cat napped, he was conveyed to his homeland of old, dancing with his beautiful young wife at the village dance, the envy of all his friends. He, courtly in his advances and she, respectful to her family, they had enjoyed a wonderful courtship which had ended in a happy marriage which promised much. Then, as Jan slipped deeper into this carousel of romance, he was suddenly awakened by a loud bang that sounded like a shotgun being discharged very nearby.

Keeping low for safety, he scanned the horizon but could see nothing, then a second report even closer and a familiar sound that he knew to be Marek's motorbike. From his secluded position he watched as Marek wrestled with his bike and sidecar on the uneven tracks as he made his way to the copse in which the pigs could be found. As Jan watched, Marek lifted a large, galvanised food dustbin from his side car and emptied its contents into the pigsty to a loud chorus of grunting and squealing.

"Well, that explains the smell of mashed potatoes" whispered Jan to himself, and he returned to his slumbers.

**

As the summer grew in stature, forcing its gentler cousin spring to fade away and the green grass changed to the colour of hay, one Sunday morning in mid-June, Jan was suddenly catapulted from his bed back to his homeland by an event which pleased and surprised him at the same time. He was awakened early by the giggling of girls outside the hut.

While Marek still slept on, Jan was curious as to what was causing the chatter. As he emerged from his hut, he was met by the sight of a dozen young Polish women walking past, wearing head dresses made of garlands of flowers. As they passed out of the camp gate and earshot of the camp, they began to sing a traditional Polish song, as they slowly walked towards the chalk stream just past the farm. Jan realised that this meant that it must be mid-summer, and the girls were going to cast their headdresses into the stream and watch them float away. If the garland floated away downstream, the girl would marry that year; if it sank, she would not. Jan decided to leave them to their fate as it was his Sunday off and returned to his bed.

With no work for either of the boys that day, and no rabbits to catch, the pair sat in the sun on the steps of their hut, chatting. Through the open windows of the community hall, they could hear raised voices and an argument.

"Kronski is a traitor!" they heard Major Bialy shout.

"Kronski is a patriot" they heard Tony Sharpe protest.

"Then why is he not here to face his accusers?" Bialy demanded.

"Because he is not guilty of any crime," countered Sharpe.

"If Major Kronski returns to Poland while it is still under the cosh of the invaders, he is telling the world that life is normal there, that normality has returned. We need him here, ready for the next war, and if he leaves, he will be abandoning his brothers and siding with the enemy."

"But he has family in Poland, a home and a chance of a normal life rather than sitting here helping to plan a war that will never come."

"You think you know us Poles. Sharpe, but you do not understand what it is like to lose everything you hold dear in

life and the extent to which we will go to reclaim our homeland, our dignity, and our right to a democratic free Poland. If
Kronski returns, others will follow, and we will have lost the
war against the invaders before a single shot has been fired."

"The world is changing," Sharpe counselled in a tone
attempting to defuse the situation, "the old ways are gone, and
a new world will emerge from the ashes of the war. Nobody
doubts the bravery of the Polish nation or its forces, but it is
time to rebuild a new Poland, and you cannot do that from a
field in Wiltshire."

Sharpe then left the hall, and as he walked past the boys,
he wished them a hurried good day but did not stop to talk,
and with that peace returned to the steps of the hut, whilst
angry murmuring continued to flow through the window of
the hall.

At this point, Kronski emerged from the single men's hut
and sat by the boys and greeted them.

"Hello captain," he said to Jan.

"I'm no more a captain than you are a major, Mr Kronski."

"No, I suppose not," Kronski replied. "Why would a major
in the Polish army spend his days slicing bacon in a chilly factory when he could be in the warm sun of his homeland?"

"Well, that is a question only you can answer."

"What made you decide to return?" asked Marek.

"I was talking to that Tony Sharpe from Cambridge about
my home, my wife and family, the town I live in, and my previous career in the army, and he helped me realise that I've
more to return to than I've here. I'd planned to bring my wife
and family to Britain, but my wife wouldn't leave her parents
in Poland, so I need to go back. I'll receive a bursary from the
British army and some cash to help me get on my feet, so I
decided to commit to returning."

"When do you leave?" asked Jan.

"Next week. I'll go to Harwich and on to Holland, from

there by train to Warsaw, and then home to my town south of Warsaw."

"Well, good luck, Mr Kronski," smirked Marek, "don't forget to write back to us to let us know that you got home safely, we'll all be interested to know that."

"I will. My wife's meeting me at the station in Warsaw, so I'll drop you a line when I have settled in at home."

"How are things with the committee?" asked Jan.

"Well, I've been kicked off the top table, so you'll find a new dining companion in the morning for breakfast," laughed Kronski. "As for tomorrow's camp meeting, I don't think I'll be attending that just so that I can be called a traitor in public for saving my own bacon."

With that, Kronski wandered off with his thoughts, and the boys sat waiting for dinner, enjoying the sun watching the world go by.

"Speaking of bacon. Marek," Jan goaded mischievously, as they strolled over for dinner while Jan told Marek about the revelations of the day.

After work that following Monday evening, Jan decided that the camp meeting might be worth a visit. Marek was working but had also asked Jan to keep him informed of events at what promised to be a highly charged meeting. It showed all the signs of being a bruising encounter, unlike the usual women's group news, religious indoctrination from Catholic Action, sewing-circle debates, and political posturing of the elite committee.

Jan took up his familiar position at the back of the hall. Leaning against the end wall, he surveyed the room for potential trouble spots. Monk was sat in the front row with a bundle of papers balanced on his knee due to no table being provided for him by the organisers, this, their usual snub to his status as camp leader.

The major called the meeting to order and asked Monk to outline to the hall those topics that had been discussed in camera before the meeting. Monk stood up and placing his bundle of papers on his chair, launched into his list of topics that he felt merited a second airing. With his back to his audience and with no translator, he launched into his messages.

"Despite frequent requests from the local community, the camp orchestra and choir still have not accepted the open invitation to perform at any local functions. The committee have assured me," he stressed in a loud and adamant voice, "that both the choir and orchestra will attend the Harvest Festival in September.

"On a related note, Mrs Goldstein has complained to me on a number of occasions that she has been refused membership of the camp choir because she is Jewish. I can assure you that her documents show her to be a Polish citizen whose religion is Christian. His Majesty's Government will not countenance this kind of alienation in its camps and I, as its nominated official, will not allow this either.

"It has also come to my attention that those ex-servicemen who are deciding to return home are coming under severe and sustained pressure to remain. As the foreign secretary has already stated, it should be your first duty to return home to help rebuild your country. If I hear of more of these cases, I will consider withdrawing some of your camp privileges which, may I remind you, are yours at my behest." With that, suitably puffed up and papers clenched to his chest, Monk left the hall.

The reaction to Monk's statement was predictable and vocal. Major Bialy stood up and waved his arms in a calming gesture trying to subdue the furore.

"The committee have agreed to the performance of the

choir and orchestra as we are now of the opinion that it is of a high enough standard not to embarrass the camp or its reputation. Although not stated by Monk, we have also agreed to allow the folk dancers to attend along with the choir to sing some traditional harvest songs.

"While we have considered the position of Mrs Goldstein, the musical director of the choir feels that her operatic training and voice would not fit in with the church choir. There is also the issue of a Jewess being present in a Christian church. Despite what Monk says, our records show that Mrs Goldstein was married to a Jew in Vienna who she met while at the opera house there. Assuming she was married under the Jewish rite, she cannot be considered married in the Catholic Church and has therefore committed the sin of fornication. It would, therefore, be highly irregular to allow her to represent the Church, in that state of sin, in our church." Jan decided that he had heard enough of this bigoted rhetoric and left the hall.

As he lay on his bed, he could hear that the subject for debate had changed. The crowd next door in the hall had become more and more audible as they sought to justify their position on the unpatriotic traitors within their midst.

CHAPTER 5
ALL IS SAFELY GATHERED IN

⧠

Next day, over breakfast, the boys discussed the previous evening's events, Jan on his way to work, Marek on his way to bed. They both agreed that it was unfair of the committee to discuss Mrs Goldstein's personal life in public and decided to make some form of complaint to somebody about the incident.

With that decided, they bade each other a good day and a good night and set off to their respective destinations. On arrival at the farm, Jan was met by Sid who was already hitching up the hay tedding machine to Dolly and Bubbles.

"We'd better wait for the dew to burn off and get the crop swathed up ready for harvesting. The barometer is falling, and rain may be coming."

Jan helped Sid complete the task and once ready, he urged the girls forward to the hay field ready to put them to work. When Jan considered it ready, he swathed the hay into billowing airy rows and allowed the sun to do its work. He returned to the yard with Dolly and Bubbles and changed over to the hay wain.

After he had given the girls a drink, Jan called Sid and they set off on the cart with their pitch forks, looking like a pair of French revolutionaries on their way to do battle. Once at the hay field, Jan set the girls to a slow walk between the swathes and he and Sid pitched the hay onto the cart from two sides. As the hay grew higher, Jan climbed on top and organised it, as Sid pitched it up.

By mid-afternoon the pair had picked up the first cart and were on their way back to the yard. On arrival, Jan was shocked to see Dyke and Chastity waiting in the rick yard with three university students to unload the cart, while Sid and Jan returned to pick up the rest of the crop using a second cart. As the two journeyed back to the hayfield,

Sid moaned, "There'll be no bloody tea tonight until we're done." Jan nodded and pressed the girls onward.

***

Over the next few weeks, hay-making followed the sporadic whims of the British summer. Thoughts of Mrs Goldstein were pushed to the back of Jan's mind and then they were gone. Attention then turned to the winter barley and spring barley crops.

"Some was for their animal feed, but most barley went for brewing," Sid told Jan.

Early August was hot and dry, and the swollen crops ripened to perfection. Eventually, the decision was taken to hitch up the binder and start the harvest. Early one day as Jan was returning from checking the sheep, he could see a column of white steam and smoke rising from the hedgerows.

The threshing machine had arrived from the contractor towed by a traction engine. It was parked up and the drive belts were attached ready to receive its first load. The contractor's men climbed all over the machines, greasing and oiling and checking the tension of the belts. Jan and Sid walked up to the wheat field, where Chastity was using the reaping and binding machine on the crop, ably assisted by Dolly and Bubbles.

Sid took over the binding machine, and Jan and Chastity started stacking the sheaves of barley into stooks to allow them to keep dry. As Jan surveyed the field, he wondered how they would be able to transport the crop to the rick yard with just two horses. He expressed his concerns to Chastity, who did not seem to share his anxiety over the matter.

"Don't worry," she assured Jan, "the contractors will start collecting the stooks shortly."

True to her word, within the hour a shiny blue Fordson tractor arrived with a trailer and three Cambridge boys. They made short work of collecting the available stooks and began the journey back to the farm.

"Where's Tony?" Jan asked one of the boys.

"Oh, he's more of an ideas man, you won't find him out here with us plebs," laughed the student as they passed through the field gate and were gone.

A long day followed that stretched into the evening. It was only when the dew came down that work in the field stopped and Sid, Jan, and Chastity returned to the rick yard with the last of the workable harvest.

As they pulled into the yard, the thresher was still working tirelessly, its pulley's spinning, its belts slapping, and the whole machine swaying rhythmically. Sacks of barley were stacked in the barn and the straw was being stacked in a straw rick by the contractor's men.

Set to one side was a trestle table with bottles of beer, cheese, and bread on it which the three new arrivals headed for straight away. As he surveyed the scene, Sid wiped his mouth on the back of his arm and said,

"We only have this contraption for three days, then they'll

be gone so we better make the best use of it. If we fall behind, we'll have to finish by hand and use that bloody winnower and we don't want that." Jan decided that, after Sid's apocalyptic warning, he would get to work much earlier next day.

Three days saw the end of the first harvesting and Jan's workdays returned to a less frenetic pace, with his daily visits to the sheep interspersed with spreading muck on the harvested fields ready for cultivation. He was able to catch up with Marek at last, and the two decided to share a beer at the Bell one evening.

As usual, Tony Sharpe was at the bar and waved the two over to him. Having learned the mistake of their last meeting, Jan kept his hands in his pockets. Tony did however stand them a beer and began to engage in small talk.

"I haven't seen your friend or her young flier in here lately."

"Well, she isn't really my friend," said Marek, "I just know her from the camp."

"Any news regarding your wife's arrival yet?" Tony probed.

"No, nothing yet."

It seemed that the conversation was running dry, but Tony chipped in again,

"Any word on Kronski?"

"No" said Marek, "we only know that he's left the camp, but I think it takes a while for the process to be completed before he gets the all-clear to return and collect his money." Tony nodded, and at this point the conversation did die.

Aware that Tony had bought them a drink, Jan decided to make the effort and opened a new line of questioning.

"So, Tony, tell us about yourself?" Jan asked, feigning interest.

"Not much to tell really. Father is a banker in the city,

Mother was a Deb, and I'm at Cambridge, that's it."

Jan interpreted this reticent reply as a sign that Tony did not want to tell them about himself, but decided he had tried and could now walk away guilt free.

As it was a nice evening, the boys sat outside on a bench and watched village life as it passed before them. This sleepy landscape was suddenly disturbed by the throaty roar of an open-topped sports car speeding across the village green towards the camp. Marta, smiling and happy with her flyer, was gone in a blur.

"Come on," said Jan to Marek, "I'll get us another drink." Marek gave an unconvincing smile and stared down at the grass, waiting for his beer.

The next day was Thursday, market day in the town, and on arrival at the farm, Sid shouted out to Jan,

"Chuck that load of scrap iron on top of that wagon of sacks of barley and wait for Dyke." Jan carefully rested his bike on top of the wagon and waited, stroking the horse's noses, and talking to them in quiet tones.

Eventually, Dyke arrived in his suit and shouted to Jan.

"Come on young-un, we have to get some money in the bank."

Jan coaxed Dolly and Bubbles to life and he and Dyke set off on the road into town. Jan was used to Sid and the many silent journeys they had shared so was surprised at how verbose Dyke was during the journey. Jan learned about his opinions on farm mechanisation and its cost, the cost of wages, the low cost of barley, but the high cost of animal feed, those interfering buggers at the Ministry of Agriculture, those interfering buggers at the Ministry of Labour and National Service, and, finally, those lazy English buggers who thought farm work was beneath them.

Eventually, they arrived at the brewery and Dyke left Jan and the girls in a shady spot while he disappeared into an office marked 'goods inward'.

After a while Dyke reappeared and instructed Jan to move the wagon to a location under a trap door. A brewery worker then climbed onto the wagon and as he did so, a chain came down through a hole in the trapdoor. The worker attached the first sack, and it was at once lifted through the trapdoors which slammed shut after its passing. In time, the whole load was taken in this way.

"Would you like me to get rid of this scrap bike?" enquired the brewery worker.

"No thanks," Jan replied in an indignant tone.

"'Come on young-un, we have to get this bank transfer in before they close for dinner," said Dyke tapping his breast pocket. So off they set to the marketplace and again Jan soothed the horses while Dyke conducted his business. Soon they were on their way home and with their load gone, Dolly and Bubbles were able to pick up the pace.

On reaching the village, Dyke instructed Jan to stop at the Bell.

"You ride on home on your boneshaker, young-un, I'm going to bide on here a while. So Jan took down his bike and started to pedal back to the farm for his dinner.

Later that afternoon, while Jan was cleaning out the stables, Chastity came out into the yard and asked Jan if he could return to the Bell as her father was having a spot of bother. Jan immediately grabbed his bike and set off for the village. On arrival he was met by a cursing Dyke and a collection of market-day drinkers, red faced and laughing.

"What the bloody hell have you done to my hosses?" shouted Dyke. "They won't bloody move."

Jan went up to the girls and uttered an instruction in Polish to them and they burst into life. Dyke and his wagon lurched forward and he was on his way.

"Bloody marvellous" shouted Dyke back at the laughing

throng. "Now even the bloody horses speak Polish!"

As the early August heat grew more intense, Jan was busy with the harvest, but for Marek life continued uneventfully until one day he received a request from the hospital buildings surveyor for a meeting that afternoon. This filled Marek with a sense of disquiet as he had a number of 'business projects' underway at the hospital and he wondered if one of these had been discovered.

After his dinner break, and while he was still clean, Marek made his way to the surveyor's office and was greeted by a secretary as he entered through the heavy, highly polished wooden door.

"Hello" he whispered, as if he was in a library, "I am Marek Bomski."

"Come in Mr Bomski, please sit down and I will let Mr Forbes-Williams know that you are here."

Marek sat on the edge of his chair, trying to guess which of his enterprises might have come to the attention of the surveyor, at which point the secretary reappeared and bade Marek to enter the surveyor's office.

Marek made his way over the deep pile carpet to the end of an imposing room where the surveyor sat behind an immense desk covered in plans and blueprints.

"Please, sit down," commanded the surveyor, indicating to an armchair without recourse to using either of Marek's names.

Marek sank into the armchair and gripped the arms as if he was about to have a tooth extracted, his mind racing, searching for excuses to questions he did not yet know.

"Now!" started the surveyor, "I understand that you are a licenced trapper for GWR?"

"Yes" replied Marek, "British Railways actually," still unsure where this line of questioning was going.

"Well, we have a problem in the wards which we hope you

can help us with. Many of the patients who have come into the hospital over the years brought their pet cats with them. This practice ceased some years ago, however, many of these cats have gone feral and are breeding under the ground floors. Now in summer, the stench is coming up through the floorboards and making life intolerable for the staff and patients.

Is it possible that you could trap these feral cats to bring this sorry state of affairs to an end?"

Marek's relief was palpable. "Of course I can, I would be happy to, it's not a problem," Marek gushed, happy to be reprieved of some imaginary crime he might have committed.

"We will be happy to pay you, say sixpence for each cats tail you take to Mr Blocker, the works supervisor," proffered Mr Forbes-Williams.

A relieved Marek only just managed to stop himself agreeing to do the task for free, but his keen business mind saw an opportunity to make money and ingratiate himself with his employers, so he was able to push this idea to the back of his mind.

"I'll bring my snares in tomorrow and set to work immediately," Marek announced as he floated, a reprieved man without a care, through the heavy door and into fresh unfettered air of freedom.

As Marek was on official hospital business, he decided not to return to work but to take a look at the task in hand. He wandered over to the hospital blocks and started to examine the lower brickwork. It appeared that some of the cast iron air grills had, over time, been broken and this made access to the underfloor spaces easily accessible for a cat. A number of these miscreants lay basking in the sun all around Marek, eyeing him up in case he should make some sudden move to end their liberty.

Marek decided that the best plan of action was to bait and snare these access points in the evening, when he was on a night shift, and visit the traps during the night. Excited by this new business opportunity, he returned to work and explained the situation to Cyril the head stoker who shrugged approval or disinterest, and the boys carried on with their daily toil.

With Jan eating at the farm and only coming home to sleep due to the harvest, Marek never really got to explain his new venture into pest control to him. However, Marek's first night shift soon came around and it was time to put Operation Cat into place. Once at work, Marek was able to take some scraps of bacon from the kitchen bins and bait around ten exit points. He then retired to the boiler house, which in the August heat was akin to working in a sauna and worked on as he anticipated a rich reward.

At around two in the morning, Marek revisited the trap sites and, to his great delight found ten lifeless bodies. With no more bacon to hand, Marek set the snares again, hoping for a second crop of greedy cats. However, on returning at the end of his shift, he found the traps empty.

"Hm" he whispered to himself in the dark, "either it was because there was no meat in the traps, or the cats were on to him."

Returning to the boiler house workshop, he cut off the cats' tails with his hunting knife and placed them in a hessian sack. He then threw the carcasses in the furnace and made his way to Mr Blocker's office to claim his bounty. Blocker handed over five shillings as agreed, and Marek signed for the reward and turned to leave.

"Oi," cried Blocker, "don't leave those bloody things on my desk. Get rid of them." Marek grabbed up the sack and made his way back to the boiler house. As he opened the door of the furnace to throw in the tails, Cyril came over to see what was going on. Marek opened the door and both men were met by the smell of roasting meat.

"Cor," said Cyril, "that reminds me of a Sunday roast dinner. What have you put in there?"

Marek didn't answer as he had had another business idea, and, in his mind at least, he was already firing up his motorbike to make his way into town.

Marek made his way to the butcher's shop after work, where he found the butcher and his staff filling the day's morning orders.

"Good morning, Marek I hope you have good news for me as I am struggling to fill my game orders for my London customers."

"Yes" said Marek, "I have come to let you know that I can resume supplying you now."

"Good," said the butcher, "duck and pheasant season don't start for a few weeks, and I am struggling to send my hotels in London any variety."

Marek, elated, kicked his bike into life and made his way home for breakfast. As he entered the camp, he saw Jan wearily cycling up the road to the farm. He decided that he would share his good fortune with him later and, feeling satisfied, went in for breakfast.

Marek knew that he needed a plan if his new enterprise was going to be a success, and so he set about putting together such a cunning one that he thought nobody would ever discover his deception.

The next evening, he set his baited traps and called into the hospital laundry to borrow a small wicker basket. He then called into the kitchen to borrow a roll of grease-proof paper. Whilst on his dinner break at two a.m. he cleared his traps and returned to the boiler house workshop where he skinned, gutted, and chopped off the tails and tell-tale heads and lower limbs. He wrapped each plump carcass in grease-proof paper, and after placing them in the wicker basket, stored them in his side car in the cool of the night. In the morning, he claimed his bounty from Mr Blocker, disposed of the evidence in the furnace, and made his way to the butchers to complete the transaction.

The new enterprise seemed to be progressing with eland. Marek was allowing his railway line stock to fatten and grow whilst keeping the butcher, Mr Forbes-Williams, and his own cash flow happy. Things became a little more difficult on his day shifts as there were more people about who might enquire about his movements. Why was there the smell of burnt hair every so often and why was there blood on the workshop floor?

But, in general the operation progressed smoothly, however, the inevitable happened and the fresh cat supply started to become depleted. Marek decided that he would now phase in his railway line stock to supplement his supply to the butcher as cat numbers had dwindled.

As he closed down the pest control enterprise, he again supplied rabbits to the butcher. Unprepared, as he handed over his first consignment of fresh produce to the butcher, he was met with a surprise.

"Ah, thank God," said the butcher, "some of those other rabbit tails were getting a bit long," he said, smiling at Marek. Marek at once realised that he had not fooled the butcher, however, clearly, both men believed that business was business.

While Marek continued his quest to be the richest Pole in Wiltshire, Jan laboured on at the farm. One day, as the second barley crop readied itself for harvesting, a car drove into the yard. Out stepped a very tall man of upright demeanour who strode over to the farm office, his sleeves rolled up as if he meant business.

After a short time, raised voices could be heard coming

from the office and Jan, for the first time, could hear Dyke losing his temper.

"'I am not sending my old gals to Belgium and replacing them with a bloody new-fangled tractor. My family has worked this land for well over two centuries and we have got on quite well thank you without your bloody tractors!"

Jan then heard the other man in a lower register trying to placate Dyke, but the fuse had been lit and after a while, Jan heard the office door close, and the chastened man left in his car. At this point, Sid appeared from behind a wagon smiling broadly,

"Did you hear that?" Sid asked. Jan nodded but did not smile as he was unsure of the etiquette in such a circumstance.

"Those daft buggers from the agricultural engineers have been coming here ever since the end of the war trying to get Dyke to modernise his farm and buy a tractor or two. I'm too old to change my ways, so I'm happy that Dyke doesn't want to change his ways either. You can't teach an old dog new tricks that's what I say." Sid spat tobacco leaf from his un-lit pipe onto the yard and that signalled that the subject was closed.

At that point, a call rang out across the yard, and Sid was summoned into the farm office. After a short while he reappeared and walked over to Jan with a concerned look on his face.

"Dyke has told me that we'll be harvesting the last fourteen acres of barley this week. There's a bit of a to-do on, so we'd better get a move on as it's already Thursday morning and the thresher will arrive on the morrow and rain may be arriving on Sunday evening. After dinner, get the girls hitched up to the reaper binder and get cutting. I'll get my missus and Chastity to stand the stooks up and I'll start bringing them back to the barn, so the boys have a head of work for Friday."

Jan nodded approval of the plan, snatched his sandwich

bag and made his way to the stables. He got Dolly and Bubbles tacked and hitched up to the machine and set off, tearing into his doorstep-size sandwiches as he made his way to the field. It was then that Jan realised that there was a gaping hole in the plan, as they only had two horses but needed two more to transport the stooks back to the farm rick yard.

Jan decided that his main task was to get the barley cut and bound so he urged the girls to work in his now familiar native Polish, and unlike normal, he chivvied them on a bit as time was of the essence. He estimated that it would take him until Saturday evening to get the crop cut and bound barring problems, which was cutting it fine to finish before the rain came. However, he pressed on regardless and waited for Sid's wife and Chastity to arrive, which they did within the hour.

Chastity made her way over to Jan to let him know of new developments.

"Sid has gone to find help; father is ringing up to try and get some university lads to come down and mother is making use of her WI contacts to try and get some land girls to lend a hand." However, she cautioned, "With the portents of rain, everybody is stretched to breaking point and those who have labour won't let it go."

Now, fully informed Jan pressed on, the newly sharpened blades sliced and chattered as the reaper sped on relentlessly bringing down the barley and binding it. After some time, Jan would have to water the girls and then press on again.

It was during one of these water breaks that Sid appeared on Jan's bike. He handed over a wicker basket containing a flask of tea and some cake to his wife and Chastity and then sat down by Jan.

"Bloody hell" he exclaimed. "That bike of yours is a death trap!

"Right," Sid continued, "here is where we are. The contractors are only coming with one spare university lad, but he is able to drive their tractor. So, if we stop cutting and standing the stooks and bring a cart down and load it for the morning, we will be sorted-"

"But, Sid, how can two of us stand up all the stooks and load it all up on the cart on our own and keep that threshing machine going at the yard?"

"I may be able to get some of the ladies from the camp to help. The kids are still on school holidays and many of the ladies come from farming backgrounds. If we take a full cart back to the rick yard today and bring an empty one back to the field tonight ready for the morning, we can load one while the other is being worked in the yard and keep the thresher working that way."

"Oh, that's a great idea!" exclaimed Chastity, "do you think they will help?"

"I don't know but I can only ask, we are where we are, and I don't see any other way out."

Sid unhitched the horses and started leading them back to the yard to pick up the cart. Chastity and Sid's wife continued standing up the stooks and Jan rode his bone shaker back to the camp to try and organise some help for the morning.

Within the hour, Jan was back at the yard with five Boy Scouts. They all climbed onto the cart with Jan's bike, and Sid, Jan, and their crew made their way back to the field.

"We'll be losing the light soon," said Sid. "Let's get this one loaded as fast as we can and get it back to the rick yard ready for the morning."

Sid's wife, Chastity, Jan, and the boys loaded the cart while Sid guided Bubbles and Dolly along the rows until the cart was full. As the light faded, they all made their way back to the yard to drop off the full cart and pick up an empty one. Having thanked the boy scouts for their labours, Sid and Jan urged Dolly and Bubbles, one last time, to take the empty cart back to the field ready for the morning.

As they made their way in the last of the light back to the field, they suddenly heard the revving of an engine coming up behind them with the angry crunching of gears accompanied by the whining of an overstressed gearbox. At once the source of this commotion was upon them. It was Marta's young man, the flier, who seemed impatient to pass the cart. The car twitched as he slung it from one side of the lane to the other, in the vain hope of finding a passing place. When it was clear that he was not going to get past he resorted to leaning on his horn in the manner of a London taxi driver in a rush hour queue.

At this point, Sid strolled back along the cart and hanging over the cart rails he shouted, "You will have to bide on young man, we will be at the field shortly."

"This is most inconvenient, and where are your lights?" the flier protested. Sid waved an indeterminate acknowledgement and wandered back to the front of the cart, sitting down next to Jan he smiled and uttered,

"As slow as you like young-un, as slow as you like."

With the horses stabled and bedded down, Jan returned to the camp and entered the canteen. On the side was a large frying pan of bubble and squeak, now cold, and some dishes containing homemade Polish sausage, sliced tomatoes with an onion garnish, and pickled cucumbers. Jan filled a plate and ate at speed, wishing only for a shower and sleep. After placing his plate in the kitchen, he made his way to the hut to pick up his towel and wash bag for his shower.

As he made to enter the hut, who should he see sitting on the steps but none other than Marek, beckoning to him and waving in a most animated way.

"Hello stranger," said Jan.

"Sit, sit," whispered Marek, "I've great news to tell you."

Jan sat and listened.

"Marta has finished with her flier," Marek explained excitedly. "I've heard that her flier has broken up with her this evening, and that Marta was going to work at the flax factory."

Marek was overjoyed that, at last, he might have a chance with Marta. Marek then added that there was more good news.

"The professor has finally managed to get a job at Oxford University through an old contact, and he starts at the beginning of the Michaelmas term, whenever that is."

Jan stood up stiffly. "This is all very interesting, and I'm happy for you, but I have to be up at the sheep by seven tomorrow morning and then have a busy day, so I'll wish you good night." With that, Jan made his way to the shower block to wash the grime and his cares away.

At the break of day, Jan and Marek made their way to the early breakfast sitting. Marek spoke in hushed tones about the exciting events of the previous day, and he laid out his plans before Jan for his approval on how he would capture Marta's heart. Both men then grabbed a lunch bag from the counter, and Jan filled an old lemonade bottle with white tea from the urn.

"Why do we all drink white tea here, we don't do it at home?" quipped Jan.

"It's because a doctor in the camp had recommended that the fresh milk should go to the children, and that the adults would get extra calcium by using powdered milk. However, it tasted so bad that the only way we could drink it was in strong hot tea." Advised thusly, Jan sped off on his bike into the dawn heading up to the sheep and a long, long day.

Jan rode as far as he could up to the downs, but, eventually, gravity played its part, and he had to dismount and walk the rest of the way. Jan was robbed of enjoying the beautiful summer morning by the urgency of his tasks. On arrival, he found Teddy and his charges in good order. He noted that several of the sheep had been tupped by Percy the ram as their backs were now marked in blue wax raddle. He knew this would mean further long weeks on the downs in isolation later in the year.

When Jan was satisfied that all was well with his flock he freewheeled down the hill as fast as he dared to the farmyard to collect Bubbles and Dolly. The traction engine and contractors were already there setting up, so Jan greeted Sid and after readying the horses he led them out to the barley field to continue his labours. The dew was not heavy, and by nine thirty, Jan was at work once more.

After about an hour, to his surprise, the Polish Boy Scouts reappeared and started standing up the barley sheaves into stooks. Then shortly after the boys' arrival the young man from the university arrived on the contractor's tractor pulling a cart loaded with Polish ladies from the camp. The ladies dismounted and immediately started loading the stooks that were standing around the field onto the cart as the driver slowly crept along the rows. Jan then noticed that Chastity was also in the throng. She saw him and waved. Jan waved back and then returned to the job in hand. Jan now felt that they had a fighting chance of getting in the harvest before the rain came on Sunday evening.

At one of the regular watering stops for the horses, Jan wandered over to Chastity and the ladies and enquired how she had managed to organise the ladies help.

"I can't take all of the credit," said Chastity. "When Marek found out about our problem he came straight up to the farm after work and offered to organise some help. It was very kind of him." Jan nodded in agreement but could not help thinking that this seemed quite out of character for his wheeler dealing friend. He lifted his hat, scratched his head, and returned to the horses.

As the empty cart returned to the field it carried pitchers

of lemonade, cheese, bread, and fruit for the ladies. They set the refreshments aside, deciding to eat while they were waiting for the next empty cart. All morning the ladies had been walking at a measured pace with their load stacked onto the cart in a rhythmic motion. As the day wore on, arms became leaden and backs started to ache, and it was at this point that the rhythm of their labour changed into a spirit-lifting song known as the *Krakowiak,* a song familiar to those from a farming background. It seemed, however, that everybody knew the song whether city dweller or rustic peasant, and all of the women broke out into song.

The sun reflected off their white headscarves and aprons as their skirts swayed in time to the song. Jan watched this scene from his reaper and was reminded of summers past in peaceful times, and his thoughts moved to his wife.

After a few moments of reflection, Jan's thoughts returned to the job in hand. He estimated that if the progress they had made so far could be sustained they stood a good chance of finishing cutting the field by late that Friday afternoon, and he could then rest the horses. This would mean that on Saturday morning they could transport the last of the sheaves to the rick yard for the contractors and the harvest would be done.

Filled with a renewed optimism, Jan urged on the girls. Their bridles jangling, their necks covered in a thin sheen of sweat, they carried out their master's bidding and pushed on. In time, the reaping was done, and Jan returned to the farmyard, fed and watered the horses, and then returned to the field on the empty cart to help the ladies finish putting the sheaves into stooks. As light faded, and with the Polish helpers gone back to the camp for dinner, Jan walked around the field with Chastity checking what was needed to be done in the morning.

As they reached the farthest point of the field, Chastity

picked up the final sheaf that had been cut and placed it in the hedge.

"What are you doing?" asked Jan in amazement. "This is where the corn spirit will live through the winter months, until we plant the new crop" Chastity explained.

With that Jan snatched up three loose stalks of barley and within minutes had woven what looked to Chastity like a corn dolly. Jan placed the newly woven braided barley on the sheaf and said,

"There they can keep each other company through the winter."

"What is it?" Chastity asked.

"It's a *popiórka*," replied Jan, "and it's where we keep our spirit of fertility for the winter in Poland, so now we'll have plenty of protection, next year will be a bumper harvest," he laughed.

The two then left the field and walked back to the farm, where Jan picked up his bicycle for his ride home. As he was about to set off, Chastity called out to him from the farmhouse garden.

"Please thank Marek for organising the help," she called. "We could not have done it without them." Jan acknowledged Chastity's request and set off home.

After a lonely cold supper, Jan made his way back to the hut, only to find Marek sat on the step in the twilight holding a bottle of plum juice and two glasses.

"Come on," he beckoned, "it's Friday evening and the harvest is nearly in, it's time for a plum juice." He smiled.

Jan sat on the steps with his friend and held the glasses so that he could pour them each a 'juice'.

"Chastity asked me to thank you for organising the ladies and scouts for the harvest. She said it was very important in helping them finish the harvest before the rain comes."

Jan lifted his glass in a salute and said, 'Cheers,' "I have to ask, how did you manage it in such a short time?"

"Well," said Marek taking a sip of his plum juice, "you know that I'm cooperating with farmer Dyke in a project up in the woods by the dew pond?"

"Yes," replied Jan.

"Well, that project is based on me supplying old hospital food as swill for his pigs in the woods, for which he pays me. The Ministry controls the production of food very tightly and all pigs and other livestock are registered as part of that control. Well, those pigs are outside of that control"

"Illegal, you mean!" Jan said in a panicked tone.

"Shush, shush," said Marek, "not illegal but outside the control of the Ministry. The mother sow is registered with the Ministry and is now back in her stie, so that is perfectly legal, it's just that her piglets haven't yet been registered.

"I offered Dyke a deal which meant that my ladies would work in the field in exchange for one of those pigs when it is fully grown. We can make sausage, smoke the bacon, and many other traditional dishes ready for winter"

"Your ladies?" cried an exasperated Jan., "when did they become your ladies?"

"It is a figure of speech, Jan, I don't mean that the ladies are mine, I was just their agent working on their behalf."

"It sounds as if, although they spent two days toiling in the field, you were doing them a favour," said Jan in disbelief.

"Listen," said Marek emphatically, "they'll get a whole pig worth a lot of money for a couple of days work, Dyke will have gotten his harvest in safe and sound, my friend the butcher will be able to supply his London customers with fresh Wiltshire bacon, they'll be happy, and he'll be happy, and I may make a small profit out of all this." With this squaring of the circle Marek was content, took another sip of juice and changed the subject.

"Have you heard any news about your wife yet?" asked Marek hastily.

"No, not yet I'll meet with Mrs Jarvis next weekend when harvest is over, and I've a weekend off at last" advised Jan.

Marek then gave a number of snippets of news and gossip gleaned from around the camp which he thought might be of interest to Jan. He started, "Professor Kaminski will be having a send-off party after the camp meeting on Monday, as he leaves for Oxford next week. Mrs Goldstein is still complaining about the choirmaster not letting her join the choir due to her operatic voice. The committee is concerned about Kronski, because, despite making numerous attempts to contact him he seems to have disappeared, and, just in case you are worrying about it, the final preparations are being made for the 'dożynki' with the dancers having to start practicing in the church hall, because the orchestra needs our hall for practice. So, as you can hear, you have not missed much while you have been working so hard on the harvest."

Jan drained the last of his plum juice and asked, "what's the news on Marta?" Enquiring in a mischievous tone to irk Marek.

"I'm treating her like a timid horse, but I'm making some progress. She's agreed to meet me at the harvest dance, so that is encouraging." With that reply, Jan handed over his empty glass and made his way to bed.

CHAPTER 6
LOVE IS IN THE AIR

Next day, Jan was up with the sheep by seven and back at the yard by nine. Sid had finished milking and the two of them harnessed up the girls, threw Jan's bike on board and made their way up to the last of the barley. To their amazement, a group of Boy Scouts were waiting for them and their empty cart to arrive.

"You might as well go back to the rick yard Sid as I've enough help here," suggested Jan. "You can oversee the last of the threshing and rick building. Take my bike, it'll be quicker."

"I'd rather walk thank you, it'll be safer!" Sid replied with a wry smile. Sid set off and left Jan and the boys to pick up the last stooks and then make their way back to the yard.

By mid-afternoon Jan noticed that the wind was picking up and the warm breeze had become a hot wind. The contractors struggled to thatch the last straw rick, but years of experience prevailed, and in no time the last hazel spar was hammered home. The sacks of barley were loaded onto the now empty wagons and pulled into the dry barn by Dolly and Bubbles. As the contractors dismantled the thresher belts, the engine driver reversed his traction engine up to the thresher and stoked up the boiler for the long road back to the yard.

As the ensemble moved off, under a slate-grey sky, the first spots of rain spat and sizzled on the engines hot body, and in a smelly cloud of oily steam, the harvest was over, and the contractors were gone as all was safely gathered in.

That evening, Jan and Marek decided that the finish of the harvest warranted a serious drink at the pub, so showered and scrubbed, they made their way to their favourite hostelry, the Bell, on the village green. As they came near to the village, they passed the village hall, and as they drew near, they could hear the strains of a Chopin polonaise coming through the open door. They decided to take a look inside to see what was happening.

As they peered through the open door, the first thing that met their eyes were two Women's Institute ladies sat behind a large trestle table full of sandwiches. Mugs were waiting to be filled from a large tea urn, which hissed and bubbled, on the end of the table.

At the far end of the hall was the camps' Polish dance group practicing with the aid of an old record player. Their leader, Captain Mróz, was guiding the dancers in a circle, their stately disposition and erect attitude not pompous but dignified, as they led the young women, their colourful dresses filling with air as they spun in unison. The men in red leather boots and blue-and-red striped voluminous trousers, blue coats, white ruffled shirts, and a felt hat with an eagle's feather in it.

The men held the women around the waist close to them with their right hand and extended their left hand up high in front of them in a haughty, balletic gesture that declared, make way for me and my lady! The men, straight backed with their heads held high glided around the hall conducting the women through the dance as if they were weightless.

The boys had seen enough, they stepped back into the pool of light that shone through the open doorway and onto the wet road and made their way to the first of many beverages.

As they neared the village green, an army lorry sped by, and from its covered rear section young men could be heard singing 'Roll Out the Barrel'. The boys gave its passing a cursory glance, then pushed open the pub door and were gone.

As the lorry approached the village hall it began to slow down, and then stopped right outside it. An imposing officer in a maroon beret jumped out of the cab and banged on the side of the truck with his swagger stick.

"Come on, you lazy load of loafers," he screamed, "two ranks in the road now!"

The young men started climbing out of the truck, jumping down on to the road, and formed two rows. They adjusted their berets, pulled their tunics down and straightened them. In no time at all two ranks of young men were stood to attention in the drizzle of a Wiltshire evening.

"Right," shouted the officer, "we are stopping here for some tea and sandwiches laid on by the women's institute before we move on to the airport. I want you to show some manners in here, so no swearing, and it will be 'please mam', 'thank you mam', and keep stum, do I make myself clear?"

"Yes, sir," came back the deafening reply.

"Right, you have twenty minutes before we move out; there is a carzy out the back. I want you tucked up in bed early tonight before you make your first jump in the morning. Now move it, left right, left right."

The sergeant turned to the lorry driver and, using his swagger stick as a pointer, said, "Driver, as corporal, you are in charge. I saw a pub back up the road. I'll be back shortly."

"Yes, sergeant major," snapped the corporal.

With his swagger stick underneath his arm the sergeant major swaggered off to the pub.

Accompanied by the corporal, the two dozen recruits strolled into the hall, joking about their future prospects and how short they might be, given the uncertainties of a parachute jump. One witty private took one look at the table of tea and sandwiches and shouted,

"Cor blimey, not much of a last supper, is it, boys?"

However, by this time most of the rest of the group had spied the slim young women whirling around at the far end of the hall. One of them, another droll wag, suggested that the girls would make a more suitable last supper, at which point one of the WI ladies chirped up.

"I'm sorry boys; we did not know the hall was double booked. We'll put some chairs across the hall to separate you from the dancers so that you can sit and drink your tea."

"No problem, madam, me and some of the boys will put the chairs out for you," said one of the eager recruits.

"What nice boys," she remarked to her companion as she sat back down.

With that, the assembly sauntered over to the dancers and spread chairs at even intervals across the hall. However, instead of moving away, they sat astride the chairs backwards with their arms resting on the backs leering at the women.

The promenading group did their best to ignore their unwanted audience and continued. When the squaddies were unable to elicit any kind of reaction from the girls, they turned to more base humour.

"I'd like to give blondie a twirl," shouted one of the boys to his friend.

"I'd like to find out what is under all those petticoats," quipped another.

At this point, Captain Mróz stopped the dance troupe and walked over to the squaddies.

"Good evening gentlemen, could I ask you all to keep your comments to yourselves, please, these young ladies are not the type of girls I'm sure you normally fraternise with."

With that said, he turned on his heels, his coat flailing out in dramatic style, his eagle feather wisping through the air in an almost audible swish, and returned to the dance troupe. As he gracefully made his way back to the dancers and assumed the start position, a chorus of 'Little Sir Echo' broke out among the squaddies, who were now becoming unruly in the extreme.

It would appear that Captain Mróz had in fact made matters worse with his polite appeal, and the squaddies' appetite for mischief had not abated. After a few moments, some of the more forward members of the military force took it upon themselves to try to grab the young female dancers around the waist and pull them away from their partners.

The male dancers, in an attempt to protect the sanctity of their female charges, reacted with cat-like speed and fists flew in an attempt to rebuff the unwanted advances of the squaddies.

As a trio of England's finest lay sprawled on the hall floor, their faces contorted and bruised, the male dancers ushered the girls up onto the stage out of harm's way, as they were sure they knew what was coming.

The remainder of the squaddies saw their cohorts on the floor and sprang into action. Without a battle plan to guide them, most of the young men decided on a frontal attack, with overwhelming numbers their best guarantee of victory. It was in this way that the battle of the village hall would enter into the annals of village history.

As splintered chairs splintered bone to the strains of a Chopin polonaise, battle commenced. Eyes were gouged, ears torn, jaws broken, and arms fractured. Eagle feathers were snapped, and blood flowed freely as fists flew. It did not take the parachute regiment too long to realise that they had bitten off more than they could chew. As a large number of regimental combatants who were on the floor stayed down on the floor, the corporal felt it would be wise to run on a rescue mission and get the sergeant major from the pub.

On arrival at the pub, he found his sergeant talking to Tony Sharpe at the bar about England's new rapid deployment force and praising it in exalted tones.

"What do you want corporal can't you see I'm talking to Mr Sharpe?"

"I think you'd better come back to the hall sergeant major; we've had a bit of an upset-"

"Upset?" snapped the sergeant major,

"Yes, Sargent Major, some of the lads picked a fight with some dancers and all hell has let loose."

"Which dancers?" Tony asked.

"The Poles sir" replied the corporal.

"My god," exclaimed Tony, "those men have fought their way out of Asia, across North Africa, up through Italy, then took Monte Cassino, liberated some of Holland, and flew Spitfires day after day. Not to mention D-Day. You'd better go sergeant major."

"Bloody hell corporal, quick march" ordered the sergeant major."

As the two men arrived at the hall, the stretcher cases were already flat out in the lorry, carried there by the walking wounded. Others were stood around nursing bleeding wounds, some white with shock even in the subdued light thrown out by the village hall. Hardly a recruit was unharmed unless they had had the good sense to stay out of the fracas. "Crikey," shouted the sergeant, "how many Poles were there?"

"Seven," shouted the corporal.

"Seven?" shouted the sergeant major. Aghast that this much carnage could be achieved by so few on so many,

"You lot are on a fizzer,' he screamed at the lorry load of pitiful humanity.

As the lorry pitched forward into the night, the strains of Chopin could, once more, be heard drifting out of the village hall as the rehearsal resumed in peace. Polish honour was once again restored and the frustrations of continual acquiescence were purged, for one evening at least.

Sunday morning breakfast for the impious few was filled with tales of the battle of the village hall and the resounding victory achieved by the dancers. As Jan and Marek sat in quiet contemplation, Marek looked at Jan.

"I'm going to make my move today and ask Marta to see Stonehenge with me."

"Good luck with that my friend. It'll be quite a test for her. If she can stand two hours in a rattling sidecar with you driving that noisy motorbike, she'll be able to stand anything."

"I'll ask her after church, and if she agrees, we can go after dinner," resolved Marek.

"Don't forget it gets dark by nine now, so keep an eye on your watch," said Jan, attempting to add more stress to an already stressful situation, smiling as he did so.

Marek scowled at Jan and uttered under his breath, "Well at least I won't be spending my Sunday with a herd of sheep"

"Flock of sheep," Jan corrected him. "Yes, even though I'm on my day off, my ladies are working hard on the downs, and I need to visit them. I'll not be around much now, so good luck with Marta and I look forward to hearing all the news later." With that the boys left the canteen and went their separate ways.

Jan unchained his bike and set off up the lane. As he passed the farmyard, he saw Chastity coming out of the dairy washroom, he waved and called out a greeting to which she responded. Chastity beckoned Jan into the yard and walked over to greet him.

"Off out for the day?" Chastity enquired.

"I'm just going up to check the sheep," Jan replied.

"On your day off?" Chastity queried.

"As I said to Marek just now, my ladies don't stop working so neither should I."

"How is Marek these days, is he still wheeling and dealing?"

"He's fine I think" responded Jan, "and yes, as you know, he's still operating a number of business projects."

At this point Chastity interrupted Jan, "Could I ask you to thank him for us, for his help with the harvest. We'd have had real problems if he'd not come up with a solution as he did. I know father will not say anything to him, but I'm sure he is glad things sorted themselves out in the way they did in the end."

"I'll make sure that I do," Jan assured Chastity. "How is your father?" Jan asked. "I never see him about the farm when I'm here."

"No," replied Chastity with a tone of pathos in her voice. "Father has a bad back after long years of manual work, so now he tends his beloved vegetable plot, which Sid's grandson digs for him, and runs the business from his desk. I do what I can to help about the place, and Mother, who was never brought up as a farm girl, keeps the books. She fills her days with socialising with the other farmer's wives in one society or another, so, we rely on you and Sid to keep things going. It's hard to find good people nowadays as nobody wants to work in the wet and cold with early mornings, you know."

Jan nodded, "Well say hello from me when you next see your father, I must go now to see my ladies. I won't forget to speak to Marek for you. Goodbye, Miss Dyke."

"Oh, crikey, Jan, call me Chastity please."

Jan smiled. "OK, goodbye Chastity have a nice day." With that, Jan mounted his bike and continued on his way.

After checking up on Teddy the donkey and his woolly charges, Jan freewheeled down the hill and straight through the gate of the camp just in time for dinner. As the mass had just ended, there was a throng of erstwhile worshipers making their way to the canteen. In this multitude he spied Marek and Marta, who was laughing and smiling at Marek's every word.

Behind the young couple the attendant chaperones Kinga and Kasia keeping the liaison within the bounds of social propriety, strained to listen to their conversation. Inside the canteen, the group divided and made their way to their respective tables.

"Well, how's it going?" Jan asked in a playful tone.

Marek answered excitedly, and as he spoke the pitch of his voice got higher and higher. "Marta's accepted my invitation to go to Stonehenge. She's been really nice to me, none of the old moody Marta. I think I'm getting somewhere with her."

With this, the kitchen hatch was slammed open, and all thoughts turned to food and a discussion about tactics for this first and most important of dates. The boys decided that Marek should keep things friendly, remember to help Marta out of the sidecar when they stopped, and leave thoughts of any future out of the conversation.

With his strategy in place, straight after dinner Marek fetched his motorbike round to the front of the hut where he waited nervously, polishing the matt green paint with a clean cloth.

"You're highly unlikely to put a shine on that, it's matt paint." Jan joked, "no matter how hard you polish."

But Marek was too anxious to pay heed to Jan's sarcasm. After a while, Marta came walking down the camp road.

She was wearing a white summer dress covered in small bunches of cherries, her long blonde hair secured in a pink headscarf.

"Well, I must say you look a sight for sore eyes," said Jan trying to contain his enthusiasm to a fatherly interest rather than sounding like an excited schoolboy lecher.

"Let me help you into the car," Marek said, in a chivalrous tone as he held Marta's hand as she stepped into the sidecar and sat down, her long legs disappearing into the body of the car.

"This is bigger than I thought it would be," Marta announced in surprise, "but why does it smell like mashed potatoes?"

Marek kick-started the bike to stifle any more conversation and the two lovebirds were gone.

Jan now planned that the rest of his first day off since the beginning of harvest should be a laid back affair. He sat in the late afternoon summer sun on the steps of the hut and passed the time of day with whoever happened by, studying camp life as it passed before him. The nuns were shepherding the young children over to the church for Sunday school, hoping to keep this young Polish seed from landing on the stony ground of the Protestantism that surrounded them. The old men sat in small groups on benches, poring over and discussing the contents of the Polish language newspapers, looking for some small nugget of information that may have been missed by all the previous readers. The debates, usually centred on when the third world war would start, the questionable patriotism of those returning home, when would it be safe to return home, and the betrayal of the Poles by the British government.

Jan had noticed that in his time there, camp gossip was not countenanced and even Frau Swartz, who was vocal in her complaining and a German, did not attract any form of reproach from her peers. Those same young girls, with freshly washed hair, sat in the sun brushing their hair dry while giggling and chatting in excited high spirits.

The young men, sullen, due to the impending Monday morning beckoning to them, also railed at the overzealous supervision directed at them by Captain Bialy and his team of ex-combatants, determined that the boys should bring no shame on the camp.

The Sunday evening mass bell began to chime, calling the faithful to prayer. Some moved swiftly, others lethargically, but most responded. Jan, awakened from his thoughts by the clanging, opted to maintain his position on the steps and wait for Marek and Marta's arrival.

As Jan waited, Professor Kaminski walked past heading towards the camp's community hall. "Good evening professor, how are you, I hear congratulations are in order."

"Good evening, Captain Kot, yes, thank you very much. I'll be glad to get back to work and collaborate with my old colleagues at Oxford. We've much to do to keep ahead of the Communists if we're to win the next conflict."

Jan decided that, in the circumstances, he would let the Captain Kot comment go and smiling, nodded agreement with the professor. As Jan watched the professor disappear into the community hut, a voice from Jan's blind side surprised him.

"Good evening, Jan, how are you today?" It was Tony Sharpe on his way to the community hut too.

"Good evening, Tony," said Jan, "off to play chess?"

"Yes I am, and to have a good old natter about what is happening in the camp, talking of which, I hear Marek has hitched up with Marta, is that true?"

"Possibly," said Jan in a noncommittal voice as he was not sure if the relationship was going to survive a two-hour side-car ride to Stonehenge and back.

"So, she's no longer with her flyer then, that's a pity. Let's hope they make a proper go of it, then there maybe wedding bells in the air."

Jan thought that this was overly optimistic but agreed with Tony. Tony ran on to the community hut his chess bag slapping against his blazer, its flap flying up in the air as it was not securely buckled. Suddenly, a small notebook with a pencil inserted in the spine flew out of the bag and landed in the gravel. Jan happened to witness this and ran over to pick it up.

"Tony!" he called, "your notebook."

Tony's disposition suddenly changed. "You'd better give that to me old chap, I don't want anybody seeing that," he said in an almost panic-stricken tone.

"Why?" asked Jan.

"Secret chess moves old chap," whispered Tony, and clenching the notebook tightly, he was gone.

As Jan reassumed his position on the hut steps once more, he heard the familiar sound of Marek's combination motorbike and sidecar coming closer and closer down the lane. As it arrived at the gates, Marek made a theatrical right hand turn gesture with his arm and the lovebirds sailed smoothly into the camp as an eagerly waiting Jan greeted them.

"So, how did your excursion go?" Jan asked Marta in a playful voice.

"Well, Marek was a revelation to me," Marta gushed, "a perfect gentleman, polite, attentive, and caring." Marek looked at Jan with a wide boyish grin and then dismounted the bike to help Marta out of the sidecar.

Marta thanked him for the daytrip but declined a meeting at the pub that evening citing hair washing and an early shift at the flax factory. Both men watched as she walked, panther like, back to her hut.

Once Marta was out of sight, Jan smacked Marek on the back and congratulated him on managing not to upset the usually feisty Marta. "You must tell me all about your day," demanded Jan.

"Only if you buy me a pint," insisted Marek.

So, the two men parked up the bike, covered it in its sheet, and strolled down to the pub and waited for it to open. Marek recounted every miniscule detail of the day in an excited mood while Jan listened intently. As the boys were chatting, it became clear that Marta's attitude to Marek had completely changed in the space of a few days. Marek was not able to pin down the reason for this change, but the boys conceded that neither of them really understood women. As they drank back their beer, they both agreed that this change was welcome.

***

As the rural calendar moved into mellow fruitfulness, Jan knew that he would be spending much more time up on the downs tending his flock. Lambing was fast approaching, and he needed to prepare his caravan for the cooler days and harsh weather to come. Sid, along with Dyke, had agreed to leave the ground fallow for a while after muck spreading, so that it would soften in the autumn rain. They reasoned that this would make the ploughing easier for Dolly and Bubbles, and as Jan and Sid would be sharing this task, -both men eagerly agreed.

So, on a bright early September morning, Jan took a bow saw from the tool shed at the farm and set off up the hill to the downs on his bike. As Jan passed the woods opposite the sheep fold, the air was full of the smell of musty leaves and the fermentation of wild sloes and apples. The foliage was on the turn and some trees already sported their bright orange coats. Jan pedalled on at speed so that he could enter the bright autumn sunshine obscured by the flushed glowing canopy of the woods.

At last Jan crested the top of the hill and emerged onto the open downs where he made his way over to his shepherd's caravan and opened the stable door. The air inside was stale and musty, as the insides had acquired a cold dampness that Jan feared would work into his bones, so he opened the window and tied back the stable door. Jan checked on the flock and

Teddy and looked for signs of new arrivals.

None were found, so he made his way over to the pig-stie copse and started dragging fallen branches over to his caravan. The illegal piglets were now plump and fully grown an indictment of British hospital food if one was needed. After Jan had dragged a number of boughs over to his caravan, he started sawing them up into manageable logs that would fit into the cast-iron stove in the caravan. Jan stacked the wood in the dry under his caravan and then continued to haul and saw for most of the morning. When a goodly amount of logs had been prepared, Jan decided to have a trial lighting of the fire. He twisted old newspapers into spills and set a pile of dry larch twigs on top. He lit the paper, and the hearth burst into life, crackling, and popping rhythmically as if the caravan had a heartbeat at last. Jan checked the chimney, and it was drawing nicely, so he decided to keep the fire going to help with the airing process. His home for the next few weeks was ready, so Jan went about checking fences, the stock, and the dew pond to make clear there were no briars that could snag the sheep. With this done, he slept in the sun and so his day passed.

Presently, after damping down the fire and closing up the caravan, Jan returned to the farm for an early finish, so that he was ready for the camp meeting. The camp canteen was abuzz with excited voices as the evening meal finished and the meeting drew closer. Many went straight to the community hall to gain the best seats and vantage points. Jan took up his normal place by the back wall, but as Marek was about to sidle up to him, Marta waved him over to a seat she was saving for him, and, just like that, he was gone.

Jan smiled to himself and prepared for the fortnightly showdown which promised to be a little more interesting than the ones Jan had missed of late. Then, the room became hushed as the great and the good of the camps committee processed onto the stage and took up their positions. Father Graboski prayed, and the assembly crossed themselves in response. With that, the meeting was called to order and first to speak, without any introduction, was Mr Monk.

Monk launched into his monotone homily at speed, anxious to get it over with and get away. Jan listened, and as he did so, he could think of no one less suited to the job.

Monk advised the assembly. "After close consultation with the committee and choir master, Mrs Goldstein is now singing in the camp choir as a soprano in the chorus. It appears that her husband had converted to Catholicism in Austria before the war, and this had been proved by an affidavit from Vienna."

Jan was not happy that this poor woman's private life had been exposed in public, but at least he thought she could now sing.

Monk continued, "It has been agreed that Mrs Kunka will remain lead soprano." A murmur of agreement about Mrs Kunka rose from the room followed by whispers of condemnation for Mrs Goldstein.

Monk moved on quickly to quell this discord. "While I know you will be holding your own harvest festival shortly, you have been cordially invited to the village harvest festival. I know many of you helped out on a local farm, and it may be nice to celebrate this bond between us." The hall was stony silent, and that told Monk all he needed to know about the decision that had already been made.

Monk then moved on to other matters. "Due to a new influx of families, the last of the single foreign workers are being moved to an old Italian prisoner of war camp to make room for the new arrivals." This comment was met with general approval, until he mentioned that the one exception to this action was Frau Swartz, who was staying with the single girls.

At this point Monk drew himself to his full height and

stilled himself for an announcement that he knew would be unpopular. He started, "it has come to my attention that there was a fracas involving camp members at the village hall recently. While no official complaint has been made, this type of disturbance does not reflect well on the camp or my running of it, that is all I will say on the matter!"

As usual, Monk then turned on his heels and walked out of the meeting, without ceremony and avoiding eye contact with any of his audience as he left. However, at the last moment, his eye caught Jan leaning on the rear wall of the hall, and he walked over to him.

"Ah Mr Kot," he said in a quiet voice that was almost a whisper, "I have taken the liberty of moving you into the family hut from Saturday, when your wife and children will arrive. Please come to the office to sign the necessary paperwork during the week." Monk then made his escape, leaving Jan in a state of shock and panic.

Jan heard no more of the meeting even though voices were raised, and tempers frayed. Jan's mind was a mass of thoughts and uncertainties. In that one moment after Monk's comment, the life that he knew at the camp and at work had seemed to unravel. Everything that had been dependable had become unstable, his freedom to choose would be replaced by seeking consensus and agreement, his money in the post office account would become their money. He would become responsible for three more lives. Who would scold the children him or his wife as they weren't his to scold.

It all became too much to bear and so, Jan decided to leave the meeting to clear his mind and think. As he turned to go, he glanced at Marek who was smiling and happy and laughing at some little comment Marta had made and Jan pondered if this new life of his would be so bad. Jan left the hall and decided that what he needed was a plan to help him organise the new life that was fast approaching, but he did not know where to go to seek help. Jan decided that finding the right person to give him advice was the first thing he must achieve the next day so with that resolve he decided on an early night.

Tuesday dawned mucky and moist and as Jan rode into the farmyard he was met by Sid and Dyke, both of whom were wearing sisal sacks over their shoulders to prevent the drizzle soaking into their jackets.

"Morning Jan!" shouted Dyke as he climbed into his car. "See you all later."

Jan put his bike into the cart shed and picked up his sack off the wheel of a cart and threw it over his shoulders as if he was the Count of Monte Cristo. "Good morning Sid, Dyke seems in high spirits today. What could possibly have happened?"

"He is in a good mood today because he has had two cheques come in the post and he is off to put them in the bank."

"Ah, that explains it, it's good that he has money coming in to pay our wages and keep the farm going. If Dyke became poor, we might lose our jobs."

"Don't you worry young-un; Dyke has more money than you and I will ever see in our lifetimes. He invests in stuff. He has milk cheques, brewery cheques, mill cheques, a posh car, and a well-connected wife who will inherit half of a Dorset farm. He has more money han God. There are two things that you will never see in life, Jan; one is a poor farmer, and the other is a dead donkey."

Jan nodded in agreement with Sid despite not having the slightest idea what he was talking about. With his sack over his shoulders to fend off the misty drizzle, he set off for the downs. It was late September, and he was expecting the cold weather to come soon, and this would mean the return of the sheep to the fold for lambing. As Jan sped out of the yard, Sid shouted out after him.

"That's another thing you will never see, a farmer on a bloody bicycle!" Jan waved his hand in a hurried acknowledgement, and slipping into the misty drizzle, he was gone.

Once he was at the caravan, Jan lit a fire and while it took hold, he searched the flock for problems. Luckily, none were found. Sid, Jan thought, was right when he said that this breed was hardy and rugged and caused little trouble. He was also right about their fertility as most were pregnant, proving that Percy the rams attention had been well rewarded with many carrying multiple lambs. Jan shrugged off the misty chill and snuggled in his inviting caravan to warm up and dry out.

He looked out of the window at the downs and the dew pond that had been his first job. The grasslands, their mossy green flush gone were now the colour of straw. How time had passed, and what a change was coming. Jan felt a mixture of excitement and dread at the arrival of his wife and the children. He still had not decided who he should talk to about his anxiety, and wondered if it would be better just to deal with it all when it happened.

As morning turned to early afternoon, the cloud lifted, the temperature rose and a warmer, gentler day emerged. Jan checked the sheep one last time, fixed some fencing, and chopped down some briers. After a while he decided to go back to the farm and see what needed doing down there, so astride his bike he set off on the swift return journey.

As he pulled into the yard, Jan saw Sid hunched over the plough, cursing and complaining. Sid had a piece of string stretched along the length of the plough with a wooden ruler to measure, and with an assortment of spanners, was trying to set up the plough.

"I don't understand it." Sid said in a frustrated tone.

"When this was put away last winter, it was set up and

working perfectly. Now it's all to cock! I think the mice or rats must mess with it over the summer," Sid jested in an attempt to calm down.

Jan walked over and helped Sid as best he could but setting up ploughs was not his forte and so his help was more moral rather than mechanical.

"Well, we need to get this bugger set up for next Monday, so I might ask my grandson to have a look at it as he is one of those new-fangled agricultural engineers and a bloody know-it-all to boot."

So, with a plan in place the two procrastinators went about their duties, Sid to his milking and Jan to feeding and mucking out the stalls. As the end of the working day drew near, Jan helped Sid wash down the parlour and clean the equipment ready for the morning. Then, after a short visit to the farm office to sign their work chits, the two left and bade each other farewell.

As Jan arrived at the camp gate, he could hear a commotion which he knew only too well was Frau Swartz complaining about her work. Jan had been told to call into the office to sign his married quarters' paperwork, so he decided that this would be a good excuse to be nosey. As usual, Marta was in attendance trying to calm Frau Swartz in German.

Jan was amazed that Marta spoke German so well and questioned her about this new skill that he had not known she possessed.

"I was a slave labourer in Germany for four years," she countered abruptly. "I was bound to pick up something other than diphtheria."

Jan was shocked by Marta's abruptness. This was not the new Marta that he had gotten used to over the last few weeks. He presumed it may have been on account of the bellicose Frau Swartz and, put her attitude down to that.

He looked at the red-faced Mr Monk. "I have come to sign

the documents, Mr Monk." Monk responded with impatience, "As you can see Mr Kot, I am dealing with Frau Swartz at the moment, can't it wait?" Jan, never one to impose on another, decided it could and decided to back off and come back at another time.

Jan moved away, bike in hand, and Marta took this opportunity to follow him and escape the drama that was unfolding at the office door and leave Monk to his fate.

"So, your wife's coming this weekend, you must be very excited!"

"I'm not that sure at present," confessed Jan. "It's complicated by the fact that the children aren't mine and I'm not sure if my wife is even mine until I meet her at the weekend."

"Well, Jan," Marta snorted in derision, "I hope that you're not going to greet her using that as your opening welcoming statement. Your wife has travelled halfway around the world with two small children to find you and be with you. If her desire was to be with anybody else or to be somewhere else, she would not be coming here!"

Jan looked down at the ground in a disconsolate manner. "I know what you say makes a lot of sense, but memories of her and our life together were the happiest times of my life and I feel betrayed by her. She was the most loyal soulmate anybody could wish for and then I find out that she has been with another man and has children with him. I'm not sure if I can go back to the old life with her with that gnawing at me inside every time I see the children: or even try to rebuild our lives."

"Listen," said Marta in an emphatic tone that betrayed her own troubled past, "all of us have been through terrible times, and all of us have had to do things we did not want to just to survive. Do you think I'd be here if I had a choice, no, I'd be back in Poland with my family. I don't even know if I have a family anymore, so what should I do? I could give up and go back and live under communism or I can try and build a new life here. Well, I choose here, and the only real difference between you and me is that you'll get to share your new life with your wife while I'll have to start alone. So, excuse me if I don't feel too sorry for you Jan."

With Jan summarily and suitably chastised the two then made their way to their respective huts in silence.

CHAPTER 7
SILENT AND UNSEEN

B ack in his hut with Marta's words still ringing in his ears, Jan removed his boots and lay on his bed to think things over. Marta's comments had stung him somewhat and he really needed to sort his head out so that when Ewa and the children arrived, he could be sure that he would not cause any more upsets. He reasoned that although he had suffered deprivation and slave labour, he had endured this with his army comrades and later in an American battalion surrounded by his co-workers. Ewa had, as far as he knew, endured her deportation alone and must have had to fend for herself during much of that time. Jan also pondered that the feelings he was experiencing of betrayal were due to the fact that he still loved Ewa, and this was the natural reaction of a man in love. He further reasoned that for Ewa to have endured so much and to have survived, she must have had to be very strong, and for this reason he owed it to her to let the facts of her journey dispel the confusion that he felt at present.

Now, feeling content to face the facts on Saturday, Jan closed his eyes and tried to drift off to sleep for a short while before dinner. However, no sooner had he closed his eyes than he felt the presence of an observer standing over him. Jan opened his eyes to be confronted by a Boy Scout, all crisply starched and shiny shoed, standing over him.

Jan sighed and asked the boy. "Do you always wait for me to take a nap before you come in to speak to me?"

The boy ignored Jan's comment and saluted him, then in a very quiet voice uttered, "Captain Kot, I'm here on a secret mission, you must not tell anybody about the meeting you are about to have with Major Bialy. Remember not a word to anyone."

Jan sat bolt upright on his bed and scratched his head in bewilderment. "what are you talking about, boy?" Jan asked impatiently as he then pulled on his boots and laced them up.

The Scout led Jan to the community hall, opened the door for him, ushered him inside, and then closed the door and stood outside to bar entry to anybody else.

As Jan walked up the hall to the stage end where two men sat talking in hushed tones, he started to become concerned that something might really be seriously wrong.

Bialy spoke first, "Ah Captain Kot, thank you for coming so quickly."

"I'd little choice in the matter," responded Jan.

Bialy ignored this comment and launched into his briefing in almost a whisper. "Captain Kot, this is Gorski."

Jan extended a hand, and the men shook. "No rank?" asked Jan with a semi-formal sarcasm.

"The less you know about Gorski, the better captain," Bialy said in a way that seemed threat centred. "Gorski is liaison office for the *Cichociemni.*"

"So," said Jan who was palpably shocked by this information. "The Silent and Dark really do exist, and what are they doing in rural Wiltshire?" asked Jan, now taking things a little more seriously.

"Gorski is following up some leads on a number of

missing persons cases among returning officers from this camp. It appears that a witness reported seeing Kronski being removed from the train two stations before Warsaw. Kronski recognised the witness, and he shouted one word at him over and over again."

"What was the word?" asked Jan.

"Cambridge," said Bialy.

"What else did the witness say?" asked Jan, who by this time had become intrigued by these reports and had lost his cynicism.

"He saw nothing else, as he was too busy blending into the crowd on the platform so that the secret police did not see him," said Bialy. "All we know is he was shouting Cambridge over and over again. You knew Kronski quite well, Kot, we would like to know what he said to you before he left for home and anything else that might help Gorski solve these cases."

Jan started to think back, searching and hoping to find some clue or a piece of information that might help. He had liked Kronski and wished to help in any way he could. He told Gorski all and anything he thought might help and as he finished, he wondered what would happen next.

Bialy answered that question for him. "Now listen captain, only we three know what has been said in this meeting," he said sternly, "not a word to anyone, do you understand?"

Jan nodded, and for once he actually took Bialy seriously and left not saying a word. As Jan walked over to the canteen, he began to wonder if he had been harsh on Bialy. Jan had always belittled his intrigues and suspicion of an invisible enemy, but now it appeared that that enemy was amongst them unseen and unknown. Jan sat in his normal seat and was joined by Marek who was still on cloud nine with his blossoming relationship.

"You look worried today," Marek quipped. "Still nervous

about the arrival of your new family?"

Jan decided to keep his secret and nodded that that was the reason for his downcast manner, but inside his mind was racing. Was there a traitor sitting at one of these tables, was there a clandestine assassin of the Silent and Dark watching him now? Suddenly the arrival of his family seemed the least of his problems.

Jan looked across at Marta, happy and smiling again, and hoped that his wife would be that pleased to see him at the weekend. As he and Marek got up to leave, Jan was approached by one of the camps nuns. " Hello, Sister Danuta, what can I do for you?".

She leaned forward and asked, "Can I have the names of your children so that I can put them down for Sunday school?"

Jan looked at the nun and had to admit that he did not know his children's names or their ages.

Sister Danuta looked at Jan aghast and turned to walk away.

"I'm sorry," called Jan after her, "I'm going to leave all that side of things to my wife." Jan looked at a laughing Marek who was able to make fun of him for once.

"Will they go to Saturday school, are they baptised, all these questions and no answers." The pair started to leave again, and as they did so, a smiling happy Marta linked arms with both of them, and the three left together.

As they made their way to their respective huts, they met Tony Sharpe making his way to the camp hall for his chess game with the professor.

"Good evening to you all, I am glad I have bumped into you. I am having a farewell party on Friday night at the Bell, so I would love to see you all there. Just off for one last game of chess and a catch-up chat, so can't stop. Hope to see you all on Friday."

The trio waved him goodbye and carried on.

"There is a chill in the air," said Marta.

"Yes, it is getting cold in the mornings on my motorbike," agreed Marek. Marek looked at Marta, she was like a sparrow draped in a thin cotton overcoat. "Is that the only coat you have to see you through the winter?" Marek asked.

Marta grinned. "Yes, but don't worry, I can put on another jumper and wear my work clothes over it. I am made of sterner stuff than these English girls."

With that, Jan left the pair to their canoodling and went to his hut for his much-delayed nap.

When Marek eventually came into the hut, the two sat and chatted about their hopes for the future. Jan trying to come to terms with the arrival of his instant family and Marek dreaming of sharing the good life of a successful businessman with Marta.

Marek, for once in a reflective mood, summed up their thoughts with profound wisdom and sage advice. "It seems to me that the only thing that is constant in life is change. Look at you and me and how our lives have changed. Look at the people around us, arriving and leaving, finding work and homes, or going back to Poland to restart again. The professor, washed up one minute, now has a job at Oxford University; even English people constantly have change in their lives. Look at Tony Sharpe, one minute working in the fields, next back at university studying."

At that moment, Jan sat bolt upright on his bed. "I have to go out for a minute, I'll be back," he said pulling on his boots and he left the hut leaving Marek to dream alone.

Within a few minutes, Jan was back.

"What was the rush?" asked Marek.

"I remembered that I hadn't put the children down for Saturday school, so I had to go and do it."

"Crikey, you really are becoming domesticated, and there

you have another example of change."

"It's late," said Jan, "time to sleep."

As the week progressed into an unremarkable Wednesday without incident, Jan went about his business, and as he did so he thought how the nights were drawing in, the temperatures were falling away, and the seasonal changes were taking hold.

At home in Poland his wife would have been pickling cabbage and cucumbers, with peppers in oil. He would be smoking the sausage she had prepared, fruits and vegetables would be stored, and the log pile would have been at its highest under the cottage eaves. Ploughing would be starting, cultivation, then planting and the whole pastoral cycle would start again. Farm life in England, Jan thought, was similar in many ways to that in Poland but there was no urgent scrabble for survival. In Poland, if your harvest failed for a year you were poor; if it failed for a second year, you starved.

As Wednesday rolled into Thursday morning, Jan arrived at the farmyard to be met by Sid who had a job for him to complete with some urgency.

"In early October, the sheep will be coming back to the fold." He explained, "There're two reasons for this, young-un. Firstly, the grass will have grown back and what will be there will have some goodness in it to build them daft buggers up for lambing and the coming winter. Secondly, with their short coats, they will be out of the worst of the autumn storms behind the high hedges.

"I want you to prepare the lambing pens in the old wooden lean-to barn and fix the leaky roof so that it will be dry for the stock."

Jan was happy to put his mind to something that would take his thoughts away from his own upcoming trials. He decided to ride his bike up to the paddock and take a look at what was required before gathering his tools and setting to work.

On arrival at the paddock, he was able to see a low building running along the hedge line. It was open at the front and its sloping roof was supported by three walls made of stone. The pan-tiled roof sloped down to the back wall and was overgrown by the hedge which had pushed its way under the tiles in a number of places dislodging them.

Now clear as to his next move, Jan returned to the yard and gathered his tools and equipment. He made his way back with a sack of tools and a ladder. Once back, he climbed onto the roof of the barn and gingerly surveyed the damage.

As he turned to get a closer look at the front tiles he was met by a magnificent vista. The land was gently sloping away to the north into the river valley, to the right of the lane opposite the fold was the wood, further down on the same side was the farm, and in the middle distance he could see the camp.

Opposite the camp, on higher ground, was the camp church. The field it was in sloped gently back up the hill to the fold paddock, and in a patchwork of russet and orange hues, wisps of smoke could be seen rising into a gin-clear blue sky over the village in the far distance. After a while of pondering, Jan thought that he could do a lot worse than bring up his new family in this area.

Jan then began the task of tackling the overgrown hedge with a mattock and reinstating the tiles, his mind drifting back to the previous evening and the dramatic events that had occurred. The passing of time had distanced him from the cross-examination in the hall, and he again began to wonder if the intrigue Bialy was so concerned with wasn't just a conspiracy theory in his mind. Jan then started to wonder if he hadn't been sucked into this imaginary world of espionage and spy networks, and that all that was needed was some common-sense reasoning, and it would transpire that Kronski was actually safe at home. Jan put the matter behind him and toiled away on the roof for a while longer.

When he had cleared the offending branches, he lit a bonfire and warmed himself for a while. With the roof now uncovered, he was able to reset the tiles to make the barn watertight once more. He then raked up the old straw from the floor of the barn and threw it on the fire. He stood and watched as the dense white smoke rose at speed into the sky to declare that the barn was as good as new. With his task sorted, Jan returned to the farm. He arrived just in time to see Sid leaving for the day.

"That's good timing," said Sid, "I thought that you had forgotten that you had promised to do the milking for me today."

"No," said Jan, "I just got a bit delayed. See you tomorrow morning, Sid, have a good day." Jan counted himself lucky that, even though he had forgotten, he had made it back in time, keeping Sid happy and their friendship intact.

His mind was a whirl of family problems, espionage problems, and wife problems, and he found a certain sanctuary in the farm and in his work colleague who was undemanding, uncomplicated, and simple to reason with. Jan called the cows in from the field and set about losing himself in his work. He passed a number of hours without deep thought or reflections, and so, lost in work, the farm acted like a balm on his brain and his troubles melted away. However, eventually he had to accept the fact that he would have to return once more to the source of his torment for dinner and an update from Marek.

Thursday was market day in the town and Marek had been on a shopping spree. As he sat down opposite Jan he was like a child at Christmas, impatient for the meal to be over so that he could delve into his sack of toys. At intervals, he would turn to see if Marta was looking at him, then disappointed like a forlorn schoolboy when she was not, he would reengage in conversation with Jan. Marta, it would appear, was more interested in talking to her friends about their day than eyeing up boys in the dinner hall.

"I have bought Marta a present," Marek announced in excited tone. "If this does not make her like me, nothing will," he reasoned.

"I think she already likes you," Jan said, "I don't think you need to buy her expensive gifts."

"No, I think this is the right strategy I propose to present the gift to her after dinner in private."

"Well good luck," Jan said. "Just be careful, you know that Marta is a proud woman and is nobody's fool."

"Stop worrying Jan," Marek countered, "she can't fail to not like my present. I will be in her good books till Christmas at least."

Dinner finished, Marek charged over to Marta leaving Jan to his own devises, so Jan decided to return to his hut to enjoy one last evening of bachelorhood.

Jan lay on his bed and looked at the ceiling, whilst pondering how best to make his new family feel at home in the camp. He had looked at their new home in their hut in the family section of the camp. It was basically a hut divided into sections with an internal linking corridor down one side. A central communal area housed the pot-bellied stove, some tables, and a couple of saggy armchairs where the neighbours could commune.

Their room housed a wardrobe a set of bunks plus a double bed with a heavy curtain which gave minimal privacy, running down the middle of the space. The walls were made of hardboard and the door frame was of pressed steel construction. All of the partitioning was given rigidity by a wooden frame of the merest strength. The only suggestion of style in all of this austerity was a pair of bright yellow-and-white check curtains which seemed to say, 'welcome, come on in'.

As Jan pondered, he resigned himself to the fact that Ewa would probably want to have a say in domestic matters, and so, he decided to leave things be until her arrival. He was snapped out of his musing at this point by an excited Marek who came rushing in with a broad smile from ear to ear.

"It went well, I see?" Jan commented with a smirk. Marek nodded, and the rest of the evening was taken up with a blow-by-blow account of Marek's gift giving.

Friday dawned bright and dry, but the clear blue sky brought a portent of what lay ahead in the coming winter. This particular mid-September morning had an edge and a chill to it that made Jan pull his work coat tightly closed at the collar. As he and Marek hurried to the warmth of the canteen, they saw Marta walking down to meet them with her entourage. Jan noticed that Marta was swathed in a red, woollen, full length coat with a black fur collar. He looked at Marek who was smiling broadly. Clearly, this was the famed coat gifted to Marta by Marek.

"You look cosy and warm this morning, Marta," said Jan.

"'Yes, I'm so lucky to have the kindest, most caring boyfriend in the world," she swooned.

So, it's official, thought Jan, Marek is now the kindest most caring boyfriend in the world. Jan reasoned that persistence had paid off and that he had misread the situation and was content to be happy for the pair. Breakfast was, as always, a segregated affair and confined to the early starters. Although he was not an early starter, Jan preferred the quiet of the early breakfast. It also gave him time to get to work early and pre-pare for the day ahead. Jan picked up his dinner bag from the counter, filled his lemonade bottle with tea from the urn, and Marta and her beau and Jan left the canteen and re-emerged into the cold morning. They said their goodbyes and headed for their respective modes of transport. Marta for the bus to the flax factory, Marek to kick-start his motorbike for the cross-country trek to the hospital and Jan to his bike for a slow pedal to the farm.

That day, Jan was on ploughing, and so he was expecting a strenuous day behind Dolly and Bubbles in the furrows. However, as always, he needed to visit his flock to check that all was well. As he left the farmyard, he stood in the bike saddle to get extra purchase and speed for his assent of the hill up onto the downs. His breath reappeared in steaming gasps as he sped upward and ever onwards towards the flock.

On arrival at the shepherd's caravan, he opened up the door and grabbed a mattock from his tool chest to chop some brambles he had spied around the dew pond. As he descended the steps, he saw to his amazement, a large dog sleeping under the caravan. The dog, seeming to sense that it had been discovered, stirred and then stood up. It was wagging its tail excitedly, as if it was greeting its master. It was as large as a big collie-dog and was black and white with large nut-brown paws, a feathery tail, and on its nose running up to its forehead was a white blaze that took the shape of a lily.

Jan's surprise at finding the dog was closely followed by his consternation at finding a dog. What about his flock, the pregnant ewes, and the chance that this dog had been harassing them? Jan ran up onto the high ground that surrounded the dew pond and scanned the flock for problems, but he could see none. A closer inspection confirmed this fact and set his mind at rest. It would appear that Lily, for that is what he had decided to call the dog, was calm around the stock. On his return to the caravan, there was the dog sat on its top step surveying the scene like a sentinel. As Jan approached, Lily gave a submissive grin which Jan likened to a smile and his heart was lost to this new stranger in his life. As Jan reached out to stroke Lily, he was still not sure if he was choosing the dog, or the dog was choosing him.

It was unusual for a dog to take to a stranger in this way

with such speed, and Jan could only assume that this was just in the dog's character. With a chance to feel the dog for the first time, Jan discerned that she, for that was what Lily was, was under-weight but was generally in good condition. He reached into his sandwich bag and removed the sausage from between the doorsteps of bread and offered it to Lily. She took it from his hand and ate it with the delicacy of a lady of breeding and gentrification. Although smitten by the dog, Jan knew that a dog in this condition must belong to someone, and his natural tendency to adopt her was tempered by a desire to help her find her way home.

Jan knew that Dyke would not allow her on the farm and that Monk would not countenance a dog in the camp, let alone Bialy, so it would be easiest for all if Lily found her way home. However, this was a problem that would have to be solved later as Jan had a day's ploughing ahead of him and the bulk of his dinner was now in his new friend's belly. Jan locked the caravan and left Lily sat on the top step guarding the flock and set off to the farm to pick up the horses for a day in the fields.

Back at the farm, Sid had already tacked up the horses after he had finished milking, and so, Jan was soon on his way to the stubble field to continue the ploughing. Jan had decided not to mention the arrival of the dog, in part, because she may have disappeared as fast as she had arrived, and, secondly because he knew that Dyke did not like dogs on the farm, so off he set for a day of hard grind in the fields. As the horses clopped up the lane, Jan's thoughts turned to the next day and the arrival of his wife and the children. He felt a mixture of excitement and trepidation as he still tried to juggle in his mind how his life was about to change.

Earlier in the week, he had resigned himself to wait and see what would happen. However, now their imminent arrival focussed his mind, and he felt waves of blind panic wash over him in between moments of calm reason. Jan eventually started to become annoyed with his continued pre-occupation with his situation and decided to put it out of his mind for that day at least. "What will be will be" he said to Bubbles and Dolly as he attached them to the whipple tree on the plough. Lifting the plough onto its jockey wheel and urging the girls on, he lost himself in his labour and directed all of his nervous energy back into the soil. The labour was arduous, but the task was simple enough as the plough flipped over the stubble, burying it and revealing fresh, moist brown earth. It occurred to Jan that it was like the turning of a page, the old that had been written was gone, and the fresh new page was revealed ready for a new story to begin. Though not prone to philosophical musings, Jan thought that, sometimes, the simplest message carried the strongest meaning.

As lunchtime approached, Jan allowed the girls to cool down by easing their pace. Leaving the plough at the far end of the field, he unhooked the whipple tree, walked them back to the gate, and put their feed bags over their heads. He then, in turn, sat on the water bowser provided for the horses and ate his denuded lunch.

The afternoon saw more toil but an early finish, as the horses needed to be rested, groomed and stabled before the end of the day. At three o'clock, Jan unhitched them and led them back to the farm, groomed them and put them in their stables with their feed. He then went to the farm office, collected his wages and signed his chitty. Pedalling as fast as he could, he made it back to the camp just before the post office closed and was able to deposit the bulk of his wages with Rosemary before she cashed up. Then, after a shower, he put on his best clothes, ate dinner with Marek then the two of them set out for the pub and Tony Sharpe's leaving do.

For Jan, this would mark the end of his bachelor days and the beginning of a different life. By six thirty, the boys were in the pub, which was already filled with rowdy university types and their girlfriends who were mostly local girls. Marek was alone as Marta had never liked Tony. She had told him that Tony was always prying into her relationship with her flyer and would often drink with them all evening despite her attempts to get rid of him.

The boys pushed their way to the bar and attempted to catch the eye of James.

"The usual boys," James said as he arrived with two pints of IPA. This, thought Jan, was the mark of a good host as he handed over the money.

"Have one yourself," proffered Jan.

"Not now, thanks, I'll need to keep my wits about me tonight. I've a feeling that it'll be a busy one and Pat's in the kitchen preparing the food Tony ordered."

Jan nodded an understanding, and the boys edged their way towards some window seats that were still vacant due to their distance from the bar. Placing their drinks on the table, the boys took a look around the bar for familiar faces, then picking up their pint glasses, now slippery with condensation from the hot room, they quenched their thirsts.

Tony was nowhere in sight, but Jan could hear him holding court in the lounge bar with notable members of village society including, to Jan's surprise, Dyke. Dyke's voice was unmistakable as he pontificated on matters of farming and the labour shortage.

"You see," Dyke said, "these foreign chaps are all right. I have a good one, a Pole he is, but I was lucky. What I want to know is when'll we get some good honest British workers back on the farm, with hearts of oak, willing to toil for their country to put food on British tables?" Dyke continued his sermon to all and sundry in the lounge, which was periodically interrupted by murmurs of agreement and approval.

As the boys sipped their beer and chatted, they heard

another familiar voice close at hand; it was Chastity. She was moving from table to table speaking to the villagers who sat there like some erstwhile Florence Nightingale, administering comforting words and understanding. After a while, Chastity arrived at the boys' table and sat on the empty chair, which until that point had been staring back at the boys, confirming their status as strangers in this close-knit village. It was a relief to the boys to at last blend into their surroundings.

"Hello, boys," Chastity chirped cheerily, "one last boy's night out before the missus arrives, Jan?"

Jan smiled and raised his eyebrows as if in submission. "Things will be a bit different from tomorrow," Jan mused, "I don't think you'll see me in here very much from now on." They all laughed in unison and Chastity turned her attention to Marek.

"And how are you love birds getting on?" Chastity probed in jest, "Not out tonight I see. She should keep you on a tighter lead in case you stray."

Marek was not sure how to react to this comment given their past history. He was confused as to whether Chastity was making fun or inflicting a barbed comment out of jealousy. Chastity sensed his disquiet and jumped in immediately.

"I'm sorry Marek, I'm only messing about with you," she said softly. "I may have had one too many gin and tonics."

Marek, now sure of his ground, brushed off her comment and with a smile said, "I don't think one more'll hurt," and grabbing up the glasses he made his way to the bar for another round.

As the bar clock struck ten, it was barely audible over the singing and lively chatter of the assembly of villagers and university lads. All at once the lounge door was pushed open by farmer Dyke. His cheeks had taken on a rosacea hue, and his eyes were moist and tearful. He glanced around the bar and eventually spied Chastity sat with the boys, and without an ounce of propriety he shouted,

"Are you coming home with me, our Chastity, or are you staying here with them bloody Herberts?"

The bar erupted in loud laughter and students cheering.

"I've my bike, Father; I'll see myself home," Chasity shouted back.

"You see that you do, and do it safely, and don't accept any help from any of these randy oiks either."

Once more, the bar dissolved into guffaws and cheering students which hastened Dyke's exit from the bar, and with that, a sense of boisterous order returned to the proceedings. After a while, as the combined effects of alcohol and a long day's ploughing began to take its toll on Jan, he suggested that it was time to go. Marek and Chastity agreed and the three made their way through the throng and out into the cool autumn night air.

As Chastity threw her leg over her bicycle saddle with little or no shame and prepared to set off, she gave out a curse of annoyance.

"What's the matter?" Jan asked.

"My carbide lamp isn't working, but it's OK, I know how to fix it. Sid told me that if the gas generator stops working all I have to do is pee on the powder, and it will start to work."

"Does it have to be pee?" Jan asked in disbelief.

"No water will do," Chastity informed him,

"Then why don't I just go back into the bar and get you a glass of water?" Jan reasoned.

"By the time you fight your way to the bar, I'll already be sorted and, on my way," said Chastity. "Right, Jan, you hold the handlebars and both of you turn your backs to save my modesty," Chastity instructed.

The one thing that was singularly in short supply at that moment was modesty, thought Jan, but the boys complied with Chastity's wishes.

No sooner were the boys' backs turned they could hear the rustling of the folds of a cotton dress closely followed by the slither of silk on bare skin, then the crunch of gravel as Chastity perched, legs akimbo, over the device. At that point, the door of the pub was pushed open, and the trio were bathed in the warm yellow light that escaped the smoky interior.

"Good evening, vicar," Jan said in a loud tone judged to warn Chasity of the approaching cleric and his good lady. However, it was too late, Chastity was mid-stream and stopping was not an option. As the pub door closed behind the vicar and his wife, the worst of the illumination was gone, which went some way to saving Chastity's embarrassment, however, there did not appear to be any embarrassment.

"Good evening vicar, I'm having a little trouble with my light," Chastity warbled with indifference.

To which the vicar replied, "Ah, Chastity, as the good Lord says, Chastity, let there be light, and there was, and it was good!" At that, the vicar and his wife walked off across the green as if what they had witnessed was nothing out of the ordinary and carried on the conversation they had been having as they exited the pub.

As a newly illuminated Chastity set off home, followed by the boys at a stately pace more suitable to their alcoholic intake, the raucous party began to abate as James attempted to call time.

He began by appealing to the lads to "drink up and look lively" but to no avail. His second plan of attack was to throw tea towels over the pumps and collect every empty glass he could lay his hands on. As it appeared that this device was not having the desired effect on his happy guests, James began to place a firm but friendly hand on their shoulders and guided them two at a time towards the now open door. In time, those few remaining became aware that they were in a near-empty bar and began to leave of their own volition.

Tony stood in the doorway and hailed James. "Goodbye, James, old boy, I will see you next summer when I come down again, I'm a bit squiffy, so I must go back to our camp now." At this, Tony disappeared into the still night and was gone. James gave a sigh of relief, slid the latch on the door and he and Patricia began the clean up and cash counting.

CHAPTER 8
LOVE OF THE YARD

Jan and Marek made it safely back to the camp, and as they climbed the steps into their hut they noticed that there was a dim light showing from a window at the far end of the community hut. Jan looked at Marek and gave a nod towards the lit window. "The committee must be planning the reinvasion of Poland," he said sarcastically. Marek laughed and the boys turned in for the night. As they lay on their beds the silence of the night was punctuated by sporadic screams from groups of university students laughing, singing and joking as they passed the camp on the way back to their own smaller hutment. This was situated just past Dyke's farm down a long narrow sloping lane and as the students disappeared down this lane their voices became muffled and then slowly fell silent.

Jan and Marek talked about the day to come and the challenges that it would present, however, they had no idea just how large those challenges would turn out to be and the impact it would have on some members of the camps community.

***

The next day started normally enough and just by chance both boys had that particular Saturday off work, so they took the later breakfast which was a bustle of young children and mothers. The early breakfast, with its quiet early risers contemplating the long day ahead of them, was much more to the boys liking. After breakfast the pair wandered down to Monks office to try and find out what time Ewa and the children would be arriving. On arrival, they were met by a frenzied Mr Monk beckoning them to come through the door, a phone jammed under his chin speaking to an as yet unknown caller. As Jan and Marek looked at each other in amazement at being invited into Monks hallowed office space, the phone conversation went some way to explaining this easement of Monks rules.

What they heard was Monks voice in staccato uttering;

"Body yes railway line ye- rabbits yes professor yes pub celebration yes, motorbike yes skivvy yes RAF yes." Monk frantically scribbled down random words in haste and after a few more frenetic moments he placed the receiver down.

His face was red, his breathing fast and laboured. He slumped back in his chair and wiped his forehead with his hanky. He stared at the boys.

"Well, the balloon has certainly gone up on this one," Monk said in a tone that was a portent of the news to come.

"What balloon, where?" asked Marek, not aware of this particular English idiom.

"Tony Sharpe has been found dead on the railway line down by your rabbit warren," Monk whispered in a way that suggested the murderer may still be in earshot.

Jan and Marek were truly aghast to hear this sombre news. Both men stood in Monks office trying to piece events together.

Jan turned to Marek. "How did a merry evening of fun and humour turned so suddenly to tragedy?" he asked.

"How do they know he was murdered?" asked Jan, "He was pretty drunk when we left the pub, is it possible that he just wandered onto the tracks and got hit by a train?"

"No," said Monk with some authority, "I have already suggested this to PC. Roberts the village bobby, but he assures me that if Sharpe had been hit by a train there would not be much evidence to pick up if you understand me."

Both men nodded and looked at each other in dismay.

"Inspector Love from the constabulary is on his way here to make further enquiries and he would like to speak to you Marek, Marta, and Major Biala. There is a rumour among the university boys that Tony may have had enemies here in the camp, but they could not be sure."

"Enemies," asked Jan. "What enemies? Tony played chess with the professor, spent time with everyone, and was well-liked around the camp."

"It appears that once while drunk, Tony made a passing comment about a secret Polish underground organisation that his mates thought he seemed in fear of."

Jan's mouth went dry, and he began to swallow hard, but when he tried to remark on Monk's statement no sound came out.

Monk noticed Jan's choked reaction, and said, "I know, Jan, I am as shocked as everybody. Now, Marek, you must stay on the camp, Marta will be interviewed at her work, and the major will be seen by Inspector Love as soon as he arrives from the students' camp. Please do not speak to anybody about this in the camp in case you implicate yourselves or create gossip which may cloud the truth."

"You mentioned the professor?" Jan asked.

"Yes," said Monk, "he will be interviewed by Oxford constabulary this morning. They have tracked him down to some university or other."

"Right" Jan replied.

With that the boys turned and walked away. They sat on the steps of their hut and waited to see what would unfold.

"Damn!" Jan cursed. "I forgot to ask what time Ewa will be arriving."

"I'd leave it for now," advised Marek. "We're both here now, so we'll see her arrive. Monk looks fit to burst, and I don't think he'd appreciate another visit from us at the moment."

Sitting on the step in silence, gave Jan time to think this situation through. He was hiding a secret which, in the circumstances, he was wondering if he should share with Marek.

Marek noticed that his friend was quiet. "Are you alright?" he asked, with a concern that did not surface that often from this entrepreneur who lived life on the fine line between legal and criminal.

"Yes thanks," Jan assured him, "it's just a lot to take in on top of Ewa and the children coming and all the changes at the same time. I'll be fine once they arrive, that'll take my mind off of Tony." Jan decided to keep his own counsel before seeing how things played out. He was not being interviewed by the police and apart from a passing word he had not had much to do with Tony. As Jan tried to calm his anxiety, the same emotion seemed to be surfacing in Marek.

"What can they want with me?" he asked nervously. "I'd no business dealings with Tony apart from a chat in the pub. I never really spoke to him."

"I wouldn't worry Marek, it's probably just routine questions to prove where you were etc." Jan whispered.

"I was with you," Marek protested, "why aren't they asking you where you were then?" Jan shrugged, and the boys gaze returned to the camp gate and the imminent arrival of Inspector Love.

A short time later a black saloon car swept through the gates and stopped outside of Monk's office. The driver got out, walked round to the passenger's door, opened it, and out stepped Inspector Love. He was tall and thin with grey hair and dark, piercing eyes that peered out from under the brim of his hat. Without acknowledging the driver, he hurried into Monk's office and disappeared from view.

He emerged a short while later with Mr Monk and made straight for the boys who were still sat on the hut steps.

"Mr Marek Bomski?" Love said, in a deep threatening tone which had the twang of a London accent about it.

"That's me," said Marek.

"Before we start our interview, I'd like to see your motor-cycle and sidecar please and then we'll go to Mr Monk's office."

Monk stepped into the fray at this point. "Don't worry I'll be with you at your interview Marek to see that everything is above board, and to advise you when questioned by Inspector Love."

"I'm not worried, he can ask me whatever he wants, I've nothing to hide."

"Right then chum," snapped Love, "let's have a look at this bike, shall we?"

Marek led the inspector, Monk, and Jan round to the back of the hut, where Jan and Marek pulled the tarpaulin off to expose the bike. Love pulled a notebook from his coat pocket and studied a drawing on one of the pages. He examined the tyres on Marek's bike and then exclaimed ."Ah ha!"

Monk reacted to Love's eureka moment with interest. "What is it inspector, have you found something?"

Love turned to Monk and said, "These tyres match the tracks we found at the murder site-"

"You know Mr Bomski has a contract with British Rail to clear rabbits from that stretch of line, and in addition, he goes to work that way, don't you?"

Marek nodded with some haste to confirm Monk's defence of him.

Then Monk's acute mind focussed on Love's comment. "So, it is a murder then?" enquired Monk.

"I meant crime scene," retorted Love.

"So, you're sure there's been a crime committed then."

" Mr Monk! It's too soon to be sure, and we can't say that categorically until we have examined all the evidence. Speaking of which, I would like to take a closer look at the sidecar please. Can you move the bike into a bit more space?"

Marek and Jan pushed the bike onto a flat patch of grass and then stood back so as not to crowd the inspector or his investigation.

"Hmm," mused the inspector, "it's bigger inside than it looks, and why does is have that strange smell, what is it? I can't quite place it, ah yes, mashed potatoes."

Marek jumped in with a plausible reason for the smell, before the inspector delved deeper into this line of enquiry. "I sometimes carry potatoes in it which I buy at the market on a Thursday when they are cheaper."

"I see" said Love with interest. "I would suggest that if you could get a sack of spuds in there, you could likely get a dead body in there. I think we should go back to Mr Monk's office for a little chat."

"Now come on, inspector." Monk implored, "I can assure you that Mr Bomski has an impeccable character."

"That is not what the local bobby says. I understand that Mr Bomski has his fingers in a number of very dodgy pies around here. I think we should have our little chat now."

Back at the office, Monk and Marek took a seat, while the inspector paced up and down pondering his next line of enquiry following the evidence presented by the motorbike. Eventually, Love launched his inquisition,

"Mr Bomski, where were you at around ten o'clock last night?"

"I was at the pub in the village attending Tony Sharpe's

going away party." Marek answered in a firm, calm voice.

"Do you have any witnesses who can corroborate your last statement?"

"Yes."

"Can you tell me the names of these witnesses, Mr Bomski?"

"The vicar, his wife, Chastity Dyke, everybody in the pub including James the landlord, and farmer Dyke," Marek countered, in a tone that suggested that his alibi had a cast-iron ring about it. "Oh, and Jan Kot, who is sat outside at present," Marek chipped in for good measure.

Inspector Love made for the door and snatching it open, he invited Jan in with a beckoning sideways nod. Jan entered the office and finding no seat, leaned against the wall by Monk's desk.

"Mr Kot, can you tell me who saw you at the Bell last night" Inspector Love snapped in a way that was calculated to catch the responder out.

Jan responded with alacrity. "Yes, the vicar, his wife, Chastity Dyke, everybody in the pub, including James the landlord and farmer Dyke, oh, and Marek Bomski," Jan added for absolute accuracy. The inspector made notes at a feverish pace and then moved on to his next point of enquiry.

Love spun around on his heels for dramatic effect, and pointed his pencil at Marek as if probing.

"'Mr Bomski, did you ever see Mr Sharpe writing in a small notebook?"

Marek thought about this question for some time and then replied, "No, never."

At that point, Jan interjected with some additional information which he calculated would help get Marek off the hook. "I once saw him drop a small notebook in the camp and I called after him and returned the notebook to him," Jan disclosed, in the spirit of one doing everything they could to be helpful.

"Did you see what was in the book as you picked it up?" Love asked in haste, like a gun dog nearing its fallen prey.

"No, I didn't see, but Tony told me what was in it."

Love's eyes widened, "And what did he say was in the book?" the inspector asked.

"Secrets," said Jan.

"Secrets!" shouted Love in disbelief. "What kind of secrets?" Love spluttered.

"Chess secrets," replied Jan.

"Chess secrets?" countered the inspector.

"Yes secret chess moves, he told me, the ones that he used against the professor in their weekly games." As the inspector scribbled furiously in his notebook, Jan began to get the distinct impression that he had not helped Marek that much.

Love turned to Marek and, adopting a serious tone, said "Mr Bomski, tell me what you know about an organisation called the Silent and Unseen?"

Marek thought for a minute and then replied with candour, "Honestly, not much, I believe they were active in Warsaw during the uprising, but I would imagine that, by now, they would have disbanded."

Once more, Love probed. "We have information that a cell of that organisation is active in this area. Do you know anything about that Mr Bomski?"

"No" answered Marek.

"You see Mr Bomski, I think that it's possible that you may be a member of that organisation and that you were sent here to dispose of Mr Sharpe, then, mission accomplished, you bundle him into your sidecar and dump his body on the tracks."

"Inspector Love!" shouted Mr Monk. "This is pure conjecture and a total fabrication of the facts. Mr Bomski was sent here just after New Year by a British government displaced persons organisation, not some secret Polish organisation. How did he know that six months later Tony Sharpe would appear here? Mr Sharpe was also part of a scheme run by the government to place university lads in agriculture to help the food effort. Also, I witnessed Marek and Jan return to the camp. They must've left the pub a long time before Mr Sharpe and returned to their hut here. I'm sure the other members of the hut can verify this fact and the time they returned."

"Well of course they will," insisted Love, "they're all in this together, the whole lot of them, these two, and Bialy."

Monk snapped back with tangible anger, "Inspector Love, you had better have more than hunches before accusing anybody of murder."

Jan pushed himself off the wall by his elbows and looked towards the inspector. "Inspector," he asked quietly with an aim to calming things down, "you seem so sure that Poles are involved in the death of Tony, why? Why not a fight between university drinkers that went wrong. We heard lots of shouting and screaming after we went to bed, enough to mask a serious fist fight."

"I have evidence that leads me to believe that Poles are involved in this, but I do not want to say what that evidence is yet."

Once more Monk leapt to the boy's defence. "If you're so sure that these men are guilty, then you would not be afraid to divulge this big secret piece of evidence. If they are guilty, then they already know what this evidence is and keeping it from them would serve little or no purpose." With Monk vouching for the boys and half the village as witnesses it was beginning to look less likely that they were involved.

However, Love still had what he considered the kingpin of the crime to question, and so, he asked Monk to send for Bialy.

Love turned to Marek , "You stay on the camp, chum, until I say you can go; I haven't finished with you yet."

Monk asked Jan to run and get Bialy for him. The two boys left the office, and as they looked out across the road, they were aware of a large crowd of people queuing outside Rosemary's post office, watching what was going on.

"I think the secret is out," said Jan with a nervous laugh.

Jan left Marek at their hut and made his way to the community hall where Bialy was holding an impromptu meeting of the security committee. Jan made his way over to the table, and looking at Bialy, he said, "The inspector wants to see you now."

Bialy stood up, straightened his tie, buttoned his jacket, and marched off, his heels clicking on the wooden floor of the hut. Jan found it hard to keep up the pace and had to adopt a running skip.

"What has been said," enquired Bialy of Jan.

"Nothing," replied Jan. "Tony Sharpe is dead, they think it's murder but don't seem to have proof of who's done it, that's all." Jan raced these words out as fast as he could in order to get the whole message across before Bialy reached the office at his blistering pace.

As Jan slowed to take up a place on the steps with Marek, Bialy said, "Kot, I'll need you by my side in the office."

Jan wasn't sure if he should be flattered or fearful, but he said, "Of course," and followed Bialy to the office.

As the two men arrived at the closed office door, a murmur rose from the intrigued members of the post office queue. Bialy opened the door without knocking and entered. He sat down before being invited to do so and in a thick Polish accent said, "Now what's all this nonsense?"

Jan was shocked; he had never heard Bialy speak in such an affected way before.

Monk turned to Jan and said, "thank you Mr Kot you can go now."

"But don't you go leaving the camp till I say so, chum," Love ordered.

Bialy interjected, "In fact, Mr Monk, I would like Captain

Kot to stay as my interpreter as I have trouble with English."

"Captain Kot is it?" asked Love, with a leer that had secret organisation written all over it.

"No, I haven't held a commission for ten years; Mr Bialy just forgets sometimes that our service for this country has ended." Jan now felt a new intensity build in the room.

Love launched into his questioning with no pretence of trying to build bridges. "So, Bialy, tell me what you know about Tony Sharpe" he snapped abruptly. Jan could tell that Bialy did not like the manner in which he was addressed as his pursed lip quivered.

"Major Bialy," snapped Bialy in his best parade ground enunciation.

"Oh, major is it, captain is it, looks like we have a proper little army here."

Jan sensed that Bialy's ire might get them into deeper trouble, and so he sought to pour oil on the troubled waters. "You must remember, inspector, that these men have spent over ten years in the service of Great Britain, and they still live in close contact, these lapses are to be expected."

Bialy, sensing that Jan was cleverly playing along, launched into his testimony in Polish, which Jan then recounted in English.

Jan began, "Mr Bialy was a friend of Tony Sharpe. He and the professor played chess with Tony, on camp, several evenings a week."

Love sprang his next question which Jan translated for Bialy and then recounted his reply.

"They talked about camp life, life in England and family life in Poland, chess and European politics."

Love looked at Jan. "Did he ever see Mr Sharpe writing in his little notebook, or read out of it?"

Jan once again spoke to Bialy. 'Nie," Bialy replied.

"No," said Jan.

"Yes, thank you, Mr Kot, even I got that one," Love said with sarcasm.

Love continued, "Ask him if he has seen anybody strange in camp lately, any visitors or people that he did not recognise."

Jan asked the question as requested. The reply left Jan unsure how to proceed, so in the end he made the decision to answer verbatim.

"No one is allowed on the camp unless they sign in, so if they are not in Mr Monk's book, then they did not come in. We have regular visits from the Red Cross and Salvation Army who trace our loved ones, and the usual horde of godless Protestant groups trying to lure our people away, but they are kept at the gate."

Jan, while translating, was also struggling with an inner turmoil which had been with him since the news had broken about Tony. It was he who had gone to Bialy a few nights earlier and told him that he suspected Tony of being a communist. That Kaminski's last word 'Cambridge' was a warning to his friend to be passed back to those in the camp, that Tony who was at Cambridge University was a mole. That the unknown man, who had appeared with Bialy and then evaporated into thin air, may hold the key to Tony's murder. But uppermost in his thoughts, was the concern that he was wrong. What if Tony was innocent, and what if he, Jan, had condemned Tony to death on a hunch that turned out to be wrong.

As Jan's internal struggle continued, he was brought back to reality by Monk, who interrupted Love's interrogation.

"Inspector Love," Monk cried in frustration, "you're no farther forward now than you were two hours ago when you arrived. Your only tenuous link to these two men is a notebook which both men have seen but never read. If you have nothing else to go on, I suggest that we call it a day, and all get on with our lives."

Love turned on Monk, "Now listen here, there's more going on here than any of you know. I'm not the only one involved in this case. Mr Bomski's young lady is, as we speak, being interviewed by detectives from Special Branch. Now you can either take this seriously and then we can all get on with our lives or we can all take a ride to Salisbury and continue there."

"Special Branch" Monk gasped. "Counter terrorism," Monk blurted out as if searching for clarification.

"Exactly," Love confirmed, "so, can we all now start cooperating and get to the bottom of this?"

For a while the room fell silent before Bialy broke the soundless tension.

"Jan, tell the inspector that as far as I'm concerned, Sharpe was one of the few people here who has shown us any kindness, or taken any interest in our welfare. The fact that he invited the two of you to his party is testimony to the fact that he treated us as equals, something not everybody else here does. The thought that one amongst us may have killed him is abhorrent to me, and if I could help him catch the murderer of Mr Sharpe, I would."

Jan repeated Bialy's comments, and Love thought for a moment before turning to Jan.

"You say the two of you went to the pub. Why did Mr Bomski's girlfriend not go?"

Jan answered in an instant, "She didn't like Tony. She said that, when she was with her flier, Tony would hang around them all the time talking about aeroplanes. He was always talking about propeller-less engines to her boyfriend, and that annoyed her as she never got a chance to be alone with him."

Love made notes at a furious pace "Go on, go on," he urged Jan.

"That's it," Jan said, "she just didn't like him for that reason, and so, she didn't come to the pub." Love paused and looked out of the window, turning over what he had just heard.

After a time, Love looked at Jan and said,

"you'd better get your chum back in here for a minute."

Jan walked across the camp road to the hut where Marek still sat on the steps. Jan tried to bring Marek up to date as fast as he could before they got back to the office.

"He wants to see you again, this is bigger than we thought, and Marta is being interviewed at work by Special Branch detectives."

Marek's *Laissez-faire* attitude suddenly changed to one of real concern. What an hour and a half ago seemed trivial was now turning into a serious problem with really grave consequences. Suddenly, life in this rural idyll had turned into a nightmare. They had been visited by the hard, unyielding outside world that surrounded them, a world that they had forgotten about over the past few months. Now, that world that seemed so alien and dystopian was focussing its steely stare on their quiet community and was seeking them out.

Marek was now concerned about Marta, and whether she was being put under pressure. It occurred to him that migrants might not be given the benefit of the doubt in the same way that English people would. As the boys approached the office, the door was snatched open, and Love appeared with a piece of paper. Ignoring them he beckoned his driver over.

"Sort this out constable, look lively, quick as you like."

With that, the driver set off on his errand.

"Right, you two, in here," Love snapped, and the boys walked into the office to face their inquisitor once more.

The mood in the office had lightened considerably when Jan and Marek settled down on the office chairs to continue defending their innocence. An extra chair had been found in the house of Mr Monk, and the boys sat next to Major Bialy who stared straight ahead without acknowledging them. Jan took this body language to be conveying a subliminal message that said, do not react, say nothing, stick to your story, however, Monk was now smiling. Love was relaxed and had dropped the hard-man attitude that he had never really mastered that morning.

"Right then, you two," Love began, "I've heard from the detectives who have finished speaking to your young lady. They are satisfied that she was not in cahoots with Sharpe, and they'll be taking no more action. I've despatched my constable to verify that your witnesses can vouch for you as Mr Monk has."

"Cahoots!" Marek protested. "She didn't even like the man, why would she be in cahoots with him?"

Bialy gave Marek a long glowering stare, and Marek fell silent.

Jan looked at the inspector and asked what he thought was a perfectly reasonable question. "So, now that you're happy with our stories, can you tell us what was so important about the notebook?"

"No, I cannot," the inspector snapped.

Marek, who would not be daunted, kept up his pursuit. "Is that because you don't know or don't want to tell us?"

Before the inspector could answer, Monk interrupted him. "I'm sure the inspector has made his position perfectly clear Mr Bomski, let's not pursue the matter any further." Marek took the hint and fell silent.

In time, the constable returned. Without saying a word, he handed the inspector a piece of paper which was studied at length by the recipient.

"OK," said Love, "you're all free to go, but please stay in the area in case we need to make further enquiries."

With that the inspector left and the four men gave a collective sigh of relief. As they all stood to leave the office, Jan turned to Monk, "Mr Monk, thank you for standing up for us and helping us to prove our innocence."

"Mr Kot," Monk replied, "my only concern here was for my own reputation in running this camp and the need to keep the camp out of the gossip and intrigue that would have ensued if any crime had been committed by any of its occupants. The fact that, in doing so, I was instrumental in clearing you of any blame is purely coincidental."

With that, Monk picked up the chair that had come from his front room and left. All three men were left speechless and in a state of disbelief, as they left the office.

"Follow me," Bialy instructed as they made their way out through the door. Jan and Marek did so, in the hope that Bialy might be able to enlighten them as to the drama of that morning.

When the group reached the community hall, the whole security committee was waiting for them sat around a table.

"It goes without saying," Bialy whispered in Polish, "that nothing can leave these four walls and must never be talked about to anyone; that includes Marta," Bialy cautioned as he looked at Marek.

The boys nodded their agreement. Bialy then began, "It's thanks to Jan that Sharpe was exposed as a Soviet spy, the Special Branch were informed, and a decision was made at the highest level to neutralise him. We were lucky that he was not only spying on us, but also on Squadron Leader Kite, Marta's old boyfriend. Because of this, Special Branch liaised with our own intelligence services to carry out the mission. Unfortunately, the British definition of neutralise isn't the same as the Polish one. While our leaders in London, on both sides, thought Sharpe was to be arrested, down here we took this word literally and liquidated the traitor. He had been responsible for several of our finest leaders, who had returned to Poland to continue the fight from within, to disappear.

"When the mistake was realised, Sharpe's body was taken down to the railway track and dumped to make it look like a tragic accident. I'm assured this is what'll appear on Sharpe's death certificate. The only problem we had was making sure that Special Branch in London was sure that Marta was not working with Sharpe. After their interview this morning they were satisfied that she had played no part in his subterfuge, so they rang Love, and he let us go."

Jan then interrupted Bialy during his monologue. "Why was Love asking all of us about the book with the chess secrets in?"

"It's my understanding," said Bialy, "that Love isn't so highly thought of, even down here. He was sent to the countryside because it was thought that he could do the least damage out here. He was in charge of investigating matters in the village to give the appearance of due procedure being carried out. In reality he was given the job because they knew he would not be able to fathom the mystery out, but would be visible in the village, taking statements, etc."

"But the book, what about the book?" Jan asked again.

"Sharpe wrote down his notes in it, the book was not full of chess secrets, but real ones. It was full of notes on jet engine designs, swept wing configurations, important personnel in the camp, and when they were going home and to where. Some of those who returned to Poland even gave him details of their missions because they trusted him so completely. Now he's gone, but we must be wary, there may be more even now watching us."

Jan thought long and hard for a few moments and then asked one final question in the hope of making sense of the morning's spectacle.

"So, the operation to arrest Sharpe failed and he was killed. Why was there such an effort put into covering this up?"

Bialy slipped back into a whisper, and leaning forward, he confided, "The British government, at present, are trying to maintain good relations with the Soviet Union for purely economic, and strategic reasons. It is a changing world, and they don't want to chuck the baby out with the bathwater until they are sure of their, and the Soviets position in a number of areas. This charade today was to protect that relationship, and, to some extent, save Sharpe's family any embarrassment. It's enough to lose a son but to brand that son a traitor would be unnecessarily cruel."

Marek, who had been sitting quietly, finished off the meeting with one final question himself, also in a whisper. "Did Monk know what was going on here today?"

"No," Bialy answered abruptly, "he's no idea what's been going on here, only you two and this committee, who're also sworn to secrecy know, and that's how it must stay.

Due to many of our best men being transferred from military duties into the Polish Resettlement Corps once they find work, our active numbers are becoming fewer and fewer. Once they leave their military service, they can no longer take an active part in security matters, and so we must act decisively while we can and eradicate our enemy before we lose our immunity. All I can tell you is that the British Foreign Office makes use of our networks as its eyes and ears in the east, and for that reason, you must remain silent as many lives depend on it."

The boys stood up nodded in agreement and walked out of the hall and into the autumn morning's sun. They returned to the step, not sure what to say or do. After a short chat murmuring under their breath, it was decided to play dumb, stick to the tragic death story that had played out around the village and say no more to anybody who was not in the know.

CHAPTER 9
THE CALM AFTER THE STORM

As the boys sat and pondered the extraordinary events of the morning, not to mention the incident of the night before, their minds were confused as to what to feel. Tony had been a friend to them both, he had been approachable, generous at the bar, and even though he had some little eccentricities, the boys had always felt that this was common in his class of Englishman and not unusual.

However, as they mulled over his betrayal whilst sat there on the steps in the sun, it became clear that Tony's behaviour was all part of his deceit and that his real loyalty was to his Soviet handlers. He was probably responsible for the death of some good men. Those whom he supported were, even now, holding their countrymen and families under the ideological cosh of communism. It was this that made it easier for the boys not to mourn his passing, but to consign his memory to the shadowy shroud of 'a casualty of war' and leave it there.

Despite this shock, one more thing was leaving the boys with a sense of disquiet. Since their arrival at the camp both of them had paid little heed to Bialy and his cohorts, characterising them as tin soldiers, who could not let go of their days of glory. To now find out that these men were in fact, to some extent, operational, left both men with the impression that the past was reaching into the future. This strange feeling was slightly unnerving, as both men thought that all of that elitism and rank that had played such a large part in their lives back in Poland, had somehow followed them to Britain. In the ensuing conversation both agreed that they wanted no part of this old regime and that their time in Britain would be spent adapting to British values, its way of life and its culture. Those who wanted to live in the past would have to do so without their support, and when the last military personnel had finally transferred to the Polish Resettlement Corps, the old ways would be gone forever.

The boys then set to change the subject and put the matter behind them. As if by magic the next subject of discussion then emerged through the gate on her bicycle; it was Mrs Jarvis the Red Cross lady.

"Oh my God!" shouted Jan, "they're here, I had forgotten all about Ewa and the children because of the upset of this morning."

Both men got up and ran across to Mrs Jarvis who recognised Jan and steered towards him.

"Good morning, Mr Kot, I am glad to find you, I have news for you."

"I have news for you does not sound like I have your family for you," quipped Jan. "Has something happened, has Ewa changed her mind?""

Mrs Jarvis dismounted her bike in a ladylike fashion and began to speak. "As you can see, I am without a car due to a mess up with the petrol coupons allocation this month, so I am afraid that I will not be able to bring your family up from Havant until next weekend."

Jan thought back to his own journey up from Havant in the back of an army truck. "Could they not get on some kind of military transport up here like I did?"

"Well Mr Kot, I think it would be very poor of us to expect your wife and children to sit in the back of a damp, cold, draughty lorry all day. Anyway, the Red Cross is a civilian organisation, and officially, the military aren't supposed to help us with transporting refugees in peace time."

"So how did I manage it?" Jan enquired in a manner calculated to prove Mrs Jarvis wrong.

"You broke the rules Mr Kot, and luckily you didn't get caught" Mrs Jarvis parried with a smile.

As the three spoke, Mrs Jarvis assured Jan that this was just a minor hitch, and that she was confident his family would be with him by the following Saturday afternoon.

"Thank you, Mrs Jarvis, for letting me know and goodbye until next weekend," said Jan with the air of a man reprieved on the steps of the gallows.

Mrs Jarvis made her way to the community hall to help bring other families together.

"Well," said Jan, "I'm free now this afternoon, I think I will ride up and check the flock."

Marek looked nervously at his watch, "if you want to wait until after the late Saturday dinner, I can take you in the motorbike, it'll be easier and quicker. I just want to wait for Marta to see how she feels after her questioning."

"OK, I'll wait, and we can go together." With that decided the boys returned to their step and waited for Marta to arrive on the dinnertime bus from town. Rosemary, the postmistress had just left on her bike and the boys knew that it would still be an hour before the bus arrived. Jan looked at his watch and suggested that he get two cups of tea to help them pass the time.

As he made his way to the canteen, he happened upon the

major who was going to the early lunch.

"When Marta gets back, please bring her to see me, captain, will you?" Jan agreed but was not sure if it was his place to do so.

He fetched two cups of strong brewed tea from the urn in the canteen, and just managed to escape before Father Graboski launched into grace. Jan hurried back to Marek to break the news to him about the major. Marek was not a happy man when he heard the news. He insisted that he should be first to speak to Marta to check on her well-being and, not until then, would Bialy have the chance.

As the time passed slowly by and the tea grew cold in the cups, both Marek and Jan grew tired of sitting on the hard wooden step and decided to wander out to the bus stop.

"I'm glad that Ewa is not coming today, this has been such a bad morning. I don't think I'd have coped too well. At least now things will calm down and blow over a bit before they all arrive."

"I can understand that, I'm worried sick and I only have Marta to think about."

Jan noted this rather tender comment from Marek and decided to press him on it.

"Sounds like things are getting serious with you two, it's only been a couple of months, but you seem taken with Marta."

Marek stared up into the sky as if looking for the right words to say as he had never needed them before. "I think I'm taken with her, she is easy on the eye, clever, hardworking, and she wants to be successful as much as I do. I think we could have a great life together, don't you?"

"Yes, I do, but is this love of Marta you are talking about or the love of the potential of Marta?' Jan probed in a fatherly tone.

"Oh no, definitely Marta," Marek shot back at speed to

quell any doubts in Jan's mind.

With that settled, the boys sat on the grassy verge and waited until they could hear the whining gearbox of the single-decker bus transporting its precious cargo of tired camp dwellers back for the rest of the weekend off.

In the Polish church behind the hedge in the field, the boys could hear traditional harvest festival songs being sung by school children being conducted by Mrs Kunka the lead soprano. She was swift to chastise and scathing in her criticism of those who could not hold a note, a tune, or the words. If this was not a misuse of power, thought Jan, he did not know what was. Marek saw Jan's contorted look and enquired,

"Will you be sending your kids to Mrs Kunka?"

"I'll leave all of that to Ewa, but if it's my choice, I would rather they did not go. I think we're in England now and we should forget the old days and move on, but who knows what Ewa will do."

Marek laughed. "Surely you'll have a say in your children's education?"

"That is the point," Jan answered stoically. "They aren't my children they are Ewa's."

Marek felt a wave of embarrassment crash onto his heart. "I'm sorry, Jan, I forgot that."

So, with the agonising choir practice to accompany them, the boys sat in reflective silence until the bus arrived.

Eventually, the whining of the choir was replaced by the whining of a red bus, its shiny red livery and gold lines easily distinguished from its green rival in these local lanes. First off, the bus as the doors concertinaed open was Marta, with her arm round a sobbing Frau Swartz trying to pacify her.

"Let's not go to Mr Monk yet, why don't you have a rest, you'll feel better then. I'll bring you something to eat later from the canteen."

The frau snuffled her agreement from behind her lacy

hanky and Marta's eyes rolled back in her head as she smiled at Marek.

"I'll catch up with you in a minute," she said quietly, "go in for dinner, I'll see you there."

Both Marek and Jan, who were both desperate to get to Marta before Major Bialy, declined and said they would walk with her and then escort her back to the canteen. Kasia and Kinga started to make fun of Marta, jibing that she had had police protection in the morning and now her own escort around the camp.

"You must be very valuable to someone," said Kinga.

"We'll take Frau Swartz to her room and sort her food out," Kasia offered. "You get off with your guards and have dinner, we'll be along shortly."

The boys were grateful for this, but instead of the canteen, they steered Marta behind the closed post office to interrogate her on the morning's events out of sight of prying eyes.

"Bialy wants to see you as soon as you arrive, but it's important that we speak to you first."

Not wanting to implicate Marta in any of that morning's conspiracy, they carefully asked her to tell them what had happened at her work. Marta did not seem fazed or disturbed by her encounter with the Special Branch that morning.

"They asked me for my identity documents which I didn't have. I explained that I never carried them just for work, so somebody from the offices brought out their paperwork with my photo attached and that seemed enough. They asked me about Billy, and I answered all their questions. They seemed quite happy. They said that they may be in touch again, but for now that was it."

"Right," said Marek, "but Billy who?"

"My Billy, William Kite, my ex-boyfriend," said Marta unaware that the boys did not know this basic information.

"Did they mention the professor or me, or Bialy?" Marek

asked trying not to sound overanxious.

"No, they asked me how well I knew Tony Sharpe, and I told them not at all as I did not like him because he was nosey. They asked me if I knew that he had died last night, and I said no I did not, however, that wouldn't change my opinion of him, and that was that."

Marek then furtively led Marta and Jan from behind the post office towards the canteen for dinner, and on entering, passed Bialy leaving the dining hall.

"May I have a word with you alone a moment, please, Marta?"

Marta turned and followed him back out of the canteen, while the boys made their way to the single-men's table, with Marek looking back nervously to see what was happening outside.

After a while, Marta reappeared smiled at the boys and sat down with Kinga and Kasia, waiting for grace to be said by Father Graboski. Dinner appeared to be a rather rushed affair, with the ladies clearing the tables with indifferent speed, to the annoyance of those who liked to slurp their soup when it was cool. With the repast consumed in record time and with the tables already being scrubbed, Marek and Jan left the canteen and waited outside for Marta and the girls.

"What did he say?" they asked in unison.

"He just asked me the same questions as you boys did earlier and seemed happy with my answers. Right!" said Marta, "I'm going to check on Frau Swartz, wash my hair and get some beauty sleep. I'll see you boys later, perhaps for a drink?"

With their orders received, Jan and Marek walked back to their hut to pick up the motorbike and sidecar. Jan climbed in, and Marek kick-started the bike io life. As Marek drew level with the front of their hut he stopped and dismounted, disappearing into the hut, leaving the bike spluttering as if gasping for air. Jan, who by now knew the temperament of the bike, reached over, pushed in the choke a little and at once the asthmatic bike breathed easier and ticked over happily.

Marek reappeared, holding an old warehouse coat and an open-faced leather helmet which was fitted with a chin strap. He tossed them into the lap of Jan in the sidecar and the two set off.

"Are we expecting company?" Jan asked intrigued.

"Possibly, if everything's gone to plan this morning," Marek answered.

"But nothing has gone to plan so far, why should anything change now?" Jan complained scornfully.

"We'll see in a minute," said Marek as he opened up the motorbike to get a good run up at the hill onto the downs.

As the boys neared the dew pond and the caravan, Jan noticed the sweet sickly smell of burnt hair hanging in the air, a smell that reminded him of the terror of war and sights that he would sooner forget.

"What in hell is that smell?" Jan asked Marek, sure that his friend was the cause of the nauseous odour and would know its source.

"Well, do you remember those little piglets that I was looking after, they are not so little anymore, and so, Dyke, and I decided their souls should be despatched to piggy heaven, so that we could have the earthly bodies to make sausages and hams with."

"You mean slaughtered, don't you? Not gone to piggy heaven."

"Slaughtered is such a harsh word, and it also means that you require a licence, whereas if the pigs died of natural causes, no licence is required."

"What were the natural causes that were able to kill six pigs?" Jan asked.

"Unfortunately, they got hit on the head by a pole axe and then had their throats cut by a very sharp knife as they fell to the ground. It was a tragic accident, I'm glad that you did not have to witness it," smirked Marek, who had by now given up all pretence of shame or guilt and was counting money in his counting house of a brain.

Marek stopped the bike by the caravan and noticed Lily sitting on the top step on guard duty.

"A friend of yours?" Marek enquired of Jan.

"Yes, she's my new workmate, I found her here yesterday and she seems to have adopted the flock and me." Jan pulled out some meat scraps in a paper bag and gave them to Lily. The dog devoured the scraps with vigour, her tail wagging and her eyes bright and happy to see food and Jan or was it just the food Jan wondered.

Once Jan had checked the flock with Lily and made some more fuss of her, he and Marek set off again over to the copse on the motorbike. What met them was a scene of carnage, blood and guts were everywhere. Jan noticed the butchers van from the town and one of the Saturday boys in a blue and white pinstriped apron hastily loading whole pig carcasses as big as himself into the back of the Morris van.

"I got a half firkin of blood for you here. The butcher says he'll make the black puddings tonight and you can pick them up on Monday. Here are the cleaned intestines from the shop, we'll keep these shitty ones and sort them out."

The boy pointed at an enamel bucket of bluey silvery intestines that were squeezed into it, and then he pointed at a pigs carcass leaning against a beech tree.

"That one's yours," the youth declared as if wishing to wash his hands of the illicit corpse. "We'll clean up and it'll be like nothing was ever here" the boy said, in an assured way that suggested this was not the first time he had attended a crime scene and helped pigs shed their mortal coils and attain spiritual freedom.

Marek's pig carcass was leaning against its tree as if waiting for a bus, its dull eyes stared wistfully into the far distance looking for its imminent arrival. Its blond eyelashes gave it a somewhat human countenance. Jan was amazed at how human the pig seemed with its forward facing eyes and lashes, its lifeless face frozen with a strange rigor mortis smile on it. Jan felt that at any moment the pig might light up a cigarette while it waited patiently for a bus that would never come.

Marek saw Jan staring at the pig. "Are you OK?"

"Yes, this isn't the first dead pig I've seen, but the ones at home were smaller piglets when they were despatched. I've never seen them this size, they look almost human."

"Exactly!" Marek shouted in an excited manner which left Jan wondering what hair brained scheme he was about to hatch. "Give me a hand with this coat and helmet, will you? This is the disguise we're going to use to get our friend Mr Pig back to the camp kitchens for processing."

Jan soon found himself wrestling with a brown warehouse coat and a pig that, despite being dead, was resisting his attempts to dress it in the coat. Several attempts later, he managed to button up the shroud on the reluctant pig to hide the open cavity of the guts and chest and soon he had the leather helmet strapped under the pigs chin. The boys then carried the pig, which was a dead weight that surprised them both, and threaded the deceased passenger into the sidecar.

The pig sat happily with its post-mortem smile, its dim eyes still staring into the far distance. Marek kick started the bike, Jan sat on the pillion and Mr Pig relaxed on his final journey in the sidecar. As the boys made their way back down the hill towards the camp, they happened upon PC. Roberts cycling around his beat in the late afternoon sun. As Roberts saw the trio slowly pass by, he gave a dutiful salute to acknowledge them and began to pedal on, unaware that he had just become a material witness to a crime. Jan, in an attempt to add a touch of realism to the charade, lifted the pigs trotter sheaved in its brown sleeve and waved back. Operation Pig had passed without incident, the camp had received its reward for a day's toil in the harvest field and Marek was already working on his next project.

Marek throttled back the bike, thrust his right arm rigidly out like a trafficator and turned gracefully into the camp. As he coasted quietly towards the kitchen at the rear of the canteen, Monk stepped from his office to see what was going on. He gave a half-hearted gesture that passed for a wave and now sure of who had come into the camp, returned to his domain.

As the motorbike pulled up at the rear of the kitchen, eager hands lifted the carcass from its final resting place, stripped it of its apparel and hurried into the kitchen. There, lined up, were a number of white aproned men waiting to dissect their prize. They held boning knives, saws, and meat cleavers and set to work at a frantic pace. As the carcass was broken down into smaller and smaller portions each man moved to his own kitchen bench and carried on cutting and carving.

Overseeing this operation was the head cook, who had a list of what she required from this pork windfall. After about a quarter of an hour, Boy Scouts started to appear at the kitchen door and were despatched to particular huts with baskets of meat where it would be hot or cold smoked to preserve it. The cold autumn air hung heavy with the scent of fruit woods flavouring the raw meat. Fires tended by old men with decades of experience of cold smoking, turned the different pieces of cold flesh into a symphony of tastes as it absorbed apple and cherry wood smoke.

Lastly, out came the garlic-flavoured sausages from the kitchen, these hot smoked with juniper and, for those with a distinguished palate, milder pear wood. The pigs' brains and head were made into brawn, the trotters reduced to jelly, and the bones boiled for soup, while the ribs went into the oven and were baked. Within an hour the hefty carcass was gone. With a look of approval, the head cook surveyed her kitchen, congratulated everyone, and announced,

"The only thing we didn't use was its squeak." The assembled staff laughed as they began to clean up the crime scene.

Dinner that evening was roast pork fragments, baked ribs with roast potatoes and salad. The canteen was abuzz with the gossip of the day's events with Jan and Marek limiting their comments to their tasty erstwhile passenger. After the evening meal, Marta rounded up Marek and Jan and the three set out for the village pub.

"Where are Kasia and Kinga?" Jan asked.

"They are saving money, so they are staying in. Next Friday is the village harvest festival dance that they want to go to, so by staying in they will be able to have money for a drink then."

"Ah," said Jan, "if it is Saturday I don't think I will be going as Ewa will have arrived and the children will be in bed."

"Oh, my goodness!" exclaimed Marta. "I forgot your wife, so she didn't make it today, what happened?"

"It was a mix-up with petrol coupons," said Jan in a humdrum sort of way, "but all things considered, it was probably for the best." Marta nodded in agreement and the three made their way to the gate.

As they approached the camp gate, an ever vigilant Monk stepped out of his office door to see who was coming and going. Seeing the thirsty trio, he entered into small talk, which was rare for him.

"My word!" Monk exclaimed,."Off out for some more air? I would have thought that motorbike ride the three of you took earlier would have been enough fresh air for one day. I do have to say it did you good Marta. Earlier when I saw you, you looked a little pale, now you have a much better colour."

Marta looked at the boys

"What motorbike ride, where?" she asked in a confused state.

The boys could not answer as they were laughing so hard. "We'll explain later." said Jan. "Let's just get to the pub for now."

It was quiet in the pub as James was downcast, and not his usual self.

"I suppose you've all heard about poor Tony, have you?" James asked.

"Yes," said Jan, "it's a great pity."

"The talk in the village is that he was so drunk that he got lost on the way home, tripped on the rail tracks, and hit his head. He lay there unconscious until the milk train ran over him killing him. I told the police this morning that when he left here he was alone, and he was well oiled. If I had known what was going to happen, I would have let him stay here the night. However, it's too late now. There is nothing we can do."

It was at this point when the mood was so low that Marta remembered the motorbike ride question.

"Sorry to change the subject but what was all that about me taking a motorbike ride this afternoon?"

In an attempt to break the solemn mood, the boys explained to Marta that she had been mistaken for a dead pig. Although she saw the funny side of their story, she felt it only right that she should slap both men around the head as payment for their cheek, and having done so, the three dissolved into laughter.

As James returned with their drinks from the far end of the bar, he was bemused at how their mood had changed, but thought it a welcome uplift to the prevailing mood in the bar. Jan went to pay for the round, but James put his hand up to stop him.

"This is money left in the kitty behind the bar by Tony from last night. I offered him the money back after the end of the party, but he turned it down. He said to keep giving the locals free drinks until it ran out. So," said James raising a glass of whisky, "to Tony!"

"To Tony," the trio said in muted tones, both Jan and Marek finding that particular toast and drink quite hard to swallow.

This, once more, dampened the mood. Marta, who was in ignorance of the real facts of events chatted in a lively manner, but the boys sipped in silence as they listened to her.

As the evening slowly passed and the bar filled up, the main topic was Tony and his demise. The most popular theory was that which James had spoken of, but others included robbery with violence, possible murder by a jealous boyfriend in the village as none of the village lads liked Tony, and failed kidnapping which was the rank outsider among the assembled good men and true. The boys had lost that Saturday-night feeling and sat as if going through the motions. Around nine in walked farmer Dyke, he looked around the bar, saw Jan and Marek sitting with Marta and shouted at James,

"Get those three ruddy Herbert's a drink and put it on my bar bill" as he disappeared through the lounge door. It was only at this point that both men remembered that Dyke would have been the recipient of a rather large amount of 'cash in hand' that day and Dykes gift of a drink was his unspoken gratitude.

Jan pondered for a moment on the character of the farmer he had now known for seven months. Dyke was outwardly harsh but seemed to have a heart of gold. Maybe, Jan reasoned, the harsh outer shell protected him from chancers and advantage takers, who might exploit his kind nature. Whatever the reason for his thick skin, Jan liked Dyke. He was firm but fair and as long as you pulled your weight, he left you alone.

"I suppose you will be buying the next round with your share of the piggy profits?" Jan teased.

"Well, by the time you take fuel, time, and wear and tear on my sidecar into account, I have probably lost money, so I think the next one should be on you. My investment here is in goodwill and the encouraging of my customers feelings of loyalty, for a future business venture."

"Always the dreamer," Marta sighed with a fake sigh, "but I can't help believing him." Jan stood up to go to the bar,

"Well, as you can't buy drinks with dreams, I'll get these in then."

As the trio walked home in the cool September night, Marek noticed that Marta had not buttoned up her coat.

"Wrap up my love," he said with the tenderness of a love-lorn beau.

"I'm full of pork dinner," Marta said, rubbing her stomach. "I'll have to walk it off before I can button up my coat as I don't want to stretch the buttonholes."

"Then let me put my arm around your shoulder to ward off the chill," said Marek who smoothly manoeuvred himself between Jan and Marta and took up his position as official boyfriend. The three slowly walked back to the camp, reflecting on the momentous events of the day. Marta was oblivious to the real drama, and as they turned into the camp, the air still hung heavy with the pungent aroma of fruitwood smoke and illicit pork.

Sunday was not the best of days, but Jan rushed down his breakfast, grabbed a bag of scraps, and set off for the downs to check on the flock. As he rode past the farmyard, he saw Sid coming out of the dairy. Sid beckoned him over with the vigorous waving of an arm. Jan slowed down and turned into the yard. As Jan dismounted Sid launched into his enquiry,

"Bit of a bloody caddle yesterday wunt it? What's been going on down there?" Jan took a deep breath and gave Sid the accepted version of events.

"I'm not being funny, but I never liked that posh bugger anyway, although I wouldn't wish him any harm," said Sid, which seemed to Jan to be a somewhat contradictory statement.

"Off to check the flock" said Jan in an attempt to put an end to any further questioning.

"See you tomorrow then, and you can fill me in on the details," said Sid and the two exchanged farewells and parted.

Jan took a leisurely cycle past the woods, and as the road began to steepen he decided to walk rather than struggle on by pedalling. All around the signs of autumn were visible. Women from the camp were in the woods picking blackberries, rosehips, hazelnuts, mushrooms and fungi. Unlike the pork, these food items were the free bounty of Mother Nature and were a useful source of additional flavours to enhance the dull Ministry of Food menu. This abundance of fruits including, sloes, wild plums and apples, and a solitary iron pear tree, hidden in the corner of the woods, were carefully guarded by the camps young Scouts. If it appeared that the locals may have discovered them, picking parties were quickly organised to harvest the produce before it could be appropriated by rival foragers.

To this wild harvest, a wealth of potatoes, carrots, onions, garlic, and other vegetables that were being harvested for winter stores at the camp was added. It could be seen that the camps gardening and food committee were a highly organised and talented bunch who made the most of very little. Jan walked on, and as he did so the sound of excited chatter from the woods died away into the distance.

As Jan arrived at the caravan, he was greeted by a smiling Lily.

"Are you pleased to see me or my treats?" Jan asked her as she sidled up to him. They spent an hour or so checking the pregnant ewes and fences, and checked for sheep caught in any briers that Jan had missed. Then, Jan spent some time with Lily, making a fuss of her and rubbing her behind her ears which appeared to be her favourite. He wished he could take her home to the camp but that was not allowed. Lily might be able to stay at the farm in the winter, but he had to find some way to keep her without Dyke finding out.

However, Jan decided that that was a problem for another day. He gave Lily one more stroke and, leaving her in charge, rode back to the camp for a rest before dinner. As he passed the woods, he noticed that the foragers had gone and the woods were, once again, silent, and lifeless. They were probably preparing their bounty back in the kitchen before church he thought. He remembered that if you did not wash and cook blackberries quickly, they developed a white hairy bloom that made them unappetising. Often, when he thought about these rural pursuits, his mind was taken back to his childhood and his mother, and he pondered what had become of his parents. He had Mrs Jarvis on the case, but she was trying to bridge a nine year gap and upheaval on a titanic scale. Maybe Ewa would bring news he thought, this he felt was another positive of her arrival next week.

For Jan, Sunday dinner was followed by a snooze on his bed. Marek and Marta had gone for a walk, so he was alone for a change. Although he lived in a room full of single young men, his relationship with them was not as close as that with Marek. While friendly, they had none of his issues to deal with like family, and most seemed bent on just having a good time with the money they earned with little thought given to the future.

As he lay on his bed, Jan reasoned that this would probably be his last lazy Sunday for quite some time, so he shut his eyes and drifted off. But sleep was to elude him on this particular Sunday because, just as he was about to slip away, Marek came in cursing and complaining about women to himself and slumped noisily onto his bed. The old, overstretched springs rang out to announce his arrival on the mattress with a high pitched squeak akin to fingernails on a blackboard. This piercing, high-pitched disturbance, bought Jan back to consciousness and with that his quiet Sunday was over.

"What's wrong?" Jan asked in a controlled tone that he hoped masked the fact that he didn't really care. At this invitation, Marek launched into a lengthy monologue about ungrateful women, and unreasonable arguments which left Jan overwhelmed by its complexity and twists and turns. In an attempt to bring some clarity to events, Jan distilled Marek's oration down to a simpler more understandable summary.

"So, you've had an argument about a coat," Jan uttered with a lucidity that appeared to elude Marek.

"Yes," protested Marek. "I spent a fortune on a winter coat, which Marta assured me she loved. On our Sunday-walk today she wore an old coat which she used for work. I asked her why she wasn't wearing my coat and she said that the weather was too warm to wear it. I disagreed with her and said, 'What was the point of spending all that money if she wasn't going to wear the coat'. Marta then shouted at me that just because I'd bought her a coat that didn't mean I owned her or could tell her what to do. Then she stormed off back to the camp, leaving me alone in the lane calling after her, I really don't understand what I have done wrong."

"Right" said Jan, "you know Marta is a strong and independent woman, maybe she felt that you were putting her under pressure to do what you say, and she didn't like that. Give it a while and she will calm down and everything will be all right again." Jan hoped that his advice would be enough to settle Marek, however, he knew Marta was sharp of tongue and quick to anger and he wondered if his prophetic advice was anything like what would really happen.

The evening meal in the canteen was a stressful affair for Marek, with furtive gazes in Marta's direction followed by prolonged periods of feigned disinterest in her when she looked at him.

"Listen" said Jan in an attempt to stop the silliness. "After dinner, just go and apologise to her and everything will be all right."

"I'm a proud man, and I can't just give in to a woman when I think she is wrong, I have to stand up for what I believe."

"Then be prepared to stand up alone for the rest of your life" Jan cautioned Marek. "You're telling me that you would break up your relationship all for a stupid coat?"

"No!" said Marek who by now had no idea what he was thinking.

"Then go over there, apologise, and rediscover the love that you really have for her, not the dislike you are harbouring in your heart at the moment," Jan implored.

As Jan finished speaking, Marta and her friends got up to leave. Marek picked up the piece of cake from his plate and hurried off to catch up with the girls. Within a few moments he was back smiling.

"How did it go?" Jan asked.

"A piece of cake," said Marek, who then sat down and finished his piece of cake.

With the equilibrium restored in Marek's relationship, the boys withdrew to the hut steps for a 'cordial'.

"I'm worried about Ewa arriving next week," confided Jan to Marek. "I haven't seen her for nine years, and what with all the confusion around her name, marital status, and the kids, I'm not too sure of how it'll work out."

"Well," said Marek rubbing his chin like Rodin's Thinker, "a wise man once told me that you need to rediscover the love if you want to be happy, try that."

Jan gave Marek a light cuff round the ear. They both laughed and decided to have another 'cordial'.

Monday morning came far too quickly, but so much had happened over the weekend that it felt like a fortnight since Friday evening. Jan grabbed a leftover sausage from the kitchen trolley and placed it in a brown paper bag for Lily before taking his own lunch from the counter and leaving for work.

When Jan got to the farmyard Sid was waiting for him with his lunch bag slung over his shoulder.

"I'm tagging along with you today," Sid said. "Chasity is cleaning up after the milking and I'm coming to see the flock with you."

"Well, I'm honoured to have such esteemed company on this lovely autumn day," quipped Jan.

"Less of your bloody cheek," admonished Sid, "Chastity says you're having next week off on account that your missus and the kids are coming, and I have to look after the flock."

Jan was shocked as he had not asked for it, but pleased that he was not only having a holiday but that he would have more time to deal with his new arrivals.

As the two farm hands set off up the road, the initial topic of conversation was about the ploughing and how much was left to do, then eventually, the death of Tony Sharpe surfaced. Sid was unaware that Jan had been intimately involved in the enquiry, so, oblivious to this fact, Sid launched into a list of speculative causes of death he had gleaned from villagers over the weekend. Jan listened intently as the pair walked up the hill, content to let Sid think he was the acknowledged expert on the subject.

For Jan, being in the company of Sid was a cathartic experience. Sid was uncomplicated. He held strong views on the order of things in the countryside and his place in it. As Jan listened to him rationalising the weekend's events, a peace came over him. This feeling was based on the belief that Sid's simple, solid country philosophy was the bulwark against the aggressive progression of modern life and all its perceived evils. Jan really felt that the village represented an oasis of reason in a sea of chaos, and he wanted to see his new family grow up in its benign bosom.

CHAPTER 10
REUNION

❦

As the two men neared the top of the hill, Sid touched on the subject of Jan's new family situation. Sid questioned Jan with the lightest of touches, careful not to overstep the polite line of enquiry into that of prying. However, Jan felt it was proper to let Sid know his new situation as it might, at some time, impact on their working relationship.

After a while, Jan had made Sid aware of all the facts surrounding his new family and its imminent arrival.

"Crikey," said Sid, "you're in a right old pickle aren't you."

Jan smiled in agreement but told Sid that he thought things would work out. Sid then came up with an idea that was out of the blue and Jan did not see coming.

"Why don't you ask Dyke if he will let you move into a tied cottage?"

"Sid," said Jan, "what's a tied cottage?"

"I live in a tied cottage," Sid explained, "the one I live in is a house which is owned by Dyke. I pay a lower rent than most in the village, it's close to work, and me and the missus save money which we can use when I retire."

This seemed the perfect answer for Jan, who was beginning to feel that things were, maybe, going his way at last. He loved the village life. There was a school for the children, a job on the doorstep and a chance to save and build for the future. Jan was about to ask more questions when Sid exclaimed,

"Bugger me, there is a dog in the flock!"

Sid was about to run into the flock to drive the dog away when Jan grabbed his shoulder and stopped him in his tracks.

"It's OK Sid, I've adopted that stray. She is no trouble and is good around the sheep." Jan whistled at Lily, and she came running up to them, tail wagging and giving them both her submissive grin.

"Watch out!" shouted Sid. "She's going to go for us!"

"It's fine Sid," assured Jan, "that's just her happy face, she's smiling at us because she's happy to see us." Jan took the bag of titbits out of his pocket and fed them to Lily and then started to make a fuss of her.

"Where are you keeping her?" Sid asked in astonishment.

"She turned up here just before the weekend and, as far as I know, she sleeps under the caravan and watches the sheep from the steps."

"Well buggered if I know," said Sid "I've never heard of such a thing before."

"I know it's crazy, but I just know she is OK, and I'm going to ask if I can keep her with me during the day and let her sleep in the cart shed at night."

"Dyke won't be having any of that malarkey on the farm, you best keep the old girl a secret and out of sight if you can."

Jan was upset to hear Sid's advice but thought it best to follow his counsel and keep Lily off the farm for the present.

The two then started to check through the flock, Jan giving Sid advice about particular sheep, especially those close to lambing. It was as they patrolled the stock that Sid noticed that some of the ewes had bite marks and blood on their hind legs.

"Ere you bloody go!" Sid said with an accusing eye cast at Lily, "armless buggery!"

Jan inspected the injuries, and they did look like bites. "I can't understand this," Jan said in dismay, "there must be some explanation. Come on, Sid, let's go to the caravan and get some iodine for the wounds."

As the two reached the caravan they were met with a gruesome sight. There on the steps was a young dead dog fox, its snout covered in blood, and its neck snapped as clean as a carrot. Lily proudly stood over her quarry, giving her grin.

"All right," said Sid to Lily, "I was wrong, I know when I'm beat."

Jan was so happy that Lily had not let him down and that Sid was now also a big fan of this beguiling waif and stray.

The two men caught the injured sheep and treated their wounds. Jan suggested that they light the fire and make some hot tea to help keep the damp air out of them and the caravan. As they sipped the tea, they discussed Lily's possible previous life.

"Well, she isn't a sheep dog because she made no attempt to help us catch those injured ewes, but she is good around stock, and brutally good at killing possible predators."

Jan agreed with Sid and explained that, when he was in France, there was a breed of mountain dog that followed the sheep in the mountains. If wolves attacked the flock, these large dogs could be on the wolves in seconds with their powerful jaws and great size and strength to drive them off.

"I know she killed a young dog fox, but I think a wolf would be stretching it," said Sid in all seriousness. "Another thing is, she's in good condition, shiny coat, bright eyes, healthy teeth, and sociable around people, so, her last owner must have been good to her, so why did she leave and pick you?"

"Maybe she sensed that I was alone," laughed Jan. "Perhaps you're right Sid, she may be missing from someone's home, and they are fretting over her loss. Do you think that we should report her to the police?"

"No, bugger that, they'll lock her in a cage, and she'll be treated very badly. You keep quiet, young-un, I'll put the feelers out and find out what I can. Anyway, you might come up here tomorrow and she'll be gone for good."

"Speaking of the police," quipped Sid, "Dyke has started finding vegetables missing from his patch. He thought my nephew was helping himself but it's not him. That bloody twister you know hasn't got anything to do with it, has he?"

Jan leapt to Marek's defence, "I think he's more of a procurer and gamekeeper come poacher than thief. He has an eye for a deal when he can find it, but I think that's it."

"Don't you mean poacher come gamekeeper?" Sid suggested.

"No, I know what I meant," said Jan grinning.

"Well, Dyke has taken measures to protect the veg now, so I think the problem will solve itself in the next few days."

"Wow! What has he done to do that, rigged up a shot-gun to a trip wire?-"

"I suggested that, but Miss Chastity said no. I think if a man is going to steal another man's hard-earned veg, he deserves some 4-10 shot up his ass. Anyway, Dyke has put some barrel rims down in the rows. Next time the 'procurer' comes along and steps on one of them steel rings, it will poleaxe his bloody shin. That should stop the bugger in his tracks."

Jan smiled at Sid in agreement and the two carried on eating lunch, throwing the unwanted crusts to Lily and slurping on their tea. Sometimes, thought Jan, life is good.

After work, Jan pedalled back to the camp, and as he rode through the gates, he met Marek coming out with a sidecar that looked more like a cornucopia. The wheeled horn of plenty overflowed with carrots, cabbages, strings of onions and garlic, parsnips, and cauliflowers. Jan raised his hand to stop Marek.

"What the hell is all this?" Jan asked, afraid that Marek was indeed the veg procurer.

"These are vegetables from the growers in the camp. I sell them to the local hotels and split the profit with the growers. On top of that I move a couple of braces of rabbits at the same time and everybody is happy. My only problem is the camp stocks are dwindling, so I'll have to curtail my hotel business shortly and find a new scheme."

As Marek finished speaking, Marta arrived in her old work coat and stepped astride the pillion. Jan braced himself for more fireworks, but none occurred.

"Marek has promised me dinner in a hotel this evening, but I'm not going to wear my lovely red coat on this stinky old motorbike" Marta squealed in excitement. A relieved Jan wished them a good evening and bade them farewell. It had been a good day he thought; let's hope it stays that way.

After Sid and Jan's trip up to the caravan, it was decided that during the week of Jan's return to work, the sheep and the caravan would return to the fold for the lambing. It was also decided that, before his holiday, Jan would take on the last of the ploughing and Sid would run the dairy. In this way, it was hoped that during Jan's absence, the workload on Sid would be lighter. Holidays were always taken during seasonal lulls which made the job of covering farm duties much easier, but this was not the case on this occasion. In the week leading up to his holiday Jan rose early and ate the early breakfast. He checked the flock, fed Lily and had the girls at work ploughing by nine thirty. This hectic routine stopped him thinking about the momentous events that were creeping nearer and nearer with each passing day.

***

Finally, it was Friday and Jan signed out at work and made his way home, getting there just in time to pay his savings into the post office and Rosemary's tender care.

It was Friday night and so it was the Harvest Festival dance night. Jan had kept back some of his wages for one last evening of entertainment and so he showered early, got dressed, and then went for dinner. Over the months, he had gone to village jumble sales and church bazaars and had managed to acquire a number of good quality shirts, a couple of ties, and two pairs of trousers which had expanded his wardrobe considerably. With dinner finished, he made his selection, dressed, and lay on his bed waiting for Marek, who was still in the shower. All the young men were combing their hair, which was caked in bay-scented hair grease, into the latest Hollywood styles. They were excitedly speculating about who might get lucky, who might get into a fight, and who would get the first dance with a village girl.

Marek eventually came back from the shower and donned what could only be described as a zoot suit.

"How do I look?"

"Like a gangster who's lost his violin case."

"Great," said Marek, and the pair left for the dance.

They met the girls at the gate and set off. The walk to the village hall was a lively affair with pushing and shoving and much laughter. On arrival, Marek pulled five tickets from his pocket, and handed them to the two old ladies who were on the door.

"Wow, where did they come from?" Jan asked in surprise.

"I was owed a favour," said Marek smoothly.

As the excited group entered the hall, a large poster proclaimed; 'Fresh from a sell-out tour of Europe, Frankie Fellows and his Musical Merrymakers are here for one night only.

Carriages at ten thirty!" The five friends quickly found a table near the stage and staked their claim to it. The girls then put their coats into the cloakroom each receiving a ticket in exchange. On their return, and with sufficient bodies now bagging the table, Jan went for drinks as Marek had stumped up for the tickets.

James was at the helm on the bar with a local farm-worker the size of a small outhouse as his assistant. As James loaded Jan's tray with his order, Jan looked at James, nodded towards the assistant, and raised his eyebrows.

"That's my insurance policy," said James.

"Insurance policy?" Jan asked.

James lowered his voice. "Some of the village lads are not so gentrified and like to push their weight around at these events. I hope I'll not need him, but if I do, Eustace will be ready to break bones and those boys know it."

Jan paid his money and carefully made his way back to the table, safe in the knowledge that they were under the collective care of James and Eustace.

As the hall filled to capacity, the chairman of the hall committee got on stage to make a short speech. He then introduced the featured musical act, repeating the words on the poster verbatim. From the back of the stage and in a flourish of green baize curtains the headliner act entered followed by his Musical Merrymakers. The impact they made was wholly underwhelming, as there was more Cricklewood than Hollywood about the boys.

Frankie wore a black dinner jacket combo with a high wing collar shirt and black bowtie. His quartet was similarly suited but as an added accoutrement the drummer had a Woodbine hanging out of the side of his mouth. As Frankie moved to the front of the stage and grabbed the microphone, the hall lights dimmed, and two follow spots worked by Frankie's crew burst to life. Unfortunately for Frankie this intense light highlighted the fact that he was sporting a toupee. His side hair had acquired a lustrous silver shine while his top hair was dull and flat auburn. As Frankie put some energy into his first song the toupee developed a life of its own flapping and lifting like a hairy fascinator.

In a wasteland of international culture, Frankie was however, a breath of fresh air. His voice was not trained but adequate. He hit the high notes solidly and was melodious in his presentation. Frankie was several levels above your average shower singer, but sadly, the 'big time' would not be beckoning anytime soon. The only drawback in his act was that he insisted on speaking to the audience in a fake American accent with serious Wiltshire undertones. However, if you could get past the faux American, he was entertaining, and the five revellers agreed value for money.

Jan waited for a slow song and made his way to the bar for more drinks. It was easier to pass through the throng while they were clinched in a slow dance than when they were moving around. Jan approached Eustace with his tray of empty glasses and while the bar keeper refilled them, they struck up a conversation. Jan started by heaping praise on Frankie's act and the tight sound that the quartet was producing.

"Do you know which places in Europe they toured?" Jan asked, thirsty for more information.

"Tour, in this case, has a rather broad meaning," said Eustace.

"What do you mean?" Jan enquired with intrigue.

"Well, the five of them are ex ENSA entertainers who spent the war years travelling around the camps as part of a show to keep the troops happy-."

"ENSA?"

"Entertainment National Service Association," Eustace explained. "They went all over the world, but this lot never got past Bielefeld. Frankie is actually a milkman in town and he and the boys do this for pin money."

With the glitz somewhat buffed off the entertainment, Jan returned to the table to share his newfound knowledge with his star struck companions.

"Would you like to dance?" Kinga asked.

"I need to be a bit more drunk than this to dance but thank you for the offer. You go and find a nice, rich local boy and dance with him."

Kinga took the advice and eyed the crowd. She saw the secretary of the Young Farmers dressed in a tweed suit. "He looks rich." So off she went.

Kinga walked up to the young, bookish man and said, "My friend over there bet me that I would not ask you for a dance," and she gestured to Jan. As she did so, Jan, unaware of the gameplay, waved at the pair.

"Well, I'd hate you to lose a bet on my behalf," the young man said, so off they set for the dance floor with Kinga smiling at Jan as the pair glided by him to a waltz.

This left only Kasia and Jan sat at the table. Kasia looked preoccupied, and after a short spate of chit-chat, she said, "Do you mind if I ask you something serious?" Jan, who was always ready to lend an ear, agreed without question.

Kasia took a sip of her drink and began. "You know if you know somebody really well, and you know that they are being dishonest, should you tell somebody?"

"Well," began Jan, "you know that I am best friends with Marek right, so I completely understand. I believe your first obligation is to your friend. That is one of the defining things about any friendship."

"Thank you," Kasia whispered, and that was the end of it.

The evening was a raging success. Eustace was not required in his bone-breaking capacity and the ten thirty finales came far too soon. As Jan walked home with his friends, he could not help thinking that he was going to miss this freedom from adult responsibility. The night was dank and cool, but the friendship was warm enough to keep it at bay. As Jan slipped into bed, he decided to offer himself up to fate, and so, content with his place in life, he fell asleep.

The next morning, Jan heard Marek leave for work, and as the motorbikes' gurgling disappeared out of hearing range, Jan fell back to sleep. On waking, Jan was galvanised into action by the impending arrival of his wife and family. He showered, took the late breakfast, stripped his bed, and took the bedding to the laundry room. He packed his bag and moved up to the married quarters. He hung his clothes up then chose the top drawer of the chest for the rest of his belongings before waiting on the step under the sullen sky, where he waited and waited. Being further into the camp, he had no view of the gate and any comings and goings that might occur. For some reason, it did not seem right to wait on the single men's hut steps. Maybe he thought he had put those days behind him.

Dinner came and went, and Jan carried on waiting. At just after two, a uniformed Boy Scout came running up to Jan and saluted.

"You're to report to Mr Monk's office." Here we go, thought Jan, what has gone wrong this time? He ambled down to the office, knocked on the door.

Mr Monk shouted, "Come!"

As Jan entered the office, he saw two young children sat on chairs. They were swinging their legs rhythmically, both looking tired and confused.

"Ah Mr Kot, your wife has finally arrived, I'm just completing the formalities."

"Hello Ewa, I'm so happy that I've found you at last," Jan blurted out, realising that he had not planned any kind of welcoming oration.

"Did you find me, or did I find you?" Ewa said through thin, pursed lips, which showed no sign of happiness at the meeting, or pleasure in her arrival.

Jan was taken aback by this obtuse statement and in an instant he knew that the previous nine years were not a gap but a canyon.

"Please sit down Mr Kot, while I complete my paperwork, there will be lots of time to catch up later." Jan sat in silence, confused, and stunned at the reception he had been given by his wife.

"Right, Mrs Kot."

"Mrs Kot-Dudek," Ewa interrupted.

"Quite," Monk said correcting himself and, sensing his interviewee's prickly nature, proceeded with caution. "These are your children I assume?"

"No," replied Ewa, "they are orphans who were secretly smuggled out of Russia in 1942."

"By you and Mr Dudek?" Monk asked almost in a whisper, afraid of what anger the question might provoke.

"Yes, but he wasn't their father either. He was a soldier in the newly formed Polish Second Corps, and he helped me escape with them." Ewa stared at the back wall of the office; it seemed as if she could see those long ago events clearly placed before her.

"Do you have official proof that these children are legally yours?"

Ewa pulled a dog-eared envelope out of her case and handed it to Monk. Monk perused the documents for quite some time and then handed them back thanking Ewa.

"So, they are called Mary and Joseph Kot-Dudek, and that is how they are to remain?"

"Yes, I promised the soldier that they would keep his name, and in the event that something happened to him, his name would live on."

"A most laudable sentiment," Monk conceded, as he carried on. "How did these children come into yours and Mr

Dudek's care?" Monk enquired, although with the presence of official paperwork, there really was no need to pursue that line of enquiry.

"I was trained as a nurse and worked in a small Catholic hospital in Russia. We didn't have much but that was all there was in the area. Every so often, Soviets would tour the orphanages looking for children who had come of age. When this happened, we would hide them if we had warning of a visit until the squads had left the region.

When Germany invaded Russia, everything changed suddenly. Military personnel were forming up and preparing to leave Russia to link up with the Allies. There was a rule that military men could take their families with them, so I found a captain who had come to us for some minor treatment, got him to agree to take me with him, grabbed the priest from the hospital who forged a marriage certificate. Just at the moment we were about to leave for the collection point, the twins, who were two months old, were brought from the orphanage. The orphanage was very crowded and had very few supplies, so we agreed to take the two orphaned twins using forged birth certificates which the same priest did for us, and we were a family."

"You left Russia with Mr Dudek?" Monk asked, now intrigued rather than carrying out any official enquiry.

"Yes, we travelled together as far as Iran in a military convoy, then I carried on into India and since then I have never seen him again."

"Do you have any information about the true parents of the children?" Monk asked.

Ewa stopped to think, casting her mind back. "I only know that their mother was making her way to our hospital when she went into labour, so she stopped at a farm to ask for help. The farmer's wife sent her son to get help from us, so two nuns rode bicycles back to the farm to help and when they got there, they helped the lady with her birth. So that they could work in privacy, they spread blankets on some hay in the stables and the twins were born. The woman was very weak, and delivering the twins was too much for her frail system as she died soon after. Because the babies were born in a stable, the nuns decided to call them Mary and Joseph.

"The farmer took the nuns and babies back to the hospital by cart. After being checked out, they were sent to the orphanage until their return on the day we took them."

While he listened to all of this, Jan was awash with emotions of happiness, sadness, and relief. Relief that Ewa was not another man's wife and that she had remained true to their marriage vows, sadness at the ordeal that she must have gone through over the past years, and happiness at not having to address any previous relationship issues so that eventually they might be able to forge a strong relationship once more. However, Jan's vision of their future was based on pragmatism rather than emotional stability and a shared love of each other. He had not considered the deep mental scars that dwelt within Ewa and his vision of their future did not match that of his newly found wife.

With the paperwork stamped and the ration cards handed over, Ewa and the children were free to go with Jan to the new family room. The walk to the hut was a long long silent one but informative in a number of ways for Jan. As Jan bent to pick up Ewa's suitcase, she picked it up and said, "I'm fine, thank you."

As they walked, the children stayed silent and made no attempt to play around. Now Jan was no expert on children, but he had seen enough to know that this was not normal. When the four arrived at the hut and stood before it, Ewa gave a very loud sigh.

"Is everything all right?" Jan asked when he patently knew that it was not.

"I'm sick and tired of living and moving from one hut to another, I'm sick of prying priests and nuns, committee members, and welcome meetings. I just want a home which I know is mine for good."

At last, Jan saw a chink of light in this otherwise dark situation. "I might be able to get a tied cottage at the farm where I work, and if I can, we can move out of here soon."

Ewa looked at Jan. He was hoping for a smile or at least some indication that this was a good thing that he was doing for them. "You work on a farm?" Ewa said disparagingly. "You were a captain in the army and now you work on a farm," Ewa goaded.

Jan was somewhat taken aback as this was not the young, carefree nurse he had left in Poland. She appeared to have contempt for everything and everybody that surrounded her. Intrigued, however, he asked, "How did you know that I was a captain in the army?"

Ewa snapped back, "Well I spent a lot of my time looking for you and every time I tried to trace you the records showed your rank and military status, simple really."

Jan had not thought that he and Ewa would be running into each other's arms at their first meeting, but he had not expected a stone wall of indifference. However, Jan felt that he could not let Ewa's inference in her last statement go unchallenged.

"As soon as I was released from the prisoner of war camp, I started searching for you, and I never gave up until I found you. How was I to know that you had changed your name?"

Again, Ewa snapped back, "It would have been better if you had not abandoned me in Poland. Why did you not come back when it was clear that we were losing the fight against the Nazis and the Soviets? Why did you leave me to fend for myself and not come back?"

Jan was stunned by this comment. "Ewa, all of the time

that has elapsed since the beginning of the war, I was focussed on my survival during the fighting and then staying alive in the labour camps. In my mind, Ewa, you were safe back in Poland, maybe working as a nurse in a city hospital. Your nursing skills would have made you valuable to whoever was in charge, and I had hoped that this would have afforded you some protection." Jan sighed and realised that the trauma of the war had been greater for Ewa, who had been alone, than for him who had been surrounded by his fellow soldiers. Jan knew that he would have to tread carefully while he tried to put things right.

"Listen," he said quietly, "I know life's been tough, and it's still going to be, but here, in England, we can start to build a safe future for us and the children. I know working on a farm is not what you would expect me to be doing, but we are foreigners, and we cannot choose what we do here."

Ewa did not respond, she just started to walk into the hut and snapped, "The children need to rest."

Jan braced himself for any reaction Ewa might give to the living quarters as he led her into the hut. As he pushed open the door, she took one look and snapped her orders.

"Joseph, top bunk, you, bottom bunk," she said, pointing at Jan. "Mary, with me on this bed." Jan had been wondering about how to approach the sleeping arrangements so he would at least have one less thing to worry about now.

"Right, the children and I need to rest, you can come back later at mealtime and show us where we go." Ewa directed Jan to leave the room with a single digit of her waving hand, and following her direction, he did so and closed the door.

Jan walked out of the family hut and made his way to the relative sanctuary of the single men's hut. There he found Marek lying on his bed with not a care in the world. At that moment, Jan envied him more than anything else and would have traded places in an instant.

"Here's the family man! How's it going then?" Marek asked in a cheery tone unaware of the dire state of Jan's life at this present moment.

"The family man isn't happy because his wife is already angry with her husband."

"What have you done so soon to make her angry, she's only been here an hour?"

"She came angry, and from what I can see she's going to stay angry for the rest of our married lives."

"Are you sure she is not just tired?"

"Oh, she's tired, tired of me. She has accused me of abandoning her in Poland and making my own getaway. She's accused me of doing a menial job on a farm when I should be in some other more satisfactory but as yet unknown job. The children won't even look at me, let alone speak to me, and just to add insult to injury I'll be sleeping in a child's bed tonight."

Marek sat up and indicated for Jan to sit down on his bed. "Now it seems to me that Ewa has a lot of pent up anger that she has been hanging on to for the last nine years. If I was you, I'd let her spend a few days getting rid of it and weather that storm. If, after a week or two, things have not changed, then you'll need to talk to her and decide how to move on with your new life together."

Jan thought for a moment and desperately pleaded, "How do I do that?"

Marek calmly replied, "You'll have to ask her what it is that she wants to make her happy, how she sees your future, and make sure you include the children in your chat. Ewa has had no control over her life for years, she's been told by others what to do, where to go, and how to do it. It'll be your task to make her believe that those days are over, and things will quickly change for the better."

Jan sat thinking about the wise words Marek had just

imparted. "How do you know all this stuff?" Jan asked in amazement.

"Because I had the same conversation with Marta about two months ago," Marek said smiling.

Jan sat and pondered his next move, and he reasoned that he would have to weather the storm and hope that as time went by, Ewa would calm down and become more approachable. There were so many questions that he wanted answers to. Jan thought though, that these questions would have to wait until there was some resemblance of calm between them. It was at this point that the ever resourceful Marek came up with a possible solution.

Turning to Jan he said, "You say Ewa is a nurse?"

"Yes," replied Jan.

"OK, leave it with me. I can't promise anything, but I'll make some enquiries and get back to you in a few days' time."

An intrigued Jan agreed and hoped that whatever it was that Marek had up his sleeve would go some way to getting Ewa in a better frame of mind. Jan and Marek passed the remaining time before the evening meal chatting about Ewa and the possible causes of her angst. However, it is the nature of most men that while professing to understand the female sex. they really do not have a clue, and so, it appeared to be the case on this occasion.

In time, Jan had to leave the sanctuary of his old hut and its memories of happier times and return to the harsh reality of his present situation. He walked like a condemned man on his way to the gallows, back to the family hut. As he knocked on the door of their room, he braced himself for whatever situation he would face behind it.

"What now!" an irascible voice demanded to know from behind the door.

"It's me," Jan said quietly in the hope that Ewa would remember that the walls of these huts were paper thin. Ewa opened the door and beckoned Jan in.

"Thank God, it's you," she declared. Jan's heart leapt for joy as for the first time that day Ewa was happy to see him. However, these green shoots of a thaw in their relationship were soon to wither and burn in Ewa's frosty gaze.

"What's wrong?" Jan asked in the most supportive and concerned voice he could muster.

"Since you left," Ewa began, "I've had nothing but interruptions. First, the Sunday school teacher tries to sign up the children, then the Saturday school teacher wanting to know when the children would be starting lessons. After that, not one but two different groups of people who claimed to represent religious groups in the camp wanted me to sign up for their weekly meetings. Just as I thought it couldn't get any worse, one of the nuns in the camp wanted Joseph to start altar boy duties tomorrow, and the choir mistress, Mrs Kunka, wanted both children to start practice this evening."

"So, what did you say?" Jan asked, somehow sure he knew the answer.

"I told them no and sent them away," Ewa proclaimed, sounding pleased with herself. Jan nodded animatedly to show his approval while also knowing that this was social suicide for the family in this close-knit camp.

Nonetheless, Jan saw a chance to gain Ewa's trust if he showed a united front on these family matters with Ewa. It would bring them closer together and demonstrate his support of their family and the choices she had made.

"I've never really bothered with all that stuff since I've been here," Jan proclaimed hoping to curry favour with his wife.

"I know!" Ewa snapped, "that's what everybody who came here has been telling me." Jan now was unsure if that was a good or bad thing, and so, he kept quiet and waited for Ewa to speak to give him some indication of which way this conversation was going. Ewa did not keep Jan waiting long.

"I don't intend to sit in this camp and become part of this world. We are in England, and we should live like English people, not live in the past."

Jan, now certain of his ground, happily replied, "I agree. This is a lovely country, and if you are prepared to work and not be choosey about what work you do you can make a good life here."

Ewa looked at Jan and said, "So, we're agreed then, we are moving out as soon as possible?"

"Yes!" exclaimed Jan, as a wave of regret washed over him at the realisation of what he had just promised Ewa as he fell into her trap.

As they walked towards the canteen for the first time that day, Jan felt that he had a family and that he could now be truly called a family man. He and Ewa had, in a few moments, decided on a number of issues about their future in perfect harmony. This discussion had cemented the fact that the pair had a future together and that they both accepted that fact. Jan was not so stupid, and he realised that he had had hardly any real input into those decisions, but Ewa was happier now and that was a good thing.

As they entered the canteen, Jan led the way to the family tables. As they sat down, it soon became clear that word had got around quite quickly and the four appeared to be *persona non grata*. Those who sat near them had turned at an angle away from them so that no eye contact could be made. Nobody in the throng made any attempt to speak and Jan looked at Ewa with a nervous smile.

"It appears that news travels fast," Jan said.

Ewa looked at Jan, and in a voice so loud that Marek could hear it on the single men table, she announced, "Good! Now I won't have to pretend that I like anybody here." The pre-grace chattering fell silent, then whispers of condemnation spread around the room like oil on water. Now sure of their status and position in the scheme of things, Jan and Ewa said grace with the rest of the room and began to eat.

Engulfed by a wall of silence, Jan decided to at last try to have a chat with the children. Children were a mystery to Jan. He had only ever had to say nice things about other people's babies, and appear interested when mothers spoke about their children, filled with pride at some minor achievement. So, Jan launched into this conversation at a disadvantage.

"What would you like to be when you grow up?" Jan asked Joseph. He watched the boy consider his answer but what followed left him in utter shock.

"Mother says that I'm going to be a doctor," said Joseph. It was not the response that shocked Jan but the manner of its delivery. Joseph spoke English with a home counties accent.

Mary then piped up, "Mother said that I'm going to be a teacher," in a similar accent to her brothers'. Jan was flabbergasted at this and looked at Ewa for some kind of explanation.

Ewa obliged. "Well, you see," she said, "as soon as I arrived at any camp, I made it known that I was an English-speaking nurse, and I was usually placed in a Commonwealth hospital. These usually had schools attached to them for the staff and families who had come to work in that particular part of the British Empire. I would negotiate for Mary and Joseph to attend these schools so that I could work longer hours as they were usually desperate for trained staff because of the war."

Jan was amazed at Ewa's resourcefulness and thought that she could probably give Marek a run for his money. Intrigued, he carried on with his questioning.

"So, how did you learn English when you did not speak it before the war?" Ewa smiled as if she was remembering some happy period in her life. "As soon as I was under the control of the British army, I started taking any lessons that were on offer. I worked with British and Allied nurses and doctors and read *Readers Digest* magazines in my spare time which were left around the wards. I realised that I was a quick learner, and so, I started to learn to write as well. When the children were old enough to go to school, I was able to help them for a while but then they took over and started teaching me." It was at this point that Ewa's smile turned into a laugh.

Jan looked at her happy face and for a second the young Ewa shone through. Then, as the reality of their situation once again emerged, the smile was gone in an instant and Ewa's brow was once more riven with frown lines.

Once the evening meal was finished, Jan was once again filled with hope.

"I'd like to introduce you to my friend, who has been a real support to me at different times." and he led Ewa and the children over to the single men's table and got the attention of Marek.

"Marek, this is my wife, Ewa, and our children, Mary and Joseph." Marek stood up, wiped his hands on the chest of his shirt to ensure that they were clean, and extended a hand, held Ewa's hand and kissed it, and greeted Ewa in Polish. Ewa responded in English, and Marek aware of Jan's rule on speaking English, continued in the vernacular.

"It is lovely to meet you at last. Jan has been so looking forward to you coming," Marek said, committing perjury in order to raise Jan's stock in Ewa's mind.

"Oh really," Ewa said in surprise, "Jan hasn't mentioned that, have you, Jan?" Jan squirmed and Marek instantly understood that crime really didn't pay. Luckily, Marta arrived and introduced herself in English, spoke to the children, and suggested that Ewa and the children should follow her to the single women's hut.

"I can tell you how things work around here, who to watch out for, who to trust, and who to avoid." Pointing at Marek, Marta said, "this one would be at the top of any list of who to avoid." Ewa smiled once more, and Jan felt that things were at last going well.

"What shall I do?" Jan asked as this was his first day as a husband who had to take other feelings into consideration.

"Do what you've been doing for the last nine years and hang around with your mates." Ewa smiled a cheeky smile, and Jan was happy to comply.

"Try not to get into any trouble while we are gone," added Marta, and in that moment a lifelong friendship was forged.

Instinctively, Jan started picking up scraps of meat for Lily and then gave out a cry, "Oh no! I've forgotten about Lily."

"Who is Lily?" Ewa enquired.

"She's my dog; I keep her up on the downs by my caravan."

"He has a caravan?" Ewa asked Marek.

"He does," replied Marek with his eyes wide open. "I'll tell you what, why don't you ladies have your chat and Jan, and I can take the kids up to see the sheep and meet Lily."

"Is it far?" Ewa fretted.

"It's only a short ride on the motorbike and sidecar" Marek assured her.

"But is it safe?" Ewa clutched her brood to her side as she saw all manner of disasters.

"Jan can sit on the pillion, and the kids can sit in the sidecar."

"Is there room for two in the sidecar?" Ewa demanded to know.

"It's bigger than it looks," said Marta.

With all these things settled, Jan and Marek made their way to the bike and the ladies went off to their hut for a chat. With a swish, Marek took the cover off his pride and joy and primed the carburettor ready for start-up. Jan lifted Mary and Joseph into the sidecar, and he climbed onto the pillion.

"It smells like potatoes in here," Mary complained.

"Everybody says that," said Marek evasively.

Jan then wondered what Mary would say if she knew that last week a dead pig was sat where she was right now. He reasoned it was best not to mention that, and in a cloud of blue smoke they were gone.

CHAPTER 11
A SOMBRE OCTOBER

As they were losing the light, this had to be a quick trip, which suited Jan. He wanted to get back with the children and see if he could keep the momentum of Ewa's happy phase going for as long as possible. Perhaps, he thought, breaking the ice with Marta and the girls would make her feel more at home and generally more amenable. As the four intrepid travellers arrived at the caravan, it was almost dark. Jan lifted the children out of the sidecar and all four walked over to the caravan. Lily was there smiling her grinning smile and turning in circles of happiness to see them. The children ran up to her and petted her.

"Is this our dog?"

"Yes, but she has to stay up here and guard the sheep for me at the moment."

"Oh!" Mary and Joseph complained.

"Don't worry, next week she will be coming down to the farm with the sheep for the winter."

"Hurray!" Mary and Joseph cheered, while Marek, who knew Dyke's rules, gave Jan a questioning sideways look. Jan gave him a sort of 'what else can I do' stare, and they changed the subject.

Jan could see that Sid had been up and had not forgotten Lily, as there were some bones under the caravan that had been picked clean by her. Also, and Jan thought this was nice of Sid, Lily now had a bed made of hay under the caravan and some corrugated iron sheets placed around the base of the caravan to keep the worst of the autumn chill off her. Jan gave Lily her second dinner of the day and then they all embarked on the homeward journey.

As Marek picked his way downhill along the sunken track off the downs the white chalk glowed with the hue of honey in the dull beam of the bikes front light. Whilst the damp chill air was racing past the sidecar it threatened the delicate chests of any who were not made of hardy stock, but Jan had no concerns as the children were screaming in pleasure. He hoped that Ewa would understand as easily that the children had not been exposed to some cough inducing-miasma on the way home.

As Jan walked back to their hut, he felt that with their introduction to Lily and the response they gave he may have gained the confidence of Mary and Joseph, so he decided to ask the children about the situation that they found themselves in.

"Mother says that we must make the best of a bad job," announced Mary.

"Mother says that beggars cannot be choosers," Joseph added.

"Your mother says quite a lot doesn't she," said Jan.

"Yes, she tells us not to worry and that she'll not let anything hurt us," Mary said, mimicking her mother's reassuring tone.

"I'm sure she won't," Jan assured them. "I think she loves you both very much," Jan whispered.

"Mother said that she has to learn to love you again, didn't she Joseph?"

"Yes, she did," Joseph replied.

Jan was shocked by the candid honesty of his charges, and he wanted to ask them one last question that he hoped would not betray their newfound friendship.

"Do you think she will learn to love me again?" Jan asked tentatively.

"I think so," said Mary, "especially when she meets Lily and if you let her play in the caravan like you let us do." Jan smiled and opened the door to the family's room.

"Here you are!" Ewa cried with mock excitement. "You must be freezing. Come over here and let me put a blanket around you both." The children said they did not need a blanket, but Ewa said she was cold just looking at them and it would make her feel better.

Jan watched all of this from the doorway unsure if he should enter or give them room to sort themselves out.

"Come in, Jan you're causing a draught," Ewa commanded. Jan did not care about the bossy comment because it was the first time that she had called him by his name all that day.

Jan sat on the bottom bunk with the children as they recounted their adventure on the downs. After Ewa had been regaled with stories of dogs, rides on Teddy the donkey and the speed and smell of mashed potatoes, Jan decided maybe he should enquire how her time with Marta and the girls had gone.

Not wanting to appear too inquisitive he broached the subject carefully.

"So, how was your meeting with the girls?" Jan ventured as his opening gambit.

"Oh, they introduced me to Mrs Goldstein and Frau Swartz and the six of us drank tea and talked. Did you know that Marek has been swapping rabbits for calming pills for Frau

Swartz with a doctor at the hospital, but now the rabbits have
thinned out he has had to stop?"

"No, I did not," remarked a surprised Jan.

"Did you know that Mrs Kunka has never spoken to Mrs
Goldstein since she was allowed into the choir because she is
jealous of her operatic voice?"

"I heard something but I'm not quite sure what," Jan said,
barely keeping up with this Pandora's Box of information that
he had appeared to have opened.

Ewa went on, "Did you know that there is a man who was
suspected of murder living in this very hut?" Jan was aghast
at this terrible news.

"Who?" Jan demanded to know.

"You silly," said Ewa, and she began to laugh.

Jan began to laugh too, and for a short while, life seemed
normal and ordinary. However, life suddenly became extraordinary again.

"The children need an early night; they have been travelling all day. Where's the bathroom?"

"We'll need to go over to the shower block." Jan, sensing
that this was not the answer she was hoping for suggested,
that he would take them all.

Ewa carried the children's wash bags and a towel, and
the family set off. The children, who were observant through
necessity, had already worked out which building it was and
were racing towards it. As they drew away and out of earshot,
Ewa sprang a question on Jan that was to make the preceding
few hours feel like wedded bliss.

"How long has Marta been pregnant?" Ewa asked.

"Marta isn't pregnant," Jan answered in a banal tone as if
the very fact was unthinkable.

"Jan," Ewa said with her best bedside manner, "I'm a nurse
and I know pregnant when I see it. I would say that Marta is
at least four months gone."

Jan began to choke on his words as he tried to make sense of this bombshell.

"But Marek would've told me, he's my best friend, he wouldn't keep something like that from me."

"Maybe Marek doesn't know," Ewa said in a low, foreboding voice. The deep tone of those whispered words filled Jan's mind with a myriad of questions.

"Hold on a minute," Jan cried in protest, "Marek and Marta have only been together since harvest finished in September. I remember he took her to Stonehenge on their first date. It's November next week, so they have only known each other just over two months, so she can't be four months pregnant. It's impossible."

"It's not impossible if she was pregnant when she started courting him," Ewa reasoned.

Jan stopped in his tracks, rooted to the spot as if the complexity of this problem and the ability to walk could not be carried out at the same time.

"No" Jan protested. "Marta would not do that to Marek. They love each other, they are a pair, and they have shared dreams and ambitions for a good life together here in England."

Ewa took Jan's hand in hers, "Listen, Jan," Ewa said quietly, "Marta is a girl alone in a foreign land, she's a voluntary worker and as such, if she gets pregnant, her contract is terminated, and she's sent back to Soviet Poland. You cannot condemn her for trying to salvage something of her life by telling lies to Marek."

Jan looked at Ewa and thought long and hard before he spoke. "Ewa, Marek is not stupid, and Marta can't hide this for much longer. Marek is a proud, proud man and he will not accept Marta's deception. That'll be the end of them."

Ewa looked down at the ground in disappointment. "Then all we can do is try to help where we can and comfort them when the inevitable happens."

The pair continued their slow walk to the shower block in silence, and on arrival family duties helped dispel the problem for a while. However, this devastating predicament was not going to disappear. The potential to destroy Jan and Marek's friendship if Jan did not handle this crisis carefully, was a real concern to Jan. Jan had a high regard for Marta but Marek was his only real friend who had helped him immeasurably in his first year in England.

On returning to their room, Ewa put the children to bed and then the couple tried to discuss the problem quietly using metaphors and mime so that the children were not able to understand. Jan started the debate.

"If, you know who is," and here he made a sign mimicking a swollen belly, "I am not sure if my conscience will allow me to say nothing."

"Yes, I understand that Jan," sighed Ewa, "but why wade into troubled waters when you can stay out of them and see how things develop?"

Jan countered, "But how'll I face him. We'll see them both tomorrow, and knowing what we know, I'm not sure how I'll react."

"Look," whispered Ewa, "it's been a long tiring day, let's get some rest and think about it tomorrow with fresh eyes. Anyway, I have a bigger problem tonight as I'm sharing a room with a murder suspect." Jan gave a grin and lay back on his short bunk. It was going to be a long night, he thought.

Next morning, Jan was awakened by the whispering of children who were trying to be quiet while they climbed out of their beds. Jan lay with his eyes shut. If there's one thing that is guaranteed to wake a person up, it's somebody saying "Shush, be quiet," he thought. It was nearly November, and their room was cold, so he sat up in bed, put his finger to his lips as a sign to be quiet. After gesturing to the children to put their dressing gowns and slippers on, and after dressing himself, he took them to the huts communal area to sit by the stove. Jan gazed out through the condensation covered windows. The sky was dull, and the slate-blue clouds shrouded the dawn. Jan looked at his watch.

"It's 7:45 and time to get ready for breakfast," he said to the children, so after one last warm by the stove they returned to their room.

Ewa was sat on the edge of the bed. Jan and the children greeted her and told her it was time for breakfast.

"Hold on, everybody," Ewa said, "it's Sunday today so we'll be going to church, so no breakfast."

Jan was aghast. "But I thought that you did not believe in all that stuff," he said with a palpably disappointed tone in his voice.

"Listen," Ewa berated him, "my faith is the only thing I was able to bring with me from home. It's my one link with our families, who I hope will be praying for us now, as I'll be praying for them later. I've no interest in the politics and status hungry religion mongers who use it for personal betterment. I just simply have a religious faith which I keep close to my heart and soul and which I wish to pass on to the children, and you if you want."

Jan fell silent for a moment, "I understand what you're saying and if that is how it is going to be, then that is how it is going to be. If that is what God wants, then I'll stay hungry and miserable until one o'clock."

Ewa's eyes rolled back in her head. "You great big baby, you haven't changed one bit," she chastised as Jan rubbed his stomach in the throes of imagined hunger pains.

The room fell silent, not a peaceful one but an awkward one, as both Jan and Ewa realised at once that this was the first time she had referred to their past life.

The silence was broken by an embarrassed Ewa who announced, "Right, it is Monday tomorrow, so we need to enrol the children in the village school. Then we need to buy a wash basin plus a jug so that we can bring hot water to our room at night and in the mornings. I need to find work and we need to concentrate on getting out of this camp and into our own home."

For years, Jan had wandered aimlessly from the army to a prison camp, then to the allies' camp, followed by this refugee camp. Now, at last, his aimless journey was over as he had rediscovered someone who gave his life meaning, direction, and purpose. Ewa was a dynamic powerhouse of a woman with strong views, deeply held beliefs, and a pragmatic attitude to getting what she wanted. Jan counted himself a lucky man.

Later, as they walked down to church, Ewa spoke to Jan whilst the children played ahead of them.

"Listen, Jan," Ewa began, "I'm sorry about how I was yesterday. I was tired, weary of travelling, angry, confused, and nervous of meeting you. I wasn't sure if you would still like me, let alone love me. The war has made me hard. I'm no longer the fresh faced girl who had her whole life before her. In Siberia, I had to learn fast to survive. I never even take an empty tin can for granted. You can cook a hot meal in a tin can, a hot meal that may save your life. Then there were the children; I just did not know how you would react to the news and how confused you must have been."

"Ewa," Jan said quietly, "when I was a prisoner of war in Southern Germany, one winter night we had a heavy snowstorm, and as I walked to work at the cement works early in the morning, I looked up and saw a million stars and a bright moon shining down. As I walked, I saw a snowbank illuminated in the compound lights. I snapped a twig off a bush and wrote your name in the snow. That day the weather cleared, and a hard frost set in. When I returned home that evening your name was still there carved in sparkling frosty snow. Every day I would look forward to seeing your name as I passed by as it was like meeting you for a few moments every day.

"Then one day a thaw set in, and when I came home that night your name had melted away. It was like I had lost you all over again. That day I decided not to do that again as I could not bear the thought of losing you again.

"Listen," said Jan softly, "a wise man once told me that I would have to learn to love again."

Ewa took Jan's hand, "And do you think that you will be able to learn to love again?"

Jan squeezed Ewa's hand and said, "I have no need to learn to love again because I think that I have never stopped loving you."

"You are still the kindest, gentlest man I have ever met. I'm glad the war did not steal that from me too," Ewa said looking into Jan's eyes. "Together we'll be stronger and fight for our family's future and make a good life for us all."

Ewa stood on tippy-toes and kissed Jan on the cheek.

Jan stopped in his tracks, not sure how to respond, however, as he looked at Ewa's tiny figure staring up at him smiling, he instinctively wrapped his arms around her, hugging her tightly. "I'll never let anything or anyone hurt you or harm you again," Jan promised.

With that, the couple walked on to church in the dull, drizzly morning not minding one bit because after nine years they had found each other at last.

As they walked, they met up with Marta and the girls, who were also accompanied by Frau Swartz and Mrs Goldstein.

"We just couldn't leave Frau Swartz alone," Marta told Ewa, "we're afraid what she might do."

So, the whole throng entered the church, and the girls began to sit at the back.

"Not there," Ewa ordered, "up the front."

Marta whispered, "Ewa that is for the important people, we always sit at the back."

"Not anymore" said Ewa and the whole group de-camped to the front few pews.

The response among those already seated was one of shock. Major Bialy's wife turned around and, assuming her status within the congregation, pointed at Frau Swartz and said, "What's she doing here? She's a Lutheran."

"She is a recent convert," quipped Ewa, and the whole group began to snigger.

The church was filled with an audible communal gasp, so Mrs Bialy turned around to face the altar. The mass was an uneasy affair with a number of noses put out of joint by the interlopers, but no matter how poisonous the stares, Ewa stood her ground. As the Mass ended and the normal procession of the great and good from the camp were beginning to stand up, Ewa stood, genuflected, looked at Mrs Bialy and said, "See you next week."

And preceding the procession, the group walked out of the church.

As the group left the church and made their way back across the road to the camp, their mood was electric.

"I can't wait to tell Marek about this when he comes home from work," shrieked Marta.

The group made their way to the dinner hall and moved to their respective seats. This was a convention that even Ewa did not challenge as it did make practical sense. Today's dinner was a much happier affair for Jan as he and Ewa had become closer. Ewa seemed to have found her feet in the camp and made friends. The children were now talking to him, and he was adapting well to fatherhood and married life. He thought that if Ewa wanted to organise and plan their day-to-day living and also their future aspirations, he was happy to go along with that.

If the day ever came when he just could not agree, he would have to cross that bridge when he came to it. The only thing that had not changed since Saturday dinner was the shunning of the family by their fellow diners. In fact, since the church incident, it appeared to have gotten even more vitriolic. Ewa showed no sign of caring about this and carried on talking to Jan and her brood with indifference.

As the family returned to their room for a post-dinner rest, Jan, who was in awe of Ewa's devil-may-care attitude, decided to broach the subject. He took the safe route. at first, in case he should upset Ewa's newfound friendly disposition towards him.

"I've never bothered to fight against the establishment in this camp as I've just let it wash over me and ignored much of it, so why do you stand up to them so vehemently?"

"I could really do without causing all this trouble for us, but I'm driven by one thing. Ever since I was attached to the military and their wives and families, I've been judged by them. Despite their façade of Christian piousness, when they saw me alone with two babies they thought the worst. They thought that I was an unmarried mother or something much nastier. None of those religious bigots ever took the time to ask me if I needed any help during our long travels together through real hardship. I'll never understand how we had all suffered so much in the Siberian forests on our own and yet, as soon as we all came together during our escape, the old village mentality took over.

"What was even more annoying was the fact that when one of their children got sick, suddenly it was call for nurse Ewa. These were people who, like us, had lost everything, and yet their biggest worry was getting on to the camp committee or church committee. When I used to tell them that the old life was gone and we needed to adapt, I was told I was un-patriotic and that I should do everything I could to preserve the old ways.

"That is why I fight back, and that is why I want to get out of this place as fast as possible." Ewa's dander was now raised, so Jan backed off, however, he felt that he did understand her a little better.

Luckily for Jan, at that moment Marek came in, he knocked on their room door. He entered as requested and, wiping the cold drizzle from his steamed-up goggles, he began to speak.

"Hello all,, how are things going?" Marek asked in a cheerful tone, hoping for good news.

"Everything is fine, thank you, Marek," Ewa replied.

Marek then asked Jan if he would like a lift up to the downs to feed Lily the dog.

"Can we come too?" the children pleaded with Marek. "Not this time kids," Marek replied. "Me and your dad are going alone today because it is cold and wet, and I want to have a quiet chat with him."

Jan felt a shard of ice-cold fear run down his back. Was this it, had Marek found out about the baby, was he going to have to deal with this alone? He looked at Ewa for a gesture of support, but she in turn made the wrong kind of gesture and said she thought it was a grand idea. As they walked outside, Jan tried the flimsy excuse that he did not have a coat. But Marek reached into the sidecar and pulled out a brown coat.

"Hang on!" Jan exclaimed. "Isn't that the coat the pig was wearing?"

"Don't worry Jan," said Marek, "he won't need it now!"

With no support forthcoming from any side, Jan threw the coat over his shoulders in the manner of a cape, climbed into the sidecar, and sped off to his inevitable fate. He waved goodbye to Ewa and the children with a forlorn look on his face and disappeared into the drizzle, with his brown coat flapping in the wind in the manner of a superhero.

However, Jan did not feel much like a superhero as he was about to be faced by the hardest decision he had had to make for some time. He was sure Marek was going to ask for some advice about the situation with Marta, and even at this late stage, he did not know what he would say. Should he lie to his best friend, should he plead ignorance, should he tell him to follow his heart, Jan just did not know. The boys pulled up by the caravan and Lily was predictably happy to see them.

Jan picked out the bag of titbits for her and made a big fuss of the dog, which sadly smelt like a damp one. As Jan unlocked the caravan so the boys could keep dry, Marek took dry wood from under the van with which Jan lit a fire. As the fire crackled and spat the caravan became cosy and warm with Lily curled up in front of the stove to warm up and dry out. This did nothing to enhance the smell inside the caravan, so Jan opened a window a crack to allow fresh air in to offset the aroma of drying dog.

Suddenly, and without warning, Marek pulled a piece of hospital steak out of his coat pocket and threw it at Lily. Lily looked at the steak and then at Marek, as she was not sure if it was for her or had been dropped by mistake.

"Eat it, Lily it's for you because today we are celebrating." Thank goodness, thought Jan, he is taking it well and is happy with the situation, the problem is solved.

Marek then withdrew a small bottle of bimber from his inside coat pocket plus two shot glasses. My goodness thought Jan. He's pulling out all the stops, even if it's a bit early to wet the baby's head. Marek pulled closer to Jan, handed him a glass, and filled it to the brim.

"Jan, I want to talk to you about my situation with Marta." Jan took the measured approach and said, "yesss. . ."

"Well, over the last few weeks, I've seen signs that we're going to get closer."

"I know about the signs," said Jan.

"You do? That's great," said Marek dismissively and then continued. "Our future is heading for a more stable period.

We're getting serious in our relationship, and I've decided to make our relationship more secure for Marta."

Suddenly the clarity of the situation dissipated into the drizzle through the open window. "Relationship?" a puzzled Jan enquired of his friend.

"Yes!" Marek shouted. "I'm going to announce that Marta and I are to get married at the pub this Friday evening."

"Because . . . .?" Jan asked, expecting to hear news of the happy arrival.

"Because we love each other and want to spend the rest of our lives together," enthused Marek.

Jan knocked back the shot of bimber, and as he did so, he felt his head fill with cotton wool and his ears start to ring. Was this the bimber or the shocking news that was making the blood race around his brain? Marek, seeing Jan's empty glass, re-charged it and drank once more to a happy life with the one he loved. Jan was speechless. What should he say, what should he do? He took the cowards way out and decided he could not be so cruel as to destroy his friend's moment of happiness and so said nothing.

Jan scrabbled for a coherent sentence. He felt that at this time he needed to say something positive to Marek. "How does Marta feel about all this?" Jan spluttered, realising that he did not seem so celebratory.

"She'll be happy, of course!"

Jan took a deep breath. "Will be happy, you mean that you have not asked her yet?"

"No," enthused Marek, "I'm picking her up from work on Thursday and taking her to pick out an engagement ring," Marek crowed.

Jan was suffering from a verbal impairment that meant that he could only cry, "Wow. . . wow. . . wow. . ." over and over again.

"I knew you'd be happy for us," Marek declared in an

ecstatic voice fit to burst. Jan tried to gain a moment of composure and come up with something else rather than just 'wow'. "I can't wait to tell Ewa," Jan wheezed with a voice now numbed by bimber.

"Make sure she keeps it a secret, nobody else must know. I want it to be a surprise for Marta on Thursday."

"I think that I can guarantee that," said Jan.

As the light began to fade, the two inebriates decided it was time to pack up and return home for Sunday tea. Lily was turfed out of her toasty fireside spot and had to make do with the bed under the caravan. Jan closed the window, damped down the stove and locked the door. He threw the coat over his shoulders and took his place in the sidecar which, by now, had collected a puddle of water in its metal seat. Jan cried out in shock as the cold puddle worked its way through various layers of clothing and then made contact with his person.

"Get a move on. Marek," he called out, and so, Marek kicked the bike to life and the pair made a slow descent back to the camp. As the bike pulled up outside the family hut, Marek whispered, "remember to tell Ewa, not a word to anyone."

Jan nodded agreement, threw the wet coat in the sidecar, and went inside. As Jan entered the room, he was surprised to see that Ewa was not there. The children were alone and reading old worn out copies of the *Readers Digest*.

"Where's your mother?" Jan asked.

"She had to go over to Marta's room as they are having problems with Frau Swartz. Mother says that the frau is having a turn," announced Mary in a parody of a grown-up.

Jan instructed the children to stay in the room, to which they both gave him a look of disdain, as if they needed him to tell them what to do when they were already under orders from their mother. Jan ran across to the single women's hut and found Ewa speaking to Marek in the corridor.

"I've some rolling tobacco in my store at work, I'll see if I can swap it for some tablets." He spoke in haste, turned and ran out shouting, "I'll be about an hour."

Ewa watched Marek race off and her face turned from one of concern to one of sadness. "He's a lovely man," she said to Jan, "it's a pity that he's going to have such a hard time of it."

Jan took Ewa away from the door, out of earshot of the girls. "It's going to get a lot harder for him later in the week," Jan confided, and he tried to tell Ewa about the afternoons events. Ewa put her hands up to his face to stop him.

Ewa told Jan to stay out of the way, take the children for tea, and organise some food for the girls and her, as they would stay with Frau Swartz back at her room.

Jan went straight to the canteen, and after a short conversation with the cook in the kitchen, he managed to procure bread, pickles, garlic sausage, and some poppy seed cake. He rushed back to the girls' hut with the food, and then went to collect the children for tea. As the three sat and ate in silence, the attrition of the weekend seemed to have subsided, and several diners asked after Frau Swartz's condition. Jan was surprised at this welling up of bonhomie, and as he delivered her perilous situation to one old lady, he came to understand why.

"There, but for the grace of God, go I," she replied.

With Sunday tea over, Jan took the children back to their room and then over to the shower block to ready them for bed. He told them to read, while he sat on the bed and pondered this difficult situation in peace. He reasoned that on the evidence of that evening, Marek had a good heart, and although he was about to be badly hurt by Marta, Jan felt his good heart would win over and he and Marta would somehow survive this schism. Jan agreed with Ewa that Marta was helpless but wished she had been honest from the start with Marek. Jan, having put the problem to rest, picked up a *Readers Digest* and began to read.

At around seven, Ewa came back to the room and beckoned Jan to the stove area. Most of the hut's inhabitants were at mass, and so, this afforded them some privacy. Ewa began,

"I'm really worried about Frau Swartz. Marek was able to swap some tobacco for some medication which will last for a few days, but just as the tablets begin to take their full effect, they will run out."

Jan nodded in understanding but decided that he needed to tell Ewa about Marek's plans despite Ewa's obvious concern for Frau Swartz.

"Listen," he said quietly, "I know you are worried about Frau Swartz, but I have something I need to tell you. Marek does not know about Marta being pregnant as the big news today was that he plans to ask her to marry him on Thursday."

"Oh, my goodness" Ewa exclaimed in a muffled cry of exasperation, "what do we do now?"

"I really have no idea," Jan replied. "Do you know what, though, Marek is a good man at heart, and, I think, in time, he will come to terms with this problem and the relationship will survive."

"I hope you are right," Ewa sighed. "Come on, early night tonight, we have a busy day tomorrow."

"But it's only seven o'clock," Jan protested.

"Well, you go and sit on the steps in the drizzle, or stay here on your own, but I'm going to bed." Jan found it hard to argue with that kind of reasoning and went to their room. Monday had all the hallmarks of a late October day, damp, grey, and soulless. At the village school, it was decided that the children would start after Christmas. Mrs Irwin, the head teacher, would have to get confirmation from the County Education Committee, but due to her own perception that both children were 'bright', she did not think this would be a problem. A walk back to the camp for dinner through the drizzle meant that the children had to stay home with Jan.

Ewa went to town on the bus to buy all the things that she felt were required for civilised living. Jan had withdrawn some money from his post office account so that Ewa could browse and purchase at will.

The inclement weather meant that the trio at the camp were confined to barracks for now, so Jan asked the children about their past lives in foreign lands to fill the time.

"In India," Joseph volunteered, "they have a bird called a shite hawk!"

Mary cut Joseph off short. "Joseph, Mother said you must not use that word, the correct name is a kite."

Joseph apologised but seemed happy that he had been able to use the expletive just once more whilst out of his mother's controlling ear.

This posed a new problem for Jan, how was he to control the children? Was he to chastise them when they were naughty or was that going to be left to Ewa? In his mind, shite hawk was no big sin as he had heard much worse in the army. He would need to ask Ewa where the line should be drawn and who should draw it. For now, he contented himself with saying that the children should always obey their mother, and he moved on swiftly.

However, it was not long before the tables were turned, and it was Jan who became the subject of intense questioning.

Mary turned to Jan and asked, "Did you miss Mother while you were apart?" Jan was somewhat surprised by the directness of this line of inquisition but did his best to answer.

"Yes, I did every day, and worried that she was all right." At this point, Jan decided that things were getting a bit too serious for young minds, so he stopped talking about the years apart. "But now," he said in a mock excited voice, "I have her back and both of you too, so I am happy again."

Around six o'clock, Ewa burst into the room laden down with packages and bags. Among the booty were a wash basin and jug, an English dictionary, exercise books, pencils, crayons, colouring books, and a host of other things that she deemed necessary. She announced that on Thursday they would all be going into the town as there was a jumble sale at the corn exchange. She hoped that they would be able to buy winter coats for all of them in the sale, because as they had lived in hot countries this was one thing they lacked.

"Have you had a good time?" Jan asked politely when she clearly had.

"Oh, yes," Ewa enthused, "it's the first time that I've been on my own for so long. I had tea in a restaurant, wandered about, saw the town which was friendly, and the people were very polite to me in the shops."

Ewa's face was pink with excitement, as if the trip to town had been the tonic she needed, as she had come back infused with optimism and an even more positive attitude. Jan was pleased to see her so happy and avoided the Marek situation for the rest of the evening so as not to spoil her day.

CHAPTER 12

DARK DAYS

T hat evening, Jan was able to deliver hot water to the room for washing, and the family were able to luxuriate with floral soap, not the hard green stuff in the shower block. As the little family sat in their room after dinner, with the children colouring and Ewa mending socks, Jan felt a great sense of contentment.

Ewa took one of Joseph's shirts and inspected it. "This shirt collar has been frayed since South Africa, I might get one more year out of it," she sighed.

"Why don't we buy him some new ones in town on Thursday?" Jan suggested, in the spirit of, money is no object,

"Don't be silly," Ewa snapped, "we don't have money to burn. Maybe if you get a better job, we can loosen our belts then."

Jan fell silent. He took this comment personally and it hurt that Ewa felt that he was not doing enough to secure their future. Ewa, who despite her incisor sharp tongue, was aware of the frailty of men's ego's, retraced her steps in quick time and, in an effort to pacify Jan, whispered,

"Jan, I know you're working as hard as you can. Three days

ago, you did not even have a family to think of. I'm happy that we're settling in together nicely. We can't have everything at once, I know that."

"Yes," Mary shouted out, "and beggars can't be choosers."

"The whole family burst out laughing, and contentment returned to that small room in the lea of the Wiltshire downs.

Thursday came around quickly, and Jan could feel his holiday dissolve before his very eyes. That morning, the family caught the mid-morning bus into town and made straight for the corn exchange where the jumble sale was to be held. After queuing for half an hour, the doors were flung open and soon Ewa was trawling though mountains of clothes with a practiced eye. A penny here and a penny there soon saw a large amount of children's clothes filling a brown paper bag which Jan was in charge of. Ewa seemed to have a shopping list in her brain which she slowly worked through.

Eventually, winter coats were all that remained unticked. At the coat rail, there was a competitive crowd of like-minded women, all tugging at seams and inspecting linings for damage that could be used in the negotiation that was to follow. Ewa was not a large lady or very tall for that matter, but what she lacked in stature she made up for with smartness. While all the ladies crowded around one side of the coat rail wrestling with the coats and each other, Ewa simply stepped behind the rail with her back to the wall and simply picked the coats she wanted in sublime isolation. Such was the feeding frenzy around the rail, none of the other women had thought of this simple tactic. Happy with her purchases, Ewa gave Jan a nod of the head towards the exit, and they left the throng to fight over what was left and went for a cup of tea while they waited for the bus.

As they gazed through the café window at the market traders packing up their wares, in the distance, a familiar cloud of blue smoke began to rise above the stalls.

"Look!" Jan whispered to Ewa. "It's Marek and Marta and they are parked outside the jewellery shop." Ewa wiped the steamed-up window with her gloved hand so that they could get a better view in the fast-fading light. Both Jan and Ewa held their breath as they watched the drama unfold across the marketplace, both hoping for a happy outcome but both fearing the worst.

At first, the signs were promising as Marta was smiling and giggling, and Marek was the happiest Jan had ever seen him. Then, Marek gestured towards the shop window and the illuminated trays of rings shining in the displays. Suddenly the smile and the colour drained from Marta's face, and as this happened, Marek's smile dissolved into a look of bemusement. He was clearly confused by Marta's reaction to his exciting news. Then, Marta extended an arm and placed her hand on Marek's shoulder, speaking to him in a gentle manner, her lips moving slowly to convey this, the hardest of messages. Marek raised his hands up to his head; the furry cuffs of his motorbike gloves covered his face, hiding his reaction.

Jan was near to tears at this hopeless scene.

"Come on, we'd better pay and get over there," Jan urged.

"Wait!" Ewa begged Jan. "We need to see how this finishes before we charge in like a bull in a china shop."

As the pair continued to watch, they saw Marek turn away from Marta, his dejected head face down, he sat astride his bike, slammed his foot on the kick-start which produced copious amounts of blue smoke, revved up his bike in anger he raced off alone. Marta was left in tears on the pavement, the blue smoke and her pale face lit only by the jewellery shop's glittering, sparkling displays.

"Quick!" Ewa commanded. "Jan pay the bill, and bring the children along in a minute. I must go to Marta before she leaves."

Ewa ran off across the square to console Marta while Jan

took care of the bill, collected up the shopping, and the children, and struggled across to the jewellery shop where he found Marta sobbing uncontrollably on Ewa's shoulder.

As Marta hid her face on Ewa's shoulder, the sombre group made their way to the bus stop and waited. In time, the bus appeared and as Ewa led Marta to the rear out of sight of prying eyes. Jan paid and started to make his way to the rear of the bus which, by now, was lurching forwards and backwards in the traffic. With no hands free to grip the handles provided, it was a perilous journey, however, he eventually slumped into a seat with the children. The children drew stick men on the misted-up bus windows to pass the time during the slow journey home. Once at the camp, Ewa took Marta straight to her hut while Jan took the children and packages to their room. As dinnertime approached, Jan decided that he would stay clear of the girls and concentrate on getting the children fed. He felt that at this time of heightened emotional stress the last thing Marta needed was another man standing dumb and helpless in the corner of the room.

After dinner, Jan took the children's damp coats and placed them on chairs around the stove with a myriad of other steaming over garments. Jan put the children to bed and sat on his bunk thinking about what was happening, and how to help his friends. Eventually, Ewa crept back into the room. Jan slipped out and returned with a bowl of hot soup that he had been keeping warm on the stove.

"Oh lovely" Ewa exclaimed thankfully.

"How's she doing?" asked Jan.

"She's full of remorse and so unhappy. At one point she said that there was nothing for her here now," Ewa said despondently.

"Look," Ewa said, "the girls are with Marta, but Frau Swartz is still playing up and Marta is in no state to help her, so I'll spend the night with the frau and check in on Marta once in a while, is that OK?"

"Of course it is. I'll see you in the morning, and hopefully by then we'll have a clearer picture of how the land lies."

With that, Ewa grabbed her sewing box and a bag of jumble and left the room. Jan felt the strongest of urges to kiss her goodbye and wish her a goodnight, but he settled with a squeeze of her shoulder, just in case she thought he was getting too forward.

Jan sat back on his bunk and began to think about this rollercoaster of a week. On Saturday, he had had the problematic arrival of Ewa to deal with. Luckily, when she had settled in and taken the time to explain her own feelings to Jan, the pair had found some middle ground on which to grow their new lives together. But now his best friend, whom only a few days earlier was ecstatically looking forward to a future with the one he loved, found his life in tatters. It was beyond Jan's comprehension to understand how these events could have unfolded and then unravelled so quickly in the space of a few days.

Sleep evaded him until the early hours of the morning, and as he was about to drop off, he heard the familiar sound of Marek's motorbike burble into life and quietly fade slowly away up the lane. It was at this point that he realised he had deserted his best friend in his hour of need, and the subsequent guilt of this meant that he would not sleep for the rest of that night. Jan knew that there was not much he could say to Marta to make her feel better and he was secretly relieved that Ewa had taken on that role.

However, he thought he could try and speak to Marek and maybe help to lessen the pain. Hopefully, help him see through the bad things and find a way to rebuild his relationship with Marta. He decided that he would meet him after his return from the early shift and have a heart to heart with him.

At seven, Ewa returned to the room and lay on the bed for

a short while and spoke quietly about her night with Marta. It did not make easy listening.

"So, how is she?" Jan asked, knowing from the look on Ewa's face that, she too, had had a sleepless night.

"Well, she's confused, upset, disappointed, afraid, and also sorry that she lied to Marek. She told me that in the beginning, she'd made a hard business decision to be with Marek as her best chance, and that she would tell him the baby was his. But then she got to know him. He was kind, gentle, and funny, and he'd such respect for her that he would not countenance any kind of physical relationship. As she grew fonder of him, it became harder to tell him the truth because she was afraid of losing him. Now she doesn't know what to do. She sees no future for her here, unless Marek calms down and takes her back."

"Let me speak to him when he comes home from work. Maybe I can make him see reason, now I know how Marta feels."

"That would be nice if you could. If we cannot get them back together there's no telling what Marta will do." With this decided, they woke the children. Jan fetched the hot water for their wash and then the family went to a late breakfast.

At around two thirty, Jan began to hang around the camp gate. He held a bag of scraps in his hand for Lily. Eventually Marek approached the gate, his trafficator arm extended at ninety degrees to the horizontal. Jan waved him down by waving Lily's doggy bag. Marek recognised this sign, spun his bike round, and stopped to let Jan step into the sidecar. Jan couldn't see Marek's face due to his scarf and goggles, but the absence of a wave or any other friendly body language confirmed Jan's worst fears as to Marek's disposition.

The noise of the motorbike made it almost impossible to

speak, so it was not until the friends reached the downs and a happy Lily that they had the chance to communicate. As Jan lit the stove in the caravan, Marek opened up.

"Well, I'm sure that you've heard the news?" Marek murmured in a despondent tone.

"Yes I have. In fact, we met Marta at the bus stop in town and she told us. She was very distressed." Jan was careful not to mention any prior knowledge of events so as not to complicate things with his friend.

Jan opened his tactical defence of Marta. "Ewa has been talking to Marta and, she tells me that Marta's very upset that she lied to you and would do anything to make things right between you." Jan waited for Marek's response, knowing this would set the tone for the rest of their chat. However, no response was forthcoming as Marek just sat in the caravan, rubbing Lily's ears and making a fuss of the grateful dog.

Jan attempted to tease some kind of answer from his friend. "How do you feel about that?" Jan asked Marek quietly as if he was afraid of the answer he might get. Marek just shrugged his shoulders, which only conveyed the sense of hopelessness and turmoil that had overtaken his mind and his ability to think logically. Jan knew that he would have to think again if he was going to reach into his friend's sorrowful soul to try to help him.

As the dim October light faded and the two friends sat in the caravan bathed in the orange glow of the fire, Jan decided that he had nothing to lose and made a more direct approach.

"Look," Jan said in a voice that seemed deafening in the silent caravan, "would it help if we all met in our room tonight to discuss things over a cup of tea?"

The crestfallen Marek looked at Jan, then at the floor, and mumbled, "How could I believe anything she says to me now?"

It appeared that his more direct approach was working, so Jan pressed on.

"You must believe me; Marta's very sorry. She didn't mean to lie to you but as the two of you grew together, she found it harder to find a way to tell you the truth."

Marek took a deep breath and seemed to answer in an extended sigh.

"No, I need time to think what to do next. Should I move away, try to rebuild my life with Marta, or just stay at the camp and get on with life without her?"

Jan patted his friend on the shoulder to show that he understood. This reassurance seemed to make Marek open up somewhat.

"You see, I would've done anything for Marta as I was planning to build my world around her. I would've tried to give her everything that she ever wanted. I was prepared to make any sacrifice just to make her happy, so why can't I sacrifice my pride to do the same? This is my quandary, and I need time to sort this problem out in my mind before I make any attempt to speak about it to Marta."

The pair sat in silence, and as the crackling of the stove grew quieter, it signalled the end of their chat and a return to the camp and reality.

As the boys turned into the camp, they were greeted by the familiar sight of Frau Swartz railing at Mr Monk outside his office door. With Marta confining herself to her room and Kinga and Kasia attending to her, the frau was left unattended and unsubdued. In the cold damp evening air, Frau Swartz's hot breath, picked out by the office light, was an effusive indication of the frau's vitriolic verbal attack on Monk.

Jan indicated to Marek to stop by the office. Although Jan did not want to, he felt that he'd have to be the one to try to calm Frau Swartz down and get her back to her room. Marek, stopped dropped off his passenger, and with a cursory wave, went to store his bike and lick his wounds on his bed in peace. Jan advanced towards Mr Monk and the combatant frau. Monk, seeing that Jan was about to speak, raised his hand to stop him.

"It's all right Mr Kot, I'm used to this, just let the woman have her say and she will leave in time."

So, Jan stood back behind Frau Swartz, just to her left side, and listened to her ranting, ready to subdue her if she became violent towards Monk. What Jan heard left him feeling the deepest sympathy for this forlorn and forgotten lady who had been left alone to deal with trauma that would make most people buckle under its weight. In a camp which was full of sad tales and tragic memories, this had to have been one of the saddest Jan had ever heard.

Much of what was shouted, Jan had already heard at other episodes of her regular ranting, but this time without any restraint. Frau Swartz was able to replay her terrible story in chronological order, retracing her journey across Europe to this cold, damp doorway in Wiltshire.

It turned out that her family were of the German upper class.

"My father was a doctor and my mother a civil servant in Berlin., the frau screamed. "I'm a woman of such standing and I'm forced to work in a stinking flax factory when there are other jobs that I could easily do."

"Frau, you've signed a contract, and nobody has forced you to sign it and come to England."

However, what followed did tug at Jan's heartstrings and made him realise that the Frau was depressed with good reason.

"I'd a happy life in Breslau, with my husband and son. I went to cocktail parties, theatre visits, summer holidays on the Baltic coast, and winter holidays at my sisters in Austria."

The frau lamented that all of this was now gone, wiped away by the war, leaving her homeless and alone in an alien country, hated because of her race and loathed by even the lowest of the low.

Jan continued to listen as the wretched woman recounted her final days of the war. She spoke, through her sobs, with a German accent that, even in her broken English betrayed her upper-class credentials.

"My husband was lost on the Russian front," she started. "We had all heard that the Soviets were worse than animals, so as they began to advance towards us, I decided to take my son and head for my sister's in Austria, as I'd heard the Americans were there. I took my son's old pram from the garage and packed it with what little food we had, some medical supplies and as many clothes as I could along with towels and blankets. It was February and very cold. We all knew the war was nearly over and I thought that if I could head west I could escape the Soviets and keep my son safe."

After another fit of uncontrollable sobbing, Frau Swartz wiped her eyes with a lace hanky which was tightly gripped in her hand, breathed in a long gulp of air, and continued.

"It was cold, and my son was wearing as many clothes as he could. We had to walk for days, and I joined a column of others fleeing and trudged along in a smelly line of the lost and homeless. At last, we reached Dresden where, on the out-skirts, we found a soup kitchen. It was the first hot food we had found for days."

At this point the distraught storyteller stopped and stared into the light through the office door. It was as if she was unsure if she had the strength to go on, knowing what pain-ful memories lay in wait if she continued. However, somehow she summoned up the strength, took another deep breath and faced her demons.

"At the soup kitchen some black marketers overpowered me and stole my pram with all my possessions in and ran off. No matter how much I shouted, nobody helped me, nobody even looked up from their soup. I clung to my son and hugged him. It was for him that I remained strong."

Monk stood fidgeting uncomfortably in his office doorway, looking at his pocket watch from time to time. Undeterred, Frau Swartz found the inner strength to carry on.

"I'd been warned that it was not safe on the roads at night, so I made my way into Dresden before dark and found a church hall to sleep in. That night, the air raid siren sounded, and we were shown to a shelter where we were told we would be safe. It stank of sweat and human waste, but I knew that we'd, at least, be safe. Later, we suffered a power cut, and the ventilation fans stopped. It soon became unbearable, but it seemed that the air raid had finished so I took my son back up onto the streets. Everywhere was fire, heat, and smoke, even the bricks were glowing in some places. I headed with a group of others who knew the way to the River Elbe.

"As we ran one by one, they gasped, as if the air had been sucked from their lungs and then they dropped down dead. My son and I were protected from the heat by the layers of clothing we were wearing for a while, but soon the heat grew too much, and a scorching wind held us back. At last, I saw the river and thought that we would be safe. I covered my son inside my coat and held his hands with mine. As the firestorm grew stronger, I had to lean into the wind to keep moving forward towards the steps to the river.

"Suddenly, I lost grip of my son's hand, and his small body was sucked from under my coat and swept away into a side street which was an inferno. There was no scream, no cry. In a second, he was consumed, and I lost sight of him. My only reason to live was taken from me. At that moment, a number of buildings collapsed, and the dust cloud momentarily stifled the flames. In a second, I was down the steps and out of the worst heat but struggling to breathe. I lay down hoping to die, but I was cursed to live, and this is my punishment for letting my son die. What can I do, what can I do?"

Monk took one last look at his pocket watch and then spoke.

"My wife and I also lost a son in the flames of Dresden on that night. We thought he was safe and that his war was over too, but it was not to be. I suggest that you do the same as his mother and I have had to do and learn to live with it. Now I will bid you a good evening, Frau Swartz."

With that, the cold-hearted Monk shut the office door on her. The poor woman fell to her knees screaming and pounding the gravel road with her fists. Jan leapt into action and bent down to pick her up off the ground. He braced himself to counterbalance her weight, but there was no weight. Frau Swartz was like a sparrow. Jan could feel her angular bones through her gabardine coat, so he helped her back to her room where Kinga and Kasia took over. Jan, in the manner of a country doctor, prescribed soup and lots of it and left the girls to tend to his patient.

Jan returned to his family room and sat on the bed.

"How did the meeting with Marek go?"

"Wait one moment, I just have to calm down a bit, I am so angry."

Ewa sent the children out to the stove area to draw so that Jan could speak plainly and not in riddles. "Oh, my goodness, what happened," a concerned Ewa asked, "Is Marek OK?"

Jan then recounted the evening's events to Ewa and the two sat in disbelief.

"I've only been here six days, and I have to say that I find Monk to be distant and aloof," Ewa said.

"I agree, Monk's attitude might be connected to his own family tragedy. Do you know what, I've never seen his wife, although I know she's here because the cleaner's told us that she's around the place."

Although concerned, Ewa was more interested in Marek's plight at this time than Monks, so she pushed Jan to tell her how their chat had gone. Jan gave her a rundown of their conversation and concluded that Marek needed time to come to terms with things, but that he felt he would eventually calm down and come around. With that said, they gathered their small family and headed for the canteen. Neither Marek nor Marta attended dinner, and it was left to the girls to cater for Frau Swartz and Marta and Jan take sustenance to Marek.

As Jan and Ewa lay on their respective beds after dinner, Ewa pointed out that the next day was Saturday October the 31st and that the next day was All Saints Day.

"Shall we go to the remembrance service in the morning at the church?" Ewa asked, sure of a negative response.

"We can't visit our own family's graves, but at least we can say a prayer and try to remember them here."

"I don't see why not," Jan acquiesced in his new found spirit of family friendly decision-making.

"Maybe Marek would like to come?" Ewa probed.

"No, I don't think so. It's his day off, but I think he'll spend it on his bed thinking deep thoughts."

"Ah yes, of course."

Jan had been avoiding this question all week, but decided that now, as they were on the subject, he would enquire about their respective families in Poland and what Ewa knew. He decided to tread carefully, not wanting to reignite the firecracker that was the Ewa of six days ago.

"I've tried to find out about our families in Poland, but without success," Jan tiptoed.

"Me too," was Ewa's blunt reply but Jan had been hoping for more. Then Jan had an idea.

"I know that Major Bialy still has contacts with Poland. He owes me a favour, so I'll ask him tomorrow if he can help." Ewa thought that this was a good first step, and the two agreed that after the mass Jan would approach the major privately.

Saturday morning was cold and cloudy with squally

showers of cold rain sweeping across the camp. Jan looked out of the steamed-up window and wiped away the condensation with his bare hand.

"Don't do that!" Ewa chastised. "It'll smear the window and I'll have to clean it again."

"Crikey" lamented Jan, "it's not even eight o'clock yet and I have been told off, and I can't have breakfast!"

"Why can't you have breakfast?" Ewa quizzed Jan.

"Church?"

"It's not that sort of mass. We won't be having communion today."

Jan cheered in playful mood and sang, "We can have some breakfast, we can have some breakfast" to the children, both of whom rolled their eyes back into their heads in embarrassment.

"That's enough," Ewa commanded, "Jan, you go for hot water, and you two make your beds." Ewa snapped her orders expecting no dissenters.

Clean and dressed for church, the family went for the late breakfast but there was still no sign of Marek, Marta, or Frau Swartz.

"I'll take Marta some breakfast after ours," Ewa whispered to Jan.

"Marek can get his own," hissed Jan, "the lazy bugger should be up by now."

"Jan Kot, I don't want you to use that kind of language in front of the children, or worse still just before church," Ewa scolded.

With breakfast over, Jan took the children back to the hut to wait for church, while Ewa took a plate of food to Marta. At the single women's hut, all was quiet. Frau Swartz's room door was closed and, so as not to wake her, Ewa crept past silently.

Kinga and Kasia were at work and their doors were ajar, displaying two crisply made single beds with the faintest whiff of Californian Poppy perfume wafting from within. Ewa arrived at Marta's room, tapped on the closed door, and entered. To her surprise, Marta was not there, and all that was there was a suitcase on the bed. Ewa placed the food on the side table and moved the suitcase, it seemed full. Ewa felt guilty but stilled herself and opened the case. It was packed with all of Marta's meagre belongings, folded and pressed as if Marta was planning a trip.

Ewa picked up the plate and returned to the room to tell Jan.

"Perhaps she's gone to work this morning after all," suggested Jan.

"Not in her state. She wouldn't have gone to that stinking flax factory," Ewa reasoned.

"Well, maybe she's gone to look for lodgings and has packed her case ready to go for when she finds somewhere," Jan supposed. Ewa was not convinced by this explanation either but thought it was a possibility.

At ten o'clock the family set off for the memorial mass at the camp church. Ewa took the rear most pew and ushered her family into it. Jan gave her a surprised look.

"I just can't be bothered today," she said, and they all sat down.

The mass began, and as a certain equilibrium had returned to the congregation, it appeared to be passing without incident. However, later on, Jan became aware of a hissing sound coming from the door. He looked around and there, peering through the partially opened door was Chastity. Jan put his finger up to his lips as a sign to Ewa to keep quiet, as she had also heard the hissing, and he sidled out of his pew and stepped out into the cold, tin porch of the church.

"Jan, we must find Marek as soon as possible, something

fearful has happened, I've checked but he is not in his room."

"What is it?" Jan asked urgently.

"Sid came to me a few moments ago to tell me that two policemen had asked to borrow a ladder from the farm. When Sid asked them why they needed a ladder, they told him it was to cut a young woman's body down from a tree in our woods. They said that she was a young blonde woman in a red coat!"

Jan gasped; his shock was palpable, and he stuttered as he tried to explain where Marek might be. He decided that he could not let his friend face this tragic event alone and told Chastity that he would find Marek.

"I'm sorry to trouble you, but I only know one woman who is blonde and owns a red coat," Chastity said close to tears.

"You get back to the farm and I will find Marek. His bike is there, so he won't be far away," Jan stuttered, still unable to comprehend the devastating news that had been delivered.

While Chastity drove off at speed, Jan ran as fast as he could to the single men's hut. He kicked open the door and, finding Marek's bed empty, swivelled round to find someone who might know of his friends whereabouts. Jan fixed his eye on one of the young men reading a Polish language paper, and pointing at the empty bed he bellowed,

"Where is he!"

"Shower," replied the shocked young man.

Jan was gone as soon as he heard the word uttered. He ran to the shower block to find his friend, but as he arrived at the block Marek appeared through the door on his way back to his hut.

"For God's sake, get your coat and come with me. We need to get your bike started and get down to the farm woods now!"

As Jan was speaking, he knew that in a minute he was going to have to break the devastating news to his friend that his girlfriend was dead.

Jan felt sick with nerves. He was close to tears as Marek came back to the motorbike in his heavy waterproof coat.

"So, what's the hurry?" Marek asked.

Jan swallowed hard, but no words would come out. He swallowed again and this time the words did not fail him.

"Marek, Chastity's just told me that a young woman has been found hanging in the woods."

"That's terrible, but what do you want me to do?"

"Marek, the young woman is blonde and wearing a red coat!"

"Oh my God!" Marek screamed like a man demented. He threw the cover off his bike and kicked it to life. "Come on, come on!" Marek shouted at Jan. Jan jumped into the sidecar and the boys sped from the camp as fast as they could go.

In what seemed like just a moment, they had arrived at the woods. Marek was off of the bike and had vaulted the stile before Jan could even get out of the sidecar.

"Marek, wait, wait!" Jan called after his friend, but there was no stopping him. Marek was screaming like a wounded animal.

"This is all my fault, all my stupid pride. I have killed the only woman that I have ever really loved for my petty pride!"

At last, Jan caught up with Marek, as he could not run as fast in his cumbersome biking coat. Jan grabbed the coat and managed to get an arm around his friend pulling him backwards.

"Let me go, let me go!" Marek screamed. "This is my fault, I've caused this."

"No, no, it's not your fault," Jan tried to reason with Marek but there was no helping him. Marek threw off his heavy coat and the two friends sprinted through the leafless, dead woodland, slipping on the rotting leaves and vaulting over the first fallen boughs of winter. Then, there in the distance, they saw a small group of policemen stood by an ancient yew tree, its dark canopy seemed to suck the grey daylight out of the wood.

The policemen worked in reverential silence under its dark shadow. One was positioning the ladder, another was drawing a rough map of the scene and a third, the local sergeant stood helplessly looking up into the tree.

As the boys neared the tree, the full horror of the sight that awaited them became all too apparent. There, hanging in the tree was the body of a young blonde woman, her head was obliquely placed looking back over her right shoulder. It was as if she was looking back at a past that could no longer hurt her anymore. It seemed as though, in that tree, she had found some-place where pain could not reach her ever again. Her blonde hair covered her face and fell down over her red woollen coat. There she hung like the last apple of summer, the reddest, sweetest, glossiest fruit shining in the dark tree. She was just waiting to be relieved of her burden and to fall to the ground where she would return to the cold winter earth.

Marek fell to his knees and wailed uncontrollably. "My God, my God, this is all me. I did not deserve you and now you have left me for-ever." His head buried in his cupped hands so as not to see the full horror caused by his stupid, conceited pride.

Jan placed his hand on his friend's shoulder to steady him. "You mustn't think like that, you cannot blame yourself, nobody could have guessed that things would end this way."

Marek crawled on his hands and knees closer to the tree, a pitiful soul in an act of contrition.

"Excuse me, sir, please keep your distance for now," the sergeant requested of Jan, fully aware that Marek would not hear him in his grief.

Jan had to bodily drag Marek back from the tree, and holding him down on the muddy woodland floor, he restrained him with all his strength.

"Let me go to her," Marek begged Jan, "let me stay with

her and keep her safe and warm. She cannot stay here alone in these cold lonely woods; I must stay and protect her."

This was the final straw for Jan, who found this pitiful sight too much to endure. The tears that he had been holding back for so long poured down his cheeks.

"It's no good Marek," Jan sobbed, "she's gone, you can no longer help her, Marta has left us."

At this moment, the sergeant slowly made his way over to the two distraught men. "Will one of you gentlemen be able to identify the deceased?" he asked in hushed tones.

One of the constables then climbed the ladder and drew his pen knife. He slowly began to slice at the flax webbing that suspended its delicate burden.

"Steady now, boy," the sergeant urged.

When it seemed appropriate, the sergeant and the constable took the weight of their fragile charge, and then with one last cut, she was released and gently lowered to the ground. The body was covered in a blanket to preserve her modesty, and the younger constable approached Jan. "Are you ready to identify the corpse sir?"

The Ssrgeant raged at the constable, "The deceased, you idiot, the deceased."

The constable turned to Jan and apologised. "I'm sorry sir, I did mean the deceased." Jan waved a dismissive hand and went to move forward. Marek held Jan's leg to stop him.

"I must do it, not you. She was my girlfriend, and I was the only person that she really trusted, I must do this one last thing for her," Marek said quietly.

Jan stepped back, nodded that he understood, and beckoned his friend to move forward.

"Now, in your own time, sir, can you tell us who this young lady is?" the sergeant asked gently.

Marek crawled forward, gently brushing some dead leaves off the blanket as he knew Marta would not have liked them there. Then he delicately tucked the blanket around her neck, as if to keep her warm, and gently stroked her long golden hair just one last time.

"Sir?" the sergeant gently urged.

Marek slowly pulled Marta's golden hair from her face, and as he did so, he began to shake uncontrollably, crying in a guttural way that made his whole body shake like a man in a frenzy.

"Sir, can you formally identify this young lady please?" the sergeant pressed.

"Yes," replied Marek, "her name is Frau Swartz."

Jan dropped to his knees as if in prayer in a mixture of shock and relief. The two men clung to each other and cried as they embraced. Both men sobbed without a care for who saw them as tears rolled down their cheeks. Jan slowly bent forward and, truly, it was Frau Swartz.

Her face had lost its care-worn lines and she looked as if she was a teenage girl again. At last, she had found peace, and would now be happy with her son and husband, thought Jan. Maybe she was looking down on this desperate scene from above, and Jan was pleased that if she was, she knew that he and Marek had been able to add a small measure of dignity to her final journey on earth.

As Marek and Jan composed themselves after the shock of the last few moments, Jan realised that at that point, Marta must be somewhere in the area deciding what to do next.

"Marek, you must go at once and find Marta. You can't let her slip from your grasp again. This tragedy means that Frau Swartz is again with the ones she loves. Make sure that the same happens for you and then her death will have had some small meaning."

"But we must stay with Frau Swartz, we can't leave her here alone in the woods," Marek pressed Jan.

"Don't worry sir," said the sergeant, "we'll stay with the

deceased. You run along and find your young lady. We'll call at the camp later with some paperwork to fill in, but that's enough for now."

Marek and Jan both stood up and, facing the frail frame of Frau Swartz, made the sign of the cross respectfully, turned and slowly walked away.

Now the race was on to find Marta before she did something that would put her in harm's way. The two friends left the shadows of the wood and Marek drove his bike back to the camp with the same urgency as the outward journey. As the boys arrived at the camp gate, the town bus arrived, and the Saturday morning workers got off to return to the camp. There, crossing the road arm in arm with Kasia and Kinga was a stony-aced Marta. Marek pulled up in the middle of the road, stood in the saddle of his bike, and screamed, "Marta! Marta!"

She acted with indifference and continued into the camp.

"Go, go," shouted Jan to Marek, which he did with some urgency but not on the bike.

Marek dismounted and ran after the three girls into the camp. This left Jan sat in the sidecar, blocking the lane and stopping the bus from moving. Jan hurriedly struggled out of the sidecar and pushed the bike into the camp to allow the bus to continue on its way.

CHAPTER 13
TOGETHER AGAIN

A s Jan pushed with all his might, he was able to get the bike onto the grass verge outside Monk's office. Mr Monk came out to see what all the fuss was about and saw Jan wrestling the handlebars of the bike.

"Oh dear, problems?" Monk enquired of Jan.

"Not with the bike, but I need to tell you that Frau Swartz has been found hanging in the woods up the road this morning."

"That is a great pity," Monk said sadly. "I suppose that means that I'll be filling in forms all afternoon and will have to cancel mine and Mrs Monk's trip into town today."

Jan was seething with anger at this last comment. After the previous emotionally exhausting couple of hours, he had had enough of sitting on the fence and decided to speak out.

"Mr Monk, is your pity directed at Frau Swartz or at your loss of a day out with your wife?"

"The latter obviously," Monk replied. "I would not shed one tear for Frau Swartz or any of her kind. Her war-mongering race has been responsible for the death of millions of people and the destruction of much of Europe. I find it strange that you, of all people, should feel sorrow at the passing of a single German woman. You are a victim of that woman's former government, a government that she surely voted for. How can you feel any pity? Good riddance I say!"

Jan exploded. "Yes, I'm a victim, but she was too. When you are alone in a foreign country and after suffering so much for so long, there should be a tendency to help your fellow man. That help is part of human nature because you are both sharing adversity that was not caused by you or anybody around you. With that fraternity of care, we can all heal and begin to live our lives again as normally as possible. It seems to me, Mr Monk, that your son wasn't the only person who died that night in Dresden. I think you died too as your heart has been left empty of feeling or compassion."

Jan spun round and marched away from the office still fuming. Monk withdrew to his office in silence and closed the door. Such was Jan's rage that he forgot that Marek's motorbike was abandoned on the grass outside the office. He made his way straight to Ewa to let her know what had happened and to try and find out about the results of Marek's attempt to rekindle his relationship with Marta.

As Jan neared the family's hut, Ewa emerged with the children on their way to lunch. He ran up to them and started to speak. Ewa could see from Jan's concerned look that he had bad news, so before he could say a word, Ewa put her finger up to her lips to stop Jan speaking and then told the children to run on ahead.

"These little ones have heard and seen enough for a lifetime," Ewa whispered, "I don't really want them to hear any more. So, what was all the excitement about that you had to rush off with a female stranger before church had finished?" Ewa asked feigning intrigue.

Jan stopped walking steeling himself to deliver Ewa the bad news.

"Ewa, Frau Swartz is dead. She has hung herself in the woods by the farm. That woman you saw is the farmer's daughter. But the strangest thing was that Frau Swartz was wearing Marta's red coat, and so, we all thought it was Marta in the woods. Marek was going crazy to think that he had caused her death, but when we found out it was the frau, his only thought was to find Marta. The last I saw of him he was running after her in the camp."

"Right," said Ewa taking control. "You take the children to dinner, and I'll find out what is going on. Marta shouldn't have too much stress in her condition, so I'd better check in on her." Jan did Ewa's bidding, as his wife made off for the single women's hut.

On arrival, Ewa knocked on the door and a quiet voice said "Come in." On entry, Ewa was met by a sea of faces all looking to see who was coming in. Marek had his arm around Marta's shoulder, Kinga and Kasia were sat on the bed administering moral support, and Marta was sat pale and gaunt, her red eyes wet with tears.

"How are you feeling?" Ewa asked in her usual bedside manner.

In Ewa's case this 'manner' was a thinly veiled signal for everyone else to leave.

"I'll be back later to see you," said Marek, "when you've rested."

"And we'll be back after dinner," the girls assured their friend.

"Can I just check you over a minute?" Ewa asked of Marta. "In your condition you shouldn't get too upset, it's not good for you or the baby."

She did the normal check of Marta's pulse and questioned her about any strange feelings or pains. Ewa then laid Marta on the bed, raised her feet on some pillows then sat down and asked Marta to tell her if she could what had happened.

Marta began, "Yesterday evening, after Jan had left the frau with the girls, I had gone in to sit with her to calm her down. A girl at work had offered me a room in her mother's house to rent so that I could escape the camp and the gaze of the Ministry of Labour. I packed all my belongings ready for the move. I decided not to take the red coat as it would be a constant reminder of Marek and the life that had eluded me. So that it would not go to waste, I gave the coat to Frau Swartz to help keep her warm in the coming winter months.

"As I handed over the coat, she broke down once more and told me that this was the first act of kindness shown to her since her arrival in Britain. Frau Swartz put the coat on and snuggled up with the collar around her neck. It was the first time that I had seen her smile, and in this way, I hoped that the coat would keep someone else happy.

"The next day, I rose and took the early breakfast and went to work. After work I went to my workmate's house to see the room. When my friend's mother realised that I was pregnant, she wouldn't have anything to do with the bargain and refused to rent the room to me. So, I had to return to the camp to work out my next move. I realised that I was fast running out of options,"

"Can I ask you about the father of your baby?"

"As soon as I realised that I was pregnant, I told my boyfriend. He became very angry and within a couple of days had disappeared and had managed to get posted to some airfield abroad. With no one to help me, I went to my employer, his parents. On breaking the news to his mother, she dismissed me and insulted me by suggesting that 'with a girl like me, it could be the child of any number of men'. I was paid off, sent away, rejected by the father who, by then, was abroad and keeping out of the way. Alone with my problem, I got a job at the flax factory before anyone could tell I was pregnant, and the rest you know."

Ewa now began to move carefully. "How are things with you and Marek now?"

Marta smiled,."He's full of remorse, full of plans, and has told me we'll leave the camp soon and rent our own cottage nearer to our work. I'll leave work and he'll take care of me."

"That sounds wonderful, but what about the Ministry?"

"Marek has told me to let him worry about that, so I am," Marta confided, knowing full well that whatever it was it would most likely be illegal.

"Well, it sounds like things are sorting themselves out for the best now so that is good news. I'll leave you to rest and you can receive your guests."

Ewa quietly closed the door, and as she passed Frau Swartz's room, she paused, placed her hand tenderly on the door, and then returned to her family.

When Ewa got back to their room, the children were having an after-dinner rest and Jan was sat with his head in his hands pushing his finger through his hair repeatedly.

"Are you ok?" Ewa asked.

"Well, I'm just a bit confused really. I have been here since March and I thought that I had found paradise, somewhere that we could raise a family happily and safely. Now in the last two weeks, there has been a murder and now a suicide. it's as if the hatred of the last war has followed me here and I just cannot escape it, it just follows me."

"Jan, there'll always be hate, there'll always be sadness and in a few years when we are all living a better life there'll still be disappointment, hate, and grief to deal with. What is important is that we face those trials together."

With that said Ewa, kissed Jan on his forehead and put her arm around his shoulder and gave him a big, warming hug.

As the two sat on the bottom bunk, Ewa suddenly became aware of the smell of cooked food.

"That is so sweet of you, have you brought me some dinner again?"

"No, actually, that smell is the bag of scraps I have brought Lily for her dinner," Jan said guiltily.

With that, Ewa jumped up cuffed Jan around the head playfully and chastised him saying, "Well you'd better go and feed your girlfriend before it gets dark then, hadn't you."

She slumped onto her bed, and indicating to the door, said, "Go on, off you go."

Jan left at a pace while he was still in Ewa's good books. As he went to unchain his bike, he saw Marek reclaiming his motorbike and walked over.

"I'm sorry that I left it there, but there was a lot going on and I didn't know where the key was."

"I'm sorry I left you sat in it in the middle of the road when I ran off, and I'm also sorry that I didn't tell you there is no key."

The boys both laughed out loud.

"Listen, why don't I take you up the hill to feed Lily and I can teach you how to start and ride the bike?"

"OK!" said an excited Jan and the two mounted the bike.

"All you do is switch on the ignition, as it's cold put the choke on, advance the throttle, make sure the clutch is disengaged, give it some throttle and kick it over until it starts."

"I'll tell you what," said Jan, "you drive."

The boys made off, and as they passed the woods, they seemed darker and more malevolent than they had ever seemed before. Where once happy people harvested nature's bounty, now there were only tragic memories. Marek sped on and the pair emerged into the late afternoon's watery sun. On arrival at the caravan Lily was, as always, on her steps on duty. She descended to greet the boys and partook of her feast. As Jan petted her, he realised that her ribs were disappearing. It seemed that Sid and he were both feeding Lily, but she was not telling either of them what the other was doing.

"All this feeding will end next week when you are down in the fold, no more two meals a day then," Jan mocked as he rubbed her ears and made a fuss of her.

Marek looked at the dog. "Sorry, Lily, no time for fireside chats today, I've to get back to my girlfriend and plan our future."

The boys descended from the downs in the last of the light, and Marek dropped Jan off at the gate.

"Where are you going?"

"I'm a businessman, and I am off to call in some favours," said Marek and he disappeared into a cloud of smoke of his own making, like a genie out of his oil lamp.

Favours, thought Jan, it's time that I called in one of mine, so he made his way to the community hut where he knew the security committee would be meeting prior to tea, just like clockwork.

Jan walked into the hall, and in what appeared to be an attack of déjà vu, there were the security committee sat at their green baize table all staring at him as they had done on the day he arrived.

"Captain Kot, what can we do for you?"

"Well, you may remember that a couple of weeks ago I was able to help you sort out a little problem you were having at that time. Well, you mentioned an extensive network which I shall not mention here. If I give you two addresses, is it possible that that network could be put to use safely to determine the whereabouts of some people close to me?"

"Leave your details with the corporal and we'll see what we can do. If that is all I bid you good afternoon."

As Jan turned to walk out Bialy, called after him. "Captain Kot, not a word to anybody in this camp, please, or everybody will be using our service,"

"I was never here," quipped Jan. He thanked the committee and left for his hut.

Dinner that evening as usual was a silent affair for the Kot family. However, it had been noticed that Frau Swartz was not dining, and this fuelled the rumours that had already started to circulate. The absence of Marta was not yet causing comment, but Jan reasoned that if Marek did not make his move soon, the gossip would start, and Monk, or worse the Ministry, would get involved. As if to highlight this point, as Kinga and Kasia disappeared with a plate of food and a cup of tea, all the older women nodded and whispered in their direction.

This, Jan thought, was a sure sign that even if the old ladies could not see the fire, they were getting their first whiff of the smoke. However, with consummate timing, Marek arrived and walked over to the family where he sat in an empty chair which symbolised the exclusion zone around them.

"I've been a busy boy and I've good news. I've found Marta a job at a hotel in town; the owner owed me a favour. Marta will wash up in the kitchens in the evenings for as long as she can but when that gets too much she can stop and stay at home."

"That's great, how'll you swing this with the Ministry and Monk?"

"Easy! The British Home Office will want our new address for our alien's identification. Well, we'll have a new address. We'll claim back our ration cards here and move. Monk only has to know that Marta is moving out of the camp, not the flax factory."

"But surely the Ministry of Labour will know that Marta has left the factory?" Jan stated in an attempt to expose a flaw in Marek's cunning plan.

"Since you have been here, how many times have the Ministry checked up on you?"

"Never."

"Me neither. I've checked around and not one of us has seen anybody from the Ministry all year. It seems that as long as you are in work and are not costing the British taxpayer any money, you are left alone."

At this point, Ewa decided to chip in. "How'll Marta keep her pregnancy a secret when it becomes too obvious?"

"Right!" Marek shouted.

"Shush," Ewa urged him.

"Right, my friend will give Marta a contract. It appears that the service industries are short of workers, and so, the flax factory will be shown this contract. They'll let her go to the hotel job, but if the Ministry does check, the owner of the hotel will confirm Marta works there. He'll not mention the baby as agreed by us, and so Marta will not be sent back to Poland."

Ewa probed deeper for a gap in Marek's deception. "What about when you both run out of your two-year contracts? Then the three of you will have to return to Poland, just like Jan and I will be expected to."

"It'll never happen," said Marek with confidence. "All of the refugees who are in the camp can stay, so why can't we? It's not as if the country is being flooded with immigrant workers. I hear that even workers from the Caribbean are coming to fill the gaps. Also, lots of the Poles here are going to Canada, and soon America, and other territories desperate for labour. If push comes to shove, we'll do the same."

"How is Marta now?" Ewa asked.

"She's better thanks, now that I've told her my plans. She's also grateful that she'll only have to keep her secret a bit longer."

"So when will all this happen?" Jan asked.

"Early December, ready for the Christmas season at the hotel, Marta can keep going to the flax factory until then. After that, we'll leave the camp and move into an old porter's lodge in the hospital grounds that I'm organising to rent."

It really did appear that Marek had thought of everything, but how had he done it in just a few hours, thought Jan.

"Marek, you really are an amazing businessman. How did you pull all this together so fast?"

Marek lowered his voice. "To be honest, most of this was already in place, ready for the engagement announcement. Marta hated the flax factory and so, as a surprise, I got her the job at the hotel as a chambermaid and cleaner. The porter's lodge was almost organised, so I've just confirmed that this afternoon. The only change now is Marta will have a light job until after the baby comes as a washer-up. The only thing I had not planned for was a baby but now that is sorted."

Now that Ewa and Jan were fully informed, Ewa decided to go and see Marta to check up on her and have a chat, leaving the boys in charge of the children.

"Don't let that pair get into any trouble," Ewa instructed.

"It's not my first time looking after children," Jan retorted.

"I was talking to the children," Ewa laughed.

"Hold on, I still think, despite the sad events of the day, that there is much to celebrate." Marek said, "You all go to Marta, and I'll be there in a moment."

So, Jan and his little family sauntered slowly up to Marta's room and tapping on the door, went in. Ewa was surprised as there was a room full of visitors. Kinga, Kasia, and Mrs Goldstein were sat around chatting to Marta. Ewa slipped into her role as matron.

"I thought I told you no excitement and lots of rest," she scolded Marta.

"There's no excitement here with this lot, they are the most boring people I know, and as for rest, they're so tedious that I'm nearly asleep."

Everybody laughed, and the new arrivals found seats on the bed and on the extra seating provided by the girls. Shortly afterwards, Marek arrived carrying a crate with half a dozen bottles of IPA. He also had lemonade, glasses, cheese straws and, most importantly, a bottle opener.

"Need I ask?" Jan enquired.

"Yes, James owed me a favour, so he lent me the glasses, but I paid for everything else."

So, glasses were charged with shandy for the ladies, lemonade for the children, and beer from the bottle for the men.

Before the festivities began, Jan felt it only appropriate that the assembly of friends should remember Frau Swartz and her tragic passing, and so, he stood to speak.

"There's a very fine line between sanity and madness, and it's often those around us who stop us from straying over that line. I'm just sorry that between us, we could not have done more for the frau. If the truth be known, I think she died that night in Dresden and this was her purgatory. Well, I hope now that she's happy with those who loved her." He raised his glass and toasted and remembered Frau Swartz.

"Do you know what," Marek said, "I never even knew her first name."

"Heidi," said Marta, "her first name was Heidi."

The room fell silent, as if knowing her first name somehow made her seem closer in their memories.

"Thank you, Jan, for those touching words, but now to the business at hand. Earlier today I asked Marta to marry me, and she has graciously agreed to do so."

At this point, Jan jumped up again. "And I'd like to ask you all to raise your glasses once more and toast the future Mr and Mrs Bomski!"

The assembly did as asked and with a cheer, they broke out into the celebratory song 'Sto Lat'.

"Is he going to keep doing that all night?" Marek asked Ewa.

"Probably," she smiled.

This toast was followed by an impromptu concert of operatic arias from Mrs Goldstein that left the room speechless. As Mrs Goldstein grew in confidence each aria became more and more complex. Her audience could see that, as she achieved the highest of notes, her face lit up with joy and emotion; it was as if this particular songbird had finally escaped from her cage. A memorable evening was had by all, and more bonds were created, and memories made that would last a lifetime.

As the chatter died down, the partygoers disappeared to their rooms at the end of the evening. Marek, Jan, Ewa, and the children all said their good nights and left Marta to get some rest. As the group stepped into the evening air, they were met by a bitter cold blast and an ink-black sky studded with stars. The contrast between the warm room full of cheer, and this steely black cold almost took their breath away.

"It's a good job that the girls are coming down on Monday," said Jan.

"Which girls?" Ewa enquired.

"He means his sheep," laughed Marek. "I swear he has names for them all."

"Well, as long as one of them isn't called Ewa that's OK. Is one of them called Ewa?" An agitated Ewa stared at Jan who winced under her withering scrutiny.

"I don't think so, but there're so many of them and only so many names, it's hard to tell." Jan smiled at Ewa and the little family said goodnight to Marek and went into their hut, leaving the now lonely Marek to make his way to his single men's hut.

As the family entered their room, they saw that because the door had been closed, there was ice on the inside of the windows. Swirls of frost had grown in the cold, covering the windows in a lacy lattice.

"Leave the door open, Jan, and go and put some coal on the fire. If there's one thing I'm not getting used to again, it's being cold." Jan did as instructed.

"No wash tonight, you two, straight to bed," Ewa told the children, which was greeted by cheers and laughter by both.

"This might explain why everybody else in the hut keeps their doors open with a blanket hanging down the doorway," Jan suggested to Ewa.

Ewa switched off the room light and the pair made their way to the stove area. Ewa lowered her voice,

"On Monday I'll go and buy some heavy curtains to replace these cotton ones. We'll need to put up with this until we move."

"I'll talk to Chastity about a farm cottage on Monday too. At least in our own place we can keep it as we please, summer or winter."

The two then sat and planned their future away from the camp, some of it dreams, some of it harsh reality. At that time of evening, most of the older hut dwellers were in the community hall listening to choir concerts, musical events and sketches, or talking about the politics of the day, so peace ensued.

Since Ewa's arrival ,she had adopted a strident attitude towards the camp's society. Jan had been happy to keep himself to himself and not make waves, but now he had reassessed his own attitude to his living companions. While never stopped from attending, Mrs Goldstein, Jan, Ewa, and many of the other younger camp dwellers, who were on the periphery of camp society, saw no value in living in that world. While it was true that this community, which had turned its back on English society, was run with efficiency and order, the camp dwellers had to sacrifice certain freedoms, some willingly, some not so willingly.

They assumed their place below the hierarchy of the committee, attended the lectures, both political and religious, and signed up to the Saturday schools, choir, orchestra, youth groups, and sewing group. Ultimately, the one thing that made this community untenable for Jan and the rest was the committees unwavering conviction that at any moment, a promised third world war would start. This would see them marching back into Warsaw behind the Polish flag.

This patriotic fervour meant that anyone who did not subscribe to this delusion, was marginalised by the community, and labelled unpatriotic and in the case of servicemen, traitors. Jan and Ewa were not about to hand their and their children's futures over to some old men in a smoke-filled hall, who sat and dreamed and schemed about a future that would never come. It was this absurdity that kept Jan,and the others separate from the milieu within the camp.

For most, the camp was heaven on earth. Familiar, safe, a haven after the terror of war, and full of happy times, but for a few, it was claustrophobic, suffocating, and restrictive. It was this which drove Jan, Ewa and Marek to look beyond the gates and seek a better life in a country which had opened its doors to them. For Jan and the others to ignore this offer of a better life would be crass stupidity. However, for the majority of the camp, life outside was full of fear and insecurity as clinging to the past was the only certainty in an uncertain world. But here, around the warm stove, Jan and Ewa schemed and planned their escape in as short a time as possible.

The next day was the last day of Jan's holiday, and Sunday was a no breakfast day since Ewa's arrival, so the day did not start auspiciously. The frost of the night before still clung on outside, but the sky was blue, and the sun was bright. Ewa took the children to the shower block for a warming shower while Jan sat on his bunk and contemplated the previous day's events. While the day had ended well for Marek and Marta, he still felt that Frau Swartz's passing needed marking in some way. He resolved to make sure that her life should not end in a pile of paperwork in a drawer. He felt that her passing should be marked in some way.

As it was still an hour before church, Jan decided to stroll down to Monk's office to enquire about what would be organised to mark her passing. Jan knocked on the office door and Mr Monk appeared in his normal business attire even though it was Sunday.

"Ah, I'm glad you're here. I've some forms from the constabulary for you and Mr Bomski to fill in. He's not here ,is he?"

"No, but it's about that matter that I want to talk to you. I'd like to know what will happen to Frau Swartz now?"

As he started to speak, Monk sniffed in such a way as to suggest that this was just a trifle not worthy of his valuable time. "Well, the whole matter is shrouded in red tape and legal procedure as the coroner will hold an inquest into her death. He may call witnesses, he may not, and then when he's satisfie, he'll release the body to a registered undertaker of her family's choosing for burial."

"But she has no family,"

"Then, when her meagre assets are assessed, they'll go towards a simple funeral and the state will meet any shortfall."

"Will there be a proper funeral and church service?"

"No, just a simple internment, and no stone," Monk snapped as if that was all the frau deserved.

Jan thought that this was a poor way to mark a woman's life. Frau Swartz had been a wife, a mother, and a loving daughter, so her passing should be marked by a proper ceremony. He didn't know what he would or could do, but he knew he had to try to do something. As Jan wandered back to the hut, he detoured into the single men's hut to drop off Marek's paperwork. Marek was lying on his bed resting.

Marek smiled when he saw his friend approach.

"Not up the road with the future, Mrs Bomski?" Jan joked.

"No, I'm not, I've been told by a committee member that I'm not to go into that hut as it is for single women only and no liaisons are permitted with single, unchaperoned men."

Smiling, Jan extended his hand which held the bundle of papers.

"Well, this'll keep you busy for a while, it's the paperwork concerning Frau Swartz yesterday."

"Do I have to sign something and hand it back?" Marek asked hesitantly.

"No, you have to fill it in and hand it back and the sooner the better."

Marek placed the papers gently on his bed. "That might be a problem. You see, I can't write in English."

"What do you mean, you can't write in English? You are a businessman, an entrepreneur, a wheeler-dealer, you must write in English."

"Well, you see," Marek said softly, "there's not much call for records, invoices, or receipts in my game, it's all a bit more formless."

"I think that you mean dodgy. OK, come to the hut after church and I will help you fill them in."

"I won't be going to church, I never do."

"However, you have just got engaged to a Polish girl; I'll see you there in a minute."

A short while later, Jan gave Marek a broad grin as he looked to the back of the church and saw him skulking there with Marta and the girls. Jan took his seat alongside his rebellious wife at the front, trying to avoid any eye contact and ignoring the sound of hissing steam released from those around him. No mention was made of Frau Swartz during the service, but the priest gave a robust defence of Catholicism and the battle against the pagan East. With Jan having survived this tedium and the sacraments received, he, Ewa, and her brood jumped up and, ignoring protocol once more, walked out.

As Jan was about to leave the church, he looked across at Marek, lifted his arms, so that his wrists seemed to be invisibly handcuffed and laughed. Marek gave a look of disdain and made to stand up. At this point he was forcibly restrained by Kinga and Marta who had come down on the side of protocol. He had to wait for some time before he could chastise his friend, then they were separated again for dinner.

After all the events of the last few days, Marta's room had become a dissident's enclave. This had several positive aspects to it as Marta could rest and Ewa could attend to her. The other young women in the hut were not great fans of the committee either, so everybody was out of their curious gaze. As long as Jan, who was married to Ewa, was there, Marek could be considered to be chaperoned. Mrs Goldstein was also a welcome visitor who, at last, had found some friendly companions with whom she could talk and moan and complain to about her petty treatment by the choir committee.

The children read, drew, and coloured pictures quietly while they absorbed all the gossip and comments made by their elders. While the girls nattered, Marek and Jan filled in their paperwork and then announced that they were going to Monk, then on to feed Lily. This went unnoticed by the girls who were deeply engrossed in some matter of critically important camp gossip. Thus ignored, the boys dropped their paperwork into Monk's office and, as the long shadows of the afternoon chased them up the lane, they made their way up onto the downs.

Lily, as always, was pleased to see them. The job of spoiling the dog went to Marek while Jan checked the flock. It soon became obvious that the sheep were coming down to the fold just in time, as some of them were fit to burst. Jan knew that the next day the journey back down the hill would have to be a slow meander to minimise the stress on the pregnant ewes. Before he set off again, Jan checked the caravan over and loaded the unused logs into the van ready to be transported back down the hill. They would be useful for keeping him warm on the long, lonely, cold nights to come.

Marek kicked the bike to life and off they set, back to the camp. On arrival, Jan helped to cover the bike, and the boys walked back to Marta's room. When they entered, the ladies were still talking and as they did, Mrs Goldstein spoke a few words of German to which everybody laughed. Having missed the beginning of the story, Jan had no idea why they had laughed but this gave him an idea.

"Mrs Goldstein, do you speak German, or do you just sing in German?"

"I speak German, but why do you ask?"

"Well, I was thinking of holding a memorial service for Heidi Swartz and wondered if you would sing something sad in German."

"I'd be honoured to. If you leave it with me for a couple of days, I'll get back to you."

As the time was rolling around to the evening meal, the group dispersed to ready themselves. On the walk back to the hut, Jan expected a barrage of questions from Ewa about his suggestion, but none were forthcoming.

"I know why you're doing this, and I think it's a lovely idea. I don't know how you'll get it done, but I'll help all I can."

"Thank you, I just can't get over the scene in those woods yesterday. When we realised that the young woman hanging there was not Marta, we were so happy, but at the same time, grief-stricken. She looked at peace. Her face was the face of a beautiful young woman who had her whole life ahead of her. But, paradoxically there she hung, dead in a damp cold wood in a corner of a foreign country. I just can't let it end that way; I have to do something."

Ewa squeezed Jan's hand and whispered, "Quiet now, the children are coming back." With that, the little family made their way to the evening meal and then, later, bed.

CHAPTER 14
ARRIVALS AND DEPARTURES

It was Monday morning, and Jan's first day back at work. As he rode his bike into the farm, it seemed like a month since he was last in the yard. Sid had nearly finished milking, so Jan helped him wash up and they readied the churns for collection. As they worked they chatted about the events of the weekend.

"That was a rum old do that hanging in the woods," said Sid.

"Yes, it was," Jan replied, hoping that his short answer would send the signal that he did not really want to talk about it to him. Either Sid was unbelievably bad at picking up ephemeral messages, or he was just plain nosy.

"Friend of yours, wunt she?" Sid pressed.

Jan decided to stick to minimalist answers, hoping Sid might yet pick up the signal. "Not really a friend, but I knew her."

"Young girl from the camp I was told by the constable who took the ladder," probed the ever inquisitive Sid.

Jan decided to give up his stealth tactic. "It was Frau Swartz from the camp."

"Never knew her," Sid said with the pretence of disinterest and moved on.

"How is your new missus?" Sid warbled, hoping to lighten the mood on a cold November day.

"Well, she's not my new wife, I've been married to her for nearly ten years, but she is fine thank you."

"That's good," said Sid, and having decided that Jan's reticent reply must be a combination of first day back at work, Monday morning, and cold November day, he decided to stop asking questions.

After a hot cup of tea, the two men threw their hessian sacks over their shoulders to ward off the cold and set off with Dolly and Bubbles to bring the sheep back to the fold. Jan knew that Sid was a man of few words, and realising that Sid had made quite an effort at the farm, Jan opened up to him as they passed the wood. He told him about the shock of finding Frau Swartz and not Marta. He shared with him the feeling of guilt that he harboured because he was happy it was not Marta but the Frau. Then he told Sid about his difficult start with Ewa, how she was nervous and a bit spikey to begin with, but now they had grown closer. How the children were well behaved and very grown up for their age. He told Sid that he hoped to get a cottage off of Dyke as his wife hated living on the camp with all the class-conscious ex-military and their wives. After nearly an hour of Jan speaking and Sid listening, Jan looked at Sid to ellicit a response.

"It's a bugger s'no," Sid replied, and in that one short sentence, Sid managed to sum up one of the most traumatic weeks of Jan's recent life.

It would have made more sense to ride on the horses up the hill. However, due to the height of the shires and Sid's bad back, he had decided to walk, so Jan felt it only polite to follow suit. In time, the downs were reached and as the ascent was over the two men decided to take their morning break in the caravan. Sid turned to Jan after their break and said,

"We've three hours before the dinnertime bus comes through the village so that should be enough time to get these daft buggers down and into the fold."

Jan nodded and harnessed the girls to the caravan, and as if he understood what all this action meant, Teddy the donkey took up his position by the gate. Lily the dog took up her position on the top step of the caravan which Jan drove, and after he had shut the gate behind them, Sid joined him.

"You know the winter's coming when the sheep come in for lambing,"

Sid said prophetically. "I did a rough count last week when you were on holiday, and I think there could be one hundred and twenty lambs if all goes well."

Jan, in an effort to show that he was on the job, corrected Sid. "I made it one hundred and thirty-two." Sid, in an effort to win in the shepherd one-upmanship stakes smiled and replied,

"I did say roughly."

So, off the convoy set off, slowly through the crisp cold downland air they descended and then into a kinder clime where an inquisitive sheep could still find a lush green shoot or two. Once more, the slow clip-clop of the horses' hooves beat out the rhythm of country life, and it was quite a relief for Jan, who sought sanctuary in these precious moments of tranquil calm. With everything that had happened in the last two weeks, it was cathartic to sit with Sid in silence and watch the fields go slowly by. Now that Jan had others to think of, it seemed even more important that he make a home for them in this sanctuary. While it was true that over the last two weeks tragedy had visited the village twice, on both occasions the source of these misfortunes had been external, not from within the village or its community. In fact, the village had absorbed both calamities with the usual gossip and theories, closed its ranks and moved on remarkably quickly.

By late morning ,the sheep were in the fold, Teddy had once more carried out his duties faultlessly, and all the sheep now safely grazed in relative shelter. Jan was able to get Dolly and Bubbles to reverse the caravan right up against the gable end of the lean-to barn. This, Jan thought, would give extra shelter to the barns inhabitants. Also, it would allow him to view the ewes in the barn through the window, from the warmth of the caravan. When the caravan wheels were blocked to prevent movement and the girls had been unhitched, Sid had a quiet word with Jan.

Although they were alone in a field, Sid whispered and looked round furtively.

"Look young-un, don't let Dyke see the dog. He's unlikely to come out here unless there's a real problem, but he does not want dogs on the farm. I don't know why but that is how it is. The old girl is quiet enough, and she's good with the sheep, but that won't help. If Dyke sees her, it'll be the dog gone or you and the dog gone, alright." Jan gave an understanding nod and thanked Sid.

With that Sid returned to his farm duties and Jan spent the rest of the day preparing his mobile home for lambing.

Jan unloaded the wood from inside the caravan and stacked it in the dry, underneath his new home. He swept out the dried mud and old vegetation, cleaned out the stove, and laid it ready for when it was needed. He stored candles and matches in a cupboard and put new wicks in two paraffin lamps. He filled both lamps from a gallon can that Sid had given him and then stored the can under the van. Once he felt ready for anything, he shared his dinner with Lily, and then rested on his bed looking out at the flock for signs of imminent arrivals.

He checked the medical box and made a list of things that he hoped Chastity could get from the vet for him. As the light faded, he said goodbye to Lily before getting ready to make his way down to the farm. As he looked back at a happy Lily smiling her smile, he realised that she had no bed. Well, he thought, that will be a job for tomorrow.

Jan called into the office and found Chastity on the phone. He raised a finger to indicate that he needed one minute of her time and stepped back into the cold. Chastity gave a vigorous wave and beckoned Jan back in. Jan quietly closed the door behind him and removed his hat. He stood like a truant outside the headmaster's office while Chastity concluded her business. As the phone receiver crashed down it was clear that the call had not gone the way Chastity had hoped.

"If this is a bad time, I can come back tomorrow,"

"No, it's OK Jan, sit down, I'm just chasing up bad payers. What can I do for you, is everything all right?"

Jan unfolded his piece of paper and slid it across the table slowly as if it was a final ultimatum. He hoped this would lessen the shock of having to spend even more money. "Everything's fine thank you, I just wondered if you'd get these items from the vet for the medical box in the caravan. Also, I wondered if it's possible to talk to you about renting a tied cottage now that my wife and children are here. My wife doesn't like the camp or its inhabitants, and Sid said there may be a chance to rent our own place."

Chastity slumped back in her chair and made a facial expression that somebody who has just lost a bet makes.

"I'm sorry, Jan, but Mother will not allow children on the farm. If it was just you and your wife, there'd be no problem."

"Oh," said Jan disappointedly, "I'll have to think again. I'm sorry to have troubled you."

Chastity could see that Jan seemed let down, and so she felt clarification was needed.

"Look, Jan, I'm sure that your children are well-behaved and would cause no trouble; if it was my decision I'd rent a cottage to you tomorrow. However, mother's diffident. She likes the quiet home life of the lady of the manor, if you understand what I mean. To mother, children have no place on our farm. As a child, I was seen but not heard. Luckily for me I was at boarding school much of the time. However, as you may have noticed, I'm my father's daughter and boarding school just made me worse.

"Even though I live in the same farmhouse as Mother, we only speak at dinner, which she insists we all eat together, while we are waited on by our maid. Mother doesn't cook, we have a cook for that, and the maid also does the housework during the day.

"You see, mother's family are big in the Dorset County set, and her one indiscretion in life has marginalised her. She's not a bad person, but she tries to keep up appearances for her family's sake, and this, as you can see, can cause problems."

Jan was sorry that he could not get a cottage, but he was grateful for Chastity's candid response. He thanked her wholeheartedly and wished her a good afternoon.

Jan went to the cart shed to get his bike and set off in the dark for the camp. Farm life was strange. In summer you worked till it was dark, which made for some long days, but in winter the short days meant that you finished earlier. He had not needed lights up to this point that year, but he would now need to sort something out he thought. Uppermost in his thoughts, however, was how he'd tell Ewa that his plan to leave the camp had stalled. Jan sailed into the camp cloaked in shadow, but this did not stop Mr Monk seeing him and calling out to him.

"Mr Kot, can I see you for a moment, and where are your lights? You'll get yourself killed going around like that."

Jan diverted to the office in a hasty manoeuvre that saw gravel spew all over the road. Monk stood in the doorway with the light behind him. Even on a cold winters night thought

Jan, he would not invite anybody into his office.

Monk started, "While I was clearing Frau Swartz's personal effects with one of the ladies today, I found this letter written in German but addressed to you. Do you speak German, Mr Kot?"

"No, I don't, Mr Monk, but as the letter is addressed to me, I suppose it's my place to find out what it says."

It was obvious to Jan that Monk's curiosity was getting the better of him and that he was dying to find out what its contents said. Jan played along cruelly.

"I think I know someone who can tell me what it says, so if there's anything I think you should know, I'll tell you later." Jan snatched the letter from Monk's hand and made to ride off.

"Be sure you do; the letter may contain information pertinent to her death and I'll need to know."

Jan smiled as he sped off into the dark, illuminated only by the sparse camp streetlights. He went straight to his family hut and, chaining his bike, went in to greet his family. He pulled back the blanket from over the door like a conjurer making his big entrance, but before he could speak Ewa shouted,

"Sheep, sheep, I can smell sheep." She threw a towel and his wash bag at him and said,

"Shower now, and don't come back until you smell of roses."

Jan swivelled on his heels but realised that his clothes would still smell, so he turned to ask Ewa for some clean ones and was met by a bundle of clothes flying through the air. "You think of everything," he joked and left for the showers.

Once showered and smelling sweet, he returned to the room where he was greeted by a further chastisement for coming back in the cold with wet hair. In an attempt to divert attention, he pointed at the curtains and said,

"They're nice."

"Stop changing the subject," Ewa said smiling widely. "They should be nice, they're new."

Jan moved over to the curtains and felt the velvety softness,

"They even feel warm," he said.

But before Jan could throw Ewa off the scent further, she plunged straight into the question of the cottage. Jan was caught off balance, and without thinking he replied,

"I've spoken to Chastity, and she'll talk to her mother and let me know by the end of the week if there's a chance that we can have one." Jan felt terrible that he had lied to Ewa. He hadn't promised her a cottage, but he'd not been totally honest with her either. He reasoned that he now had four days to sort something out or come clean about the cottage.

Once more, he moved the subject on to another topic. He pulled out the letter that Monk had given to him and showed it to Ewa. Luckily, this intrigued her enough to drop the subject of their future housing.

"I thought I'd ask Mrs Goldstein if she could read it to me later."

"Go and see her now!" Ewa begged Jan excitedly.

"The girls aren't back from work yet, I'll catch her at dinner, then all'll be revealed." Jan still did not feel right about his indiscreet lie, and while they waited for dinner, he tried to lay some ground in preparation for letting Ewa down gently about the cottage.

"What if we can't have a cottage at the farm?"

"Well then, you can get another job where you can get a cottage. If you are going to come home every night smelling like that, I at least want to get my own home out of it. But no pigs, if there are pigs, I'm going back to South Africa."

Jan was amazed. Why hadn't he thought of that, he asked himself. He would talk to Sid in the morning. With this salve poured on Jan's guilty conscience, he relaxed a little and waited for dinner while Ewa told him about her day.

The Kot family still did not have much in the way of dining companions, so they ate and talked among themselves.

As soon as Jan could see that Mrs Goldstein had finished her meal, he moved over to her in a semi-stooped position in the hope that he would not attract too much attention. This failed, however, as everybody in the room looked across at him wondering why he was moving around in this way. Jan crouched down beside Mrs Goldstein and whispered,

"I wonder if I could come and see you after dinner in your room?"

The girls all started to giggle and made suggestive comments about the possible reasons for this liaison and any potential outcomes. Mrs Goldstein leaned forward down to Jan's level and whispered furtively,

"I'd like that as I've got something that I've wanted to say to you all day."

Jan nodded and retreated, still stooping, back to his table, followed by a chorus of laughter from the single girls' table. As Jan slid back into his seat, Ewa smirked.

"That went well."

a breathless Jan responded. "Good, do you think so?"

"No! I don't, you idiot," Ewa admonished, "why could you not have just walked over like any other human being would've done?"

Jan felt slightly crestfallen at being chastised in front of the children, however, all that dissolved in an instant when Mary piped up,

"Oh Mother, don't be nasty to daddy." It'd taken a week, but one of the children had called him Daddy, and his heart leapt in his chest with joy.

Straight after dinner, Jan and the family made their way to the single girls' hut and knocked on the doorframe of Mrs Goldstein's room.

"Come in," she sang out in a mock operatic voice. "How can I help?"

Jan gave her the letter from Frau Swartz and asked her if she could read it.

"First, Jan, please call me Julia, it's shorter and, especially around here, less Jewish if you understand my meaning. Now let me see." Her eyes scanned the letter earnestly, and once she had read and understood it, she recounted it to Jan.

"Heidi, for that is how she signed off the letter, has asked you to be her executor in the event that something should happen to her. She has money in a post office account here in the camp, which should be enough to bury her. The necessary paperwork has been filled in and Rosemary's holding it at the camp office. She's asked for a simple ceremony, in the event that something should happen to her, but she's most insistent that she should have a gravestone. She says that her only hope, and the thing that gives her comfort nowadays, is that someone from her family will eventually come to find her. She says that this thought helps her to believe that she's not lost in a foreign land but will one day be found and be alone no longer. She thanks you in advance and apologises for any trouble she may cause you in carrying out her request. That's it."

Jan sat in shock,

"It's as if she knew that I would want to mark her passing. That I would be there at her end and feel the need to organise a small tribute. I've hardly ever spoken to her apart from that last night."

Ewa put a hand on Jan's shoulder. "Maybe she saw something in you, maybe she felt that you were different, and that you could be trusted to do the right thing for her."

The room fell silent for a while, but, eventually, Julia was the first to speak.

"I've some news for you that's even more pertinent since reading this letter. I've chosen a piece of Brahms which I can now sing at her funeral, and tomorrow evening, at choir and orchestra practice, I'll see how many volunteers I can drum up to accompany me."

Jan's shock quickly turned to panic as he had never organised a funeral in Poland, so how was he going to do one in England, he pondered. Ewa could see the look of dismay on Jan's face.

"Don't worry," she said calmly, "tomorrow you can call into the camp post office and talk to Rosemary the postmistress. Sort out the money and then we can go from there."

Jan relaxed slightly. He wondered what he would do without Ewa's organisational skills and calming hand on events. Ewa had an inner strength that he'd regularly witnessed, and he admired that about her above all else.

Jan thought it too late to call on Mr Monk, even though he always seemed to be there in his office, so he decided to talk to Marek in his hut and go over events with him. When he explained to Ewa what he was going to do she stopped him in his tracks.

"Before you go off chatting to your mate, I'll need you to bring a jug of hot water for the children so they can have a wash back in their room." As the evening was chilly, Jan thought this made perfect sense and acted instantly.

Task completed, Jan made his way to Marek's hut and, sitting on his bed, told him everything.

"I find it strange," said Marek, "that Heidi Swartz picked you as it was me who had bargained for her medication, and it was me who had helped Marta cope with the continual ranting and raving. However, I'm happy to help in any way I can. I too have a strong desire to see this through to a dignified end for Julia Swartz." Marek agreed to meet up the next day to discuss progress.

Happier now that he had shared his burden with his best friend, Jan returned to Ewa at their hut.

Jan crept in quietly so as not to disturb the children. He sat on his bunk opposite Ewa.

"I'm so happy that Mary called me Daddy earlier at dinner."

"Well, you don't know this, but ever since we arrived Mary has been referring to you as Daddy, but never in your earshot."

Once more Jan's heart leapt, as until their arrival, the children had posed nothing to him but a problem to cope with. Now, in this short time it became very important to him that they liked him.

"So, what about Joseph?" Jan asked pointing to the bunk above his head.

"Give him time, he still sees himself as the man of the family and he takes that role very seriously. He'll learn to relax and let go eventually." Jan gave an understanding nod and made a move to lie back on his bunk.

"Not so fast mister, here's a basket with your work trousers and five work shirts in. Take this with you and leave it in your precious caravan. Tomorrow you can wear your home clothes to work and change in the caravan into your work clothes, then before you come home again, wash at the caravan and change back into your home clothes before returning. I don't want you stinking this tiny room out. I'll wash your shirts on Fridays ready for Monday morning."

Jan thought about this arrangement which seemed like a lot of trouble, but in a strange way, it was nice to have somebody caring for him again and he decided that it sounded like the matter was settled.

Next morning, Jan took the early breakfast leaving the family to sleep on. When he had risen, he pulled open the new, heavy, velvet curtains to be greeted by spitting rain, ink black skies, and high winds. He looked at his warm bunk and wished that he could crawl back in. However, Jan knew that he needed to push himself to leave and get to work. With basket in hand, he cycled to the caravan, greeted Lily, and let her in out of the cold and wind.

Jan's first job was to start the fire in the stove, and once the caravan started to feel warm he got changed. He hung his home clothes on a clothes hanger that Ewa had thoughtfully placed in the basket. Jan thought the very presence of the hanger meant that, subliminally, Ewa was really saying, 'Don't you dare chuck your good clothes down in that caravan'. Jan smiled to himself as this notion occurred to him. It was still too dark to check the sheep properly so leaving Lily guarding the stove, Jan rode back to the farm to help Sid.

As they worked, Jan filled Sid in on the cottage. "Chastity's refused my request for a cottage and that means that I'll have to look for another job with a cottage included."

This news worried Sid, who had grown to like his hard-working friend, who knew when to talk and when not to. "Now hold on, young-un, don't get too hasty, this job here is better than many you will find. Not every farmer is as honest and caring as Dyke. You'd better think on a bit."

With the crashing of the churns and the echo in the empty dairy, neither was aware that Chastity had come into the dairy and had overheard everything.

"Is everything all right, Jan?" Chastity asked, fully aware that it was not.

Jan, fully aware that he and Sid had been rumbled, decided to come clean and explained his problem. Chastity understood but cautioned Jan not to be too hasty.

"That's what I said," Sid added, partly to support Chastity, and partly to distance himself from any thoughts of subterfuge she may have harboured.

"I love this job. I'm grateful to Sid and all of you for making my time here so pleasant, and I really don't want to leave this farm or this area, but my life changed last week. I now have a wife and a family, and I've to do what's right for them."

At this point, Sid gave up any pretence of holding a partisan view and blurted out, "Can't we do anything? I got this one trained up lovely, he gets here early, goes home late, you tell him once, and you don't have to tell him again, not like that last idle bugger we had."

Chastity raised her hand to silence Sid. "I spoke to Mother last night and there's no moving her, but I've an idea. Would you be prepared to work with these new vacuum pump milking units that are all the rage now?"

"I could learn," Jan said, sensing that -no- would've been the wrong answer.

"Then let me make a phone call and I'll come up to the sheep fold later and talk to you." With this agreed they all went about their work.

Sid and Jan started the feeding, and a cheery Sid, who was for once, effusive in his conversation, said,

"That's good what Miss Chastity said, init, sounds like she may have a job lined up for you."

Jan, who was now excited about events himself, quipped, "Sounds like I may come up here one morning and find you replaced by a vacuum pump."

Sid, who was no fan of technology, progress, or anything new-fangled, fell silent. Jan laughed and, after slapping Sid on the back, carried on feeding.

By eight thirty, it was light enough to check the sheep, so the two men went up the road to the sheep fold. They toured the field looking for signs that some might be near to lambing, but none were obvious. As they walked, Sid gave Jan a lecture on the subject of lambing signs.

"See these daft buggers here; when they're about ten days from lambing, their tits go hard. Then, their lady parts get saggy, and when you see them wander off alone, that's when you get them into the lambing barn."

Jan nodded attentively, although inside he wanted to

scream that sheep in Poland were exactly the same as English sheep, and that everything did not change at the channel. That Polish sheep had tits, saggy lady parts, and liked to be alone to lamb. However, Jan kept quiet and walked alongside Sid with his hand behind his back like a doctor making rounds on the ward.

Ward rounds completed, Jan and Sid went back to the caravan and had their morning break. As Sid pushed another log into the stove, he looked at Jan.

"Shame we can't teach that bloody dog of yours to put wood on the fire."

Jan smiled at the thought of this, and said, "Well it's going to be a long winter. I'll see what I can do."

Jan went outside to the water bowser, filled the kettle, and before long tea was brewing and toast was toasting. Suddenly the weather that day did not seem quite so bad. Work in the winter was at a slower pace. There was an unwritten rule between employer and employee, that during this quiet time, as long as no liberties were taken nobody expected the same frenetic activity as was usual in the spring and summer months.

As the men sat in silence, Sid caught sight of Jan's home clothes hanging on the wall by the stove chimney and erupted into laughter.

"Bloody hell, Mr Hoity Toity. Bloody businessman with his office clothes and work clothes."

"Home clothes, Sid, home clothes," Jan responded. "My wife's rather house proud. Imagine how it would be if we actually had a house," Jan mused.

"Well, my missus makes me get changed in the outhouse summer and winter, at least you can get changed in the warm," Sid sniggered.

With that, the door of the caravan opened and suddenly Chastity was climbing in to join the two men.

"Cup of tea please, no sugar, and if you haven't got milk, none of that powdered stuff."

"Miss Chastity," Sid blurted, "I'm your dairyman why would we have powdered milk?"

Despite the unwritten rule, both men felt rather vulnerable being caught at break and tried to make it seem that it wasn't as warm and comfortable as it seemed. Chastity was a kind woman who understood the way of things and made light of the situation.

"Well, now we're all here for the committee meeting I can start. I've spoken to the Farmers at Grove Farm, and they have a proposition for you. In the new year, they're having a new parlour fitted, but their old dairyman doesn't want to train up on it at his age. This new parlour will cut milking time by over half, so they're keen to press ahead. However, they don't want to lose their own man as he's a good worker and has worked there since he was a boy. Jan, if you're prepared to train up on the new equipment you can do the milking for them. Then, when you have finished there, you can work here for the rest of the day. They've told me that they'll let you have a tied cottage, but reduced wages if you agree."

Jan was beside himself with joy as this meant that he could go home to Ewa that night and tell her some good news.

Before he could speak, Sid leapt to his feet and shouted, "That's bloody marvellous, he'll take it!"

Chastity calmed Sid down and said, "Don't you think we should let Jan decide that?"

Sid, who was so happy that he would be keeping his old friend said, "Look at that young-un's face, of course, he'll take it, he's going to be working for farmer Farmer."

Jan nodded in agreement, "Where do I sign?" he said, and the three finished their tea to celebrate.

"OK, so that's settled. Now, Jan, I see you have got a dog."

"Well, actually, the dog has me," quipped Jan. "She turned

up in early summer and has stayed at the caravan looking after the sheep. It's not a sheepdog, but when young dog foxes started attacking the sheep, she killed them, just like that. I know your father doesn't like dogs on the farm, so I'd planned to keep it at the caravan caring for the sheep."

Chastity stroked Lily, and the two seemed to bond instantly just as Jan had.

"What's her name?"

"Lily."

"Because of the marking on her head? Well, you know what I'm going to say. Don't let Father see her or, lovely as she is, she'll have to leave."

At that point, Sid involuntarily grabbed Lily, and held her to his legs as if to protect her from removal.

"Father rarely comes over here so I'm sure it'll be fine, just be careful."

At this point, Jan felt the urge to ask if Chastity knew why her father was not a fan of dogs, but considering what she'd just done for him, he kept quiet.

Chastity left the men to their break and returned to the farm to ring farmer Farmer. Both Sid and Jan then started weighing up the pros and cons of the offer whilst finishing their tea. After a while, Jan made the point that they had stopped for quite a while.

"That's all right, young-un, when we were talking to Miss Chastity that was like work, so we can now carry on with the rest of our break."

Jan was often amazed by Sid's simplistic reasoning, but, on this occasion, let it pass. With no lambs imminent, Jan returned to the yard with Sid and spent the rest of the morning sawing logs for the house and for the caravan. He took an early lunch so that he could catch Rosemary at the post office to sort out the money for Frau Swartz's funeral. Luckily, as it was a weekday, the office was quiet, and Jan could speak to

Rosemary without interruption or interlopers.

Rosemary began by paying her condolences to Jan, and then she handed him an account book which held a total of one hundred and twenty pounds. Both his and Frau Swartz's names were on the book.

"Right," Rosemary said in a business-like tone, "as and when you require cash you can come in and remove the cash from the account. If there's cash left in the account, then that belongs to you as you're a joint account holder."

"Thank you." And he left in silence.

Jan crossed the camp road to Monk's office and banged on the door. Monk opened it and stood in the doorway. Before he could speak, Jan launched into a monologue which barely disguised his anger.

"Mr Monk, the letter in German was a letter requesting me to be Frau Swartz's executor. We hold a joint account at the camp post office which'll pay for her funeral. I'll arrange for her body to be brought back from Salisbury and she'll be interred here in the village. That was her last request. In this way, if her sister or one of her family eventually come looking for her, they'll find her in the village churchyard."

"Mr Kot! I'm not sure if this is all totally legal and above board."

"Mr Monk, do you really think that the British government is going to shed any tears over one last, dead German woman. On the contrary, I think that I'm doing them a favour don't you?"

Monk, aware that his own surly attitude towards Frau Swartz may have had some bearing on her suicide, simply replied,

"Quite so, Mr Kot" And he closed the office door.

Jan, now out of time, decided to return to the farm and his work. He replenished the farmhouse log pile in the coalhole at the rear of the big house, then, hurriedly built up his pile of logs under the caravan until the light began to fade. He checked the sheep one last time and said goodbye to Lily. Lily now had a straw-filled box screwed to the top platform of the steps, so that she could carry out her duties in some comfort. He returned home, washed, and changed ready for dinner and to share his good news with Ewa.

As Jan imagined, Ewa was ecstatic that he had been able to secure them their own home, even if she was slightly confused by the deal.

"I don't understand why you're not at the farm you work on, but that is just a minor detail. Still, living in the village means that once the children start school in the new year, I can find a job and increase our income," Ewa gushed.

As the family walked to dinner, Marek and Marta caught up with them and Marek also had some good news.

"Guess what? Our hospital has its own mortuary. Today, a funeral car arrived to pick up a patient who had passed away. I approached the driver, who told him that once they had a death certificate, they could pick up Frau Swartz from Salisbury and hold her body until the funeral. So! Simply get the death certificate, talk to the vicar, and Bob's your uncle."

Jan could not believe that it would be that simple, but he was grateful to his friend for once more keeping his promise to help.

"Tomorrow," Marek added, "I'll call round to the funeral director in town and give them your details and advise them that you're dealing with the Frau's final wishes."

The group stepped out of the cold, dark, drizzly November evening into the warming atmosphere of the canteen, took their seats and waited for grace to be said.

As Julia Goldstein took her seat on the single women's table she looked across at Jan and Ewa and put her thumb up. This caused a wave of murmuring and whispers around the room, which took some time to abate. Ewa, now soon to be the master of her own home, smiled and waved back without a care for her dining companions feelings, and an even louder wave of murmuring erupted.

After the meal was over, Julia stood up and marched over to Jan and Ewa. Standing erect and in a somewhat theatrical stance, she said loudly,

"I met my friend, the organ player at the church, on the bus and she's agreed to play at the funeral. I'll keep you informed. She's telling the vicar to expect a visit from you. I must dash; I've choir practice." Julia spun around on her heel and made a flamboyant exit stage left.

"Now that's how you deliver a message in the dining hall," Ewa said to Jan.

Tuesday was a wet and angry day with high winds and sheets of rain lashing the hedges and sheep in equal measure. As Jan and Sid worked about the wet and windy farmyard, the caravan seemed a haven of warmth and comfort. Once the jobs around the yard were complete, the two men visited the sheep and again took their break with Lily.

Sid looked at the sheep crowded under the high hedges.

"You see, young-un, they don't mind the wind, but they get nervous because they can't smell anything properly due to the gusts. It makes them fearful, this caddly weather, so they keep close to the hedge to lessen the chances of attack."

Jan nearly choked on his sandwich as he'd never heard such a fanciful load of rubbish in his life. However, Sid had delivered this pearl of wisdom with such conviction that Jan just nodded and made a noise that had interest woven into it and then changed the subject.

Suddenly, the quiet lane was filled with the revving of a lorry engine and the clanking of gears. The pair looked out of the window and saw a lorry stopped in the gateway loaded with hazel sheep hurdles. Both men put on their work coats and went out to the driver.

"You Sid?" the driver asked with very little respect or interest.

"Yes, who wants to know?" Sid asked in equal measure.

"Well, I do, don't I?" the driver snapped, with a tone guaranteed to upset Sid. Despite the cold, Jan could see this getting heated, so he interjected,

"They for us?" Jan asked, pointing at the hurdles on the back of the lorry.

"Might be, might not be" the quizmaster of a lorry driver replied.

"Well, are they, or aren't they?" Sid shouted. "Because if they aren't ours, bugger off."

"All right, grandad, keep your hair on," said the driver, consulting his clipboard and then confirming that ten were indeed for them. "I'll wait in the lorry while you get them off," the driver said to Sid as he untied the load.

"Then you'll wait all bloody day, you cheeky bugger, because they will still be there when we go home."

"I dunno," the driver complained, realising that he had met his match and hauled himself up onto the flatbed. In no time, the hurdles were in the lean-to barn and the driver was taking his particular form of wit and customer service to the next farm on his clipboard list.

"Lovely, now we can nail these up to make the barn nice and cosy for the old girls when they start to lamb."

"Do you have the hammer and nails?" Jan asked.

"No, they're in the workshop in the yard," Sid said in a way that suggested that Jan was about to have a wet walk back to the yard to fetch them, so off he went.

On his return, Jan was welcomed with a nice cup of tea and a piece of Sid's wife's lardy cake, which made the wet, windy journey worth it.

Sid warmed his hands by the stove. "I don't know what these young buggers get up to now-a-days. If I'd spoken to my elders like that, I would have got a good hiding."

Jan looked at Sid and consoled him. "I'm pretty sure that day is not too far away for him." They both smiled and ate their cake in silence pondering the youth of today.

Then, for the first time since Jan had known him, Sid confided in Jan.

"You see, young-un, I don't like change. The sheep have arrived back down here for lambing like they do every year, but now you are departing. I like things steady, with no surprises. If I'm being honest, change scares me. You aren't afraid of change. You're, how they say, adaptable. You'll leave old buggers like me in your dust later on."

Jan was touched by his work friend's rare show of candour. "Listen ,Sid," he said quietly, "the sheep will still be here, I'll still be here, the farm will still be here, even Lily'll still be here. Not much will change around here, so don't you worry."

CHAPTER 15
FINAL FAREWELLS

◦

B
y Tuesday evening, the funeral arrangements were gathering pace. Julia Goldstein had managed to get a bassoon player, two violinists, an oboe player, and a cello player to accompany her. The organist, who would also be playing was putting together a simple arrangement for this eclectic mix of instruments which they would practise in the church. The vicar had agreed that as long as the death certificate showed that Frau Swartz's suicide was due to her unsound mind, he would carry out a full service with burial in the churchyard. This was due, in some part, to Marek naming the vicar and his church as the address where the funeral directors should take the coffin when a day was decided, without asking the vicar.

Jan divided these cold, damp days between the sheep fold and the farmyard, checking, feeding, milking, on occasion, and keeping the farm neat and tidy as Dyke liked it. Ewa spent her days, sewing mending, and minding the children. If the weather was dry, she took them to the library or museum in the town, especially on market day.

On market day she looked for bargains that would make

their lives a little easier. She dreamt of new curtains for their cottage and making and preserving Polish food on her cooker once more. The days of communal hardship were coming to an end at last, and her family would thrive in the freedom of their own home. Little more than three weeks had passed, and yet that time felt like months, and although the children were settled, they were not country folk at heart. Clean and tidy, warm and dry were their requirements, not muddy farmyards or foraging for wild fruit. Ewa did not mind this as she was trying to raise doctors or teachers, not ploughmen or milk-maids.

On Thursday evening as Jan and his family prepared for another silent dinner, Marek came bowling over to their table.

"The undertaker's received an interim death certificate for Frau Swartz that means that we can start planning a date."

This kind of announcement made quietly, would usually elicit a tremor of mumbling, but the delivery of this particular message brought an uproar to the dining room as it appeared that Polish people organising the funeral of a German did not sit well with the gathered throng.

An elated Marek returned to his table while Ewa looked at Jan.

"Once again, that's not the way to deliver an unpopular message at the dinner table, you men!"

Jan felt a hundred eyes burning into the back of his head. Ewa just did not care. If the organising of Frau Swartz's funeral was going to upset people, Ewa thought that that was just a bonus.

Jan, as the primary organiser of the funeral, expected to hear about this assault on Polish sensibilities quite quickly. He did not have to wait long. As he and his family left the food canteen, Major Bialy raced to catch up with Jan and confronted him.

"Why was I not informed about this, Captain Kot?"

Before Jan could answer, Ewa decided to have a go, and she went in low.

"Captain Bialy, you weren't told because you're not invited, indeed, none of you are invited."

"I'm Major Bialy, not captain," Bialy interjected harshly, and pointing at Ewa, he harangued her. "Have you no sense of shame that you're going to hold a funeral for a member of a bestial race who tried to eradicate our nation? We fought the Nazis for six years until the final victory came at such a cost to Polish lives."

Bialy's treatment of Ewa was the last straw as Jan could hold his calm restraint no longer and exploded in rage at Bialy.

"What do you mean major, 'we'? When I got to Boulogne to catch an escape ship to carry on the fight, I was told that most of the room was taken up by senior officers, not fighting men like me but bureaucratic men like you. You escaped to London and sat behind a desk pushing paper, while I was sent to a prisoner of war camp where I barely survived. The real enemy now is the Soviet Union major, not the Nazis, so why don't you go back to the community hall and push some more paper around, then maybe you'll defeat them."

Jan gathered up his family and they made their way back to their hut. Ewa was bursting with pride with the way Jan had put Bialy in his place, but she knew all their bridges had been burnt now. Life in the camp could not get any lonelier, but it would be a hard couple of months until they left. Now that Marek and Marta were leaving in three weeks, there would be even fewer friendly faces at dinner.

The backlash was swift and savage. Julia came to their room just twenty minutes later to tell them that the bassoon player had been put under pressure not to play at the service and had withdrawn. Fifteen minutes later, she had lost one of her violinists too. However, the rest of the ensemble were made of sterner stuff and held out. Later that evening, Monk was summoned to the community hall to be told that Marek was spending an inordinate amount of time in the single women's hut and the rest of the girls there wanted it stopped.

Marek was then called to Monk's office by a Scout runner and told that if this continued, he would be removed to another camp. Marek was incandescent with rage. He raced off to the community hall to have it out with Bialy.

When he got to the hall, he found Marta there, standing in front of the committee, being questioned by all the old men of the committee about the rumours of a pregnancy.

Marek shouted angrily, "Marta go back to your room and leave this to me."

Marta turned to leave. "But we've not finished yet. Stay there miss," Bialy demanded.

"Oh yes, you have," Marek shouted.

He then lambasted the committee. "Remember all the medical supplies you've had, all the extra food I've brought, all the help you've received with local groups, well, all that ends now and forever. Stay away from Marta, or the local constabulary may get a phone call about a certain incident not so long ago!"

Marek turned, and despite vociferous demands to stay, he left, slamming the hall door. He marched back to Monk's office and walked straight in without knocking. Monk stood up at his desk in shock. Marek raised his hand and pointed a finger at Monk.

"You get my and Marta's transfer out papers completed pronto. We'll be leaving as soon as the ink is dry and will fulfil our contracts living in private accommodation." Monk tried to explain that it wasn't that simple, but by then he was talking to a slammed door.

Marek arrived at Jan and Ewa's hut and found Marta sat on the bed in tears.

Marek sat down beside her and tried to comfort her. "It's OK; we'll be leaving very soon now. Jan and I can decorate the porters lodge, and we can move in."

Jan looked dismayed and muttered awkwardly, "I'm sorry Marek but I'll be at the sheep nearly all day and night soon, I can't help you, I'm really sorry."

Ewa once more came to the rescue. "I sit here all day getting bored, Marek; you get the paint and brushes, and I'll decorate the lodge for you. The children and I can catch the bus in, and you can give me a key to let myself in. Once you show me what you want, I can get it done ready for you to move in."

Both Marek and Marta hugged and thanked Ewa, who once more left Jan overcome with pride at her can-do attitude and ability to get things done. It was decided that as it was market day next day, Ewa and the children would catch the morning bus and make their way to the town. Marek would meet them at the bus stop and transport them to the lodge, show Ewa what they wanted doing, and leave it to her.

Next day, Jan had the company of his family for breakfast. It was early, and so all the camp malcontents were not there, which made for a polite and civilised start to, the day. Breakfast over, the family kissed and went their separate ways. It was still dark and spitting with rain, so the children were dressed warmly, as Ewa had no idea what condition the lodge would be in.

They met Marek at the marketplace bus stop, and he invited them to alight his motorbike. Ewa refused point blank to sit on the pillion, and so, the three of them squeezed into the sidecar.

"Come on, Mummy," Joseph said, "it's bigger than it looks."

Ewa was not by any means a lady of leisure, but this journey was just about as much as she could cope with to maintain her composure. At the lodge, Marek handed Ewa a key with a wooden tag chained to it with the word 'lodge' burnt into it.

The key was large and cumbersome so that it could not easily get lost. However, Marek made sure that Ewa knew not to lose the key as it was Victorian and not easily replaced. Ewa opened the heavy front door and was instantly hit by a wall of hot air.

"Crikey, I haven't been this warm since India."

Marek explained that the lodge had been left empty for some time and had become damp, so he had turned up the heat.

Unfortunately, he had not left the windows open a crack and the whole place was now a hot, humid jungle-like abode. Ewa reached for the living room sash window and, surprisingly, it slid down despite years of paint, allowing hot humid air to escape and fresh air to come in. She looked around. There were dust sheets on the ground, tins of emulsion paint in different pastel shades, and a selection of brushes, turps, and tin cans to wash the brushes. Each item had 'hospital property' on it. Ewa looked at Marek with a questioning glare.

"It's OK, I agreed to decorate if they supplied the stuff, it saves them money and me time."

They toured the lodge which was a single-story dwelling. It had a small kitchen with hot and cold running water and a toilet next to a bathroom where the hot water gas boiler was sited and where Marek had got one of the facilities boys to fit a shower over the bath.

Next was a single bedroom and then back to the living room. Ewa was jealous but knew she too would soon have her own home. With that, it was pinny on, and the children washed woodwork while Ewa started painting walls.

Around one, Marek arrived with fish and chips for them all.

"Wow! It all looks so neat and tidy, and you have already glossed the woodwork!"

"No, all we've done is wash it with hot, soapy water. But it looks great and will save us time. I hope that by the end of the day, I'll have finished at least two rooms and that I'll have it all done by the weekend."

As they sat eating, Marek asked Ewa about her past.

"Where did you study your nursing, was it Lublin?"

"It was in Lublin until the war, then once I was in Siberia, I worked with Polish nurses in field hospitals. Once I became attached to the Allies I worked as an auxiliary nurse for the British Army Nursing Service in Iran, India, and South Africa."

"Do you have documents to prove that?"

"Yes, I even have pay slips and a reference written for me by my last hospital."

"If I was you ,I would keep them safe for the future. You might be needing them."

The two finished their dinner before carrying on with their respective jobs. As the light began to fade, Ewa tidied up and then she and her little helpers made their way to the bus and home for tea.

With everybody planning their moves and readying the lodge, time flew by. Ewa and the children finished painting the lodge and the family saw less and less of Jan. Jan was now seeing the first signs of lambing being imminent and he was spending less and less time at home and more time in the caravan. This meant that Ewa and the children endured the now absolute silent treatment at dinner on their own.

Ewa did not care though. Her children were tough, and she was tougher. Every day that she showed no remorse was a day won by her and her family. She refused to buckle under the pressure, and maintained a dignified aloofness that set her apart from the clique that surrounded her.

However, there was some good news. Over the second weekend of November, Marek got a message from the funeral director saying that Frau Swartz's funeral would be on the following Saturday. Julia was happy about this as it gave her and her hardy band of musicians longer to rehearse. As Jan was busy, Marek cleared the final details with the vicar, and all was set to say a final farewell to Frau Swartz.

Finally, the day of the funeral arrived. Sid sat in at the caravan with Lily while Jan cycled home, showered, and got dressed into his one and only dark suit. Ewa had elected to stay at the camp with the children because she didn't want them at the funeral.

At the church, the hearse waited in the light drizzle with the coffin bearers sat inside out of the weather. As the mourners arrived from the camp, one of the men, recognising Marek, got out, lifted his top hat, and shook Marek's hand.

The man then surreptitiously handed Marek a small, brown envelope, bowed respectfully, and opened the rear door of the hearse as Marek, Jan, and the rest walked into the church.

Jan caught up with Marek and whispered, "What's that?"

Marek handed him the envelope, smiled, and said, "It's the bill."

Inside the church, Jan received a shock as word had got around about the tragic case of Frau Swartz. The church choir was in attendance, the village Scouts were handing out order of service sheets, and Mrs Goldstein and her intrepid musicians were arranged at one side of the altar. Jan looked around the church. It was not full, but it certainly was not empty. This lifted his spirits and made Marek and him realise that they had been right to go ahead with things. They smiled at each other, and the service began.

As the choir sang something slow and sad, the coffin bearers slowly marched into the church. On top of the coffin was a wreath of red and yellow chrysanthemums with a broad black ribbon hanging down. The pallbearer set the coffin down on the trestles so gently it was as if it were eggs. The four men bowed in unison and slowly marched back to the rear of the church and sat.

The vicar then stood and delivered the liturgy of the funeral. Near the end of the mass, he delivered a sermon.

"Maybe, it is time that we start the process of reconciliation. Perhaps enough time has passed that we should turn our minds to compassion and forgiveness and forget vengeance and hate. This service has been organised by people of a nation who had suffered more than most under the Nazis. Yet here they are making sure that this lady's life would not pass without being marked in some way. I wonder, if we all could not learn something from this simple act of kindness."

He then turned towards the coffin, anointed it with holy water, and returned to his seat. Mrs Goldstein stood up and moved forward. The organ mistress moved to face the orchestra, and slowly the orchestra took up the melody. All at once the church was filled with the sound of Brahms' *Ein Deutsches Requiem*. Mrs Goldstein's soaring voice filled the rafters of the church with a passion so crystal clear that the listener might think that their heart would be pulled from their chest.

The choir was impassioned and at the same time tenderly easing Frau Swartz to her final resting place in the afterlife. When Julia Goldstein had finished, it was as if the echo, in the church, lived on and refused to die away for some moments. The congregation were sniffing and wiping tears from their eyes, and as they sat there, maybe, some had thoughts of other funerals that they were unable to attend over the last years.

Now, the vicar, caped against the cold and wet, led the pallbearers into the churchyard for the final internment, and just like that Frau Swartz was at rest, waiting for a curious loved one to find her one day.

As Jan slowly walked back to the camp, he nervously slipped his finger into the sealed envelope to reveal the cost of what had gone before. He sighed with relief when he saw that the total cost of the funeral, including the stone, was forty-nine pounds, eleven shillings, and ten pence. However, this now posed a further problem: what to do with the rest of the money?

Jan decided that this was a problem for another day. Catching up with Julia, Kasia, Kinga, Marek, and Marta, he suggested that they see what was left for them on the side counter in the canteen. He collected his family, and they all walked to the dinner hall, Jan ushered Ewa and the children in. However, there was no food set aside for them as was customary when people came late from work or such.

Marek was furious. "This is beyond petty," he shouted.

"Shh..." said Ewa, "don't let them know that they've won, we can sort something out." Marek leapt into action. He ran to his hut, fetched his motorbike coat, and in a trice was gone in his usual cloud of blue smoke.

"Let's go back to my room it'll be easier to talk there." Said Marta, and so, the hungry mourners made their way to the single girl's hut.

"I'm sorry but I've to go back to work," said Jan. As he was about to turn and go, Ewa caught hold of his arm and gave him a kiss goodbye. The whole room fell silent as a shockwave of realisation shot around the small space.

"What?" Ewa demanded. "He's my husband, isn't he?" This candid assessment of her surprise kiss broke the spell, and everybody started to laugh.

"Ah, I think there is love there in that kiss," Julia quipped and with that Jan made his escape before more enquiries could be made.

Jan changed out of his suit and back into his home clothes so that he could go back to the caravan and change back into his work clothes. When he made it back to the caravan, he found Sid and Lily snuggled by the fire. On top of the stove was an enamel pie dish with one of Sid's wife's shepherd pies. It smelt lovely, and a starving Jan was jealous of lucky Sid for having such a tasty dinner provided for him. Sid picked up a fork and then the pie with a tea towel as the dish was hot. He handed it to Jan and said,

"Ere-yar, young-un, my missus left it for you, she said well done for this afternoon." Jan was at once aghast and grateful.

As Jan ate, he asked how Sid's wife knew about the funeral.

Sid then entered into a critique of the day's events. "My old gal is in the church choir, so she attended and sang with that Jewish gal. Said she had a fine set of pipes she did, and my old gal said that she was the nicest woman you could wish to meet. Voice of an angel, my old gal said. But all of them Jewish entertainers are good singers aren't they. You have that Al Jolson from Hollywood don't you, then, you have Frank Sinatra and Bing Crosby."

At this point Jan felt he had to intercede. "Well, Crosby is Irish American and Sinatra is Italian American, actually."

"So, not Jewish then?" Sid asked in disbelief. "No, not Jewish," Jan promised him, "and, in fact, Sid, Julia Goldstein is a Polish Catholic."

"So, not Jewish either, even with a name like Goldstein?" Sid said with astonishment. Jan assured him that she was not, "even with a name like Goldstein."

"Well, I'll be blessed," a bemused Sid lamented. "I'm surprised that she didn't burst into flames, a Catholic with a Jewish name singing in a Protestant Church for a woman who was a Lutheran."

Jan agreed, "Makes you realise how stupid all that is, doesn't it?"

"Ah," said Sid thoughtfully.

Back at Marta's room, the food had arrived and although not piping hot, it filled a gap. It turned out that Marek knew a man who sold hot pies from a van at the weekly football match in the town. If he had not sold out by half time, he would sell them cheaply to get rid of them. So, Marek made him an offer he could not refuse and bought all his redundant stock.

"Isn't he clever?" Marta said with pride, and the rest of the diners agreed.

"Now we're full," said Kinga, "they can clear their own tables. Maybe that'll make them think."

The assembly of rebel diners laughed and carried on eating.

"I'll miss this," said Marta. "We'll be leaving next weekend, now that the lodge is ready, thanks to Ewa and these two," she said hugging the children tightly.

"Don't worry," said Kinga, "we'll be round after work on Saturday's for cheap pies and a chat."

Although everybody smiled it was a sobering thought that everything was going to change for ever soon.

Jan had finished his dinner, and Sid had gone home for the night. While the signs of an imminent birth were not yet apparent, Jan thought he would take one last stroll around the fold before going home, so he lit an oil lamp and set off with Lily. As he walked amongst the flock, he could hear the choir in the Polish church practicing carols for the Christmas Eve mass. As he stood in the cold drizzle listening to the sad, soulful songs, his thoughts turned to his family in Poland and the many happy Christmases they had shared before the war.

He guessed that he would not now hear from Bialy about his family, but he was glad he had spoken out as sometimes things just have to be said. Jan and Lily walked back to the caravan, and as they ascended the steps, Jan noticed something different picked out in the yellow light of the lamp. Sid had rigged up a small tarpaulin sheet to protect Lily's box from the worst of the weather.

Jan looked at Lily. "He really is a big old softy isn't he, Lil's?"

While Jan got changed from his work clothes into his home clothes, Lily took advantage of the last heat from the stove, but eventually, she was banished to her box and Jan rode home.

During lambing season, as the shepherd, Jan was expected to work seven days a week. Therefore, he was excused church duty by Ewa. He ate a hearty breakfast and then made for his caravan, which had now become his retreat from fractious neighbours and a devout spouse. As he cycled past the farmyard, in the early dawn light, Chastity spied him and wandered out to see him at the roadside.

"Good morning Jan, I hear that your opera lady went down a storm at the funeral yesterday. I think that it was a wonderful thing that you and Marek did for the frau."

Jan stopped his bike and leant it against the wall. "Do you know what, like many here, I've seen my fair share of death. All of it senseless and much of it needless, but the sight of that poor young woman hanging there in the wood was the saddest thing I've ever seen. We both agreed that we couldn't let her life end in that wood, in that way, we knew we'd to do something."

"Well, your actions have certainly made an impression on the vicar. He's going to ask Mrs Goldstein if she will sing in a concert to raise funds for the church tower fund."

Jan remounted his bike and shouted back to Chastity as he rode off, "It's nice that a positive thing has come out of such a sad event, and I hope that the concert will raise lots of money." Chastity smiled and agreed, waved goodbye to Jan, and went back to work.

When Jan got to the fold, he found that life was going to get a lot busier. In the night, one of his sheep had gone ahead and lambed without him in attendance. As dawn had just broken, he had been able to see the happy arrivals from the steps of the caravan while unlocking.

There was a cold, light rain, so Jan walked down to the ewe and her two new lambs. Scooping them up, one under each arm, he took them back to the lambing barn, followed closely by their anxious mother. He placed the lambs in one of the prepared stalls on some straw and then let the mother in by untying one end of the stall and letting it hinge back. An anxious mother was a good sign as it meant that she was less likely to abandon her offspring.

Jan fluffed up some hay for her and made sure that her water bucket was full of fresh water as she would be making a lot of milk now. A bit like London busses, none come for ages, then loads come all at once, thought Jan, as more and more ewes started showing signs of imminent birth. During the day, what had started off as an amazing miracle of nature soon became an arduous battle to keep up with events.

Sid had been right. The sheep were hardy and most gave birth easily on their own, with just the odd one needing some easement or manipulation to deliver. As Jan moved the new arrivals into the barn with their mothers, he noticed something strange. As a ewe started to show signs of delivery, Teddy the donkey would stand close by as if he was comforting them. Jan wasn't sure if this was fanciful imagining, but it happened time and time again.

At lunchtime and after church, Marek arrived with the children who had been pestering their mother all morning to see the lambs. Jan was at a loss to how they knew there were lambs and asked Marek how this was so.

"Well, you see, when we all came out of church, we could

hear the lambs bleating in the next field, and the children then started pestering their mother until she gave in and let me bring them up."

"Ah, are they wearing work clothes or home clothes?" Jan said sarcastically.

"What do you think?" Marek joked. "It took me longer to listen to all the rules and instructions than it did to get here." He lifted the children over the gate into the field.

Jan invited the children and Marek into his little home while he ate the dinner Marek had brought him.

"I wish we could live in a caravan, it's so cosy," said Mary.

"Well, if your mother keeps upsetting the neighbours like she is now, you might have to," Jan laughed.

"Then you could wear work clothes all day and not have to keep changing into home clothes," teased Marek.

"Do you want a bet? I would have to change on the steps in the rain, before I came into the caravan."

The children giggled and the men smirked, but both took some comfort from this forced domestication they were willingly imposing on themselves. Both now realised how empty their lives had been beforehand. Marek looked around the caravan and observed,

"This is a single man's game, Jan, the sooner you get out of this the better."

"You're right," Jan agreed, "when I took the job, I wasn't even sure if Ewa was alive, now everything has changed."

Jan then changed the subject. " I hear mention that the church is raising money to repair the bell tower. I think that, maybe, we should give the balance of Frau Swartz's money to that fund on the understanding that, every year on her anniversary they would place flowers on her grave."

"I think that is a splendid idea."

"I will collect the money on Monday morning from the post office and give it to you, Marek, with the bill."

"I'll sort everything out with the undertaker before seeing the vicar."

With a plan in place and the children still clean, Marek decided to get them home and out of his custody, so off they set in rain-soaked splendour and blue smoke.

The surge in new arrivals had slowed, and so, as Jan took stock, who should appear but Sid. He had brought some of his wife's famous poppy seed cake and a round of chicken sandwiches.

"Thank your wife please, Sid and give her my best wishes."

"I'll tell the old gal."

Sid then gave the labour ward the once over. "Bloody hell, you! Eight lambs from five ewes. That's very good. Jan!"

"Thank you. Sid, but I can't take all the credit, Percy the ram had quite a lot to do with it."

"You daft bugger, I know that" chided Sid, "but getting them alive and all feeding is no easy task. They don't really need to stay in the shelter though, they are hardy and don't mind a bit of wet and cold."

"Yes, I remember you telling me that, but I just want to make sure that they are feeding OK and that the mothers are getting enough water before I let them out," Jan stated defensively.

"Fair enough young-un, fair enough, now how about a nice cup of tea?"

Jan took this as the signal that Sid was happy, so he put the kettle on.

**

This routine was to dominate Jan's life for some time, and family life would have to take a back seat, reasoned Jan. In the new year they would have a home of their own and any shepherding duties would be shared by Jan and a new man who Jan would be training. There was one deviation from this rigour, when during the last week of November with copious paper-work done and their meagre belongings packed, Marek and Marta decided to have a farewell party at the pub.

Jan managed to take a few hours off, and with Mrs Goldstein babysitting, Ewa was able to join the farewell get-together. Kinga and Kasia came straight from work and got off the bus at the village green. Marek, Marta, Jan, and Ewa walked slowly down the dark lane to the village with Marek holding an army torch he had acquired to light the way.

At the pub, James had a small function room adjacent to the lounge in which he had prepared and set out sandwiches, sausage rolls, Scotch eggs, and some pickles. Marek had placed money behind the bar and the friend's private function commenced. There was reminiscing of happy times, sad times, and just a feeling, for most in the room, changing times. But spirits were high and there was much to celebrate. Later, around nine, the pontificating voice of Dyke could be heard in the lounge, then after a moment's silence he burst into the room uninvited and sat down.

He looked across at Jan and enquired, "Where's that other 'mush' hiding then?"

With that, Marek came back into the room.

"Bugger me, speak of the devil and he will appear."

"What can I do for you, farmer Dyke?" Marek asked, anxious to get Dyke out as soon as possible as he had a loose tongue when he was drinking.

"Well," said Dyke, picking up a sausage roll while everybody else looked on in silence. "I've a bit of a problem. My missus has her family coming up next week from Dorset. She's holding her pre-Christmas soiree for the stuck up buggers. She wants me to get coal for all the fires in the house because she says that the logs stink the rooms out. Now I've steam coal for the boiler, but she wants coke for the fires, as it's cleaner. So,

I need you to get me some coke, can you get me some coke?"

Marek would have preferred it if Dyke had kept his voice down but suggested that it might be possible.

"Might be!" Dyke said loudly. "Is it possible or not? I need to tell the missus tonight."

"Yes, when do you need it by?"

"Next Friday night will be OK; her lot are arriving on Saturday morning." Marek nodded, and Dyke rose to leave, but as he did so he looked at Jan.

"Ah, your new boss said you and the family can go over this Sunday morning and see the house and measure up for curtains and all that."

"OK," said Jan, but he was interrupted by Ewa.

"It'll have to be in the afternoon as it's the first Sunday of Advent and we can't miss church."

"Bugger me!" Dyke exclaimed. "you can see who wears the trousers here, no wonder he hides in that caravan all week."

The gathering wanted to laugh but thought better of it.

"I'll get our Chastity to ring Farmer and tell him. James get this lot a drink!"

Moving swiftly through the door, the irascible Dyke was gone, like a summer storm that had passed before you could get your brolly out.

"You are going to be working for farmer Farmer?" Marek asked, bursting out laughing.

"Yes, I am, and he is letting us live in one of his houses, so I don't care," Jan rebuffed Marek.

Instantly the talk changed to curtains, furniture, bedding, and the like, so the boys sat and listened as they drank.

After a while, Dyke's voice rose once more above the general noise in the bar.

"Ah, a flyer, I believe, his name is MacDonald, and he was one of our boys in blue, fighting for king and country. My Pole is a good-un, I was lucky, but you can't beat a good old

British lion, hearts of oak and all that, and a cricket player most likely."

It sounded to Jan that a replacement had been found and would be arriving from Liverpool the following Friday, so there was no going back now. As the evening wound down, James cleared the food and placing it in a paper carrier bag, he handed it to Jan.

"Oh, you needn't do that," Jan said in embarrassment. "It's not for you, it's for Lily," Marek joked.

They drank up, said their good nights to James, and walked home happily, that is, all except Jan, who had to change from his best clothes into his home clothes so that he could change into his work clothes at the caravan.

"So, old MacDonald is coming to the farm," sang Marek.

"E I E I O." the ensemble replied.

There was much hugging and kissing as the girls said their farewells, and, for the first time in eight months, Marek and Jan did not know when they would see each other again.

This really did seem like the parting of the ways. No more early morning motorbikes purring off down the lane, no more clever financial plans shared, no more 'cordial' on the hut steps, no more scrapes with the local bobby.

Jan was glad for his friends that things were working out, but life would not be the same without his business dynamo of a friend close by. At the hut, Jan got changed and hugged Ewa goodbye. She in turn showed him how much she cared for him by making him wear a scarf and a bobble hat as he was riding in the cold and gloves just weren't enough.

Jan was glad that it was dark in the lane as he felt that he looked like a submarine commander on a bike. Back at the caravan, he dutifully changed, stoked the fire, shared James's food with Lily, and when he was warm, he and Lily took a tour of the fold. Teddy was stood alone and as Jan approached, he seemed to wince in the lamplight.

"Nothing to report?" Jan asked Teddy and taking no answer for an answer he retired for a spell.

Saturday passed with a few more arrivals, but also a stillborn lamb. This, Jan thought, just to prove that nature was not perfect. The sense of failure was palpable, even though both Jan and Sid agreed that nothing could have been done. Jan made it back for Saturday tea and an hour or two in his hut with the family, then, once more changed, on to his bike again and back to the fold.

Sunday was a red-letter day; it was new home day. Jan held out at the caravan until he knew church had begun, and, once he had heard the bell ring at the end, he changed and went home. Ewa was not that convinced that he could not make it back earlier, but she was so excited about the house that she ignored it on this occasion.

After dinner, the family walked down to the new farm and Jan knocked on the door.

Out came a man in his early forties. "Hello, I'm Chris, you must be Jan?'

Jan was amazed on a number of levels. First, he pronounced his name with the soft 'J', and second he was young and cheerful, the absolute opposite of all the other farmers he had met. Chris then shook hands with Ewa and said hello to the children.

Both Jan and Ewa thought that the signs were already looking good for their future happiness.

"I'll take you round to the house, shall I?"

They walked through a wrought iron gateway in a hedge, and there before them was their future home. It stood at the top of gently sloping lawns. It was the kind of house a child would draw if you asked them to draw a house. It had two downstairs windows, with a large central wooden door with three windows above just under the eaves. Ewa looked at it and could not help feeling that the house was smiling at them; she was smitten.

Chris continued, "This was supposed to be for my younger brother when he came back from the war, but sadly he never made it."

"I'm very sorry for your loss," Jan said quietly, "there aren't many who have not been touched by tragedy."

"No, that is true," Chris said stoically. "Where did you get yours?" Chris asked, referring to what action he had seen.

"Poland, France, and then southern Germany," Jan listed, at which point Chris looked at Ewa.

"Siberia, Iran, India, South Africa," she said.

"My lord," said Chris "you must have been a nurse."

"Yes, I was," Ewa said bluntly. "I didn't see the front line, but I saw what it did on a daily basis for quite a long time."

"I'm keen to modernise the farm, but as you know, Jan, my man is no spring chicken, and I want someone who can embrace change and make it work. I'll show you where the new dairy is being built later, but here are the keys to the house. Keep this set so that you can let yourself in when you want to put up curtains and move in furniture."

Chris left them alone to explore the house but as he left, he joked, "We don't have kids yet, it will be nice to have some about the place."

"What about dogs?" Ewa asked.

"Love dogs," Chris said happily.

"Oh, damn," Ewa muttered under her breath, "that's that then."

CHAPTER 16
HOME SWEET HOME

❦

"Oh Crikey," shouted Ewa, "we don't have any furniture. We have no pots, pans, cutlery, bedding, or towels!" For Ewa, the honeymoon was already over as she now had a panic attack wondering how they would fill this large Victorian house.

"Calm down, we've two months to find stuff. We can go to second-hand shops, sales, and auctions, and don't forget, we've the 'procurer in chief' on our side, I'm sure he will help. Let's just look around the place and get some ideas of what we need and then make some plans. We won't be in here until the end of January, so don't panic."

Ewa relaxed a bit and spent at least an hour looking at the rooms and dreaming of building her family's home there. "Chris is nice isn't he?"

"Yes he is a bit different to old Dyke; I think I'm going to like working here."

They heard a knock on the front door, and a lady's voice asking if she could come in. Jan and Ewa went down the broad wooden stairs into the light reception hall where stood in the doorway, was a young blonde lady.

"Hello, I'm Anne Farmer, call me Anne."

Jan stepped forward and introduced himself and the family to her.

"Would you like a cup of tea, Ewa? I expect I've some cake for the children, so let's leave the boys to talk tractors and slurry, shall we?"

Ewa was all at once swept away with the children, leaving Jan with Chris.

"'Come on Jan, I'll show you the plans for the dairy, It'll be nice to talk to somebody who isn't scowling while I show them."

"OK Mr Farmer," Jan said, not being able to bring himself to say farmer Farmer.

"Just call me Chris. I've had that farmer Farmer thing follow me since I was a schoolboy. Chris is fine, and I promise not to call you Mr Kot Jan, OK?"

"OK," said Jan, as he pored over the plans rolled out on a workbench.

After a short time, Jan drew his fingers over the plans. "It's quite simple really. The cows come in and stand on this raised platform, I wash their udders, attach the suction cups, then the milk goes up these pipes and into a stainless steel dump bucket to be cooled before going into the churn. When I've done the first eight, they leave and the other eight come in. I steep the teat cups in solution, flush them in fresh water and start again."

"You have it in one, Jan, exactly, I'm sure we're going to get on well. The system is designed to be added to, so as we grow the dairy grows. It is so exciting; no more hand milking, just wash, attach, and repeat."

Chris's optimism was infectious, and Jan was almost sorry to be still returning to Dykes farm, but he loved the old pace of life there in some respects.

The walk back to the camp was full of excited chatter.

Mary and Joseph picked which would be their rooms and Ewa started quoting Anne Farmer and her many progressive attitudes to family and life. Jan started to worry about how he would pay for it all, especially with rationing. It would not be easy, but he kept that to himself. The family ate tea together and then Jan made his way back to the caravan.

Lily was on guard, so Jan fed her, and then after stoking the stove, he lit an oil lamp, and the pair did a circuit of the field. They found Teddy standing watch over a single ewe near to the hedge. "That's one to watch Lily," Jan said, and with nothing else seeming to be happening, they made their way back to the soft orange glow of the stove.

After that evening's mass, the choir and orchestra rehearsed its Christmas carol concert. The solemn tunes drifted across the field and merged with Jan's memories of happier times. Jan loved the carols but wondered why so many English ones were so cheerful and so many Polish ones sad when they were about the same subject. As Jan sat listening he stroked Lily behind her ear as the choir mistress, Mrs Kunka, began a solo with harmonies from the choir.

She was no Goldstein, thought Jan, but as Sid would reason, maybe if her name was 'Kunkstein' she would have hit all the notes in the right order at the right time. However, the overall effect was mesmerising, and it was amazing to think that the orchestra was a mix of professionals, army band members, and keen teenagers.

They practiced for hours, going over the same sections time and time again, their tolerant conductor urged, cajoled, and encouraged. Mrs Kunka had a very different strategy with her choir, which centred on personal vilification and publicly shaming shoddy notemanship. She also had an absolute absence of any musical knowledge or comprehension of its power to please.

With choir over, Jan and Lily ventured out into the dark

and damp. Teddy had moved away from the sheep by the hedge, as she was now the proud possessor of two bouncing baby lambs. Their wet, woollen coats glistened in the amber lamplight. Jan picked them up and placed them in the barn with their mother. Jan was tempted to go home but felt he should stay just to show willing. The barn would need a clean-out in the morning, both of sheep muck and the stronger family members.

This would make more room for the newer, weaker lambs, and make space for those still to arrive. As he lay on the sofa in the caravan, he had a nagging sense that something was not right but could not pin it down. At two in the morning, Lily began to growl in an aggressive way that he had never seen before. Her flared nostrils and guttural growl was a sign to Jan that something was very wrong. He picked up his shepherd's crook to use as a weapon and slowly and quietly opened the door of the caravan.

Lily crept down the steps and looked towards the gate just a few feet away. She did not bark, but looked with such an intensity that Jan could see the whites of her eyes even in the darkness that enveloped them. Jan was tempted to ask if anybody was there, but he reasoned that no sheep rustler was going to call back,

"Yes, it's me the sheep rustler," and anybody who knew him would not have been creeping around in the dark.

Later that morning, around six, he walked down to the dairy to see Sid and told him about the scare. Sid made a couple of suggestions which he hoped would help.

"You see young-un, you have all those lovely plump lambs crowded into a barn right by the gate. They're easy to see and even easier to steal. I tell you this, if you think catching a lamb in a field isn't easy, you should try it in the dark. The other thing is, I always had my four-ten shotgun handy, and that kept away all but the most determined or stupid rustlers."

Jan was aghast. "So you mean these people are local and know you and know you have a gun?"

"Yes, that's right, I could probably take you to their homes now and they would still have sheep shit on their boots."

"So, what do I do?

"Well, tomorrow, let all but the newest or weakest sheep and lambs into the field, they are safer there. Then, on the evening, I'll go down to the pub and while I am having a drink, I'll let slip that I had to lend you my shotgun, due to rustlers, and that you are ex-Polish military, and you won't mind using it. That should do it." Jan thanked Sid profusely and made his way back to Lily who was now on full alert on her step.

At first light, Jan made a count and found no lambs missing, but this had been a wake-up call as he had not thought about crime as part of the job, just wet and cold. He liberated most of the stock into the field and like coiled up springs the lambs exploded into their freedom with aerial gymnastics and boundless energy. At nine, Jan rode down to the post office and drew out the money and closed the account.

Before she returned the book to Jan, Rosemary took a rubber stamp and, in red ink stamped each page 'CLOSED'. Jan looked at Rosemary as she sadly stamped each page. She understood the symbolism of what she was doing, and so, when she slid the book back to Jan there was a moment of silence.

Jan made his way to the family hut where he found Ewa readying herself and the children for the journey into town. He gave her the money and funeral bill and asked her to say hello to Marta and Marek for him. As Jan walked them to the bus stop, he told her about the nights events.

"You be careful," Ewa begged.

"Don't worry, I now have an imaginary shotgun. You know what, though," Jan said quizzically, "even before that I had this feeling that something was wrong, that something was missing, but I could not put my finger on it."

Ewa reacted with astonishment. "Do you know, I've been having the same feeling ever since we walked back from the new farm yesterday, but like you, I can't for love or money think what it is."

"Well, I'm sure it'll come to us eventually," said Jan, as he gave everyone a sheepish smelling hug and returned to the canteen for the late breakfast.

Out of habit, he sat at the single men's table. As he did so, a voice from the kitchen shouted that as he was not a single man, he could not sit there. Jan pointed out that as he was alone, he was a single man. The disembodied voice disagreed with this fact, and instead cited marital status as the main criteria for the seating arrangements. As Jan had been up all night he gave in and moved, but he really wished that he had had his imaginary shotgun with him at that moment.

The week moved on with an inevitability that most November weeks hold, with cold, wet, windy, stormy days and long hours of darkness. However, Friday was another red-letter day. Jan's replacement for training was arriving that day and he was meeting Dyke at the pub where he would stay until the tied cottage could be readied for him. To Jan's amazement, Chastity came up to the fold at around four in the afternoon and asked Jan if he would like to meet her father and Captain MacDonald at the pub around seven that evening.

"Is he a real captain or is he one of our kinds of Captain who really isn't a captain now?"

"No, he really is a real RAF captain who is retiring and wants to buy a farm. He is hoping that working for Father will help him decide. Oh, and, Jan, if you see Marek, tell him not to forget that coke as Mothers family will be here in the morning and the weather is set to get frosty later."

"If I see him, I promise I will remind him, but he is a family man now and I don't see much of him."

So, at five, Jan changed and went back to the camp. He ate at the married men's table with Ewa and the children and then went for a shower. He donned his funeral suit and tie, and went down to the pub. As he entered the Bell, Sid was leaning on the bar talking to some locals. Sid nodded in Jan's direction and Jan gave Sid's drinking companions a mean stare.

They all quickly turned away, and Sid gave Jan a sly grin. Jan smiled and made his way to the bar.

"Dyke is in the lounge bar; you go on in and tell him that I will be along shortly."

Jan acknowledged Sid and, slowly, with an affected cowboy swagger, sauntered into the lounge.

"Ah, here is my man now," Dyke shouted. "James, get this poor bugger a pint and one for yourself." Jan accepted his pint and stood attentively whilst Dyke held court.

Sid then joined them and whispered that he did not think that Jan would be disturbed at night from now on. Jan made a signal of gratitude by raising his pint glass in a cheers motion. Both men stood quietly while Dyke revisited his hearts of oak, cricket and the boys in blue war hero stories with the assembly. Dyke, again, while extolling the many virtues of some of the foreign chaps, waxed lyrical about his preference for a good, solid, British shoulder to the grindstone, grit.

At around eight, James came through to the lounge bar "There's a Captain MacDonald in the bar asking for farmer Dyke."

"Ah, here's my boy in blue, my one of the few!" Dyke shouted excitedly.

With that, James opened the lounge door, and stepping back with a broad gesture of the arm, he announced, "Captain MacDonald!"

In stepped the captain and the room fell silent.

Dyke felt the glass slip from his hand, but he never heard the explosion of frothy glass fragments as they burst over the flagstones of the lounge bar floor. This reaction was caused by the singular fact that Captain MacDonald was one of the Kingston, Jamaica MacDonalds, not one of the Edinburgh, Scotland MacDonalds.

The arrival of the captain caused a pregnant pause, which, before it could become embarrassing, was filled by Jan who stepped forward and introduced himself. "Hello, it's nice to meet you I'm Jan, and, you, I believe are my replacement."

As soon as the captain spoke, it was clear that he was not one of the rank and file 'of the few'. He spoke in clipped tones, his deportment beyond reproach, and his pencil moustache did not have a hair out of place.

"Jan, please, can I buy you a drink as you'll be my teacher. I think we should start on the right foot." Jan accepted graciously.

Then Sid butted in, "I'm Sid, I'll be training you too."

MacDonald started to tally, "Right, so a beer for Jan and one for Sid. Can I get anyone else a drink as I'm in the chair?"

A forest of glasses shot into the air and the room filled with noise once more. Dyke stepped forward, and looked up at this peacock of a man whose chest was adorned with a myriad of medal ribbons.

"I am Dyke, it's my farm you'll be working on; I thought that you would be British."

"I am British, everybody in Jamaica is British," MacDonald said, amazed that British people did not know who their countrymen were or where they were from.

James came in to clean up the smashed glass and, taking one look at his fellow airman's chest, said, "My God, you've seen some action."

MacDonald looked at James and said, "Flier?" James nodded. "Well I think that we're going to get on just fine while I'm here."

In that one word, MacDonald had indicated that he did not belong in a field filled with muck and sheep.

Sid whispered to Jan, "I'll give that bugger 'til Christmas."

"But which Christmas?"

"This bugger," Sid grinned.

"We shall see," Jan said, and the two rejoined the group.

While Jan was hobnobbing it with the upper crust of the village, Marek's evening was taking a dark turn. He'd finished work at six, and aware of his promise to Dyke, had managed to place a fully filled sack of coke into his sidecar. He had hidden the bike in the shadows behind the boiler house, but he now faced a problem, how to get a hundredweight of coke back to the village without being seen by one of Wiltshire Constabulary's ever-vigilant constables? He did not think that a warehouse coat and a helmet would be sufficient this time.

His plan was simple, yet ingenious, he thought. He would leave the hospital by the back lane behind the mortuary, up the track to the horse paddock, across the paddock and letting himself out of the gate, back onto the rough track that would take him to the railway line, and then Dyke's farm.

Happy with his plan, he wiped the frost off his saddle and kicked his bike into action. He slowly let his bike purr away from the buildings avoiding the streetlamps that dotted the hospital grounds. Happy that he was now out of sight in the back lane, he opened up his bike to ascend the hill. As he did so the sack of coke, which was filled to the rim, over balanced, and lurched to the side. Marek was able to grab it quickly and pull it back into the upright position before adjusting his speed to compensate for the unsteady nature of this unusual load.

Marek eventually reached the paddock where he was greeted by a group of curious horses breathing clouds of steam into the ink-black air. As he closed the first gate, he started to make his way to the second one when all at once the sack lurched to the left again. Marek made a grab for it, but with his leather bike gloves covered in frost, he was not able to grasp the errant cargo, and it spilled some of its precious load onto the field.

Marek stopped the bike, and leaving it to tick over, he raced round and scrabbled up all of the spilled coke. When he was sure he had picked up every last piece, he remounted and slowly made his way across the paddock, careful not to repeat the disaster again.

At last, and on smoother lanes, he was able to pull up at the back of the farmhouse. He knocked on the kitchen door and the housekeeper answered.

"I've been expecting you. Mr Dyke is at the pub meeting our new man, but I'm not lugging that sack of coke anywhere. Here are six coal scuttles, fill each one then I can take them to the rooms. Leave the rest of the sack in the back porch and I'll get Sid to fill them tomorrow when we need more."

Marek did as requested, then the housekeeper handed him a sealed envelope and closed the door. Marek placed the envelope in his inside jacket pocket and made his way back to town by a more orthodox route. As he passed the pub around eight thirty, he saw Jan coming out. Marek slowed and turned onto the pub side of the road.

"Lift?"

"You are a sight for sore eyes, yes, please, I've to be back at the fold by nine."

As he climbed into the sidecar, Jan noticed that the smell of mashed potatoes had now been replaced by something even less fragrant. He mentioned this over the noise of the motorbike and rushing wind to Marek, who only heard the word fragrant and replied, "It must be Marta."

Jan was dropped off at his door, said his hello's and goodbyes to Ewa, and armed with some goodies from the kitchen, made his way back to the caravan or, as he now called it, the guard house. The night passed without incident, and while Jan was unnerved by the events of the night before he felt that with Sid on his side he was assured of a peaceful night. MacDonald had told Jan that he would see him on Monday, so until then Jan and Lily had the place to themselves.

After a tour of the field, and sharing the kitchen goodies, both man and dog settled in by the stove under a star-filled sky. After midnight, Jan helped to usher more new lives into the world and transported them to the relative comfort of the straw-filled barn and out of the frost. He pondered what Sid had said at the pub about MacDonald. Surely, Jan thought, a man who had fought in aerial warfare would not be fazed by some sheep and a bit of mud.

Jan looked at Lily and said, "Well we only have to wait 'til Monday to see," so the pair relaxed again with Lily thinking of the next titbit and Jan still trying to remember what it was that was bothering both Ewa and him.

The next morning, being a Saturday, Jan went back to the camp for the early breakfast. There he saw Kinga and Kasia, and after a bit of a chat, he ate his breakfast before snatching some extra toast for Lily and mounting his bike to make his way back to the fold. As he was in his stinky clothes, he knew that Ewa would not relish a visit from him at that time of day, giving off that kind of aroma, so off he pedalled and in time reached the farm where he guessed tempers would be fraying and nerves would be jangling at the imminent arrival of the 'Dorset lot'.

To his surprise, all the windows in the farmhouse were flung open, despite the frosty morning air. Jan decided to investigate and pedalled into the yard where he could hear Mrs Dyke screaming at Mr Dyke with Chastity trying to calm the situation. Sid was running across the yard with a wheelbarrow emptying coal scuttles into it and then running back to the boiler house at the rear of the farmhouse. Jan caught up with him and asked him what was going on.

"Well, what's going on is this," said Sid succinctly. "Your mate brought some dodgy coke for Dyke so that his wife's family didn't have to smell log smoke. Unfortunately, if you check the sack in the back porch, it contains frozen horse manure, but the coke that was taken into the house last night does not."

"Well, that's good then, isn't it?" a bemused Jan said.

"No, it's not good, because the coal scuttles in the house contain thawed out horse manure and they have stunk the house out to high heaven. You tell your mate not to show his face around here for a while for his own safety."

Jan didn't know when he would see Marek again, but he would be sure to warn him not to visit for a while. Jan then left the mayhem of the farmhouse and returned to the comparative peace of the fold.

About mid-morning Jan had a big surprise because as the day was bright and sunny, Ewa decided to visit the caravan. There she stood at the gate, immaculately dressed in her best winter coat, waiting for it to open. Jan saw her waiting and jokingly shouted,

"Around these parts we climb the gates, we don't open them."

"Well, that's not going to happen." So at that point Jan thought that it would be better for everyone if he just opened the gate. Ewa picked her way across the frozen white grass, avoiding any foreign bodies that did not look like frozen white grass. She climbed the stairs into the caravan where Lily was sat in her sheltered box at the top of the stairs, smiling her toothy grin, hoping to make a good impression.

Ewa proffered a gloved hand onto Lily's head and moved on into the caravan.

"Tea?" Jan asked, hoping to conjure some good humour out of Ewa who was clearly out of her comfort zone.

"No thanks, we're off to the Farmers for a visit; I'll get a clean cup of tea there."

"It's not that bad here. I have heat, hot water on the stove, a freshwater tank and I can wash just by turning this tap on. Oh no!" Jan stopped in his tracks.

Ewa dropped the heiress in a brothel attitude "What's wrong?" she asked.

"Taps," said Jan,

"Yes, you said taps, but what about taps?"

"There weren't any taps."

"Where weren't there any taps?" Ewa asked, becoming a bit annoyed again.

"I've remembered what we both thought was odd but couldn't remember. There were no taps in any of the rooms at our new house."

Ewa sank back into her seat in shock. "You're right, I knew something was wrong but couldn't think what it was, there were no taps. I'll have to have a chat with Anne when I get there and sort something out. We can't bring up two children without hot and cold running water."

Ewa stood to leave and as she passed the lamb barn she shouted at the children, "Don't touch anything. Heaven knows what you might catch."

She looked at Jan for validation. "A bit of ringworm, maybe some scabies, worms," Jan said in an effort to raise a laugh.

None was forthcoming, so he moved to open the gate.

Ewa proffered a ladylike cheek for Jan to peck and as he did so she complained, "I can smell sheep!"

By now the princess attitude was wearing a bit thin for Jan, so he blurted out, "Well, you're stood in a field full of bloody sheep, so it's not surprising."

Ewa loved it when she was able to coax Jan into a temper, so she smiled and made her way to Anne Farmers for a sort-out chat. Jan waved them goodbye and returned to the caravan where he looked at Lily and said, "I think you made a good impression, better than mine anyway, but that was not hard."

Ewa and her brood arrived at the Farmers', and she pulled the doorbell knob. Ewa could hear a distant ringing and then Anne came to the door.

"Come in, we're all waiting for you."

"We?" Ewa asked rather shocked.

"Oh, don't worry; it's only some of my WI friends. I thought that now you are moving into the area you might like to join."

Ewa was flattered that she was being asked to join the WI, however, she had no idea what that was. "What is WI?"

"The- WI," Anne explained, "is the Women's Institute. We share recipes, make jam, raise money, and help each other to develop a social life. I thought with you being a trained nurse with battlefield experience, you were just the type of woman we wanted to attract."

Ewa was flattered at being asked to become part of an English institution and said that she would give the matter some serious thought.

"Would your children like to play in the parlour room with the other children, I'm sure the language barrier won't be a problem."

Joseph answered in his clipped home counties tones, "Yes, please, that is very kind of you. Do the other children not speak English?"

Anne Farmer's mouth dropped open. "Well, you are full of surprises, Ewa, as I had no idea that your children spoke English."

"That's because they speak when they are spoken to. They speak Urdu and Afrikaans as well," Ewa said proudly, knowing full well that her and her family's stock had been raised quite considerably in those last few minutes in WI circles.

Ewa now turned to the matter of the lack of taps. She apologised to the small assembly of village ladies and promised that it would not take long to sort out. She spoke to Anne in private as she felt it unseemly to discuss private business in public. Anne understood at once.

"You see, Ewa, you live on the camp which was built by the American's with all mod cons, kitchens, laundry, toilet blocks, boiler house for showers but the rest of the village doesn't have those luxuries. They've outdoor privies and spring water wells. Most women have a log-fuelled cauldron in an outhouse where they do their weekly wash and a tin tub in front of the fire for a bath on a Sunday night."

Ewa was aghast to hear this news as all the time she felt that she was going without, she actually had more than most. Anne did, however, have some good news.

"When the new parlour is installed, water will be brought to the site and plumbed into the house and the farmhouse. At the same time, a gas boiler will be fitted in each home and radiators will be installed. All part of Chris's drive for modernisation," Anne said proudly. "I think the best thing to do is stay at the camp until the work is completed around the beginning of March, and then move in"

"Oh, that sounds marvellous," Ewa said, and safe in the knowledge that her family would have the most modern of mod cons, Ewa returned to her new friends.

While in conversation with the ladies, it transpired that the vicar's wife was among the guests. She was effusive in her praise for Jan and Marek in handing over the cash for the bell tower fund. All of the village ladies agreed and, once more, Ewa felt the warm glow of acceptance wash over her and her family.

For Jan it was business as usual. Arrivals, releases, and the odd problem to cope with, but nothing he was not used to or could not cope with. As he sat eating his packed lunch from earlier, he looked out at the bright, clear blue sky, filled with an optimistic sun. He always thought that even on the frostiest of days, the sun had the ability to cheer people up. He thought about MacDonald. Why would anybody leave the warmth of Jamaica to choose to live in this cold, wet country?

Maybe for the same reason that he chose to fight in the RAF perhaps, Jan thought. He had a strong attachment to the country and felt it was worth fighting for. Jan envied him. While he loved England, he did not think that he would ever feel the same way about it as he did about Poland. For the first time in a long time, even with his small family around him, he missed his home.

As the light faded, Jan lit an oil lamp and did a sweep of the field. It looked like it was going to be a quiet night and, once again, he toyed with the idea of staying at home for the night. He returned to the caravan and weighed up his options. Go home and hear all about Anne Farmer and her new ideas or, even worse, how Ewa would have to bring up her family without hot and cold running water. That did it; he was staying at the caravan. There was also the danger that, if he showed up at home, he might be roped into church, given that it was Advent.

That was settled then, Jan was staying. It was not long after that that he heard the music rehearsals start up across the field in the church. However, something was amiss as there was no screaming or allegations of wrongdoing being shouted at the undeserving choristers, just calm melodies executed to perfection.

As Jan stood on the step listening to the music, suddenly Lily sprang to life from her box and stared at the gate in alarm. Jan was at once grateful that he had stayed, as he thought the rustlers were back to try their luck. As he descended the steps holding his shepherd's crook as if it was a shotgun, he heard a voice speaking in Polish. Jan reasoned that the small, shadowy figure at the gate bore him no harm, so he moved towards him, questioning his presence in Polish.

As he lifted the lamp, he could see it was the corporal from the security committee. "Put down the lamp," hissed the corporal. "If I am seen, I'll be at risk of retaliation."

Jan placed the lamp on the ground. "What can I do for you this evening?" Jan asked at a loss to understand this visit.

"I've a coded cypher from London, from one of our operatives in the east. The major told me to file it as it wasn't operational, but I decoded it and know that it's about your family."

Jan's heart leapt with excitement and then in fear, what if it's bad news, but what if it's good news. "Show me the message."

"I don't have the message as it's filed in the camp under lock and key, but I have memorised it. Before I tell you, you must promise me that you will mention this to nobody, or I will face consequences."

"I promise that this'll go no further," Jan swore.

The scared man began to recite the message. "The Kot family have survived the war. The farmer that they rented their farm from was arrested and his land has been gifted to the tenants by the Soviet regime. So, Mr Kot now owns his farm. The Shriver family also survived the war, Mr Shriver is still a doctor in Lublin and his wife is still a teacher. The political persuasion of neither couple is thought to be in support of the invaders. They're not aware of this investigation, and so, know nothing about their family in the west." The corporal ended his recital, and again, pleaded for anonymity.

Jan assured him he was safe and then asked him why he had risked his position.

"You stand up to the major and make many of us question his reasoning. I like that and I like you as do many, but we'll not say so." With that the corporal was gone, moving briskly in the shadow of the high fold hedge.

Next morning, the second Sunday in Advent, Jan presented himself for mass, bursting to tell Ewa the good news. He changed back into his funeral suit and joined his little family on the lonely walk to mass. Ewa was impressed that Jan was there, so she felt the need to start the conversation.

"I'm sorry but I have some bad news. We'll have to stay in the camp until March because the plumbing won't be finished 'til then."

"OK," said Jan dismissively.

"You don't seem too upset."

"No, I'm not, because I've some good news for you." Jan checked around to see if anybody was close by. Obviously they were not as the Kot family were the camp pariah's.

He closed up to Ewa and whispered, "Our families in Poland are safe and well."

Ewa almost collapsed under the weight of this news. Jan supported her arm, and the pair stopped walking.

"How. How do you know this?"

"Shh, I can't tell you as I made a promise to protect somebody, but it's true, and this news is only days old."

Ewa began to walk faster and faster. "We must get to church and pray to thank God that he has looked after us all and brought us through this trial."

Jan did not feel the need to rush to church, but he picked up the pace to keep Ewa happy. In church, still flustered by the news, Ewa sat at the back and sank to her knees. As she prayed, her hands were pressed together so tightly that they appeared as white as alabaster. Jan noticed that tears were trickling down her cheeks which she wiped away by extending her thumbs hoping not to be noticed by others.

He was happy that he could bring her some good news for once, but as if this was not enough, there was more. As the choir began to sing, it was Mrs Goldstein who stood to direct them. Jan found out later that Mrs Kunka's husband had been sent to work up north at short notice. She had had to follow him, and Mrs Goldstein had agreed to step in.

During the sermon with the usual rhetoric of the evil outside the gates of the camp, and the true path lying within the gates of the camp, Jan suddenly noticed a problem with the priest's reasoning: the camp had no gates! In fact, Jan thought, if Polish children had been banned from speaking Polish, or made to change their religion to Protestantism, or forced to serve the State rather than languish in camps then he would understand. However, none of these things had happened, as on the whole the British had accepted the Poles, so in Jan's opinion, the only gates were the ones on the closed minds of some of its inhabitants, not the camp.

Jan stayed in his suit for dinner but then hurried back, got changed into his home clothes, and set off for the fold with extra treats for Lilly. As he threw his leg over his bike crossbar, Ewa grabbed him and hugged him tightly.

"Thank you for today, it means so much to me, now I've one less thing to worry about."

"Maybe we can work out some way of contacting them so that they know we're safe, now we know they are still live in their homes," said Jan, then he kissed Ewa on the forehead and set off back to the fold.

Back at the caravan, Lily was fed while Jan changed back into his work clothes. Suddenly, Jan heard a distinctive voice calling from the gate, it was Captain MacDonald.

"I thought I'd walk up and see how the land lies," MacDonald shouted.

"Come in," Jan shouted back, "I have the kettle on, make yourself at home."

The first signs were good as MacDonald did not seem afraid of the stock or their muck. He was obviously someone who was used to mucking in, as he made the tea and handed Jan a cup.

As the evening crept in from the east, the temperature

began to fall. Jan suddenly noticed that Teddy was standing in the middle of the flock. He had been there since Jan left for church mid-morning, so Jan knew this was not good news. He put down his mug and ran over to the ewe. She was struggling with a breech birth with the first of two lambs.

He called out to MacDonald, "Bring me that bag with the red cross on it."

MacDonald was there in an instant. "Will we need to turn it?" he asked, betraying his knowledge of animal husbandry.

"Yes," said Jan, "give me some lanolin ointment." Jan went to work, manipulating and pushing until, eventually, he had to force his hand into the ewe, who gave a low moan of pain. "I know, I know," Jan said as he tried to calm the patient.

He eventually managed to get a thin sisal cord around the front legs of the lamb, and working with the contractions, pulled the lamb free. The second lamb soon followed now that its passage was clear.

"Captain, please go and fetch me some warm water and a sack," Jan requested, suddenly aware that he did not know his companion's first name.

MacDonald was soon back, and while Jan laid the sick lamb on the sack and massaged its tiny frame with warm water, MacDonald got the mother to her feet and tried to get her to feed the second lamb.

"I must get the mother to feed quickly or the stress may make her abandon both lambs," he said urgently.

Jan nodded, and slowly the sick lamb began to make movements but seemed unable to breathe. Jan picked it up and swung it around by its back legs, massaged its back again, and suddenly it coughed and started to breathe and struggle.

"A struggling lamb is a live lamb," Jan shouted with triumph, and after a while, the new family was coaxed into the barn by the light of the oil lamp.

Jan pulled his own hessian sack around his neck to ward

off the cold air getting to his sweaty shoulders.

As he did so ,MacDonald looked on amazed. "Is that part of the uniform on this farm?" he joked.

"It is" Jan joked back, "we should have one in your size back at the farm. I'll get you fitted out for one tomorrow." Both men laughed, partly at the joke, and partly because they had managed to save a ewe and two lambs, and that nervous energy was now releasing. Unusually, Teddy the donkey came over to the barn and stood near Lily as the two wrapped the sickly lamb in some old white sheeting.

"Well done out there," Jan said heaping praise on MacDonald. "Have you done this before?"

"Not exactly, I read about it in a book I borrowed from the library."

"Well, you are a fast learner and that'll set you fair in this game as you have the power to save life and that is not nothing."

As the two men cradled the two lambs, the mother drank water and began to show an interest in her offspring. In the distance, Mrs Goldstein's voice floated across the field giving her rendition of the solemn Polish carol called 'Minerza Chiha'.

"By the way, my name is Basil, and I won't be a captain from the end of December." He smiled and, picking up the hessian sack that Jan had used on the lamb, he slung it around his shoulders and said, "I'll be a shepherd."

As Teddy and Lily watched on, and the plaintive carol drifted across the fold, the two men knelt down, looking at the lamb in the amber light like a scene from a modern-day Nativity play.

"Look Jan," said Basil incredulously, "it's a new life."

"It's a new world, Basil," Jan corrected him, and the two men sat and contemplated their different futures.

ABOUT ATMOSPHERE PRESS

Founded in 2015, Atmosphere Press was built on the principles of Honesty, Transparency, Professionalism, Kindness, and Making Your Book Awesome. As an ethical and author-friendly hybrid press, we stay true to that founding mission today.

If you're a reader, enter our giveaway for a free book here:

SCAN TO ENTER
BOOK GIVEAWAY

If you're a writer, submit your manuscript for consideration here:

SCAN TO SUBMIT
MANUSCRIPT

And always feel free to visit Atmosphere Press and our authors online at atmospherepress.com. See you there soon!

ABOUT THE AUTHOR

MIKE KRAWIEC has a PhD in Modern History from the University of the West of England in Bristol, England. He is the son of a Polish slave labourer who came to Britain in 1948 as a European Voluntary Worker. This family history inspired Mike to study migration, the refugee experience, and nationalism in all its forms.

However, dry academic research did not inspire Mike, and so he decided to turn to historical fiction. He used his considerable knowledge of contemporary social history to create contextual frameworks, which he can suspend a fictional narrative from. His work is, in general, humorous as it observes the human condition in all its facets. However, like life, it is tinged with moments of tragedy that immerse the reader in the world that he creates.